For Len,
In memory of

RIVERS C.

A Prophetic Novel?

ALLAN STEVEN

April 2nd 2022

Counting The Spoons Trilogy: Book Two

2nd Edition

Cover artwork by Martin Gorst

Dedicated to Brenda Gibson, and her colleagues, who put a damaged boy back together and set him onto a productive pathway.

Also for friends and family, cascading down the years from my parents to my daughters, Elizabeth and Alice, and my grandchildren Aimee, Alfie and Lily.

***

Thanks are expressed to those who read a sample of Rivers of Blood, and gave feedback. Richard Welch manfully read the first draft and gave his insights; thanks Rich. Martin Gorst read it in whole and part numerous times and gave invaluable advice, and lots of time – including technological instruction; the pupil became the master. Undying gratitude Mart.

Author's Note

Prophecy hasn't been in vogue across the Western world for a significant period. Its bond with religion means it is given scant regard in these secular times. The common assumption is that prophetic utterances are the property of God. If we don't believe the old boy exists, then those who prognosticate from the mountain top are just deranged ranters and general nutters.

I contend that whilst prophecies are not cast in tablets of stone they can be perfectly respectable warnings about where our present behaviour will lead. Prophecy is born out of human reason and observation. You don't need to examine the entrails of a goat to deduce that if a teenager plays 'wag' from school persistently, and spends his time in town shoplifting and taking drugs then he's likely to face an adult life of unemployment, poverty and deprivation. A life unfulfilled, except by trouble. Of course, he may turn a corner, but probability indicates that our errant teenager will not escape the pit into which he has descended. That is prophecy. Whether or not it is God-given is between me and my conscience, and you and your conscience. Should I contend that this gift has come from the Supreme Being I am only asserting that it is the gift of willpower. I must choose to use that, and so apply my powers of reason and observation.

Would that the sentimental populace of the United Kingdom got off its collective fat arse, and exercised self-control and willpower to make the most of each individual's ability to reason. Then we might stand a chance of creating a civil society (with civility the norm), where social and economic justice reigns. We British can be intolerably smug. This affliction causes us to pontificate that civil strife and revolution only happen to 'Johnny foreigner'. Our indifference to reasoned thought and emotional self-control prevents us from seeing that we too are susceptible to the most chilling and monstrous disorder. I do not know if a Julian Marlborough *will* emerge from the primeval slime to cause mayhem on a national scale, as he does in the pages of this novel. What I suggest is that it is not beyond the bounds of possibility. If it does, it will be the product of the last fifty years spent shitting on our own doorstep. The deification of the Self in opposition to collective responsibility, manifest in good citizenship, is the excrement I am referring to. We are at a turning point in our history when Brexit, immigration, climate change and political sea changes of a particularly obnoxious hue are prevalent. They are dividing the citizens of the United Kingdom.

I do not lay claim to the status of the prophet Elijah, nor am I so sanctified that my personal prejudices don't influence the portrait I have drawn in Rivers of Blood. Politically, I have always voted for the Labour Party, with the following exceptions: Blair, the consummate soap opera act; Brown, the frighteningly inadequate schoolboy, and Miliband who is so bloody wet you could shoot snipe off him. In the 2017 and 2019 General Elections I spoilt my ballot paper. How could I vote for a man who is recorded in Parliament as having voted against his own Whip over four hundred-and-fifty times? Everybody else is always wrong, only Jeremy is ever right. History is littered with that type of disastrous leader. Oh, I HAVE NEVER VOTED CONSERVATIVE!

The ensuing tale is at your disposal; wipe your backside on it if you like; remember to use hard copy not your Kindle!

Allan Steven, Stratford-Upon-Avon, April 2019

1

"By the pricking of my thumbs, something wicked this way comes."
Macbeth Act 4: Sc. 2

Captains rarely accompany infantry patrols, but Julian Marlborough wanted one last shot. Another two hours and he would be back at base, and then it was piss-up time in the mess. A great night ahead with his cronies before the flight home to the UK the next morning, and a new life in civvie street.

The Middle Eastern sun was as bloody hot and perfect as ever. It rendered the shelled buildings of the town ahead a freshly-laundered look, belying their traumatised degradation. Each man in the three vehicles knew damn well that they would soon come under fire from the tortured wreckage of the houses, and pitted streets and alleys. The Rifles, formerly the Royal Oxsters Light Infantry, had fought in this armpit of the world for the last six months, and this was their third tour in four years.

Sergeant Billy Conway grinned at his commanding officer, with a look of adoration and worship. The men surrounding him felt similarly about the Captain. Julian Marlborough had returned to them for his final stint of service after years with the Hereford Regiment. No one knew the precise circumstances necessitating his sideways move into retirement. The rumour mill spoke of an *'over-vigorous'* approach when dealing with prisoners. Not that they cared. Each soldier present was seared through with the brutality of the ongoing conflict against Islamist extremists.

Fucking politicians bragging for years that they would wipe them out, and put an end to their Medieval barbarism; 'Cocksure' Cameron, Theresa May (but she didn't, as the tired gag went), 'Anonymous' Obama riding tandem with Hillary 'Butch' Clinton. As for Donald 'Two Chins' Trump, he was what everyone anticipated – all wind and piss. Even the Labour leader, who had succeeded Jeremy 'The Regretful Robespierre' Corbyn, had left the military to get on with their unending job; content to mimic the facile anti-war rhetoric of his predecessor. When he became Prime Minister everyone anticipated being out of the Middle East within two years. Boots went back on the ground. The Yanks went in first, motivated by the need to make use of the monumental arsenal, and to impress their emotionally sub-normal population. Where daddy leads the Brits follow.

Labour remained in government in the UK. A small majority meant they had to protect their ass, or rather count their votes. The feeling in the country remained anti-immigrant. With Brexit concluded, and freedom of movement from Europe under control, vitriol was reserved for the Muslim community. The public wanted action against them, both at home and abroad. In the spirit of handwringing the war continued overseas, whilst at home an attempt was made to foster an ecumenical spirit.

In the rear of the lead troop carrier, Rifleman Jimmy Allsop was mulling over his chat with the padre the previous evening. Bright-eyed and bushy tailed, Jimmy was a committed old-style Socialist. He enjoyed his fierce, but amicable, debates with Captain Peter Standish. They discussed Corbyn's rise and fall, and Jimmy was honest enough to admit his disappointment in the man.

"Don't you see Jimmy," said the padre, "Socialism is Christianity without God – without the love of Jesus. It always fails."

Jimmy came up with a feeble, "Doesn't have to be that way, sir."

Peter Standish leant forward in his canvas chair and clasped his fingers together.

"Socialism copies Christianity, with its commitment to the material improvement of mankind. Look how frequently we are instructed in the Bible to help the poor. The problem for Socialism is that it puts all of its eggs in one basket. While it's fixated on filling that basket with a cornucopia of goodies, for everyone to feast off equally and fairly, it neglects the life of the spirit. I'd go so far as to say it denies the existence of the spirit."

"Not all of us deny it, sir."

"Ah, Jimmy, you remind me of those old time Evangelical Christian Socialists of the nineteenth century."

"I don't know about that."

"I do, Jim. You've got the fire and zeal they had to change social conditions for the better, but you also believe that man doesn't live by bread alone." Peter Standish smiled seductively, "Now I wonder where that phrase comes from?"

A bugle sounded, its notes slipping away into the alien air of the surrounding desert.

"Time for some beauty sleep, Jimmy."

The young rifleman came to his feet.

"Ay sir, you'll need all you can get; you going home to the clatter of wedding bells..."

Jimmy cut himself short, and blushed to his roots.

"I...I...I'm sorry sir. I didn't mean to be disrespectful..."

Peter's throaty laughter cut him short.

"Oh, Jimmy, Jimmy, I'll let you into a secret – even vicars have sex. On your way, sweet dreams."

Jimmy paused in the doorway, "We'll miss you both, sir."

"Both?"

"You and Captain Marlborough, sir, leaving the army together. He's a fine officer, sir."

Peter Standish glided into profile, and said nothing.

"Good night then, sir."

"Goodnight."

"INCOMING!"

Sergeant Conway's yell shook Jimmy from his daydream. He felt the vehicle swerve to its left, as bullets pitter pattered the armour. In a trice they were piling out the back and scattering left and right to find cover. They sought safety behind the low walls which marked the boundary of once prosperous houses. Homes where Arab families had gathered for dinner, and to celebrate birthdays and weddings; no different from their western counterparts in love and devotion to their wives, husbands and children.

Julian Marlborough was ice.

"Now then, my merry men, a little light exercise methinks."

He sat with his back against the wall, legs extended, surveying the three troop carriers pounding the broken body of the town from their machine guns. The infantry was under cover, and spread in a cordon. The machine guns paused. Only a few desultory shots were returned from the town.

"Not much coming our way, sir," said Conway, "an' all lightweight. What d'yer reckon?"

The last phrase betrayed Conway's origins; a hard nut Scouser, with the city of Liverpool's propensity for coming to the point, and usually taking the piss at the same time – but not right now, this was business.

"Get Corporal Slack over here."

"Yes sir."

Conway signalled down the line, and Richie Slack crawled forty metres to join them.

"Slackie, me boy, do me a favour, me old china – you don't mind me employing rhyming slang do you? You being a Cockney cunt."

Julian Marlborough had been a fine amateur actor. He fancied himself as a master of voice. Despite the tension, chuckling punctuated the burning air.

Richie Slack's face burst into a sunny smile.

"Not at all squire, you bein' an horficer an' a gen'l'mun."

Two could play at that game.

"Jesus H!" Marlborough retorted, "You sound like a GBS character."

Billy Conway frowned, "GB who, sir?"

Jimmy Allsop blurted out, "George Bernard Shaw, sarge – playwright and socialist."

"Thank you Allsop, quite correct. And proving the point that you don't have to be a Cockney to be a cunt. Fucking armchair Socialist. Enough, enough of this witty badinage, or Noel Coward will appear as a shining apparition out of the desert…"

"Noel who, sir?"

"Sergeant Conway did you never pay attention at school?"

"I was never there, sir."

"Ah, of course. No doubt you spent your days to the detriment of the local crime figures in Liverpool City Centre."

The machine guns started again. Marlborough's professionalism kicked in.

"Don't reckon there's much opposition here. The remnants of a few ragheads from our last visit to this fair metropolis. Satellite shots show the bulk of their forces thirty miles east. Right Slackie, six men and circle left; Billy, you and six to the right. We'll keep pouring the wrath of God down on whoever's left, while you flush them out. Careful as you go, you know the bastard's penchant for leaving prezzies behind."

It wasn't worthy of the name *'firefight'*. The opposition amounted to no more than half a dozen souls, left behind for experience and martyrdom. A pincer movement, of the simplest kind, entrapped them and three were killed instantly by Richie Slack's men. Two more came out of an abandoned building, with their wounded colleague between them.

"Down, down!" Billy Conway screamed and gestured.

Gingerly, the two Arabs lowered their companion to the ground, where he lay whimpering and clutching his guts. Conway repeated himself, and the two uninjured fighters lay prone before him. Julian Marlborough loped towards them, accompanied by four men. The rest held their positions.

"All clear, sir," Conway barked. "Don't reckon there's anyone else 'ere, apart from this pair o' dick'eads."

Marlborough prodded the wounded fighter with his toe.

"Oh dear, not long for this world, methinks. Still, he has the consolation of one hundred virgins waiting for him."

He turned to the other two.

"And what have we here? Get them on their feet Corporal, and remove those ridiculous dishcloths from their heads."

The fighters were hauled to their feet, the coverings torn brutally from their faces. The assembled company was as still as the overpowering air. Every eye fell upon the Caucasian features of the figure to the right. Her long blonde hair had become untangled from its fastenings. Now that they looked closely they could see her feminine outline beneath the male garments she wore. It was her tiny choking sobs that broke the spell.

"What the fu…!" Billy Conway was gobsmacked.

Julian Marlborough stepped forward and gave her a resounding slap across the face.

"Stop snivelling, bitch."

A clear English voice appealed to him.

"Don't 'urt me. A never did nowt. They made me do it."

"What do you think I am, a fucking schoolteacher?"

Marlborough's sarcastic tone ripped into her.

"Perhaps I should tell you not to be a naughty girl, and don't do it again?"

"I'm…."

"Shut the fuck up, and don't speak unless you're given permission."

Everybody's curiosity was aroused. They gave full attention to the Captain as he circled behind her. He lifted her tresses, and whispered into her ear.

"What's your name, sweetheart?" She mumbled. "A little louder please, darling, so that all of the gentlemen can hear you."

"Suzie!"

Some of the men jumped at her loud exclamation.

"Suzie…ah, that's nice, and very pretty. You're pretty too. Now, I'll bet you have another name since you converted to Islam. I am correct aren't I, you did convert?"

Suzie nodded affirmatively, "Fatima."

"Fuckin' 'ell skipper, dat was my old school, *'Our Lady of Fatima'* – shit'ole."

"My goodness, that was brave; upsetting Sergeant Conway. So you left home to have lovely adventures. Joining a bunch of ragheads to kill me and my men."

Marlborough let uncertainty weigh upon everyone. He came to her side and wrapped his arm around her, bringing her head onto his shoulder.

"Now, my dear, tell your Uncle Julian everything, and he'll take care of you. Where is home?"

"Bradford."

"Oh dearie, dear, a northerner as well. You are in trouble, aren't you? No offence Billy, we don't classify Liverpool as the north. You are a unique entity all to yourselves."

"Too fuckin' right, Cap, we're not woolybacks."

"Quite."

Julian glanced at his watch.

8

"Tempus fugit, old girl," he declared to Suzie. "Tempus fugit. Anyone?"

"Time flies," Jimmy Allsop ventured.

"My, my, you are having a good day rifleman; a credit to the Education Corps. Pray, may I ask where your delightful accent originates?"

"Lancashire, sir." Allsop gestured to the girl, "Other side of the Pennines."

"What do you think about that Billy?"

Conway rubbed his chin.

"Good soldier is our Jimmy, Cap, but...fuckin' woolyback!"

Marlborough switched his attention back to Suzie.

"Well, me dainty duck. You are going to have to take your medicine. A traitor, a northerner, and that appalling use of grammar – it just won't do. You, my lovely, are well and truly fucked; that is, you're going to be."

Marlborough gestured to the other prisoners.

"Get rid. Billy, with me, in order of seniority I think."

The two of them dragged the girl into the ruin, her screams silenced by a punch to the face.

Around the house the men sat in desultory fashion, waiting for their turn. Jimmy Allsop wanted to cry. When Richie Slack asked for a volunteer to distribute extra water from the troop carriers he gladly showed willing. Striding toward the vehicle, he prayed fervently that her pain...no not her...that Suzie's pain would not be long.

2

"Think you we are Turks or infidels? Or that we would,
against the form of law, proceed thus rashly... but that
the extreme peril of the case, the peace of England...
enforced us to this execution?"
Richard III Act 3: Sc. 5

"**L**et's stroll down to *'The Rag'* Hugh. We can catch up on strategy as we go. Nothing better than the street for a private chinwag."

Andrew 'Freddie' Forbes – 'Freddie' because he bore a passing resemblance to Frederick the Great – led the way out of the House of Commons. Hugh Marlborough brought up the rear.

"I'm most awfully sorry about this Freddie. Been a bugger of a morning. My usual driver didn't turn up. It took the bloody taxi firm forty-five minutes to find a replacement. Some bloody toe rag who doesn't seem to have mastered the *'Queen's'*..."

Freddie interrupted, "Better get up to speed Hugh, it's been the 'King's' for quite a while now."

Regal gender didn't matter a fart, Hugh thought, but he didn't want a row with Freddie.

His replacement driver was Usman Khan, who was even less pleased than Hugh. Usman didn't like to get out of bed too early, especially when he had a drugged up fifteen-year-old girl beside him. His nephew, Qadir, was horrified by his activities. His brother Raza turned a blind eye, fulfilling his sexual preferences with comfy middle aged women.

In deference to an imaginative variety of insulting epithets, thrown at him by Raza, Usman rose early. He got on the road to Banksmore, and thence to London with Sir Hugh in the rear seat. Usman spoke the *'King's'* more than adequately, but remained sullenly taciturn on the drive, rather than his usual loquacious self.

"Thought you dealt a good hand on the *'floor'* this morning, Hugh. Marvellous crack that, calling him the *'Aging Juvenile'*."

This was Hugh's coruscating putdown of Tristram Hunt, M.P. and historian, who was enjoying a second stint in the House.

"Oh well, he's always got on my tits. Public schoolboy from Tory stock with his heart bleeding for the poor."

"My dear boy, you excelled yourself when *'Chucky'* came to his feet. I thought Blacow was going to have a fit when you referred to him as the *'lounge lizard from accounts'*. Where on earth did you dig that up?"

"Old comedy routine on the box – can't remember. By the way, that bugger Blacow is for the push, when we return to power. Quite fancy being Speaker. How in Christ's name has he managed to hold onto the job for so long? He must be older than God's dog."

"Quite. Anyway to business."

They turned off Birdcage Walk onto Horse Guards Road, and came abreast of the Imperial War Museums and Churchill's War Rooms. Soon they were on the Mall, negotiating the roundabout at Trafalgar Square to arrive on Pall Mall. Normally, about a twelve-minute walk from Westminster, but Freddie realised it might take a little longer. Old Hugh was slowing down these days. Yes, the

Speaker's Chair might be just the ticket for the old boy. Keep him out of mischief, but permit him to put that acerbic tongue to good use.

'*The Rag*' is the affectionate name for the Army and Navy Club situated in St. James' Pall Mall; 1st President the Duke of Wellington. The Military Members Club has been situated in St. James' since 1837, and on its present site since 1851. Originally, it was founded for former and serving officers of the British Armed Services and their immediate relatives. Hugh qualified as Julian's father, which rankled with him secretly. Freddie Forbes had long been a member, being a former colonel of paratroopers. His present position as Shadow Minister for Defence would probably have sufficed; that and being the eldest son of the geriatric Earl of Seaforth.

"Remember Hugh, softly, softly catchee monkee. These are the best chaps in the world, but they're loyal Englishman. What we've proposed is a monumental ask. Here we are. Let's enjoy lunch, and go easy on the giggle juice. How's that boy of yours?"

Lunch was excellent, and served to the seven of them in a private room. Freddie led off as they were attacking the cheese.

"Our chaps within '5' are keeping me up to speed."

A lean and cadaverous man, dressed in a discreet double-breasted suit, interjected.

"Got anything you can show us, Freddie?"

The Shadow Minister shook his head.

"Not consigning anything to paper, '*Frobisher*', but I can quote you chapter and verse." A murmuring encouraged him. "*Lennon* is going to turn things upside down."

This was the code name for Deputy Prime Minister Tommy O'Donnell. Hugh came up with it; he thought it appropriate for one troublesome Liverpudlian bugger to be named after a deceased member of the awkward brigade from the same city. They all operated under cover names. *'Frobisher'* was the *nom de plume* for the urbane gentlemen who had asked the question. Hugh was tickled pink by his *nom de guerre 'Winston'*. The aliases were based on simple association; Marlborough gave Churchill, gave *'Winston'*.

Freddie continued.

"Regrettably, we have to accept that *'Lennon'* is a true believer. His present boss is merely a fellow traveller, but this gentleman is a fanatical revolutionary Marxist. You don't need me to tell you that we're plagued by strikes, and the economy is going down the pan. You can get that from the newspapers. I should tell you that a palace coup is in the offing. When *'Lennon'* occupies the hot seat he intends to accelerate immigration from the Indian sub-continent, and from Africa and the Middle East. It is his avowed intent to turn Britain into an irreversible melting pot."

A brisk, no nonsense, man of muscle in his mid-fifties spoke up.

"That will mean the end of our way of life. Haven't we enough trouble on the streets already with different ethnicities at each other's throats?"

A tentative hand went up from *'Winston'*.

"If I may? Though I concur with you, *'Paddy'*, on the first point, I must disagree with you on the second."

'Paddy' waved him onward.

"Actually, things are remarkably quiet on the ethnic front. The blacks are pretty much settled to our way of life, and the bloody Indians are more English than the English. As for the East Europeans who stayed after Brexit, they make a damn fine contribution. Rather be served by a hardworking and courteous Pole than some ignorant British lout who calls me *'Mate'*. True, the Muslims are getting a bashing from our less educated brethren, but…well, they bring it on themselves, and most of them aren't really fighting back."

Freddie was concerned about where this was going with this, so cut him short.

"Not a good reason to flood the country with thousands more, and, as *'Paddy'* so rightly put it, change our way of life. If I may continue, there are other alarming issues emanating from Comrade *'Lennon's'* antediluvian creed. I have to inform you, gentlemen, that within a week of him taking office the *'Sneaky Beakys'* will be recalled to base. They will be processed through Hereford and dispersed to their original regiments, or honourably discharged if that is their wish."

Protestations broke out around the table with everyone gabbling in outrage at the prospect of the disbandment of Special Forces.

Freddie rapped the table with his empty glass.

"Gentlemen, gentlemen, I'm afraid that is not all. In the summer of next year work will begin on decommissioning our nuclear deterrent, and the scrapping of the submarines. Furthermore, each branch of the service will be reduced by fifty per cent, and maintained merely as a homeland defence force. Needless to say, defence spending will be negligible."

"This is *indefensible* madness," said a small, lean and wiry individual.

"Quite so, *'Bernard'*."

"We'll be defenceless, and with the resurgence of…"

"Ah, ah, ah, do forgive me for interrupting, but I think I anticipate what you were going to say. We must be discreet. As it happens, that will not be a problem. How can I put this? *'Lennon'* is already in bed with the *'Bear'*."

"Hope it bites his arse," grumbled *'Bernard'*.

"Oh it will, it will. The difficulty is it will take a chunk of our collective posterior with it. Time is getting on gentleman, and I have to appear in front of a select committee. One final tit-bit to wash your cheese down with. House of Lords and the Monarchy to be gone by the end of the year."

Hugh Marlborough was apoplectic.

"Can't do that, the present incumbent may be a bit of an arse, but we've managed those before. The Monarchy is the glue holding the nation together."

"How will it be accomplished, Freddie? He hasn't much of a majority."

The purr of an Edinburgh brogue held the floor.

Freddie laughed.

"I'm told that he holds the dirt on an astonishing number of his upright Socialist brothers – financial irregularities, under-age girls and prezzies. Even we know about the joker who withdrew from the leadership contest because of 'coke' and boys. In the end *'Rob'*, they'll vote with him and he'll accomplish it rather easily. No more Civil List, no more money for the royals. The King will be permitted to keep Balmoral and a few goodies. His other des' res's will be expropriated to the state. Should boost the tourist economy, opening *all* the rooms at Buck House!"

A lengthy silence dwelt upon the company. A fine clock ticked, and the Iron Duke looked down from his portrait.

The Scotsman spoke.

"We cannot permit this to happen."

'Frobisher' put his two pennorth in.

"Any chance of removing him from office? We could *'deep six'* the bugger."

Freddie shook his head.

"Not wise. He's surrounded himself with a rather formidable security team, though, how can I put this, not all of them are batting for his eleven."

"Couldn't one of them *'persuade'* him that his time is up?"

"Too risky, *'Frobisher'*. He has an inner circle of commissars; they guard the guards. Rather like the scum Stalin sent to keep an eye on his generals. If one of our chaps was caught in the act, it would inevitably rebound on us. We don't want excrement soiling the air conditioning."

A further silence ensued, until Freddie himself had to break it.

"You recall the last time we met, at the old man's house? We put certain plans into operation and reviewed others already in place. My understanding is that it has gone rather well. We have our people in the key positions. So gentlemen, time is short, and I'm going to be blunt. What are you prepared to do for your country?"

Once more it fell to the Scotsman.

"If push comes to shove, the Scottish regiments will secure the major cities outside London – Newcastle, Leeds, Manchester, Liverpool, and Birmingham. Presumably, the Navy will take care of Portsmouth, Southampton, and the South West?"

'Frobisher' came alight.

"Indeed we will. We'll station a few ships off Portsmouth, Southampton and Bristol, AND we'll help you out with Newcastle and Liverpool."

'Winston' murmured, "Save time if you just gave the coordinates for Liverpool to one of the subs in the Caribbean."

"My dear boy," smiled *'Frobisher'*, "I rather think that guns trained on the Liver Buildings will concentrate the mind a little better."

An appreciative chuckle went round the room.

'Paddy' chirped up.

"My chaps will, of course, support the Navy, and any spare will be at your disposal."

Freddie eyed a so far silent member.

"What about you, *'Connolly'*? Will your chaps be available to drop in at short notice?"

'Connolly' looked worried.

"They would be if we had transport. So far, there's been neither sight nor sound of the boys in blue at these gatherings."

Freddie and *'Winston'* enjoyed a smile of complicity.

"Not to worry, that's in hand. You'll get your transport. Well, that leaves you *'Bernard'*?"

The steely little man stared Freddie down.

"We are ready. When the time comes we will do what's necessary in Westminster, and lock-down the London area. Question!" Freddie gestured. "Who will secure telecommunications?"

'Winston' took the floor.

"We are in negotiation with the seriously disgruntled amongst the *'Sneaky Beakys'*. They have assured us that they will walk hand in hand with our fellows in Security to harness the power of television, radio and internet on our behalf."

As per, a politician said in forty words what could be said in ten, but the answer satisfied.

Freddie rose to his feet.

"Thank you so much for your attendance, gentlemen. A most satisfactory lunch. Look forward to seeing you all again at the old man's in 'Tizzers' in a fortnight."

Apart from Freddie and Hugh, they wandered casually towards the club exit, smiling and chatting about all and sundry. It was as though they had just passed a pleasant hour or two with old chums. When they entered the lobby they gathered as a group, shaking hands and saying goodbye.

An old man sat nearby showing only a mild interest in his newspaper. His eyebrows rose in curiosity, as he glanced up at the discreet group. Lieutenant Colonel Ronnie Stancliffe was long retired, but maintained a keen interest in who ran the *'show'* these days.

Each of the departing group was identifiable, and he was deeply surprised at what an august body it was: two major generals, respectively for the Scottish Regiments and the Household Division; a Brigadier General of the Parachute Regiment, and then he was even more impressed as two faces came into view from behind the others – the Commandant General of the Royal Marines and, by no means least, the Admiral of the Fleet.

He whistled to himself, and spoke inwardly.

"My, my, that must have been an interesting lunch."

In a jiffy they were gone. He returned to his 'paper, only to be disturbed by a rather noisy fellow chattering away to his companion. Ronnie Stancliffe had no idea who the former was, but he recognised Seaforth's boy, and came slowly to his feet.

"Andrew, my boy, how very nice to see you. How fares the old man?"

"Good Lord, Colonel Stancliffe. You're looking marvellous. Yes, yes, father is fine. Creaking a little, but aren't we all?"

Ronnie was about to sally forth with another question, but Freddie intervened.

"I'm so awfully sorry, sir, not to have more time for you, but I'm due in front of a select committee in forty-five minutes."

He offered his hand to Ronnie, who said, "Do give my best to the old bugger, would you?"

"Certainly will. Cheerio."

Freddie strode out of the club, trailed by Hugh.

Ronnie stood in thought.

"All that gold braid AND the Shadow Minister for Defence in the club together. Quite a glittering array."

He picked up his paper and paused.

"And they were all in civvies?"

Ronnie sat down to the crossword, but a further puzzle occupied him.

"Strange that, Andrew never introduced me to his companion. Always such a polite boy, Andrew, not like him. Still, he did go to Harrow." Ronnie shrugged, "Must have been rather preoccupied with that select committee." He buried himself in the Telegraph.

Out on Pall Mall they dispersed. Each of the seven walked off alone. Freddie raced to the House. Hugh watched them disappear; the men who held the future of the United Kingdom in their hands.

He looked the length of the street, and inhaled an England that had stood for centuries. The buildings timeless and majestic. That was it! What they were fighting for was not the illusion of an England long gone, but its present majesty great and small. Curmudgeonly old so and so he might be, and backward looking in many things, but he loved his country, and he loved her people. Rich or poor, southern or northern, Scottish and Welsh, though he wasn't too keen on the Northern Irish. He'd be damned if he was going to see them destroyed by a failed creed. Hugh would die for England.

3

"This England never did, nor never shall, lie at the proud foot of the conqueror, but when it first did help to wound itself. Now these her princes are come home again..."
King John Act 5: Sc.7

To their surprise, Captains Standish and Marlborough were placed upon a civilian flight home. Julian oozed charm at the check in desk, and before they knew it they were upgraded to business class. Striding to the departure gate, in perfect step, they drew glances. The more observant recognised them for what they were. Deep tans and lean bodies combined with straight backs spoke volumes. Some looked with curiosity, wondering what they'd been up to, others returned to their magazines.

Peter Standish stood five feet ten. His blue eyes reminded you of that feminine look Peter O'Toole had as Lawrence of Arabia. His gaze was made more penetrating by his tan. The padre's muscled physique was not as toned as Julian Marlboroughs, attributable to the greater time Marlborough spent in the field. Both possessed a strong personal magnetism, but the blonde Standish held the eye for longer. You wondered at his calm. Many a person found themselves fixated upon him, and caught out as they stared a little too long. Their embarrassment was relieved by the generous and easy smile he flashed. It revealed his generosity of spirit and compassion.

Julian had grown considerably since his school days. He was thirty-one years old, with an imposing frame. Bone, muscle and sinew strained at his buttoned up blazer, and his pristine shirt was tight across the sternum. His olive complexion had burnished across the years to a deep walnut. Jet black eyes intimidated you. There was just the touch of a squint, from peering towards too many sun-scorched horizons. Julian too had a distinctive feminine feature. At school he had been called *'titty lips'*; it would be an unwise individual who called him that now. Full and fleshy, and wet from his habit of licking them every few minutes, most found them deeply unattractive. One poor chap didn't, and approached him on Hampstead High Street on a Saturday evening. Thankfully, the ambulance didn't have far to travel, the Royal Free Hospital was just around the corner. When Julian looked at you his dreadful power gripped you, and you felt your bowels loosen; it was prey and predator.

The aeroplane levelled off at cruising altitude.

"Well padre, that's the end of that little jaunt. Back home to crisp sheets, and even crisper women."

Marlborough snorted at his own witticism. He had none of the prudish instincts of Rifleman Allsop. Just because a man wore a dog collar that wasn't going to restrain him.

"A jaunt, Julian, is that how you saw it?"

"That's what we signed up for padre, sun, sand and..."

He was going to say sex, as he recollected his activity in the abandoned town, but that might be a step too far for his clerical companion.

"Yeees," he yawned, "a bit of jaunt to keep us on our toes. I didn't find it too strenuous."

Peter Standish spoke quietly.

"We left some behind who found it a little more than strenuous."

Marlborough bristled.

"If they weren't prepared to die they shouldn't have taken up arms against us…"

"I meant some of our own boys."

"Same principle applies. They were volunteers, not conscripts; knew what they were signing up for, padre."

"Peter! The padre bit is behind me now. Soon have plenty of people calling me vicar in my new parish. It would be refreshing to hear my Christian name used."

Julian yawned again, and released his back rest.

"No worries, Pete it is. Now if you'll excuse me I need a bit of shut eye. Rather a full on session in the mess last night. Wake me when they come round with the *'scran'*."

He slumped in his seat, extending his long legs as far as space allowed. Peter heard the slow rhythm of his breathing, and saw the shallow rise and fall of his chest.

Peter Standish struggled to master himself in early life. He was the product of a working class family. His father held a critical view of everyone and everything, which was instilled into him and his brothers. His reawakening to Christianity had crept up on him. By his late-twenties he was tired of endless drinking and rugby clubs, and more than wary of young women who bought him Pyrex dishes after a two-week relationship. He'd always been a voracious reader, and one evening he leafed through an old Bible, given to him by his grandmother for his eighth birthday. Within a week he was convinced that its tenets were the only foundation upon which a fulfilled life could be lived. That didn't make him a Christian; it certainly didn't propel him to church.

The dreams began. For an entire month the same scenario. A long, dark passage with a half open door at the end, light beyond. He pushed it open, and a blinding sun engulfed him. With a hand across his brow he could make out the silhouette of a man.

In the fifth week a shift. He couldn't see himself, but knew that he was walking towards the same rock outcrop every time. The man who sat upon the rock and took him into his arms was Jesus Christ.

Peter started attending Sunday service at the local church.

The dream changed. There he was, a small child, led by the hand of Jesus. Together they walked into the ocean. He had always been afraid of water, but was tossed high in the air to plunge back down into the deep. There he turned and twisted in joy, luxuriating in the soothing buoyancy of the waves. He and Christ frolicked, and a small boat drew near occupied by fishermen. Christ towed him towards the craft and lifted him aboard. It rose on the waves to be drawn ever nearer to the seashore. Standing in the prow, Peter saw a countless multitude before him. He knew in his heart and in his mind that he was called to serve them.

Examination of calling, ordination training, followed by a curacy in a northern industrial town, and then the army. Sixteen years flashed past, and here he was on the way home to Jane, his wife to be, and a parish yet to be decided upon.

"Tea or coffee sir?"

The sultry air hostess loomed over him.

"Too much makeup," he thought.

"Tea please, black tea."

"What about your companion, sir, shall we wake him?"

Peter laid his fingertips lightly on Julian's arms, who became instantly alert.

"Ahh, thanks Pete. Time for a nibble is it?"

Looking up at the hostess he declared.

"Indeed it is, most decidedly time for a nibble."

She giggled at his innuendo, and repeated, "Tea or coffee, sir?"

"Think we can do better than that. Do be a poppet and bring us a couple of those little bottles of champagne you keep for the discerning palate."

Peter tried to protest.

"Now, now Pete permit me to treat you to a pre-nuptial drink. My friend...what's your name?"

"Karen."

"And very nice too. My friend, Karen, is going home to get married. What do you think of that?"

"Sounds like a great reason to celebrate."

"That's really amazing, Karen."

"What is?"

"We're on exactly the same wavelength. Are you married, Karen?"

"Never got round to it."

"Astonishing!"

Marlborough laid it on with a silver-tongued trowel.

"Neither did I. How about that, both of us single."

They colluded in knowing laughter, and Karen swayed away to fetch the champers. Julian leant across Peter for a quick shufti at her retreating posterior.

"Must be jelly, cos jam don't shake like that."

No offence was meant, and none taken. Peter had been around soldiers long enough to know that one of the main staples of their conversation was women. He didn't approve of the antediluvian attitude of some, but he had to accept the badinage as part of the daily round.

"You know the song, Pete?"

Julian began to sing the old Jazz standard.

"*Said it must be jelly cos jam don't shake like that...* You a Jazz man?"

"Bach and Haydn for me."

Peter couldn't resist adding.

"Heard someone describe Jazz as musical masturbation."

He smiled, but his companion didn't respond. Julian Marlborough liked to crack the jokes and be the centre of attention. He wasn't keen on *'funnies'* at his expense.

"Here she comes, our sexy trolley dolly. Just a moment darling. Need to pop to the loo, scuse Pete."

Stepping into the aisle, he took Karen by the waist and *'circused'* her like a roundabout, whilst whispering into her ear. Her laugh tinkled, and she went all girly. Under the makeup was a forty-eight-year-old woman. Julian disappeared towards the toilet, and Karen served.

"Quite a character, your friend. What does he do for a living?"

 Peter saw no reason to avoid the truth.

"We're retired army officers, on the way home from our last posting."

"Gosh, overseas long?"

"Quite a while."

Her face hardened.

"You'll find things have changed – a lot!"

Her posed smile returned.

"What business are you and Julian taking up in civvie street, isn't that what they call it?"

It was obvious that the latter had imparted his name.

"I've no idea what Julian will be getting up to, I don't know him that well. As for me, I'm a vicar."

Karen blushed, not quite knowing what to say. Peter laughed.

"Sorry, it's always a bit of a showstopper."

"No...no, that's alright. Gosh, look at the time, meals to be served. Lovely to talk to you, er, vic..."

"Peter will do."

"Peter. Oh, chicken or beef?"

"Chicken please."

"Do you know what Julian will want?"

"Here he comes, why don't you ask him."

She met Julian halfway along the aisle. They laughed in complicity. Julian resumed his seat, and replied to Peter's enquiry about food.

"Chicken...breast, a nice plump one."

Whilst they ate Peter asked Julian about his plans and prospects.

"Not given it much thought. Why do you ask?"

"Your newly-found friend was interested. She was most impressed by you being an officer and a gentleman, retired."

Momentarily, Julian's mind zipped back twenty-four hours to his badinage with Corporal Slack.

He relaxed.

"Thanks for putting in a good word, Rev. No, not much in the way of plans. Home to the manor in Buckinghamshire, and see how the old man is getting along."

He sipped his champagne in a fastidious and lingering manner.

"Your father, is he a farmer?"

Julian's roaring laughter turned heads.

"Good God no. He's M.P. for the local constituency. Sir Hugh Marlborough."

"Don't believe I've come across him. Which side of the House?"

Julian cocked a wry eyebrow, as if to say *'are you taking the piss?'*

"Dyed in the wool Tory. Not surprised you haven't heard of him. He's a real backwoodsman; flirted with Farage in UKIP's early days, but decided against them. *'Frottage'* – no class, and that surname too foreign-sounding for the old man."

They chewed on in silence. Peter manufactured conversation.

"So you're undecided about your future?"

"Mmmm, think I'll have a gap year and enjoy myself. But what about you? Marriage and a new parish. You'll have your hands full in more ways than one. Don't envy you."

"Which bit in particular are you referring to?"

"Oh, the marriage bit will be okay. S'pose I'll get round to it myself one of these days."

Peter was mischievous.

"What about Karen?"

"Ah, ah, don't think so. Have you seen beneath the makeup? Quite well-preserved, but definitely on the downhill slope. More a spring chicken man. No, I meant the religion bit. That's one hell of a hard row to hoe. I hear congregations tend to amount to one man and his dog these days. More's the pity."

Peter became alert.

"I didn't realise that you're a believer, Julian."

"I'm not…it's what you do though isn't it, regular parade. You know, Easter, Remembrance Sunday, Christmas…weddings, funerals and bar mitzvahs!"

A tinge of bitterness crept into Peter's tone.

"The Tory party at prayer eh? Or should I say the aging middle class clinging to the vestiges of a lost England?"

"Don't knock it Pete. We could do with more of it the way the liberals have torn the heart out of our country. Our true values and customs spring out of the life of the Church of England. Your influence as clergy, once upon a time, made us a civil society."

Peter was astonished by Julian's vehemence.

"Wow, I think your family has another member of Parliament in the making."

Julian inclined backwards and drained his glass. He sprang to his feet and shuffled into the aisle.

"Who knows."

With a surge of energy, he was off, and beside Karen in an instant.

The plane landed, and they lost sight of each other in the crowds. Peter made his way towards the Heathrow Express terminal – Hampshire via London, to his lovely fiancé. He caught a final glimpse of Julian steering Karen towards an exit.

4

"I like this place, and willingly could waste my time in it."
As You Like It Act 2: Sc. 4

Faisal Hussain was inured to the cold. It was his birth right as a British citizen, born and raised in the modest Buckinghamshire town of Wenbury. He stood in the lee of a wall watching the fourth form playing rugby, rather inadequately. No one could see him indulging in his one vice, secreted behind wall and trees.

Drawing upon a Black Sobranie cigarette, he shook his head. Another dropped ball, the cue for an interminable scrum. When he attended Wenbury Grammar he had been mainly academic, but he wasn't a bad sportsman. The lads in front of him were woeful. He gagged on his fag when Gerry Marsden told a boy that he was about as much use as a one-legged man at an arse kicking party. Gerry was Head of P.E., and a great friend. He was old-school. One of the few who could get away with a variety of insults that were most definitely not P.C.

Faisal swept his surroundings with an appreciative look. He enjoyed being back at the old school as a teacher. Next year he would be Head of History when Jim Bradfield retired. Faisal's special interest lay in the Tudors. It never crossed his mind to proselytise for the historical role of the Asian in British society. If he thought about his ethnicity at all it was only in passing.

The Hussains were British, and lived life according to the mainstream culture. His wife's name, Abir, suited her perfectly: serious and beautiful. She was racing ahead in her profession, making shed loads of money compared with his income as a teacher. Abir worked in high end insurance, servicing the needs of rich Buckinghamshire clients. They dressed in the prevailing style at home, in their two-bedroomed cottage in Old Wenbury. The only time they acquiesced to traditional Asian dress was for wider family occasions when grandparents were present.

Faisal attended Mosque in neighbouring Cranchurch, but paid his devotions quietly and sincerely, avoiding the wilder reaches of his faith. Abir would have none of it, and he respected her decision. Faisal and Abir lived a partnership without gender dominance.

Gerry Marsden's whistle brought him back to reality, and he nipped his ciggie out half-smoked. Boys swept past, barely visible in the steam rising from their open mouths. It was a cold Early-December, with the end in sight. Two and a bit more weeks and they would break for Christmas.

"Worra you doin boy, smoking is it? Why aren't you in class?"

Faisal laughed at Gerry's sing song Welsh tones.

"Please sir, I wasn't. Matron told me to get some fresh air."

They chuckled as they moved indoors. Gerry purred like a cat as he felt the warmth of a radiator.

"Ah, two free periods, and an opportunity to charm young Miss Munroe of the Classics department."

"You'll be lucky! She has some hooray Henry in tow."

"How do you know that?"

"Abi and I saw them arm in arm in Boots last Saturday."

Gerry scratched his arse, as only a Welshman can.

"Reckon she'd jump at the chance of the experience the older man can offer. I refer, of course, to my extensive teaching experience. Think I'll discuss dangling participles with her."

"Oops look at the time! Sixth form and Thomas Cromwell."

The voice of the Vales sang out, "Bit of a shithouse wasn't he?"

"Mmmm? Not as clear cut as that. The only shithouse, as you so delicately put it, will be my second encounter of the week with Denis Trueman."

"He's one of yours, is he? Most definitely a rum cove. I had the pleasure of asking him last week whether it was him or James Corden who ate all the pies. Couldn't catch a ball to save his life."

Gerry was nothing if not firm in his opinions.

"His views are somewhat to the right of Attila the Hun. Best get going."

"Badminton in the sports hall after school?" Gerry shouted.

"If you want another thrashing!"

Denis Trueman's father was the proprietor of a superior gentleman's outfitter in Old Wenbury, founded in the 1960's by his grandfather. It was typical of a Trueman to swim against the tide. Old Derek kept faith with classic clothing at the time when flares and kaftans became all the rage. Denis inherited his grandpa's curmudgeonly demeanour, and rather expansive waistline. There was another attribute he shared with the founder of the House of Trueman, but Denis kept that a closely guarded secret.

Like good grammar school pupils, the sixth form class was boisterous but controlled as they waited for Faisal.

"Oh my God, Johnny, have you let one go? You must have a dead rat up your arse."

"It's not me…God, that stinks. Who's dropped that?"

A chorus of denials rang out. Dave Black called for silence with his right index finger pointing accusingly at Denis Trueman.

"You dirty get Trueman. You need a pull-through."

Johnny Walsh chimed in, "Don't deny it Trueman. I've had to use the bogs after you. I'd recognise that scent anywhere…"

"What scent is that Johnny?"

Faisal's entry had passed unnoticed, unlike Denis' attack of wind.

"Phooaw…nice aftershave. Whose is that? No, don't answer. Right you bunch of ne'er do wells, down to business. Thomas Cromwell, sometime chief fixer for Henry VIII, what have you discovered from your research?"

The boys responded eagerly, for three reasons, a) intellectual curiosity, b) Faisal was a likeable guy, and c) word was that his wife was as fit as a butcher's dog.

The usual stuff came back: Lord Great Chamberlain, Lord Privy Seal, engineer in chief of Henry's annulled marriage to Katherine of Aragon.

Dave Black's hand went up, and you sensed mischief.

"Sir, his father's name was Walter. Amongst other things he was always being had up by the magistrates for watering his ale. He'd also been a blacksmith, a fuller, and a cloth merchant. WALTER…THE CLOTH MERCHANT."

A titter went around the room; everyone knew what Dave was inferring.

"Very funny Black!" exclaimed Trueman.

"I don't get it," said Faisal, "explain please."

Trueman adopted a more superior tone than usual.

"My father's name is Walter, and he owns…"

"Yes, yes, I get the point. I know your father's shop in town."

Johnny Walsh piped up.

"Have you ever bought anything from them, sir? They do a superb extra strength material. Denis' trousers are made out of it, sir."

The room exploded. The boys wept with laughter. Faisal had a job controlling himself, and his lower lip trembled noticeably.

Denis' voice boomed over chaos.

"I really don't think Mr. Hussain will ever have entered the premises. Our clothing is for the discerning ENGLISH gentleman."

Malice on his face betrayed Denis' view on what constitutes an English gentleman. The colour of Faisal's skin meant he was found wanting.

Faisal broke the embarrassed silence.

"Okay, you've had the essay title. If you start making notes, I'll come round and see you individually."

Faisal worked out his anger on a shuttlecock, to the detriment of Gerry Marsden. Dressed in a suit he looked trim, but nothing special; in shorts and t-shirt hard muscle rippled everywhere, and his six-foot frame was well-sculpted.

"Bloody hell 'F', that's the biggest hammering you've ever given me. What's got your goat?"

Faisal rubbed his neck with a towel.

"Apparently I'm not enough of an Englishman to shop in Trueman and Son, and probably not a gentleman either."

Gerry frowned; a light switched on.

"Ah, young master Trueman was it, airing his opinions. Fat, little racist bastard. I wouldn't let it bother you 'F'. You know what Wenbury is like; you know what Buckinghamshire is like! Never anything other than a Tory council since they invented them. As for M.P.'s, dress a sheep in blue and they'd vote for it…"

"And you'd probably shag it!"

"That is a calumny upon the Welsh nation!"

They dissolved into companionable laughter.

Faisal became thoughtful.

"Racists don't just come from the middle class, Gerry. They all surfaced when the Brexit vote went tits up. Followed by Trump in the States, and a bevy of nutters across Europe. The good-hearted working class played their part."

Gerry raised an amused eyebrow.

"And there was me thinking they spent all their time in and out of each other's houses borrowing cups of sugar and singing *'Knees Up Mother Brown.'* Listen mate, next time Trueman tries to wind you up get him out in front of the class, and show him a few of your Krav Maga moves. You still doing that?"

"Yep, working towards my grade 2 instructor's badge."

Krav Maga is a martial art, or rather a combination of them with the addition of street fighting techniques. It's favoured by the Israeli Defence Force, and employed by special forces throughout the world. Its basic tenet is avoiding trouble. If impossible, take out your opponent swiftly and walk away. Attacks to eyes, throat, groin and other tender parts are its principal techniques.

"You are joking Gerry? Say boo to Trueman and he'd run a mile. He's not exactly Big Arnie, is he?"

"More like Danny Devito. You got time for one in the Roebuck? I'll buy you a lemonade."

"Abi and I are off to that new Italian in the old town tonight."

Gerry sighed, "Ah, a scrummy wife and a scrummy meal. Lucky man. See you Monday then."

"Monday it is."

*

Banksmore is an expensive village set in the Chiltern Hills. The *'Manor'*, as Julian called it, was a sizable Georgian house set two-thirds of the way up a hillside. A rough track twisted a half mile from the lane to the main gate. It wasn't a remarkable property, but it gave credence to Sir Hugh Marlborough's lifelong pretensions to be an English gentleman. Hugh was keenly aware that his surname evolved out of 11th Century migration generated by the Norman Conquest. As his views on the French were as trenchant as those on other races he fostered the image of the true Englishman assiduously.

Julian stared out of the drawing room window to the valley below. Half-timbered cottages dotted either side of the lane, leading to the heart of the village. City types, architects and bankers occupied the houses; their sort of people. Log burners were going full blast by early afternoon, no shortage of money here to keep people warm. Surrounding farms supplemented the beauty of the scene. Farms that had been in the same hands for generations. Tradesmen and oiks appeared when deliveries and labour had to be undertaken. At weekends and holiday time, though, the place was overrun by ramblers and cyclists. For all their influence, and it was substantial, the locals had yet to find a way of excluding the great unwashed entirely.

Julian's eye settled on the square tower of the church, its crenulations reminded him of ancient battlements. St. George's Parish Church sat plumb centre in the village. The triangular green, in front of it, was the site for the splendid war memorial to the dead of the South African wars.

Sipping his whisky, Julian recalled that the church remained in Interregnum.

"Any progress with the new vicar?"

Hugh Marlborough glanced up from his Daily Telegraph.

"Oh, ask your mother, she knows more about these things. Sits on the PCC you know – you are still on it, aren't you darling?"

"Of course Hugh."

Theirs were lives in a hothouse, but at separate ends of the building nowadays. Time together was for public appreciation – dinners, flower shows and church attendance.

"Taking rather a long time to find a new vicar, isn't it mother?"

Deborah Marlborough was an attractive lady in her sixties. Petite and elfin like, with translucent skin and hair that fell in a natural wave. She curved subtly in all of the right places. Her piercing grey eyes always gave you their full attention, and a teasing smile was perpetually on her face enhancing her beautiful cheekbones. Deb's voice was surprisingly gravelly.

"It always takes a bloody long time, darling. You know what the Church of England is like with its arcane rules and regulations; not to mention saving a year's salary!"

She glugged from her G and T.

"He'll be our Rector, not a vicar."

"What's the difference?"

"The Rector is responsible for the Benefice. You know, overall responsibility for St. George's, our mother church, and five others in the surrounding villages."

"Dear God, does he have time to eat?"

"Oh, your father sees to that. We've got more associate ministers than you can shake a stick at, haven't we darling?"

Hugh looked up distractedly from his paper, "Mm, what?"

"Plenty of support for the Rector, darling."

"Oh yes, word with the Bishop and all that. Went to Merchant Taylors and wears a beard! Better than nothing I suppose, could be a woman."

"Darling, we're beyond all that, we've had women in the church for absolute yonks."

Debs resorted to her boarding school patois. Her eyes twinkled with mischief.

"Might get a woman as Rector."

Predictably, Hugh exploded, "Over my dead body!"

"Well darling, there are two on the short list."

"What!"

Hugh folded his paper, and leant forward.

"Now look here Debs, the PCC is responsible for telling the Bishop who they want, isn't it?"

"I believe so."

"Then you make sure that we get the right sort. We're not having the Vicar of bloody Dibley in my village."

Julian liked to side with his mother, so he stuck his two pennorth in.

"Never know, we might end up with that lay preacher who took the Remembrance service last month."

Hugh's complexion went a dangerous purple, and Deb's laugh drowned the tinkling of her ice.

"No chance Jules, he isn't ordained. Still, it's a thought, I rather like him. He brings out my maternal instinct."

"Quite," said Hugh, "he needs a firm hand. What was that bloody sermon about – love your enemy. Where did he get that nonsense from?"

"Jesus said it, father."

Deb's glass hovered mid-air.

"Darling, you are surprising at times. Fancy you knowing that."

Mother and son wrapped their arms around each other's waist. She kissed Julian on his cheek, her eyes swimming with worship.

Feeling rather put out, Hugh grumbled.

"Anyway, let's get a push on, eh Debs, see if we can't have the new man in place before Christmas."

"You'll be lucky. The mills of God grind slowly. Easter, we'll have him in place by Easter. The rota for Christmas is already done."

The glint returned to her eye.

"Jack Preston is leading on Christmas morning."

Hugh shook his head resignedly, and buried himself in his Telegraph muttering.

"S'pose we'll all have to feel sorry for bloody Herod. Good God, what has that arse of a Prime Minister been up to now..."

Jane was ecstatic, as she wrapped her arms around Peter, giving him a long lingering kiss.

"Mm," he breathed, "I could eat you for supper."

"Don't be greedy, you've already had me for breakfast – well, before breakfast to be strictly accurate. Shortlisted!"

Peter had endured a difficult year. The exception was their glorious wedding day and the joy of being with each other for ever. Given the shortage of clergy, it was surprising that he hadn't already landed a parish. Few had come up, and from the ones that had only a couple were attractive. It wasn't a question of where they would have to live, more the style of worship demanded by those offering posts. Pete wasn't an arch-traditionalist, but neither did he feel comfortable with the 'happy clappy' brigade.

Much of the year had been spent in voluntary work on the streets, amongst the homeless and the drug addicts. He was surprised at the extent of social problems in such a modestly-sized Hampshire town. As time passed he understood its causes more. Words came back to him.

"You'll find things have changed at home – a lot!"

He smiled, and wondered if Julian and Karen had got hitched.

Peter regarded himself as a Christian Socialist. The first year home left him sad at the disastrous failure of the Labour government. He'd seen old documentary footage of a female Labour M.P. preparing to contest the leadership against Corbyn.

"I stand for hope, not grievance," she said.

That was it in a nutshell, Corbyn had never known what he stood for in concrete terms, so he was agin everything.

Labour came to office without Corbyn, and the Prime Minister implemented Disneyland social initiatives. Borrowing became astronomical. Three years into power, and it was collapsing round his ears. Taxes and prices had risen, the unions were as militant as they had been in the 1970's, house repossessions were sky high, and unemployment grew exponentially.

The people on the streets weren't just from the bottom end of society. It was the young men and women in their early-twenties who touched Peter deeply. Beneath the poverty, dirt and addiction he saw a chrysalis. Deep inside each lost soul was a life rich in promise, but they were seduced into dependency for everything on the State. Lives neutered by the 1970's corruption of true Socialism. In their discontent they played the old blame game. Immigrants kept a low profile these days, even those who had been here decades. A steady stream of abuse had flowed their way ever since the referendum to leave the E.U, back in 2016.

"You know I'm not altogether sure about this, Jane?"

"I know, but there are plenty of people in the villages who need a hand up. Anyway, don't the rich need Christ, just as much as the poor? *'It's easier for a camel to pass through the eye of a needle, than it is for a rich man to enter the Kingdom of Heaven'.*"

Pete smiled at her with unadulterated love in his heart. He examined her beautiful moon-shaped face, framed by a page boy haircut.

"Logically, if they're struggling to get through the pearly gates then they need a good minister to set them on the way."

"Have I told you lately that I love you."

"Frequently, but don't ever stop."

"A week today then, you get your best frock on, and we'll go and meet the PCC."

Jane couldn't resist, "Will you be wearing one of your frocks?"

They rocked with laughter.

"Think I'll stick with best suit and dog collar, save the *'frock'* for my first service. Now, what are we having for dinner?"

Jane pressed up against him.

"Depends how hungry you are."

The interview was a formality, once Peter became known to Deborah Marlborough.

"You've a military background, Peter. What regiment?"

"The Oxsters."

She threw her head back, and bounced that dirty laugh off the wooden panelling of the parish hall. The rest of the PCC smiled submissively.

"You must know my son, Julian. Did you serve together?"

Peter shook his head inwardly, of course Marlborough.

"Yes, yes indeed. We retired at the same time; sat together on the flight home, as it happens."

Deb's mind was made up, and that meant the committee's was as well. She fancied the idea of having a dishy forty-something for Rector. His background in the forces, and friendship with Julian, clinched the deal.

Marjorie Whitlock interrupted her train of thought with a firm and incisive voice.

"Reverend Standish, may I ask you what your views are with regard to the use of modern musical instruments in church services?"

Debs gave her a haughty look, to no avail. Old maid she may have been, but she was the kindliest of women with a fierce intelligence and a deep faith.

Peter unburdened himself of his thoughts on the subject of electric guitars and tambourines. Marjorie was not entirely satisfied, but the balance was in his favour. Her cherubic smile showed approval.

"If there are no more questions, then I think we should release Peter from this interrogation."

Derek Fisher, chairman of the PCC – still chairMAN in Banksmore, none of that *'person'* nonsense, took command.

"Do have another look around before lunch, Peter. Ah, we seem to have lost your wife?"

"She's having a wander round the village, Derek. I'll join her for a stroll."

"Half an hour then, Peter, and back here for a bite. Good of you to let us grill you. Till later then."

Derek leaned back in his chair.

"Like him; want him."

Debs sighed with relief. She wasn't afraid of Derek, but didn't want a struggle with the former CEO of an investment bank.

A chorus of support broke forth from the other members.

"...and his wife," said Marjorie, "such a sweet girl."

Derek grinned, "Rather a looker, I thought, eh Deb?"

"Somewhat enthusiastic."

Her tone would have cut through steel.

"Bit of competition Debs."

Lady Marlborough kept her composure whilst seething at Derek's indiscreet remark. She brought them to order.

"So we're all agreed, Peter Standish is our stand-out candidate?"

A ripple of laughter went round at her corny pun.

"Our sort of people, I think."

Derek completed the formalities.

"All in favour…unanimous. I'll communicate our decision to the Bishop post haste. By the way, he's shaved his beard off."

"About time too, I concur with Mrs. Thatcher, men with facial hair have something to hide."

Before old Johnny Parkinson could ramble further about the great days of the *'Iron Lady'* Derek cut him short.

"Ladies, if you would attend to the food, I'll tidy up the paperwork. Bottle of scotch in that cupboard Johnny."

The ladies retreated to the kitchen. Debs took a supervisory capacity.

Derek, Johnny and the third male member of the committee were left alone. Johnny poured and Derek scribbled.

"Didn't have much to say Jack?"

"Preferred to listen, Derek."

"Do you approve of our decision?"

"I put my hand up, Johnny."

"Not the same thing."

Jack Preston was very content, but he wasn't going to tell them. He had discerned the true disciple of Christ in Peter Standish; not just a 'Sunday Servant'. Oh yes, they didn't know what they'd let themselves in for.

"Think he'll be a shot in the arm for the Benefice. Wouldn't be at all surprised if within six months he'd got Martin Russell back in the congregation."

Martin was the resident strident atheist and village know-all, though there was some competition for the latter title.

"Care to have a small wager on that, Jack?"

Old Johnny interrupted Derek.

"Might even see a bit more of young master Julian in church, him being a friend of the Rector."

Derek cocked an eyebrow.

"Now that is something I'm not prepared to bet on. That young man will visit us on high days and holidays alone. Come on chaps, I'm ready for my lunch. Marjorie's quiche is a wonder to behold, and so is young Mistress Standish. Bring the bottle Johnny."

*

Padam Gurung drove the taxi slowly along the Marlborough's uneven drive. He negotiated the crescent in front of the Manor to turn about face. He'd been here many times to pick up Sir Hugh, and take him to the House of Commons. Lucrative jobs they were, and he got on well with the Member of Parliament for Wenbury and Cranchurch. So much so that Sir Hugh made it plain to the firm that Padam should drive him whenever possible.

To his surprise Padam saw a tall young man silhouetted in the doorway of the house kissing a lady on the cheek. He recognised Lady Deborah from the occasional trips alongside her husband. Jumping out of the Mercedes, he opened the rear nearside door for his passenger.

"Good evening, sir."

"I'll join you in the front, if I may Sergeant?"

A much surprised Padam ushered him into the front seat.

Whilst they bumped down the drive he threw curious glances at his passenger.

Julian threw his head back and laughed.

"My father told me about your past career, Sergeant."

"And you must be Captain Julian, of whom his mother and father are so very proud."

"*Touché*, Sarge."

"The Royal British Legion it is then. A night out is it, sir?"

"Sort of, they've asked me to say a few words about my Middle East experiences. I expect there'll be a drink or two going as well."

They smiled at each other. Those who knew Julian would have been a little surprised at his warmth. Like most servicemen Julian had the utmost respect for Gurkhas, and the nut brown tone of their skin was irrelevant.

"You a member of the Legion, Sarge?"

"Indeed I am sir, though I don't get much time for socialising. Driving a taxi doesn't earn you that much, and I need to work all the hours God sends."

"Not your firm then?"

"No sir."

"Who's the gaffer?"

"The Khan brothers, sir. They're the main players around here."

"Pakistanis! You like working for them?"

Caution overtook Padam Gurung.

Julian went on a charm offensive.

"No need to say any more, I understand."

"It's...it's not wise to say too much about the Khans in public."

"Surely an old Gurkha soldier isn't afraid of a few taxi drivers?"

Sergeant Padam Gurung bristled.

"I'm afraid of no one sir, but..."

"But?"

"They are very bad people, sir."

"Hardly surprising Sergeant, they are Pakistanis."

"Oh no sir, that is not what I mean at all. I am a Christian sir; I worship in your village church. I do not judge a man to be good or bad by his nationality, or his religion. A bad man is such because of the wrongs he does as an individual."

"And what wrongs do the Khan brothers get up to?"

Padam Gurung held his counsel, and Julian didn't press him further.

As they drew up in the British Legion car park in Old Wenbury Padam spoke.

"Are you old enough to remember those shameful affairs in Rochdale and Rotherham, sir, and similar cases throughout the country?"

Julian's face was as hard as basalt. Flames of anger made his pupils dance. Child abuse, grooming of girls – he remembered it well.

"The Khans, Captain, they..."

"Enough said rifleman; no names no pack drill, eh. Collect me at eleven, as arranged?"

"It will be my pleasure, sir."

Cries of fear came from beneath the market square clock. It was a toss-up who heard them first; Padam and Julian exiting the Legion car park, or Faisal and Abir standing on the doorstep of *'Il Trovatore'*. The reaction was the same. Julian, Padam and Faisal ran towards the noise, whilst Abi stayed beside the proprietor, Mr. Fazio.

The scene greeting them was lit dimly by a distant street light, the walls of the tower casting shadows.

Feral youths were pressing up against someone, laughing, jeering and catcalling. A voice rent the night air.

"What you fink you're up to, cruisin'? Fat little queer. In my country we 'ang shirtlifters like you."

A dog barked, and received a kick for its pains.

"Leave him alone, please, I…"

The sound of wind escaping the victim loudly caused the assailants to laugh even more.

"'e's shit 'imself Mo!"

"Yeh, he's getting' 'is arse ready for you."

Whoops of vindictive delight filled the night air.

A commanding voice rang out.

"Leave him alone! Denis, come here son."

The authority in the voice made Julian and Padam jump, as much as it did the gang. Everyone turned to face Faisal, who came abreast of Julian.

Mo' broke the silence.

"Mind your own fuckin' business pal, if you know what's good for you."

"You've had your fun fellas, call it a night and we can all go home."

In the amber light the gang appeared more threatening than at first glance. Julian counted nine, and they weren't young kids. He and Padam exchanged a look and smiled, as Faisal stepped forward to face Mo'.

"Let him pass, please. Come on Denis."

Young Trueman took a step forward, only to be slammed backwards into the wall by Mo'. The thug was a good six feet one and well-toned, and when he faced Faisal he sneered.

"What's your problem, he your bum chum? What's wrong with you man, siding with a white boy instead of with your own?"

The gang muttered in agreement, though they were a mixture of races; white, black and Asian.

"What did you mean about hanging people in your country? You're British, aren't you?"

Julian's question caused a hiatus in the proceedings.

Mo' looked him up and down, and said viciously.

"Just cos a dog's born in a stable, it don't make it a horse mate."

Julian was beginning to find this tedious, so he became provocative.

"I'm not your mate. I imagine your mate would have a furry coat and a tail, and more balls than you - bitch."

Mo' flew forward to attack Julian. Before he realised it he was on his knees. Faisal had swayed to one side and taken him in a very painful arm lock.

"Oright man, oright!"

Faisal released him, and he clambered to his feet seething with anger. Mo' turned his back and started to slowly walk away, trailed by his acolytes. Without warning, all nine turned to attack Faisal. Padam Gurung reacted first, and felled one youth with a head butt and a kick to the groin; Julian swept another lad of his feet and stamped on his face. Faisal sidestepped the onrushing Mo' and slammed the heel of his hand under his nose shattering it. The others backed off. Nothing was said, as the injured parties were helped away.

"You're bleeding Denis. Come on, let's walk you over to the restaurant, and see if Mr. Fazio can clean you up."

They entered the well-lit doorway, and when Julian saw Abi his eyes glittered.

"Now there is a honey," he thought.

"Mr. Fazio, Denis has taken a bit of a knock. Do you have a first aid kit?"

"Of course, of course. Come inside everyone, you can have a drink while I sort him out."

Denis sat alone at a table, waiting for Mr. F. to reappear. Mrs. Fazio offered drinks, but there were no takers.

"You and young Denis seem to be old friends," Julian said.

Faisal smiled politely, "He's in my sixth form history set at the grammar school."

Julian's face was impassive. Inside his head he was coming to terms with what he'd just seen. A schoolteacher handling himself like a professional in a rumble.

"Nice work out there. You'll have to give me lessons."

Abi spoke proudly.

"He'll be a grade 2 instructor soon."

"Oh yes, which particular branch of the martial arts?"

He had a damn good idea, but wanted it confirmed.

"Krav Maga. Have you come across it?"

Julian flapped a hand.

"Vaguely."

He smiled inwardly, remembering his own training in the deadly art at the base in Hereford. He was impressed, but he wasn't going to show his feelings.

"There we are, all done and dusted. No real damage."

Mr. Fazio examined his handiwork The abrasion to Denis' cheek wasn't serious.

"What were you doing Denis, wandering about at this time of night?"

Denis avoided Faisal's eye, and mumbled that he was just walking his poodle, Minnie.

Padam caught Julian's eye, and an imperceptible smile crossed their features. Julian saw Abi watching them. She too was struggling to stay composed at Denis' illuminating information. For a moment she and Julian were complicit.

He broke the spell.

"Do forgive my manners. I'm Julian Marlborough, and this is my driver Padam Gurung late of the Gurkhas. I suspect you guess something like that by the swift and summary justice he inflicted beneath the stars."

Julian chuckled at his own wit.

Faisal came to his feet and extended his hand.

"Faisal Hussain, and this is my wife Abir. Just a plain old schoolteacher I'm afraid, nothing so brave as a soldier. The nearest claim I can make is for my grandfather. He fought alongside your regiment, Padam, in the Second World War. What line are you in Julian?"

"Oh, I'm retired and sponging off my father."

"Excuse me sir, Sir Hugh Marlborough is chairman of our governors. Are you related sir?"

"The very same Denis."

"He very kindly patronises my father's shop, sir. Trueman and Son."

Julian nodded, he knew who they were. Smiling oleaginously, Julian addressed Abi.

"Whilst we're all getting to know each other we mustn't leave Mrs. Hussain out of the conversation."

He cocked a quizzical eyebrow.

Abir felt uncomfortable with his aroused eyes on her; she found his fleshy lips especially repellent.

"I'm in insurance".

"Oh yes. Locally?"

Faisal answered for her; his pride in his beautiful and talented wife matching that of Denis'.

"For Warburg and Driffield...in the City."

"My, my, my, only connect."

"I'm sorry?" said a puzzled Abi.

"Oh nothing, I was just musing at what an evening of surprises it's been."

Faisal turned to Denis.

"Come on Denis, we'll walk to our house for the car and give you a lift home."

"Leave that to us Faisal. You don't mind the pooch in the back do you Padam?"

The taxi driver wanted to wrinkle his nose, but he couldn't afford to lose the Marlboroughs' business.

"Do you have far to travel young man?"

Denis ignored the Gurkha's enquiry, and looked at Julian.

"The edge of town."

They moved outside into the cold night air, thanking Mr. and Mrs. Fazio. Padam brought his Mercedes over from the other side of the road.

Julian was charm personified.

"Well goodnight then. Unusual circumstances, but a real pleasure to meet you both. Denis, haven't you something to say?"

Despite Faisal having saved his skin, Denis spoke through gritted teeth.

"Thank you, sir...for your help. Goodnight Mrs. Hussain."

The taxi eased away, and Padam smiled benevolently upon the Hussains through his steamed up window.

"Come on my darling, let's get home. We don't want to hang around here. There's been enough excitement for one evening...defending Denis' honour."

They giggled knowingly as they walked arm in arm down the High Street.

Padam drew away slowly, taking the opportunity to study Julian, who was lighting a cigarette in the porch of the Manor. He seemed consumed with his own thoughts, but suddenly waved a hand to the Mercedes as it departed.

Descending to the village, Padam reflected upon the evening's events. The face of his old Regimental Sergeant Major intruded, and he recollected a conversation they'd had. Young officers had just been posted to them, and the RSM expressed his doubts about one of them.

"He looks a wrong 'un to me."

"How can you tell?"

"He's a *'watcher'* Pad', which is not a bad thing. But you want his eyes focused on the enemy, not on you. Our 2nd Lieutenant was sizing us all up the moment he met us, and ingratiating himself with everyone. Trying to be all things to all men. He's storing it away for when he can put it to some use; which means, to his advantage. I tell you Pad', I've seen officers like him before, and they're bad buggers."

53

The Mercedes passed the War Memorial and Padam shuddered. This particular officer had taken a dislike to a young corporal, and accused him of making homosexual advances. He'd been a good lad, that junior NCO, a handsome boy fresh from the hills. The shame of it was too great for him, and he shot himself. Nothing was said, but it was known that the accusation was made because the boy had rejected the officer's sexual advances.

Padam's mind reverted to Julian. Friendly as he was, there was something not quite right there. During the confrontation with the youths, and after, he had noticed his intent watchfulness. At the restaurant he saw how attentive he was to the Hussains, to Mrs. Hussain in particular. What surprised Padam was Julian's vagueness about the martial art. Sir Hugh Marlborough was inordinately proud of his son. Whilst chauffeuring him, Padam had learnt a great deal about the young man, especially his regiment. That was the puzzle. If he was SAS, then he'd have an intimate knowledge of Krav Maga. Padam thought that he hadn't been at all wise in mentioning the activities of his employers, the Khan brothers. The car climbed upwards into Wenbury-on-the-Hill, and he reproached himself. He rather hoped that Julian Marlborough would not turn out to be a bad bugger.

Julian poured an Armagnac. Hearing a shuffling from his father's study, he strolled down the hall and tapped lightly on the door before entering. It was the habit of childhood years. Woe betide you if you entered the room unannounced.

Hugh Marlborough was on the telephone.

"Yes Freddie, yes you're right. Won't be long now before we take power."

He glanced at Julian framed in the doorway, and laughed into the receiver.

"Spot on Freddie. Won't be much fun for the country in the short term, but bloody good news for us. Cheerio Freddie. Yes, yes, ten-thirty in that bloody cubby hole you call an office."

He replaced the receiver, and sat there looking gleeful.

"Still hard at it, father? Don't you get fed up with it after all these years?"

Sir Hugh was quivering with emotion, and he jumped to his feet embracing his son.

"We've got the buggers, Julian, they're finished."

"Who father?"

"You haven't heard the news? There's been a coup at the *'palace'*."

"Good God father, I know our present monarch is an arse, but surely you don't approve of Republicanism?"

Sir Hugh roared with laughter.

"Forgive me Julian, I was being rather facetious, and inexact in my terms. The palace I refer to is Ten Downing Street. That bumbling and inept fool is out on his arse. His own lot have stuck the knife in."

"Will there be an election?"

"Oh no, even better, they've replaced him with Tommy O'Donnell."

"I'm a bit out of the swim these days, pray who is Tommy O'Donnell?"

"Pour me a cognac, and I'll tell you."

Julian provided his sire with a generous measure from the decanter on the bookshelf. Hugh reclined in his leather armchair, and gestured to Julian to take the one opposite.

Savouring his cognac, he mused.

"Tommy Patrick O'Donnell, oh he's a beauty. Do you remember the Deputy Prime Minister under Blair and Brown?"

"I do, a toe rag called John Prescott. Thick as a Gurkha's foreskin. Incidentally, I like your taxi driver, handy fellow in a tight spot."

Sir Hugh, waved a hand airily.

"Yes, yes, good sort...now this O'Donnell, he makes Prescott look like Albert Einstein. You know what's most amusing? Prescott came from Hull, and our new Prime Minister comes from the opposite extremity of the M62."

"Good God, father, we've got a Scouser for PM?"

"Indeed we have. You know it never fails to amaze me how gullible the electorate is when it comes to qualifications."

"Not sure I get your drift?"

Sir Hugh enlightened him.

"The news has been rattling on all evening about O'Donnell's M.A. in Media Studies from some God-forsaken former polytechnic in the middle of nowhere. As if that qualifies him for the highest office in the land. It made me smile, when I served in the Education Department under Theresa, how pathetically humble the public become when they realise you've been to public school; as if that means anything. You and I know those places aren't all they're cracked up to be. Remember that place in Dorset we nearly sent you to? The *'Asylum for the Rich and Thick'*. You've got your mother to thank for not ending up there."

Julian watched and said nothing. He knew only too well the size of his debt to his mother. He recalled with pleasure the years spent at High Heath School, Hampstead; excepting that unfortunate incident during his last year. His father's nose was still somewhat skew from where the teacher's head butt landed. Still, it was a small price to pay for getting Julian out of a very big and nasty scrape.

"Wonder where that teacher is now?" he thought. "Must be pushing seventy."

"Are you listening Julian?"

He focused on his Pa'.

"With O'Donnell in place it's a shift to the real extreme left. O'Donnell is a raving loony. He can't keep his temper, and he isn't wise enough to keep his own counsel. The end is nigh, and we're ready. Time to put this country to rights. No more hiding behind bogus social science to protect the idle and the criminal."

Hugh rose, and poured himself a small one.

"So, you liked our Sergeant cum taxi driver? He's a good man. Attends church in the village so I'm told. What was that about tight spots?"

Sir Hugh may have been advancing in years, and over-excited by the recent political news, but he had a retentive memory. Julian related the details of the encounter in the market square, and in the restaurant afterwards.

"Son's a shirt lifter eh? Better keep that from old man Trueman. He's farther to the right than us; a real hang 'em and flog 'em sort. I haven't come across your history teacher. Tell you what though, I wouldn't mind meeting his missus. From what you say, she sounds a peach. Warburg and Driffield eh? We need to update our insurances. I'll get my secretary to give old Bobby Dixon a bell. Let's put some business the way of Mrs. Hussain over lunch. Right, bedtime for me, Sergeant Gurung returns at eight-thirty to power steer me into Town. Goodnight Julian. What an interesting night it has been, for both of us. We do indeed live in interesting times."

"Goodnight father."

Julian sat alone, nursing the remains of his Armagnac. He pondered on the old Chinese curse.

"May you live in interesting times."

To most people the thought was terrifying, but not to Julian. Chaos and disorder brought opportunities.

5

"God shall be my hope, my stay, my guide and lantern to my feet."
Henry VI Second Part: Act 2: Sc. 3

Spring came early to Banksmore.

Despite the shenanigans in Parliament, the Labour Party clung to power by its fingertips. The Tories bated Tommy O'Donnell, and his responses made him look like a raving lunatic.

A sense of hopelessness gripped Britain. It was nearly as bad as the *'Winter of Discontent'* in 1979, but at least the dead were being buried. It was a return to the Harold Wilson era of beer and sandwiches with the union leaders. Except, as Hugh Marlborough noted upon attending one of these get-togethers, this time round it was an appalling Cuban red and sausage rolls; there was even a tray of pineapple and cheese on cocktail sticks.

In Banksmore hope sprung eternal, it always does amongst the moneyed class. The greatest joy was reserved for the week before Easter, and the Licensing and Installation of Peter Standish as Rector of St. George's. Bishop Arthur officiated, assisted by Archdeacon, Ingrid Lovett. The single reading from the Bible was delivered with relish by lay preacher Jack Preston. His fluid voice ran like a river throughout the church:

"Proverbs 8: 1-11, Wisdom's Call: Does not wisdom call out? Does not understanding raise her voice? On the heights along the way, where the paths meet, she takes her stand; beside the gates leading into the city, at the entrances, she cries aloud: 'To you, O men, I call out; I raise my voice to all mankind. You who are simple, gain prudence; you who are foolish, gain understanding. Listen, for I have worthy things to say; I open my lips to speak what is right. My mouth speaks what is true, for my lips detest wickedness. All the words of my mouth are just; none of them is crooked or perverse. To the discerning all of them are right; they are faultless to those who have knowledge. Choose my instruction instead of silver, knowledge rather than choice gold, for wisdom is more precious than rubies, and nothing you desire can compare with her...'"

The words per se did not offend. A congregation of well-fed dignitaries was attuned to Church ceremonies and challenging Scripture. Faces wore expressions of gravitas and intellectual superiority. The heads bearing them were elsewhere, wondering if there would be a good feed afterwards.

On this occasion Jack's well-crafted delivery forced the meaning of the proverb into everyone's consciousness. He managed to make almost the entire congregation feel uncomfortable, and offend not a few.

There were those who bridled at the thought that they were labelled simple and foolish, and they dismissed the idea that they needed to gain understanding. The implication that they may not possess discernment upset the very successful businessmen, and the injunction to give only secondary importance to their gold and silver came close to provoking a number of heart attacks. Johnny Parkinson was audibly muttering that he'd worked hard for his money, and he'd be damned if he wasn't going to enjoy the proceeds of his labour.

When Jack stepped away from the lectern there was but one beatific smile in the place, and that belonged to Marjorie Whitlock. She and Jack were a generation apart, but he shot from the hip and she approved. Bishop Arthur saved the day, by his equivocal exposition of the Scripture. Hugh Marlborough warmed to him, despite the fact that he was growing that bloody beard again.

Assembled in the church hall, bearing a plate of nibbles and a frugal glass of wine, the guests listened to the area dean formally welcoming Peter.

"We wish Peter every success in his ministry tending his flock and spreading the Gospel of Christ Jesus."

Jack Preston whispered to Marjorie Whitlock.

"He'll need all the help he can get here in Sodom."

Marjorie tittered, as a sharp-eared Deborah Marlborough threw him a filthy look.

"Oops, think I've spoiled my chances there."

Marjorie blushed to her roots, but she was enjoying every minute of it.

Peter gave a short peroration to thank all and sundry.

"Hope to see you all again on Good Friday and, of course, Sunday."

He'd be lucky, many of them would be off to their second homes in the West Country. If the long-range weather forecast was borne out, quite a few of the chaps would be on Wenbury Golf course by 08:00 hours, and arseholed in the clubhouse by 14:00.

"Splendid service Bishop. Do you know my boy, Julian?"

"Ah yes. Lately returned from foreign climes."

Julian grasped a surprisingly firm hand, and said nothing.

"What about you Bishop, been on any jollies recently? Any sit-ins or marches? How's that blog of yours, still giving good news to the great unwashed?"

Bishop Arthur was not the *'useless fart in a colander'* that Marlborough proclaimed him to be. He was an astute and intelligent man, handicapped by coming from the generation that believed it could capture souls for Christ by simply being amenable to all sorts. Arthur had forgotten to be *'in'* the world but not *'of'* it. He was aware that Hugh Marlborough was being offensive, but refused to rise to the bait.

"Bishop! Any progress on financing the *'Single Mothers and Children Club?'*"

Jack Preston wasn't going to miss the chance to press his case.

"Ah, Jack, I was hoping to have a word. Exciting news. Must have a word with this stout fellow. If you would excuse me gentlemen."

Deborah Marlborough swung through the throng to join husband and son.

Apoplectic as ever, Hugh waded in.

"Debs, what's all this bloody nonsense about some club for single mothers and their brats?"

"Oh darling, that's just Jack Preston promoting good works."

"Aiding and abetting feckless and careless women in my opinion."

Hugh spoke, as if addressing the House.

"Actually, my love, we were thinking of asking you to be titular head of the project."

Hugh was about to rant on when Debs cut him short.

"Look good in the local rag, and we can get that ghastly Mayoress to join you at the inaugural meeting – she'd turn up for the opening of a window."

Julian laughed loudly at his mother's wit. He really did love and appreciate her. Principally, because she had defended him from his father's vicious temper when he was a child. One thing Julian always admired in his father was the way he played his cards close to his chest. He had noticed that, with age, he seemed to be losing his sense of discretion and discernment. It reminded Julian of Jack Preston's Bible reading.

"Still can't take to your lay preacher, mummy. He read that passage rather pointedly, I thought. Smacks of impertinence, you know. The sort of dumb insolence we used to have to deal with in bolshie privates."

"And I'm sure you dealt with them perfectly, darling. Come on, let's jolly things along. We have the Claymore-Browne's to lunch, and I want to impress them."

"Why mummy? He's only a local farmer."

"Sweetie, Desmond's a bit more than that with three hundred of the best acres in these parts. Besides I want to charm Fiona into being my social secretary. A good lunch, and the promise of a seat on a few important committees should appeal to her."

"Room for me at table?"

"Of course, darling, I was relying on you to lead the charm offensive. I think Fiona's rather smitten with you."

Julian kept his counsel. He wasn't smitten with Fiona, but he relished the thought of tying her up and spanking her. Fiona was about fifty, with a lean and spare physique which appealed to Julian.

"Rightio Ma, on parade."

The Marlboroughs made a three-pronged attack upon the rest of the room. Soon the VIP's departed, so they were able to leave.

Peter Standish introduced an innovation for Good Friday. In the morning a small number gathered on the Green. Peter hove into view, negotiating the churchyard gates with a large wooden cross. This was to be the first time Banksmore joined in the traditional Walk of Witness.

From the four points of the compass Christians converged with their individual crosses on the centre of Wenbury-on-the-Hill. Along the way they chatted, sang, took time for prayer, and collected wayside litter. Occupants of vehicles on the busy Good Friday roads remained largely indifferent to them. Occasionally, a horn was tooted in support, and the odd 'wankers' was hurled.

When they assembled in front of St. Peter's Wenbury it was discovered that the cry of *"Allahu Akbar"*, ('God is Greater), had been yelled from passing windows at two different groups. The cries from Muslim believers puzzled them. It was a terrible irony that the Islamic world still believed they were engaged in a struggle with Christianity. How anyone could think that Western Europe was remotely Christian was a mystery. The marginalisation of the Church was two centuries old. For at least the last fifty years its influence upon the conduct of society had diminished to vanishing point.

"You see, Marjorie, what the Apologists never make clear is where the responsibility for the mess we're in lies."

Marjorie loved the sheer pleasure of minds meeting and exploring possibilities.

"Where, in your opinion, does the blame lie, Jack?"

"Firmly and securely at the door of Atheism, the *Gospel of Despair*. Look at it like this Marjorie, we Christians are a tiny minority within Britain. Our influence upon the body politic is negligible. Ipso facto, the greed, the incivility, the violence and intolerance rampant in our society must be laid at the door of the majority. The collective noun for them is Atheists."

Marjorie savoured his words.

"So why do they bother with negative and insulting behaviour towards – I won't say Christianity – Religion?"

Marjorie was a delightful old girl, and surprisingly astute, but she was imbued with that wonderful aptitude to always see the good in people. Mendacity evaded her comprehension.

"Marjorie, Marjorie, Marjorie, it's a technique as old as time. When the house is falling down around you, and you're responsible, you find a scapegoat. The Church has a history of great deeds in our society, but also some horrendous mistakes. We are a convenient minority to blame, and we let them get away with it."

"No need to say who lets them off the hook. In my lifetime I've watched the Clergy lose its nerve, and, in quite a few cases, their faith. They've become social workers instead of being on fire for the Gospel. Of course, they've been put in straitjackets by bishop after bishop, because *they* long since succumbed to the corruption of Liberalism."

"Don't quite follow, Marjorie?"

"Well, I'm teaching my grandmother to suck eggs. As you know, Liberalism is founded on the ideas of liberty and equality. All well and good, but it has become debased by conflating liberty with licence. *'Liberty Hall'*, as my mother used to say; a place where anything goes. Our people are twice intoxicated; by alcohol and by the perverse doctrine of personal liberty. They *"...bawl for freedom in their senseless mood, and still revolt when truth would set them free..."*

"That's brilliant Marjorie, you should put that in a letter to the Times."

"Oh, it's not mine dear, John Milton made that perceptive observation; Sonnet 12: *'I did but prompt the age to quit their clogs'*. You know the next part of it?"

Jack shook his head.

'Licence they mean when they cry liberty, for who loves that must first be wise and good.'

"As you know dear, I don't do anything after 1800."

They laughed at her well-used refrain concerning her interests in life.

"You're familiar with the epigram uttered by one of the victims of the Reign of Terror in revolutionary France? *'Oh, Liberty, what crimes have been committed in thy name!'*

"That terror is coming again," Jack said, "we've been seeing the signs for some time now. I don't think we know half of what's going on in the country."

"What do you mean?"

"The scale of racial abuse and attacks, and not just in the U.K. France and Germany aren't safe havens for immigrants anymore; parts of Eastern Europe are hell on earth for those of a different skin colour. I suspect the extent of racial aggravation is far greater than we are allowed to know. The irony is that each generation of Jihadists just make the situation worse. Not so much for the indigenous populations, but for their own Muslim brethren who suffer the backlash against their atrocious acts..."

A well-spoken voice interjected softly.

"Thank you Jack, you've given me the germ of an idea. Now come on, hand that Cross over to someone else, we're on the final stretch."

Peter Standish helped Jack negotiate the vivid symbol of suffering around a lamppost. To everyone's surprise it settled on the shoulder of Fiona Claymore-Browne.

6

"For you, the city, thus I turn my back: There is a world elsewhere."
Coriolanus Act 3: Sc.3

The Khan brothers' fingers were in a variety of local pies, but principally they had the taxi service sewn up in Wenbury and Cranchurch. Their portfolio included petrol stations, and the best Indian restaurants in five towns.

Head of the clan was Raza Khan, sitting behind an expansive desk to accommodate his corpulent frame. He was juggling paper work on second hand cars.

To the watching world Raza was a good Moslem. He attended mosque in Cranchurch, and observed the rites scrupulously. In his heart he was as far from God as anyone could be. Raza was a man of obsessive secrecy, both in business and his personal life. The sole intent of his religious observance was to advance himself in the Moslem community. His god was profit. He tried to remain below the radar where authority was concerned. The local police were aware of dubious dealings and activities, but nothing was yet proven.

"Usman, get your sorry person in here, now!"

His younger brother appeared with alacrity; you didn't keep Raza waiting.

"What the hell is going on, man, three cars sold at rock bottom prices, next to no profit?"

"Family Raza, all to family, well not all. One went to 'Johnny' Gurkha for his wife."

"Who the hell is 'Johnny' Gurkha?"

Usman looked puzzled. It was the nickname for Padam, surely everyone knew that.

"Gurung – one of our drivers..."

"Yes, yes, yes, I remember. If it's family, or insiders, just mark the bloody papers with that, save wasting my time. I hope you didn't give him a discount as big as family?"

"Ten per cent less."

Squealing brakes and a gunning engine sounded from the yard. They smiled at each other.

"Qadir".

The three were chalk and cheese in looks. Raza, a cunning mountain of blubber; Usman, pushing thirty-eight, not bad looking but running to seed. He was well-dressed and dripping in gold adornments.

Qadir was something else. He worked out in the gym installed in their large and secluded house in Beaconsfield. Each morning, at six, he was running, cycling and pumping iron. Qadir was five feet eleven inches of bone hard muscle, and a very handsome twenty-four-year-old indeed. His eyes were fascinating, their coal-black depths disappearing to infinity. They would change in a flash when he was in a fury. Red spots would dance like a Dervish in them. Qadir could lose his temper at the drop of a hat, and pound someone to pulp if he felt they'd insulted him.

Unlike his uncles he was a true believer. When Qadir was at Mosque he discovered his raison d'etre; to advance the cause of Islam by any means necessary. He may not have inherited Raza's girth, but he had inherited his discretion. Qadir made sure never to reveal his religio-political ends to the head of the household. Should Raza learn of his intentions all hell would break loose. For Raza the bottom line was, *"Business is business."* No, best keep quiet, for now, Raza would put a stop to anything he thought would interfere with profits.

"Boy, you are going to blow that engine up."

"Don't worry, it's not one of ours."

"Who the hell does it belong to then?"

Usman chipped in.

"It's *'Johnny'* Gurkha's Mercedes. He's not working today, and we've got two cars in the workshop. I slipped him thirty for lending us his motor."

Raza's aggrieved tone washed over the other two.

"You gave him thirty! Twenty would have done. Why the hell isn't he working today?"

Usman never paid much attention at school, but he did retain some knowledge from his *'Comparative Religion'* course.

"It's Good Friday. That's…"

"I know what Good Friday is, chapatti head. You're not the only one who went to school. Why should that interest a bloody Gurkha?"

"He's a Christian, Raza."

"What! Bugger should be in saffron robes, chanting Hari bloody Krishna, and in his own time too, not on one of our busiest days."

He turned a crafty eye on Qadir.

"You been driving his jalopy all day?"

"Except when I went to Mosque, Uncle. Before you go off on one, I started at six, and I've had a good day. We've got the thirty quid back, and a fair bit more."

Qadir sat on the edge of the desk, and Raza patted his knee with affection.

"Very good, very good."

It was Qadir's turn to moan.

"Missed my workout this morning so that Christian could go to church."

It was a matter of principled bigotry with Qadir. He didn't think Raza should provide work for Christians, or indeed anyone who didn't subscribe to Islam. He knew his uncle didn't give a rat's arse, and though he was tempted to say something he held his tongue.

"Come, we have worked long enough today. There's a table waiting for us at the *'Tamarind'*. Let's have dinner."

"You paying, Uncle?"

Raza gripped Qadir by the cheek, and roared with laughter.

"Not bloody likely, this is on the Inland Revenue."

Men brim-full of ambition, that will lead to their damnation, begin their programmes in rooms so small that you couldn't swing a cat. They secrete themselves in tight and unknown corners, and their acolytes cram in there with them. Each one a dreamer, justifying himself with the lie that his belief is the panacea for the ills of mankind. The true compulsion lies unacknowledged; the almost sexual thrill of seeing oneself possessed of unlimited power over others.

Qadir Khan held forth in just such a room, in a far corner of the Mosque. His voice was a whisper. Not because he was afraid of being heard, but because he knew that this was the best technique for holding an audience in a small space. When he attended school he

71

loved Drama. The mesmeric power of a controlled voice was the single most important lesson Qadir had learnt.

"Brothers, we stand at a time of crisis. The infidel persecutes us daily. Now they no longer have Poles and Romanians to abuse we are their target. They watch our faith schools like hawks; our women are insulted in the streets for covering their heads, and endlessly they insist on integration. We do not wish to integrate; we assert the greatness of Allah; praise be upon him. It is not we who must change our ways, it is they who must submit. I tell you...greetings cousin, join us."

A young man slipped into a corner. His features were held together by sticking plaster, whilst his nose recovered from the savage blow it had received.

Qadir resumed his theme.

"Too many of our people are cowed. We must go among them, particularly the young, and rouse them. It is we who must put the fire and sword of Islam in their hands."

An imperious contempt scarred his face.

"You have seen them, brothers, on Friday and Saturday night; you have carried them in your taxis. Blind drunk, their language foul and that's just the women!"

Qadir leavened his address with bathetic humour. Then he drew them back to him.

"Soft! They are as soft as butter, and when there are enough of us to rise in revolt we will throw them to their knees. If they will not confess the greatness of Allah we will finish with them."

Qadir's eyes blazed with the manic certainty that you could see in any tyrant throughout history.

"Go out there, brothers, and recruit."

When Mo' brought his misshapen nose into the room he had left the door imperceptibly ajar. A hidden figure moved away swiftly. Faisal strode out of the Mosque in a state of near despair. Ten minutes earlier he had spotted Mo' in the throng milling around the musalla – the prayer hall. Curiosity got the better of him when he saw the young man edge away from the crowd and disappear down a corridor. Keeping a discreet distance, Faisal followed the sound of his footsteps echoing on the stone floor. He saw Mo' disappear into Qadir's meeting room, and stealthily placed himself within hearing distance of the gathering within. Sensing it was ending he moved off sharply.

He was deeply shocked by the peroration he had overheard, and as he drove home he shook his head repeatedly.

"Surely, no one could be so mad as to think that they could overthrow the British State?"

Then he pulled himself up short. A historian should not think like that. He recalled a very British saying, *"Mighty oaks from little acorns grow."* Shuddering, he drove a little faster to get home to Abir and the twenty-first century.

Now the others were gone, Qadir threw an arm around his cousin Mo'.

"Wow man, what the hell happened to you? Your nose looks like a grape."

A sullen Mo' related the incident in the market square, some weeks before.

"Who the hell was this guy?"

"Dunno, it was too dark to see his face properly. Couldn't tell nuffin about 'im, uvver than he was a Paki like us."

Qadir's face hardened.

"I don't like that word, cousin, never use it again."

Big and hard as Mo' was he knew better than to argue with Qadir.

"Why were you picking on the white boy?"

"Oh man, you should of seen 'im. He had queer written all over him. I remember you said the bastards should be burnt."

"And you say that the guy who slammed your nose knew him?"

"Yeh, maybe he'd done a bit o' business wiv 'im."

Qadir was still and thoughtful. He wasn't particularly interested in Mo's features, but this was a matter of family honour.

"There were two other guys you said. Did you get a look at them?"

Mo' became very agitated.

"Oh yeh, big white feller, right cocky bastard. He stamped on Deggsy's face…"

"And the other one?"

"Stuck the 'ead on Jamal. I know who he is…he's that little bastard wot works for Uncle Raza."

"Be more specific, he has more than one little bastard working for him."

"That twat from the hills; face like a betel nut."

Qadir frowned in puzzlement.

"You know, used to be in their army. I' sin 'im half a dozen times in the yard. Might even have paid the bastard to drive me 'ome once or twice."

"You mean *'Johnny'* Gurkha?"

In the dim recesses of what Mo' laughingly referred to as his mind a bulb flickered.

"Oh yeh, yeh, that's right, 'im. I've 'eard Usman call him that."

Qadir shut him up.

"No one gets away with doing that to family. This is what we'll do..."

*

History is made at any time of day. What is commonly called *'the fate of nations'* is, of course, the product of accumulated actions and events. The popular phrase is a euphemism, employed to soften the blows that fall upon people when their world is thrown into turmoil. It would not do for the common herd to stare destruction in the face, and realise that it is wrought upon them by the educated, the powerful – their leaders.

So it is they are gulled with blurred words, soothing words, divisive words, rousing and inspiring words to tolerate hunger, disease, poverty, loss of liberty and death. Naturally, the movers and shakers in society are aware that the unfolding events, which they themselves have generated, may well lead to a national, or even international, crisis, but they plough onwards consumed by their atheistic selfishness. Power is their raison d'etre, and the unshakeable belief that they alone are fit to cradle it in their self-righteous bosoms. It is a truism, nonetheless, that having led their nation downwards towards the abyss they often lack control over individuals whose conduct produces tipping points in history. A single person who, fired by rhetoric or events, decides to take matters into their own hands.

Marjorie Whitlock would seem to be an unlikely candidate to sit upon the see-saw of history. That early

May morning found her in the right place and at the right time to save the life of Padam Gurung, but in the wrong company. That companion was not her Golden Retriever Luther, who at 05:45 hours was relieving himself on Banksmore village green, it was Julian Marlborough maintaining his exercise regime.

Julian descended the hill, his loping stride devouring the ground with ease. He spotted Marjorie. By the time he reached the green she and Luther were disappearing into the churchyard. Marjorie paused to put the latch of the gate in place, and smiled graciously.

"Lovely morning, Miss Whitlock."

"Delightful. Go carefully, Julian, there's traffic even at this time of the day. They drive so carelessly through our lanes."

Julian threw a mock salute and moved on, but he saw a flapping shoelace and bent down to retie it.

Marjorie followed her usual route, and skirted the church porch. Luther had other ideas, and pulled hard on his leash towards the dim recess.

"Oh do come along Luther, there's nothing in there for you."

Luther whined, pulling so hard that he broke free from her grip, and disappeared into the porch.

Marjorie called to him with the brisk authority that had once chastened a small child causing mayhem in Wenbury Tea Rooms. Luther did not respond so readily to her command. She advanced towards the porch to regain her pooch. Julian heard her exclamation one hundred metres away.

He hesitated, and thought about moving on, he didn't like his runs to be interrupted. There was something in

Marjorie's tone which pricked his interest. He jogged towards St. George's, and hurdled the gate.

"What is it, Miss Whitlock?"

Marjorie had seen blood before. Her father had been a local farmer, and she recalled the day she helped him when one of the farm hands had cut his leg open to the bone.

The sight of Padam Gurung was altogether different. He lay prostrate on the hard stone floor. His arms flung wide, as if waiting to be nailed to the cross. His face was almost unrecognisable, and his right leg was set at crooked angles. The greatest horror was just discernible in the gloomy porch. Padam's shirt had been torn open. From sternum to belly, a cross had been sliced into his torso with a sharp knife. It had not penetrated so far as to be fatal, but it added to the enormous pool of blood he was swimming in from his wounds.

"My God! Marjorie, take this."

He handed her his mobile phone from a bum bag.

"I don't know how to use one."

Julian stripped off his t-shirt, and swathed Padam in its folds. He barked.

"999, and press the green button on the left. Ambulance and police immediately. You'll need to stand on the Village Green to get a signal."

She returned to the porch.

"They're on their way. What can I do?"

Julian cradled Padam as tenderly as he could, trying to transmit some body warmth.

"Nearest house on the Green. Hammer like hell on their door, and get me a couple of duvets."

Marjorie sped away, heading for Derek Fisher's house. Derek saw her coming down the garden path, as he appeared from the rear of his property, mug of coffee in hand. Within two minutes they were in the church porch bearing duvets. The largest one was from the master bedroom. His wife, Wendy, was much surprised when Derek tore it off her with some ferocity. For a moment her heart leapt, as she thought she was about to be ravaged by the husband she knew from days of yore.

"Dear Lord!"

Derek's mug shook in his hand.

"Never mind that. Help me to wrap him. We need to keep him warm."

Derek was transfixed, so Marjorie assisted. Padam moaned, and appeared to say something.

"Never mind that old chap. Sergeant, sergeant, stay awake. You are one of my men sergeant, and I won't have you asleep on duty."

The faintest of smiles lit Padam's damaged face, as a line of blood seeped from his mouth.

The wailing sirens came closer until they were deafening. Bedroom curtains were flung open throughout Banksmore, including those of Peter and Jane Standish in the Rectory next to the church.

Derek Fisher stepped into the churchyard, and shouted, "Over here!"

The paramedics dealt swiftly with Padam, and were stretchering him to the ambulance when Peter appeared. He couldn't make out who the injured party was because of the oxygen mask over his face.

When he entered the porch he recognised Julian Marlborough, emerging like a vision from Dante's 'Inferno', His bare torso was caked in blood, and his face smeared like that of a Native American about to go on the warpath. Little did anyone realise that this was to be one of those pivotal moments. Soon, Julian would, once again, go to war.

Whilst the police interviewed Marjorie and Derek, Julian sat on a grave. Peter nipped to the Rectory, and re-emerged with Jane carrying a bowl of warm water and towels. Julian sat motionless, as Jane knelt in front of him wiping the blood from him.

A police constable towered over them.

"Don't do that madam. He's a material witness, and forensics will want to examine him."

Marjorie Whitlock had finished talking with the sergeant, and what she overheard made her furious. Striding purposefully towards the constable, the force of her personality fell upon him.

"I have told you both that we came upon the unfortunate victim by chance. If Mr. Marlborough had not acted with such decisiveness and efficiency, I doubt not you would be dealing with a murder case. For goodness sake, if you would show half of the compassion he showed to that poor man you would let Mrs. Standish clean him up a little."

The constable was about to retort, but his sergeant held up a discreet hand.

"Any relation to our local member of parliament, sir?"

Marjorie interjected.

"Sir Hugh is his father."

For good measure she added.

"If it's blood you want, you will find plenty seeping into the stones back there. Good Christian blood, spilt as it has always been spilt."

The Reverend Standish calmed her.

"Now then Marjorie, come along with me. We'll have the English remedy, a good mug of strong tea."

Marjorie's humour restored itself.

"Don't do mugs dear, but if you have a cup that would be delightful."

Jane Standish spoke from her kneeling position.

"May I continue to clean Julian up a bit, Sergeant...?"

"Sergeant Durham, madam. Yes, yes, go ahead. As the lady said, there's plenty for forensics to go on in the porch. I'm happy that he was a passer-by."

That was true, but he also didn't want to tread into deep water with the Marlboroughs.

"Jane, you take Marjorie back to the Rectory would you, and I'll help Julian."

The sight of Jane on her knees in front of Julian, washing his bare torso made him uneasy.

More police arrived, and set up a crime scene. Jane and Marjorie departed for the Rectory, passing silently through a small crowd of villagers gathered by the gate.

Peter fished the flannel out of the bowl of water, and Julian leapt to his feet briskly.

"Thanks all the same, Pete, but no thanks. Prefer the woman's touch, no offence."

Silence lay between them, until Julian spoke.

"Which of the dear departed have I been squatting on? Good grief, talk about serendipity. It's the Whitlock family grave."

He peered at the inscription.

"Isaiah 1: 4 and 7, what's that all about Pete?"

Peter looked at the biblical numbers beneath the name of Marjorie's great-grandfather.

"I'll have to look it up. May I give you a lift back up the hill, Julian?"

"Think I'll finish my run. Sun's warming up nicely."

"In that condition?"

"Nothing to be concerned about. We've seen plenty of the *'sauce'* before, haven't we?"

Julian was about to break into a stride when Peter held him back.

"Who was he?"

"Who?"

"The body in the porch."

"Very Miss Marple, Pete. It was Gurung, Padam Gurung. One of your parishioners."

Peter looked stunned.

Julian broke away and shocked him further.

"...and whoever did it doesn't appear to be terribly fond of Christians. They carved a cross in his chest. Come for drinks at six tonight, bring Jane. I'll tell you all about it."

Julian ignored the staring villagers. He noticed his bloodied lace untied again. When he rose from retying it, he stared into the distance. About a mile away, he estimated, a faint spiral of smoke drifting lazily into the matchless sky. It intrigued him, and he altered his route to investigate. Soon he was out of sight down the lane, and then into the fields. Like a fox on the scent he knew there was prey to be had.

Peter Standish emptied the bowl beside the Whitlock grave, and stared once more at the inscription.

When he entered the Rectory kitchen he could hear Marjorie relating her experience to Jane in the sitting room. That could wait. He picked a Bible off the shelf where the recipe books were kept.

"Isaiah 1, Isaiah 1: 4 and 7:"

"Ah, sinful nation, a people loaded with guilt,
A brood of evildoers, children given to corruption!

They have forsaken the Lord;
They have spurned the Holy One of Israel and turned their
backs on Him…
Your country is desolate, your cities burned with fire;
Your fields are being stripped by foreigners right before
you,
Laid waste as when overthrown by strangers…"

Peter lay the Bible upon the work surface. Glass of water in hand he walked through to the sitting room to see how Marjorie was coping, and to hear her version of events.

7

"I follow him to serve my turn upon him."
Othello Act 1: Sc. 1

Liverpool was a great city. You could feel its raw power as thousands assembled in front of St. George's Hall, opposite Lime Street Station. They chattered and swayed, as vendors cried out their wares for the unwary to buy; cheap mugs and tea towels bearing the image of their beloved.

An excited whisper passed through the crowd. They faced the imposing steps that led from the station exit. There he was, the conquering hero come home for the first time since he grabbed office. Tommy O'Donnell had arrived in more ways than one. Ironically, his train from London had been delayed due to a variety of strikes for a variety of imperfect reasons.

The police had planned to get him into St. George's Hall by a circuitous route round the back. From there he could appear through the central entrance on the east façade. Construction of the grade 1 listed Neoclassical building began in 1841; it opened in 1854.

Lines of policemen struggled to part the crowd, whilst O'Donnell strolled nonchalantly through the irregular gap, hemmed in by his personal bodyguard. Now and again he shook a hand, or called to someone, "Oright mate!"

When he mounted the wide steps he glanced upward at the statue of Benjamin Disraeli glowering down at him. Out of the corner of his mouth he whispered to an aide.

"The next time I cum 'ere I want dat Jew boy gone."

The Earl of Beaconsfield would not have been amused, nor would Queen Victoria. It is the true Liberal who respects people regardless of colour, creed or religion; extremists in one thing tend to be censorious and intolerant in others.

O'Donnell clasped his hands together in triumph. He resembled an F.A. Cup winning captain at Wembley. He milked the adoration before sitting in a throne-like chair. Two bodyguards stationed behind him, scanned the crowd.

The Mayor of Liverpool introduced him with sycophantic flattery.

"Ladies 'n' gen'l'mun, boys n' gerls..."

This great Socialist of days gone by had cut and run when former Labour Leader Neil Kinnock had reined in the extreme left wing years before. The Militant Tendency was neutered to pave the way for the party's makeover and resurgence under Blair. Mr. Mayor had gone off to the Algarve to make a small fortune. It's not only cream that rises to the top, scum manages the same trick. An expensive suit couldn't obscure round shoulders. Foxy features bore a five o'clock shadow that former U.S President Richard Nixon would have admired.

"...give a big Liverpool welcome to our own, our Prime Minister, Mr. Tommy O'Donnell."

Jimmy Allsop remained watchful over his charge. His mind churned its way through discordant thoughts. He had bought himself out of the army not long after Messrs'. Marlborough and Standish had gone. A longing to be with his young wife and baby girl was realised. A cosy home in the northern town of St. Helens; half dozen miles inland from Liverpool. The old Pilkington Glass town had seen improvement from its long dilapidated Victorian state, and he'd been both prudent and lucky.

Whilst serving in the Rifles he'd saved most of his pay, and when his hardworking parents had died he'd inherited everything as their only child. It wasn't a great deal, but sufficient for them to buy a three-storey Victorian house, near an entrance to the delightful Taylor Park.

Jimmy re-joined the local Labour Party and become active. Work was hard to find, and unemployment gave him more time for party matters. His involvement took him increasingly into Liverpool. When the powers-that-be discovered he was an ex-soldier they offered him work as a minder to local M.P., and rising star, Tommy O'Donnell. The job took him away from home, and he spent most of his time in London. Paying work was paying work.

He was thinking about Liverpudlians. Jimmy had grown up with them. Years before, their overspill had spread out to the nearby industrial towns of one-time Lancashire. He didn't dislike them, or their city, and the dockside and Liverpool 1 developments of recent decades were fantastic.

As a thinking man, Jimmy had examined the problem for quite some time, and reached his conclusion. Too many Scousers suffered from nostalgia, and it burdened them with an inferiority complex. Sixty years had come and gone, and they still wittered on and on about the Beatles. They had passed through a golden age, when the city was a player on the national and international stage. Not just the Fab Four, but numerous musical acts, and comedians, and triumphant football teams. Music, theatre and sport had thrived in the city. In the 1980's they had playwright Willy Russell going to the Oscars ceremony in L.A., nominated for *'Educating Rita'*. Every dog has its day, and by the dawn of the 1990's they were just another city. That's what they couldn't live with.

The Prime Minister came to his feet; a paunchy man with a thick black beard and a mop of unruly hair. However expensively his spin doctors dressed him he still looked like a *"sack of shit in a cheap suit."*

O'Donnell cast himself in the mould of the docker, the tough, no-nonsense, *'werkin'* man. His grandfather spent a lifetime on the docks, and his father had been a bricklayer; Tommy had been a shop assistant in a variety of *'cool'* clothes shops for the young and trendy. He was frequently sacked for his loud mouth, and disrespect for managers and customers alike. He enjoyed temporary success in the rag trade when a company made him manager of their town centre shop. When they discovered his extra-mural activity, i.e. selling stock in the town centre pubs, and pocketing the proceeds, he was given the old heave-ho.

Tommy had the gift of the gab, and entered local politics. Contrary to Hugh Marlborough's assessment, he wasn't entirely stupid. His mastery and manipulation of constitutions and regulations was a wonder to behold. Combined with the malcontent thugs he surrounded himself with, his meteoric rise to M.P. was rather unsurprising. Give Tommy O'Donnell credit he was nothing if not consistent, and he maintained his modus operandi amongst his Labour brethren in the Commons.

Jimmy had heard his peroration for the day ad nauseum – *'the time of the common man'*, *'the hegemony of the people'* etc. etc. It was a recording, whose antecedents lay with Castro, Mao, Stalin and Lenin.

He switched off, and returned to his musings. Scousers – not all of them - disgruntled and easily offended if they thought someone was casting aspersions upon them. Only too ready to express their forthright opinions about *'soft southerners'* and *'fuckin' Tories'*. A bitterness borne out of frustration that nobody flattered them anymore. Refusing to accept that they were no better and no worse than people from other cities, towns and villages across the United Kingdom. Jimmy glanced to his left, and saw a group of aging poets, actors and comedians given pride of place to enhance O'Donnell's reputation. He recognised a few, one hard, brassy, face in particular. She was the sort he blamed for the distorted view some Liverpudlians had of themselves. Jimmy couldn't recall which one of them said, *"Everyone's a star in Liverpool."*

"No they aren't," he thought. "The majority are just decent, hardworking folk like you'd find in London, Birmingham, Aylesbury, Bradford or Woking."

The new King of Liverpool finished, and Jimmy put his musings to one side.

They were staying at the grand old lady of the town, the Adelphi Hotel round the corner. 'She' was past her best these days, and certainly not of the standard when Sir Jock Delves Broughton, of the infamous Kenya Happy Valley Set, committed suicide there in December 1942. It was politic to stay there. The ordinary people of Liverpool looked upon the Adelphi with pride.

Awkward as ever, the P.M. insisted on walking to Ranelagh Place through the teeming crowd. It was a bloody nightmare, with the police having a torrid time of it. Not that O'Donnell cared, he had plans for them.

They pressed through the final crush and got their VIP a clear run to the hotel entrance when a voice shouted.

"Jimmy, Jimmy Allsop, "gis a job!""

Jimmy looked backward and recognised him instantly. It was Billy Conway, his old sergeant from the Middle East tours. He was close enough to call back.

"Seven-thirty, Billy, inside…"

Then he and the Prime Ministerial party were safely indoors.

"Pint o' bitter please, Jimmy."

The old comrades in arms stood at the bar. Jimmy ordered the pint, and a soft drink for himself.

"Gone teetotal, lad?"

Jimmy didn't take offence at the gentle ribbing.

"Strict rules, Billy, no 'pop' on duty. You know the form."

Billy brought his mouth a little closer to Jimmy's.

"Dis job, you packin'?" Jimmy gave a little nod. "What, right now?"

"Always Billy, when you're with the P.M."

Billy was impressed that somewhere on Jimmy's body a sidearm fitted snugly.

"Nice threads you've got there, mate. The money must be good."

"Bought and paid for by the guvnor, or rather the taxpayer. He insists we dress well. Saville Row, Billy."

Conway managed to sound both embittered and proud.

"Gettin' some back of wot's rightfully ours."

Jimmy sipped his lime juice and soda water, eyeing Sergeant Conway with interest.

"What happened Billy, you seem down on your luck?"

Conway's clothes were cheap and mass produced, and they looked rather old. He was pensive for a moment, before telling his story.

"Got chucked out the army, dishonourable discharge."

"Do you mind me asking why?"

Billy took a long draught of his pint before continuing.

"Thee said a got a bit rough wid sum women an' kids in Bongo-Bongo land, an' dat was it. Didn't do nuffin the old Captain didn't do, an' he got away with it. Typical eh, friggin' officer gets away with it, an' I get stuffed."

Jimmy had long since consigned those memories to the dustbin of time. Others leapt back with unnerving clarity. The officer's name escaped him, but he remembered his vicious character.

"You working?"

Conway shook his head and looked downcast.

"Land fit for heroes, eh Jimmy lad."

Like a woefully sad puppy he lifted his head, and with pleading eyes appealed to Jimmy.

"You couldn't get us sumfin in your line, could yer? I keep meself in fightin' shape."

A group of five middle-aged men burst into the bar making a racket. The largest of them, seventeen stones and shaven-headed, called out when he saw Jimmy.

"Over 'ere, lad."

"Scuse me Billy."

He wandered the length of the bar to join the men who were ordering bottles of champagne.

"What can I do for you Mr. Kinsella?"

Steve Kinsella announced to all present.

"Bit of a problem, son. Just found Kev pissed as a fart in his room. The lads 'ave kicked 'im out the back door. He won't be coming back. Leaves us short-handed like. The boss'll kick my arse unless he's got full security around him before he leaves. Wot d'yer reckon?"

Jimmy threw a quick look over his shoulder, and laughed.

"Eh lad, it aint funny. Dis is my ring piece on the line."

"Wasn't laughing at you Mr. Kinsella, just that it's your lucky day."

One of his companions bellowed.

"You always were a jammy get, Stevo."

As the laughter died, Jimmy indicated Billy Conway alone at the bar. In a quiet voice he gave the P.M.'s Chief of Security a run-down on Billy's career and his assets.

"Get 'im over 'ere, will ya."

"Pleased to meet yer, Mr. Kinsella. We've met before. My old feller used to deliver yer mam's milk, an' I werked with 'im during school 'olidays."

Kinsella's jaw dropped.

"Was Terry Conway your old man? Fuck me, small world eh."

Liverpudlians are often sentimental, and Kinsella was no exception.

"Ah, eh, your dad was a right laff. Didn't he drink with my old feller?"

"Not sure about dat. Oh yeh, thee used to sit near each other at Goodison…"

Kinsella was all eagerness.

"Do you still follow the lads?"

"Tickets are a bit out of my price range these days, sir."

Kinsella liked the 'sir' bit, and made his mind up.

"Not any more, Billy lad. Do you wanna werk for us?"

"Yes please, sir."

"Right mate, you're on the team. Best get you smartened up, the boss will have my balls for earrings if you turn up dressed like that."

Before anyone could speak, he drew ten fifty pound notes from his wallet, and thrust them into Jimmy's hand.

"We're leavin' at 1130 in the mornin'. Sort 'im out with some decent gear, Jimmy. Back to London tomorrow, then we'll get you some proper stuff Billy. Oright wid you?"

"Nothin' to keep me 'ere Mr. Kinsella…"

"We'll fix you up with some digs when we get there. You'll be able to afford it now, an' a season ticket for Goodison. Great to 'ave you on the team."

Kinsella's eyes lifted over their shoulders to view half a dozen scantily clad young ladies enter the bar.

"My lucky day again. Over 'ere ladies."

A gorgeous brunette sidled up to him.

"You Mr. Kinsella?"

"In the flesh, girls. Let the party begin. Plenty of champers upstairs ladies. The P.M. can't wait to meet you."

The jocular and excited party began to disappear.

Steve Kinsella paused in the doorway.

"Eh sarge, was our Jimmy a good soldier?"

Billy Conway stood up straight, and shouted back with authority.

"The best sir, the very best – straight as a die, and loyal."

Kinsella stared back stony-faced, and then he was wreathed in smiles, holding up a thumb before he exited.

"Jesus H, Jimmy, I don't know 'ow to thank yer."

Allsop was embarrassed.

"You looked after your lads out there, seems only fair to return the favour. Can you make 08:30 tomorrow for our shopping expedition?"

"Too right, pal. Wot about meetin' under 'Dickie Lewis'?"

This referred to the nude male statue, sculpted by Sir Jacob Epstein, that stood over the entrance of what was once a John Lewis department store.

"Perfect. You got far to travel?"

"I live in Huyton. Bit of a drag on the buses these days, they go all round the 'ouses."

Looking at his cheap wristwatch he added,

"Gettin' a bit pushed for time. Better get off 'ome, an' pack me suitcase."

Jimmy pulled two twenty pound notes from his wallet.

"Here, that should get you a taxi, now and in the morning."

"Ah eh, I can't take your bread mate…"

"Billy, it's a good earner. I'll tell you how much on the train tomorrow."

"Can't thank yer enuff, buddy."

He threw an embarrassed hug around Jimmy.

"08:30 hrs it is then. Tarrar."

The bar was empty, and Jimmy finished his drink. He disengaged himself from the garrulous barman, and took the lift back to his room. Passing O'Donnell's suite, he heard raucous goings on, and was only too aware of the debauchery that was going on within. Yes, the money was good, but these people offended his Christian and Socialist principles. In a flashback he suddenly saw himself in conversation with that other Captain, the padre. What was his name?

After saying goodnight to his little girl on the telephone, and a long conversation with his wife, he stretched out on the bed. He sighed at the thought that they were only a handful of miles away.

His mind turned to Billy Conway. Poor Billy, it was true that he'd looked after them on those dreadful tours of the Middle East, but he wasn't surprised at his discharge from the army. A puzzle agitated his mind. The sarge had always had a marked Liverpool accent, but never as pronounced as the one he'd just heard. He put it down to him being back in Liverpool and, by the look of him, having to live in pretty rough circumstances. Others were on watch that night. Jimmy drifted off to sleep, comforted with the thought that he had been able to do an old comrade a good turn.

Ex-Sergeant Conway, now a bodyguard to the Prime Minister of the United Kingdom, sat on the bus reflecting upon a good day's work. He would take a taxi in the morning, the other twenty would be spent on a substantial Indian takeaway. They pulled into Huyton bus station, and Billy lit a cigarette whilst waiting for people to disperse. Casually, he wandered to the car park, and unlocked a beat–up Ford Fiesta.

Driving discreetly, he was soon in the next town up, Whiston; many moons ago a lovely village, but long since transformed into a nondescript suburb. He pulled in at the side of the Indian restaurant. The manager greeted him with familiarity.

"How are youse, mate?"

The incongruity of a thick Scouse accent coming out of Asian features never failed to amuse him. He sank a pint while waiting for his order.

Billy pulled out of the car park onto Windy Arbor Road, that long broad highway that runs down from the village to the M62 junction at Tarbock. However, he turned left, and sat with the lights on red at the centre of the village. Then he went left again in the direction of Huyton. Within fifty metres or so he indicated for another left into Paradise Lane. Halfway down he pulled up outside a modest house.

Inside it was immaculate, as you would expect from a senior NCO with discipline. The takeaway went into the oven on low heat, and he took the stairs two at a time. Billy cast off his clothes, and slipped on a Djellaba; a long and loose-fitting robe with full sleeves, acquired on holiday in Morocco. Once in the bathroom, he carefully removed the plastic bath panel. He reached inside and withdrew an object wrapped in thick waterproofed material. Back in his bedroom he unwrapped it to reveal a laptop computer. When it was fired up he sent a simple message, *"Our lucky day."* Then he restored the computer to its hiding place, and went downstairs to enjoy his meal.

Andrew 'Freddie' Forbes let the telephone ring, whilst he put down his copy of Kipling's *'Kim'* and a balloon of fine cognac.

"Forbes here."

He recognised the voice.

"He came home a winner."

"Thank you for letting me know, *'Lester'*. I had every confidence putting my money on him. Goodnight."

More than satisfied, he returned to his armchair. Swirling the golden liquid, he sniffed its gorgeous bouquet. As he swallowed, he looked down at his book and smirked.

"We'll teach the bastards how to play *'the Great Game'*, Rudyard old boy."

*

"Good of you to be punctual, Mr. and Mrs. Rector."

Julian laughed, and they responded in like manner.

"This cocktail is a special of mine."

"Not for me, thank you. Have you something soft?"

Julian was about to make a *risqué* response, but decided it might be too near the bone, so to speak!

"Off the singing syrup, Jane, thought you liked a tipple?"

"Normally I do, but…"

Peter couldn't restrain himself, he was bursting with joy.

"We are pregnant…I mean, Jane is pregnant."

"Good grief! I truly hope you don't mean *'we'*. A miracle in Banksmore would be too much for the residents to cope with. Congratulations, and if you'll pardon my French, bugger the cocktails. Champagne, champagne, champagne!"

He flew from the room, and returned just as quickly brandishing a bottle of vintage Louis Roederer. His mother and Fiona Claymore-Browne brought up the rear.

"Darling, what are you doing?"

"A celebration mama, we have a pregnant lady on the premises."

"Well it isn't me. Fi darling, you haven't been up to no good have you?"

Fiona responded in that rather odd voice of hers, terribly clipped cut glass English but with a lightness of tone that turned everything she said to a cushion of air.

"Chance would be a fine thing."

"Come on Ma, don't play the fool, it's Jane. She and Peter are going to have a baby."

Debs raised her eyebrows in mockery.

"I KNOWWW. I'm not senile yet, Julian."

She embraced Jane lightly, kissing her on both cheeks, and then did the same with Peter. The embrace was a little tighter, and the kisses lingered a fraction too long. It didn't escape the notice of anyone in the company.

"Many congratulations, how exciting."

Fiona moved in to offer congratulations.

"When is it due?"

"Late December."

Julian dispensed champagne. The toast was to health and happiness.

Settling into armchairs, they relaxed at the end of what had been a fraught day.

"How is he? Does anyone know?"

Peter had checked on Padam Gurung around mid-day, and then again at five.

"Padam became fully conscious around three this afternoon, Fi, but they've sedated him. His injuries are severe. Thankfully he's out of danger."

Julian piped up.

"I gave him the once-over when Marjorie and I found him. The left eye looked nasty, and I'm sure one or two ribs were broken. It was his leg that concerned me most, broken in a couple of places, I think."

Fiona spoke quietly.

"Is it true...about his chest?"

"Yes, whoever attacked him carved a cross in him. Oddly, the hospital said that was the least of their worries. A couple of bits needed stitching, but most of it was so superficial that they only had to clean it and dress it to prevent infection."

Peter looked pensive.

Debs lay back and took the tiniest of sips from her champagne.

Jane was perched on the edge of her seat.

"Why would anyone want to do such a dreadful thing?"

Julian was whimsical, to begin with.

"Well, it might have been our resident atheist, Martin Russell…"

"Really Julian!"

"Sorry mama, just my little joke. State this country is in, it could have been any one of a number of people – plain yobbos, someone with a personal grievance who knew Padam was a Christian…Muslims…"

He allowed it to hang in the air as bait.

Fiona spoke first.

"Would they do such a thing?"

"Who Fi?" asked Debs.

"Muslims."

"There are certainly enough of them in the area darling. Mind you, most of them vote for Hugh at election time. The ones in business are deeply Conservative, little and big 'c'."

"I find it difficult to believe that any truly devout Muslim would have done such a thing…"

Julian snorted derisively.

"Come on Pete, with our experience, we know that they're just the ones who would."

"I was going to say, in this area. As it happens, I'm getting to know the Imam at the Cranchurch Mosque rather well. He's a very moderate sort of chap, and I believe that most of his congregation follow suit."

Debs looked troubled.

"What is the point of your exchanges with this gentleman?"

"Usually, as you know, our ecumenical work is based upon interaction between the various strands of Christian faith. I thought it was about time we became more inclusive. I approached the Imam about engaging with us in inter-faith discussion. We'll be joined by the usual suspects – Methodists, Baptists and Roman Catholics. Interest has also been expressed by Sikh and Hindu representatives in nearby towns."

"Will they be discussions for leaders only, or can the laity get involved?"

"Good question Fiona. We're ironing out the details at the moment, but we're aiming for a series of public meetings to be held at our respective venues. St. George's will host the first next month."

Stillness fell upon the room. Debs and Julian looked away, their faces set in stony fury; Peter and Jane looked calmly ahead. Fiona sat there, knees together and glass in hand, and said,

"I think it's a terrific idea. Count me in."

Julian's voice resembled a stiletto being inserted into flesh.

"Peter, did you look up the biblical reference that was chiselled into the Whitlock grave?"

"I did, it's…"

"So did I, "*Your fields are being stripped by foreigners right before you, laid waste as when overthrown by strangers…*"

He spat it out with venom, and added for good measure.

"Do you think it appropriate, when our whole way of life is under siege, to engage with those who would destroy us? To ignore the Word of God, expressed through his own prophet?"

All eyes fell upon Peter, who drank slowly from his glass.

"I'm afraid you misinterpret the Scripture Julian. Isaiah was telling the people of his time that their woes were caused by their rebellion against God and His ways. That was why the foreigners were sent amongst them. It is the chastisement of God for their wickedness in turning their stony hearts against their loving Father."

Debs was having none of this, she didn't want a full-blown theological and political row in her drawing room; she wouldn't allow even Hugh to do that.

"Goodness me, look at the time. Sorry to be so inhospitable, but I've got to be in Old Wenbury by eight-thirty. Jane, Peter, may I give you a lift down the hill? Hugh is terribly keen to be involved with the single mother's initiative, and we also need to discuss how we're going to support the Gurungs whilst the breadwinner is *hors de combat*. There are four children, I believe."

She was bustling them out of the room.

"Oh, Fi darling, could you spare me another ten minutes? I'll be back in two ticks; Julian will keep you company."

Julian's innate good breeding restored his equilibrium, and he eyed Fiona. She really wasn't bad for her age.

"I say Fi, you're keen on horses aren't you? We've got some marvellous prints in the Snooker room, let me show you. Bring your glass, here let me top it up."

They went along the corridor, and into the room. Julian closed the door and turned the key in the lock.

"Why are you locking the door Julian?"

His most charming smile lit up his face, and he stood up against her, pulling her to him by her waist.

"You really are a most attractive girl, Fi, and I've always wanted you."

"Oh Julian, I really..."

He kissed her deeply and luxuriously, and she was putty in his hands. Fiona was lifted onto the Snooker table and relieved of her pants in one motion. She thrashed wildly as he plunged into her again and again.

"Over you go Fi."

Without warning the image of Padam Gurung's burnt out Mercedes flashed before his eyes. In a furious temper he declined the easy pink and risked the tight brown.

8

"The web of our life is of a mingled yarn, good and ill together."
All's Well That Ends Well Act 4: Sc. 3

Imam Shirani was indeed a moderate man. His faith was like the sacred river Alph in Coleridge's poem 'Kublai Khan; it ran *'though caverns measureless to man'*. Unlike the next line, it did not drain into *'a sunless sea'*.

Shirani was a man filled with great joy, and he felt that he and his family were blessed to live in Britain. The only time he got grumpy was when he heard British people complaining about, what they saw as, their hard lives. He would snort in derision, and be sorely tempted to interrupt their moaning in supermarket aisles and say,

"You think you've got problems? Try living in Pakistan, or Somalia, Syria, Nigeria etc."

He resisted the urge to point a finger at their groaning shopping trolleys.

Shirani also kept quiet about something else, an opinion that it would not have been wise to express openly in the Muslim community. He was a great admirer of both the Indians and the Jews who had settled in Britain. Sure, he had religious differences with them, but what he approved of was the way they conducted themselves. In his view, most of them accepted the prevailing culture of the country that had given them refuge. They pursued their personal beliefs in the privacy of their homes, temples and synagogues. He wished that some of his brethren would show similar respect for the prevailing British values, and refrain from seeking to overthrow the way of life that emanated from those mores.

The Imam knew better than most that the historical spread of Islam was achieved by fire and sword. That was the past. How an educated person could assert that you can promote true faith by *forcing* others to accept it was beyond him. Like any good Muslim, it would be a day of joy for him to see the crescent moon flying over Ten Downing Street. It had to be by the consent of the people, otherwise you were just storing up trouble for the future. The battle of wills in the Middle East would continue *ad infinitum* if men and women of violence clung to the status quo. He feared that inflicting their dogma on the West through terror might eventually create a backlash upon his people whose only precedent was the Holocaust.

After much prayer, he decided to accept Peter Standish's offer to participate in inter-faith discussion.

Sitting there with Faisal Hussain he was even more convinced of the necessity to reach out. If what he was hearing was true, then misguided men like Qadir Khan would bring the roof down on the entire Muslim community.

"Thank you, young man. You were wise to share this knowledge with me."

"What will you do?"

"I will think, and I will pray, and I will ask Allah for guidance. Rest assured, He will speak and I will act according to his Will. Now, how is that wife of yours?"

Faisal was embarrassed, but true to his convictions.

"By consent, by consent."

"*Touché*! Keep talking to her and praying for her. She will come back to the fold; of that I am convinced."

Faisal looked at his watch.

"Oops, nearly the end of lunch break, I must get back to work."

"Do, do, don't be late. There are many in our community who are very proud of your achievements. Off you go."

Faisal departed, with the customary salutations.

The old man sat still with closed eyes. Within seconds he knew what was asked of him, and he picked up the telephone. A short conversation ensued. He noted in his diary that Raza Khan would call on him at ten the following morning.

9

"False face must hide what the false heart doth know."
Macbeth Act 1: Sc. 7

It wasn't his religion, or the colour of his skin, that got Mo' got into endless trouble. A lack of education, wilfulness, and an inferiority complex plagued him. He overcame this through a penchant for violence. His only other occupation was as a delivery driver for the *'Tamarind'* restaurant owned by his Uncle Raza.

Outside the front door he was regaling two other delivery boys with the story of retribution inflicted upon Padam Gurung.

"Yeh man, you should o' seen 'im. 'is face was one fuckin' mess, an'…"

"Mo', get yourself inside, your Uncle Raza wants a word."

The manager of the *'Tamarind'* looked nervous.

The back office was crowded. Raza sat behind the desk munching his way through a plate of starters. Usman stood behind him, whilst Qadir reclined against a wall. The manager ushered Mo' in, and stood with his back against the closed door.

Raza examined his samosa then chewed upon it steadily.

"You are one big, dumb bastard, boy."

Mo' tried to respond…

"Keep it shut, boy. Tell us again, Sunny."

The Manager was not family. He needed his job, so he had already reported what he'd overheard.

"He's been banging on for days to the others about what he did to that driver of yours."

Mo' tried again to get a word in.

"I never..."

Raza came to his feet, holding up his enormous frame by placing his hands on the desk.

"I tell you boy, shut the fuck up. If Sunny says he heard you, he heard you. Rather believe him than a goat brain like you."

Everyone was agitated, apart from Qadir who remained impassive. Raza bawled at Mo'.

"You tell me boy, you tell me everything, or your balls will end up hanging from Usman's rear view mirror."

In a faltering voice, Mo' related the events of the Market Square when his nose had gone west.

Raza interrupted.

"Who gives a wolf's willy if he's a *gandoo*? You should have just stuffed his arse with chutney and left him to his poodle."

No-one passed comment.

"Why are you always causing me trouble, boy? Go on, let me hear the rest of it."

Mo' tried not to look at Qadir. He would tell everything, well almost everything – no way would he implicate Qadir in the attack. He had only heard what had been done to the Gurkha, because he hadn't actually been present. Mo' knew that if he blabbed the entire truth he would get sliced as well.

"It was a question of honour, weren't it..."?

"Boy, you wouldn't know honour if it jumped up and bit you on your *lun...*"

"FAMILY honour!"

Raza calmed down. He spread his capacious bulk into the office chair, waving a hand airily at the boy.

"We took a real stompin' Uncle, they shamed us. You should of seen my nose."

"Qadir told me, said your face looked like a swollen *pudi.*"

Mo' wasn't keen on having his features compared to an over-ripe vagina, but he took it.

"Yeh, Unc', dat's true. So I figured we should do somefink about it, an' dat driver of yours was the only one I recognised..."

"Whoa, whoa, whoa, before you finish this fucking Bollywood script speak proper English, and not this crappy street language. I know you can."

Mo' replied in standard English, as good as any you'd find up the road in Sir George Gilbert Scott Grammar School; a tribute to his parents who had managed to instil one useful lesson into him. From here on in Mo' blurred the edges.

"Dead simple really. Late one night I got together three of the boys, and we rang for a taxi. Asked if we could have your Gurkha boy specially; said he'd driven us before and what a great guy he was. Got him to pick us up outside the restaurant..."

"What? This restaurant? Boy, oh boy, you are stupider than I realised. Get on with it."

"Told him we were going to a party in Watford. Should have seen him, his eyes lit up at the fare. Before we got to the M25 we asked him to pull over so I could take a piss. Then we jumped him...the rest is in the papers."

106

Raza spoke softly.

"Whose clever idea was it to carve a fucking cross into him?"

Mo' was breathless, even he had been frightened when one of the attackers described to him the malice in Qadir's eyes as he emblazoned Padam's chest with the Christian symbol.

"One of the guys, he's a bit…you know."

"No, I don't fucking know. What you trying to do boy, start a fucking Crusade?"

In the shadows, Qadir gave a thin smile. Yes, indeed, that was exactly his intention.

"Newspaper says they found his Mercedes burnt-out in a field in the middle of nowhere. What did you all do, walk home through cow shit? Somehow, boy, I don't see you as a member of the Rambler's Association, too much of a lazy bastard."

Mo' struggled with his temper in the face of his uncle's repeated insults.

"We'd planned it all out before, and knew where we'd end up. Another of the gang picked us up, and drove us home."

Raza clapped his hands sarcastically.

"Well freeze my piss! You're Julius Caesar, Napoleon and Alexander the Great all rolled into one. Now you listen boy, I'm not saying you did wrong – family honour must be upheld – but you've put us all at risk. My restaurant, my driver! Don't you think someone will have seen something…?"

"It was two in the morning Uncle…"

"I don't care if it was forty-two o'clock on fucking Mars. You don't do anything that puts my business at risk. And now Sunny says you can't stop blabbing about it! From now on you keep that big mouth shut; not another word. Fucking police have been round to see me already. Fortunately, I really did know nothing."

"Can I go now?"

Raza screamed.

"I'll tell you when you can fucking go, you insect up my asshole. No you can't."

He sat back breathing heavily.

"I'm a driver down, and one who had a luxury vehicle. Here's what you are going to do. Sunny, he's off the takeaways, he's driving for me now, AND boy you are on early starts and late finishes."

Begrudgingly he added.

"You're a good driver, boy, and I know that you can be personable when you try; you're not as stupid as you pretend to be. Now you can go."

Sunny stepped aside, and Mo' opened the door. Raza had one last surprise for him.

"Mohammed."

Mo' looked over his shoulder.

"Report to the yard at five-thirty tomorrow morning. You have a long drive ahead of you, and a very important person to drive down to Wiltshire." He wobbled with glee. "You're going to pick him up close to the scene of your crime in my Lexus. Let's hope no-one went for a piss at two in the morning and looked out of their window. Go boy, go…and you scratch my Lexus and I guarantee that your balls will catch fire."

Usman exclaimed, "Stupid prick, he's about as much use as a lid on a pussy!"

He reached over Raza's shoulder to liberate a samosa. His hand was smacked for his trouble, and he withdrew it quickly.

"Never mind all that. You telephone our sister; she's got bigger balls than that husband of hers. When that boy of hers gets home she's to tell him it's suit, collar and tie in the morning, and a shine on his shoes like the head of that bald bastard who runs the *'Jacaranda'* in High Wycombe. Make sure she gets him to the yard on time. I don't want our M.P. complaining again."

Usman was eyeing the food.

"I mean now, paratha breath, fuck off and call her. Jeez, am I the only one with brains in this family?"

Qadir hadn't moved, and he remained unresponsive. Raza fondled a half-eaten samosa, and then dropped it back onto the plate. One problem sorted out, but a greater one in front of him.

He'd met with the Imam, and returned to his office deeply troubled. Hearing that Qadir wanted to take over the world had shaken him, and he wasn't certain how best to address the issue. Weary as he was, the old cunning came into play. He would have agreed with Freddie Forbes' policy of *'softly, softly catchee monkee.'*

Raza laughed lightly.

"Hell of a day, eh Qadir?"

Qadir thought it politic to give some sort of response.

"They don't realise the responsibilities you bear, Uncle, you being head of the family."

Raza wasn't as green as he was cabbage looking, and he thought,

"Non-committal little bugger."

He chewed on the edge of a samosa in a disinterested fashion.

"What about that Mo', eh? Silly boy wants to start a war," and his laugh was hollow.

Qadir held his counsel.

"Good country this, you know nephew...you never knew the old country did you? Boy do I remember. Electricity always going on and off, no running water in the village. To get anything done you had to pay this bastard and that bastard; bombs going off and governments changing, and always having to watch what you said in case some crazy kid with his head stuffed full of wild dreams reported you."

Raza sat, quietly immersed in memory.

"I tell you nephew, and I've never told anyone this. When I saw my mother turn on the hot water tap for the first time in this Britain, and fill a clean bath for us all to wash in, I cried. I was twelve-years-old and I cried. My mother didn't have to carry water anymore and wait an age for it to boil. Simple things Qadir, just simple things we take for granted... and the chance to work and build a future for your family – what greater honour is there?"

For the first time he looked up from his musings, and held Qadir's eye.

"And I tell you this nephew, I will not see that way of life destroyed, because some kid has ideas he doesn't understand and wants to tear the world apart because of them. I may not be the best Moslem, Qadir, but I try to be a good Moslem. My family, my friends and my community are everything to me, and I will rip the heart out of anybody who does anything to put them in harm's way."

Stroking his beard, he looked away. With a smiling face, but cold eyes, he held Qadir's gaze again.

"Listen to me talking! I'd have made a good Imam. Good man, Imam Shirani, you can learn a lot from him."

They stared each other out, until Qadir lowered his eyes in deference to his elder. Raza eased himself to his feet, and waddled over to Qadir.

He placed an arm around his shoulder.

"Ay, ay, ay, a long day. Do me a small favour Qadir."

He stiffened, wary of what his Uncle was going to ask of him.

"Tell Usman to ring your Auntie Amira again. That boy of hers, when he returns from Wiltshire he's to come to our house in Beaconsfield. He can live with us for a while until we can sort his head out. You're a good boy Qadir, the son I never had. I know *you* won't let the family down."

Qadir padded smoothly from the room. He had got the message loud and clear, but his mind was working overtime.

"Imam Shirani, what had he heard? And from whom had he heard it?"

His first thought went to Mo', but he dismissed it out of hand. His young cousin wasn't the sort to confide in Imams. There was a blabbermouth somewhere, and a price to pay

*

Raza need not have worried about Mo's aptitude to be civil, when the need arose. The next night he arrived at his new quarters in Beaconsfield like a dog with two dicks. He sat opposite his uncle at the kitchen table filling his face with a well-earned dinner.

"Yeh, yeh, picked him up on time – some place he's got there in Banksmore - and got him down to dis..."

"The word is *'this'*, boy..."

111

"Yeh, yeh, THIS even bigger place in Tisbury, int that what it's called?"

Raza considered another speech lesson, but let it lie.

"Should of sin dis place we went to; man it was like a castle. I..."

"Yeh, yeh. I've seen hundreds of places in my time, boy. If you must tell someone, tell Qadir."

With that he waddled out of the room.

Mo' shovelled another forkful into his mouth, and an amused Qadir eyed him.

"What was so special about your *'castle'*?"

Mo's fork remained suspended mid-air, and a crafty look laced his features. He finished the mouthful, and dropped the implement onto the plate with a clatter.

"Got a few fings to tell you, cuz, that might interest yer."

He anticipated an enquiry from Qadir, but got none.

"Dis place in Tisbury, well I say *in* cos it was just outside, fuckin' big drive up to the house, went on for miles. An' yeh, it was like a castle. Loads of cars outside. Rollers, a Bentley, a Maserati – shit man, they was amazing. Dis guy, looking like a fuckin' penguin, comes out to take the M.P.'s case. But listen to dis, dese two guys drive up an' when they get out o' their motor they're like in dese amazing uniforms, an' more medals on their chests than a Lahore copper..."

"Army, Airforce, what?"

"One was deffo Army, didn't recognise the other uniform, but man they were serious dudes."

Through a mouthful of dhal he spluttered.

"Nearly forgot, the M.P. slipped me a tenner – two fives – an' dis was stuck between 'em."

He passed a slip of paper to Qadir. The word *'CASTLE'* was written on it, with two telephone numbers printed below. His initial instinct was to think that they were related to the imposing residence of the Earl of Seaforth. Looking again, he was puzzled. The landline number was preceded by the London area code. Without fuss, he slipped the paper into a pocket.

"So you've had a good day, Mo'? Long trip in the Lexus, a fair tip, and now a billet in Beaconsfield, if you'll pardon the alliteration."

"The what?"

Like his Uncle Raza, Qadir was tempted to provide an impromptu English lesson. He decided on a glass of water instead.

"Got sumfin even better to tell you."

Qadir finished filling his glass, and took a delicate sip, only then did he turn to face Mo'.

"When I picked dat geezer up I saw sumfin."

Qadir was becoming irritated with Mo's man of mystery act. He imitated his uncle's mode of address.

"Spit it out then, kebab head!"

Mo' was aggrieved.

"No need for dat cuz."

Qadir pulled up a chair and sat beside him. It was the nearest thing to an apology.

"What did you see?"

Mo' punctuated the air with stabs from his fork.

"Got to Banksmore, 6.30, an' went up the drive like Unc said. Turned the car round, an' before I'd even stopped dis M.P...."

"His name's Marlborough, Sir Hugh Marlborough."

"Yeh, yeh, he's comin' down dese steps in front of his house. So I do like Unc says, an' I get out to put 'is suitcase in the boot. Just as I slam the lid down dis voice shouts, *"Hugh, Hugh,"* an' der's dis fit woman standing in the doorway waving his briefcase. Bit wrinkly, but I like older women, bit of room to wobble around in, know what I mean like..."

"Get to the point."

"Right, yeh. Well, he was about to go an' grab his case when dis big bastard in running gear comes up behind her, kisses her on the cheek and scoots towards us wiv de briefcase in his hand. Chucks it to Sir Hugh, an' runs off down the drive wiv a *'have a good trip, father'.*"

Mo' sat there with a look of serene satisfaction on his face.

"And that's the *sumfin* else you had to tell me?"

Qadir rarely swore.

"Fuck me, Mo', I'll bet Sky News will pay for that."

"Ah, aven't told all – yet. Recognised him straight away, didn't I?"

"And?"

"He's the one who stomped Deggsy when we was 'avin' fun wiv dat shirtlifter an' 'is doggy. Tell you what, he is a big bastard. Should of sin the muscles on 'im – rock 'ard."

Qadir rolled his glass between his palms.

"We gonna sort 'im out, Qadir, like we did dat Gurkha boy?"

A glint appeared in Qadir's eyes. Oh yes, something would have to be done, it was a question of honour. He wasn't going to share it with Mo', who would only end up dropping them in the shit with Raza, and probably the police too. Besides, this would take some thought, they wouldn't be bashing about some no-account taxi driver this time.

"Big bloke, eh?"

"Oh yeh, looked as if he could handle himself."

Qadir went to the sink and swilled out his glass.

"You recognised him, Mo'. Did he recognise you?"

"Nahhh, he never broke stride, hardly even looked at his pop."

But Julian Marlborough *had* cast an eye over Mo', and it came to him just as he exited the drive and started the daily descent into the village.

10

"Tis ever common that men are merriest when they are from home."
Henry V Act 1: Sc. 2

Billy Conway was most definitely enjoying himself. On his days off, he liked to breakfast late and read the newspaper. He would stroll around the corner, from his taxpayer-funded flat in Fawley Road, into West End Lane. On these glorious summer mornings, he sat outside his chosen café, munching, reading and watching the world go by. With the full English inside him, and another read about Everton's woes, he sat back with his second cup of coffee.

West Hampstead was a great place to live, full of young and vibrant people, and older folk who dressed smartly and wore well. On any given day you might run into stars of stage, screen and television. Put the package together, and you couldn't ask for more from the *'Smoke'*. Not that Billy was impressed by theatricals, after all they were only actors, not people of any real importance. What Billy didn't know was that someone was watching him.

In an upstairs flat, across the road, a curtain twitched lightly. Julian was buttoning up his shirt, whilst the prostitute he had just spent an hour with was occupied in the bathroom.

"Hey, don't open the curtains."

Much to his own surprise, Julian heard himself say, "Sorry."

She was such a delight that he'd been blown away, in more ways than one. After trawling the internet, he had chosen her. He had to come into London anyway to meet his father for lunch. The grumpy old bugger was starting to ask questions about how long he intended to idle away his days in Banksmore.

Charlotte was far more than he expected. She had a beautiful and educated voice that matched her lively and intelligent mind. Her thirty-year-old body was to die for, and she gave it with a generosity that nearly convinced him he was having sex with a girlfriend. They lay side-by-side for the last fifteen minutes, and enjoyed the most delightful conversation. He hadn't given her his real name, of course, and he realised that Charlotte wouldn't be hers. In other things she had been more forthcoming.

In reply to a question she must have been asked a hundred times she said, "I had fifty thousand pounds' worth of student debt; cleared it in eighteen months."

"Where did you go to university?"

"I read law at Durham."

"Profitable profession to get into."

"Which?"

"Both."

Charlotte rested her head on one hand.

"This one pays upfront; law is a bitch to make a living at early on, and it can take such a long time to progress."

He stroked her silky, bronzed body.

"That's a gorgeous tan," she said.

"Yours is rather nice."

"Mine's natural."

Julian looked quizzically.

"My dad is Spanish."

"Where did the refined accent come from, is that natural?"

Charlotte didn't take offence, you couldn't afford to in her business; not unless they turned nasty, and she didn't think *'Roddy'* was going to be trouble.

"The real McCoy, honed at my very expensive girls' boarding school."

When she told him which one, he rocked so hard with laughter that she had to shush him. He'd known a few *'gels'* from that place before her time.

"Sorry."

He let the curtain fall back into place.

"See anything interesting?"

He had, but he wasn't going to disclose the details.

"Only you."

He folded her in his arms and kissed her lingeringly. She responded warmly. He really hadn't expected this generosity of behaviour.

She glanced at her watch.

"Sorry, I'm afraid we'll have to stop there."

"Okay. Thank you, that was fun."

Charlotte led him to the front door, and peered through a spy-hole. She hid her naked body with the door, and reached out to open it. Julian laid his hand on hers.

"Question. Do you do outcalls?"

"When I get to know someone well."

"What about me?"

"Not against the idea, but let's see each other a couple more times first. The main thing is, I need to be certain that you won't cut me up in some dark and lonely place."

Her laugh tinkled, but she meant it.

He couldn't resist stroking her breasts one last time.

"I might eat you."

Charlotte was sharp, very sharp, and her throaty laugh uncannily resembled his mother's.

"I think you've done that already. Bye for now."

Julian descended the stairs, and came out onto the pavement. He ignored a leery grin from the East European shopkeeper, who was reorganising his produce in front of the shop window. He felt like a million dollars, and ready to deal with his father's demands, but first he had something to do.

He turned left, and walked one hundred metres before crossing the road. Once over, he made a right and strolled past the shops and cafes, knowing full well that in a minute he would pass by Billy Conway. He had no intention of accosting Billy, he wanted to see if his former sergeant would recognise him, and he wasn't disappointed.

"Fuck me backwards with a tube of Smarties!"

No one looked up at the profanity; that wouldn't be cool amongst the left-leaning trendies of West Hampstead.

"Skipper, Skip!"

Julian halted, and looked at Billy with an affected air of bewilderment.

"It's me Cap', Billy, Billy Conway."

Julian went into am' dram' mode.

"Good God, it can't be. Billy, Sergeant Billy!"

He grasped his hand in genuine pleasure.

"What in God's name are you doing in London, Billy, casing the joint?"

"I've gone up in the world Cap'. Got time for a coffee?"

"Reveal all, Billy, reveal all."

It was past mid-day, so they moved down three doors, and sat outside with a glass of wine whilst they caught up.

The curtain across the road twitched, and Charlotte peered through a barely perceptible chink. Her next client was late, a decent old sort – retired headmaster from a local prep school, who wasn't getting any because his wife was disabled. Nice old boy, clean and still fairly trim. Like all prostitutes, there were times she had to grit her teeth when she opened the front door, and saw what was waiting there. Her *'fee'* deterred most toe rags; not everybody could lay their hands on £220 for an hour's sex. She caught sight of old *'Lionel'* crossing the road, and over his shoulder she saw *'Roddy'* and a male companion laughing heartily.

"Hope he's not Bi," she thought, "and moving on from me to him."

Somehow she didn't think so. She would be pleased to see him again, not because she had fallen for him in the slightest way. It was just that it was nice to do it with someone now and again who was attractive and knew what he was doing, and what he wanted.

"Come on then *'Lionel'*," she said out loud, "come and rip the gym slip off me."

Julian invited Billy to join him and his father for lunch. It amused him to think what his father's response would be when he learned that Billy was one of Tommy O'Donnell's security team. In the event, Billy declined claiming call of duty for later in the day. When Julian departed, Billy blew out his cheeks. That was a close one, he couldn't afford to be seen in the company of a Tory M.P.

Draining his one and only glass of wine, he was startled by the blast of a car horn. Looking up he saw an elderly man caught in confusion in the middle of the road, drivers on both sides cursing him.

"Bastards," Billy thought.

It seemed to be the way everyone behaved these days; incivility and rudeness was rife. He strode into the middle of the road, arms outstretched.

"Alright, alright, give him a break. You'll be his age one day."

Billy picked up a shopping bag for the old geezer.

"Here you go grandad, let's get you on the pavement. There we are, everything shipshape and Bristol fashion."

"Oh thank you. I get a bit puffed these days if I have too much exercise."

'Lionel' tottered away.

"Mind how you go. I hope I'm getting as much exercise at your age."

Billy managed to get through his front door before he doubled up laughing. The dirty old sod. Billy had seen where he had come from, and he knew all about what went on upstairs behind that door. He'd run into the girl in the café and wine bar a few times; a right little cracker. Good for you, grandad. He wondered if *he* might be able to pay her a visit, on expenses of course. Then he considered if Julian had visited her more than once, and he smiled as he thought of the lyric from a song, *"Who's watching who?"*

Father and son lunched in Great Peter Street, at the old man's favourite venue. He gave Julian an ear bashing about getting some work, and not expecting to live off him for the rest of his life. In passing, Julian mentioned his unexpected encounter with his old comrade. Hugh didn't seem to take it in, so he dropped the subject. It was a lengthy lunch, lasting well into the afternoon. They went their separate ways around four.

Julian was disinclined to return to Banksmore just yet. For a second he thought about spending a little more of his father's cash. Maybe he should let him finance an early evening visit to Charlotte. Perhaps not, he didn't want to look too keen.

For a while he wandered around Westminster, and saw that security was tighter than ever. He noticed a greater preponderance of beggars on the streets, and how the roads and pavements were in a shocking condition. If London was like this, what was the state of the rest of the country? Once, he stepped aside as a demonstration marched towards Westminster. It was an odd sort of protest, made up of what appeared to be shopkeepers and small businessmen, chanting about scandalous rates and taxes.

One cheerleader bellowed, "What do we earn?" and the reply came, "Whatever we can, whatever we want." "How do we earn it?" "Working hard."

Julian had read in The Times that in 2017 Comrade Corbyn had decided that when he came to office he would put a ceiling on what a person could earn. Idiot! No idea about human nature. If all the money in the world were divided equally, there would be inequality again two minutes later. However, Tommy O'Donnell had tried to implement the policy.

Somehow the day disappeared. He took a trip on the river, and noticed the paucity of cruise boats, and how few tourists there were. Astonishing for London, the once thriving capital, but it wasn't a welcoming place anymore. He took in a film, had a few drinks in a bar and got talking to a girl, but her gimp of a boyfriend turned up.

Gradually, he made his way over to Marylebone, and hopped onto a Chiltern Line train back to Wenbury. The evening rush had died down, and there were only three other people in the carriage. Julian had enjoyed a great morning, but the rest of the day had left him feeling disgruntled.

The smell of cigarette smoke wafted up his nostrils. He looked across the aisle to see a yobbo with his filthy shoes up on the seats, smoking a cigarette.

"Excuse me, there's no smoking on trains."

The overgrown layabout took a drag, and exhaled.

"Go fuck yerself."

Julian was fastidious in folding his Evening Standard, and placing it carefully on the seat. He stood up, walked two steps across the aisle and punched the obnoxious youth once in the face. Said party slid to the floor, and lay unconscious. The other couple in the carriage hid behind their Ipads, but Julian detected satisfied smiles on their faces.

When they reached Wenbury all three of them stepped over the prone body. At the barrier, Julian heard the lady speak to a railway employee.

"Excuse me, I think someone's been taken ill in the last carriage."

As the couple went past Julian heard,

"About time someone did that. Knock some civility back into people, that's the only way we'll put this bloody country right."

He was pleased, and suddenly felt it had been a good day. Reclining in a taxi he noticed it was one of the Khan's fleet.

"That's what I'll do tomorrow," he thought, "pay a visit to Sergeant Gurung and see how he's getting on."

*

Stars align themselves. Not as a result of mystical nonsense, but because chance arises logically out of a previous set of circumstances. The balance of probability pays out now and again. So it was that Peter Standish and Julian found themselves visiting Padam at the same time.

When they entered his room they discovered Faisal Hussain bedside. Faisal had recognised the injured soldier from his photograph in the newspaper, and decided to pay him a visit. Standish, of course, was ministering to a parishioner.

"Hello Sarge, how's it going? I know you."

Julian addressed Faisal.

"The Market Place."

Peter Standish extended his hand to Faisal.

"Peter Standish, Rector of St. George's Banksmore. Do you live locally?"

Faisal explained his circumstances, before they gave their attention to Padam.

"What did the doctor say, Padam?"

"My eye socket and ribs are much better, thank you minister. They are discharging me tomorrow, but with this leg I will be in a wheelchair for some while. The fractures were very complicated. Won't be driving any taxis for a month or two; not sure how we are going to manage at home."

"You're not to worry about that, the parish is rallying around..."

"Doesn't your wife work?" Julian interjected.

"A little bit of cleaning here and there, but with the children she can't be out and about all the time."

"With you stuck at home to keep an eye on them perhaps she'll have a bit more time. Leave it with me, I think that we can find a few more clients for your wife to keep tidy."

"I'm grateful, sir, you are all so very kind."

Remember, Mr. Gurung, if my wife and I can do anything you have our number. Even if it's just a lift here and there. If you'd excuse me now, a pile of books need marking. Always a joy!"

They shook hands, and Peter held the door for Faisal who paused.

"Forgive me asking, are you the priest who is initiating these inter-faith discussions?"

"I am."

"My Imam has mentioned it at the Mosque. Not everyone is pleased."

"How do you feel about them?"

"Oh, I'm very interested, I'd like to come along. When is the first meeting?"

Peter looked over his shoulder.

"Would you excuse us; I'd like to have a brief chat with Faisal."

Julian and Padam were left alone.

"Quite a bashing you took there, Sarge. Ever been banged up like that before?"

"A few bumps and bruises over the years, but nothing like this."

"I had a ride in one of your taxis yesterday; the Khans that is."

He observed Padam's face closely, as it hardened.

"Any ideas, Sarge?"

"Ideas sir, about what?"

"Don't come the old soldier Padam, you know exactly what I mean."

Padam looked deeply into his eyes, and asked himself, "Can I trust this man?"

The balance fell in Julian's favour; the old soldier conflated officer and a gentleman with honour.

The story he told was similar to Mo's, but the youth had omitted one detail through ignorance. Padam's assailants thought him unconscious. Oddly, it had been the fire-like pain of the cross being carved into his chest that brought him out of his stupor. He kept his eyes closed whilst the cruel punishment was inflicted, and with steely resolve he avoided crying out. When Qadir had finished he caught a glimpse of his profile through narrowed eyes. As the group walked away down the church path he heard a laugh, and a voice.

"That'll teach him to mess wiv your cuz an' his mates."

"What have you done with his Mercedes?"

"Left it in a field, Qadir, burnt out."

"You idiots, if my uncle finds out he'll wring your neck for destroying the best car in his fleet."

Padam drifted into unconsciousness.

Julian laid a hand on the brave man's arm. Inside he came to a resolution. He felt the eyes upon him, and relaxed into a smile.

"How is the chest wound?"

"I wear it as a badge of honour, sir, the mark of Christ crucified…"

"And He is with you."

Peter Standish re-entered the room.

Julian held his tongue.

"Leave you with the Padre, Sarge. Good to see you looking better. Oh, let me have your telephone number, will you?"

"I've got it Julian. I'll ring the Manor when I get home. Will you be there?"

"Not sure, but you can leave it with mother if I'm not. Rightio, leave you to your ministrations. By the way, are you still going ahead with that inter-faith thing you were talking about?"

Peter nodded.

"Best of luck," Julian said ironically.

When the door closed he stood in the corridor and muttered to himself.

"Time for me to engage in a few inter-faiths *'activities'*."

With determination in his stride, and cold fury in his eyes, he exited the hospital.

11

"Cry havoc! And let slip the dogs of war."
Julius Caesar Act 3: Sc. 1

Thunderstorms were predicted for days. The heavens opened, and the baking hot and arid July came to a temporary halt.

Mo' settled to his new routine after a few weeks. Now that he had done penance for upsetting his uncle, he was no longer at it all hours. Today was a late shift. The rains began around four p.m., and the country was still taking a lashing at six. You could barely stand upright in the whipping wind; Mo' was inundated with fares. It was nearly midnight, and rain and business had slackened off. The streets were deserted. He parked up, and got out of his cab for a ciggy.

Julian bided his time. Like the good soldier he was he put in plenty of reconnaissance. Over a fortnight he kept tabs on the Khans, specifically upon Mo's habits. There was a café opposite the taxi rank in Wenbury-on-the-Hill, and he varied his times there to observe who turned up and when. Two doors down was a Chinese restaurant, which he frequented for a few evenings to keep watch during the light summer nights. It didn't take long to work out Mo's shift pattern. He waited for the opportune moment.

The storm was raging when he slipped out of the Manor, waterproofed against the elements in plain, dark clothing. The route to Old Wenbury was via fields and footpaths. When compelled to emerge into civilisation he looked no different than the few other individuals struggling to get home from the pub.

He was the only occupant of the long and narrow street, in Old Wenbury. The Market Place was a curious construction; an open-sided space beneath a huge clock tower supported by brick pillars. A single person could secrete himself behind them. His plan might or might not work first time, but he was prepared to try it until it did. By Julian's reckoning Mo' would be near the end of his shift. One evening, he took the precaution of following him home in the estate Land rover. Mo' was still parking his sorry carcass in Beaconsfield.

Taking out a disposable mobile phone, Julian rang the taxi firm. It was answered quickly, and he affected a Cockney accent.

"Yeh, yeh can I get a taxi mate. To Beaconsfield, guv. Tha's right, down on the Broadway. Where am I? 'angin' abart in the Market Place in Old Wenbury. Ten minutes? Yeh, yeh, fanks mate."

It might come to nothing, but if so it would do for a dry run – well, hardly dry, and he snorted to himself.

The storm passed. It was a beautiful summer night. You would see more stars in Banksmore, because of less urban light disfiguring the sky, but it was still breath-taking. Everyone had gone to bed, an enforced early night because of the weather.

Julian peered down the street from behind the column, and breathed in the air of centuries. The tower encased him, as it had done for others over two hundred years. Higgledy-piggledy houses revealed a crazy-paving perspective in the soft glow of the amber streetlights.

Most of the dependable edifices were built during the Regency.

An atavistic spirit swept through Julian; this was his land where people could sleep safe and sound. He knew that when these properties were constructed the streets of England had been far from safe. But the people of this land had struggled and died, and worked and persevered to make it what it now was. He had no intention of letting that be swept away. Instinctively, he knew that he was not acting for any one class of persons. Rich and privileged he might be, but he had fought alongside men from the industrial towns of the north, and Welshman from their scarred valleys. He was only too ready to acknowledge that the country was theirs also. The fight must go on; it was his turn to persevere.

He heard the taxi approaching. What else could it be? It pulled up at the opposite end of the Market Place and reversed into a space. Julian flitted within the covered area, and emerged onto the narrow footpath behind. Stealthily, he padded the twenty metres to where the taxi was parked, coming close to its rear end. Half-hidden behind the corner column he tried to make out the driver. Mo' opened his driver's door and threw an empty coke tin onto the cobblestones, it's impact shattering the serene stillness. It was him, it was him, tempted by a final fare which would leave him a short hop from home.

The car door closed. Pulling his hood downwards, Julian did his best to disguise his face. It didn't really matter, because this would take seconds. He stepped towards the driver's door, whistling loudly. Julian wanted Mo' to hear him coming, and he wasn't disappointed when he heard the electric buzz of the car window opening.

He stood slightly behind Mo's seated position.

"Orwight mate, you for me, Beaconsfield?"

"Yeh bruv, hop in."

The movement of Julian's hand was so swift that Mo' had no idea that it had actually moved. The carotid arteries are major blood vessels in the neck that supply blood to the brain, neck and face. There are two of them, one on the right and one on the left. Julian gripped the collar of his shirt and twisted it tight around his neck to interrupt the supply. Within ten seconds Mo' was unconscious. Easy - Julian had learnt that in the early stages of his Krav Maga training, long before he advanced to the deadlier arts of Commando Krav Maga.

A gag was drawn from his pocket, and it bit into Mo's mouth; a length of strong cord was unravelled from his waist, and he tugged the body out of the car almost lovingly. Supporting the dead weight under the armpits, he propped Mo' up against one of the Market columns and bound him to it with the cord. A Fairbairn-Sykes knife – a remnant of his active service days – appeared in his hand, and Mo's trousers and underpants were shreds around his ankles.

Julian reached into the sleeve of his coat and withdrew a supple cane, nearly the length of his arm. Without further ado, he gave Mo' a ferocious six of the best; the body and head jerking violently in pain. The weals on Mo's backside dripped blood, but the flow was about to become more profuse. Squatting down, he took out the knife again, and with great deliberation he carved a name into Mo's flesh with a delicacy worthy of a great surgeon, it read: "PAKI." He had one more task, which was accomplished with the aid of an aerosol can of red paint. On the wall above Mo's head he repeated the word inscribed on his buttocks. This time he added letters to each Capital, and spelt out a message to set the land alight:

P - *aedophile*

A - *nd*

K - *iller*

I - *mmigrants*!

Without a backward glance, he loped across the road, and into an alley. Back to the anonymity of the footpaths. The eyes of a fox blinked at him, and the creature wisely gave him a wide detour.

The ambulance pulled away, as Chief Inspector Simon Reynolds of Thames Valley Police was waved into a parking space by a constable. He wondered why someone of his rank had been hauled out of bed to deal with a common-or-garden assault. When he saw the inscription on the Market wall he was in no doubt.

"Sergeant."

"Sir?"

"I don't care how you do it, get that covered up."

"Forensics will want to examine it, sir..."

"I know, but I want a screen around it now."

Simon looked at his watch; 0730. Dear God, it was inevitable that someone had passed by and seen it, if only the dog-walker who had discovered Mo' and called for assistance. Damned thing was incendiary; of that he was certain.

He had been around long enough to know that the figures on race hate crime had been massaged for years. The public were dissuaded from believing that a major problem existed. Earlier in the year he had been sent to Berlin for a Europe-wide conference. Late into the night, in the hotel bar, he learnt that most Western Europeans governments were pulling the wool over their citizens' eyes. Their East European colleagues didn't seem to care a fig, and admitted openly that they had an internal war on their hands. More than a few made it clear that their sympathies lay firmly with the racists.

"Another world," he thought, "another century – the sixth!"

The police had been unprepared for this, but Sergeant Jeff Durham showed initiative. A nearby shop was undergoing internal renovation, and the builders had started early. Simon saw a couple of them carrying large sheets of MDF in his direction. He stopped them and commandeered the wood. Before his constables could move to assist, one cheery chap strode over towards Simon Reynolds with his MDF.

"'ere you go, mate."

A thin young man with lank blonde hair down to his shoulders, wearing jeans and a tatty t-shirt looked up at the racist words and laughed.

"Something amusing you?"

"Fuckin' brilliant that. Some clever bastards about."

Jeff Durham addressed him.

"How's it going these days, Tony, any cases pending?"

The young builder looked sullen.

"No, no I haven't. Got regular work now. All that's behind me, getting married next month."

The Sergeant looked around.

"You got a motor here, Tony?"

An extended finger pointed to a rusted and ancient BMW parked across the road.

"Tax, MOT and insurance up to date are they?"

Tony looked decidedly shifty, as Jeff Durham came close to his ear.

"Some things are best kept quiet about, son. You catch my drift?"

"Can I get back to work?"

"Mind how you go, Tony, mind how you go."

"Old friend of yours, Sarge?"

"Known our Tony, sir, since he was at school. Not a bad lad, but can't keep his thieving hands to himself."

"Well let's hope marriage settles him down."

"We can but hope sir."

"Tell me about the victim."

Durham rather relished what he had to report.

"Taxi driver, sir, works for the Khans."

"Good grief, that's the second of their men who's been assaulted in the last few months. Has someone got it in for them?"

Durham wouldn't have minded if they had; parcel of trouble the Khans, in his experience.

"Any progress on the first assault, sir?"

"Proving a mite intractable, Jeff. You'd think the three wise monkeys lived in Wenbury."

Jeff Durham liked the Chief Inspector; he appreciated his dry humour. Never swore either, which was more than a tad unusual in their milieu. Rumour mill said he was a Christian and a lay preacher, here in Old Wenbury. Curiosity got the better of him.

"Excuse me, sir, is that your church round the corner?"

Simon smiled, he was only too happy to bear witness.

"It is indeed, Sergeant Durham, St. Andrew's Old Wenbury. Thinking of joining us Jeff? You'd be more than welcome."

The officer shifted uncomfortably from right foot to left.

"Sundays are for shopping and golf, sir. Anyway, I only believe in what I can see."

A wry grin lit up Simon's handsome features. The same porous argument. He thought of the old saying, *"There are none so blind, as they that will not see."* This was neither the time nor place for a theological, or indeed existential, discussion.

"Best tell me what you saw when you arrived, Sarge."

Jeff described the sight of Mo' gagged and bound and the bloodied weals on his backside.

"...and you saw that for yourself, sir."

He pointed toward the now hidden proclamation on the wall.

"There's another thing, sir. This beating, whoever did it carved the acrostic on the wall into his buttocks."

Simon raised an eyebrow.

"ACROSTIC eh?"

"We're not all thick plods, sir. I'm a Times crossword man."

"Apologies Jeff, that was unforgivably judgemental. There's something on your mind, what is it?"

"You mentioned the attack on the Khan's other driver, sir, and whether there might be a connection. Thing is, the first victim had a cross cut into his chest, and this one has the word *'Paki'* incised into his derriere."

Simon was one step ahead.

"You think the connection might not be as obvious as we first assumed?"

The sergeant gave a small shrug of maybe, maybe not.

"If I'm reading you right, Jeff, you've got the word *'revenge'* flitting through your mind."

"Right sir."

Simon turned half away, and the words he spoke barely carried on the dry air.

"Dear Lord, I hope not." He faced Jeff and whispered, "Religious?"

"That was my thought, sir."

A constable called to them.

"Sir, sir, forensics have arrived. They'd like a word, sir."

A little way down the street, Tony the builder peered through the plate glass window of the shop they were tarting up.

"The fuckin' *'filth'*, never give it a rest, do they."

He couldn't give a fiddler's fart about their threats, Tony was inured to their behaviour. That graffiti on the wall was fucking amazing. He clicked all the right buttons on his mobile to post the photograph, he had taken earlier, onto Facebook.

An older man appeared in a doorway.

"I'm not paying you to fart about on your phone, get that timber sawn up, and then paint the toilet walls."

Tony said quietly, "Fuck you – Polish twat," but he did as he was told. Occasionally, he checked to see how many *'likes'* he was getting on Facebook.

*

Hot summer evenings, when no-one wants to go to bed, are a bitch at the best of times. When trouble stirs the torrid air they are even worse. Within eighteen hours Tony's Facebook post had gone viral, not just in the United Kingdom but worldwide. The majority *'disliked'* it, but the *'likes'* were in multiples of thousands. The incident, in this average little town outside London, was national and international news. Politicians of all hue were pontificating. BBC and Sky had lined up the usual suspects to discuss its ramifications; their language a mixture of sentimental abstraction and clichés.

A sizable population of Asian origin resided in the county town of Buckinghamshire, largely peaceable and integrated. On the last evening of July, they were in a ferment. The situation was not improved by gangs of white youths rolling around the streets laughing and jeering at Asian passers-by. In more than one place the foul inscription of Julian Marlborough's invention was replicated on walls and doors.

Extra police had been on the streets since mid-morning, but they were unprepared for the suddenness with which violence erupted. The difficulty they faced was that the rioters had no need to go from door to door whipping up a blood lust, they were able to do it through social media. Not something that bothers the parasites who make their fortunes out of the technology, and live far away in their rich ghettoes.

They came roaring off their estates – white, Asian and black alike – tooled up, and determined to damage something and someone. It began with sporadic and individual fights, as parties ran into each other, on their way to the centre of town. If the police had been out in number they may have been able to *'kettle'* small groups early on, and keep the violence and damage to a minimum. Moderate Asian groups had attempted a peaceful protest, making their way to County Hall to hold a silent vigil. They became the eye of the storm as everyone congregated around them. It didn't take long for the surging crowds to engage in inter-racial battles. Wagons full of police were drafted in from Oxfordshire and Northamptonshire at great speed to support their Buckinghamshire colleagues. At one stage a number of military policeman joined their ranks from nearby RAF stations.

When the dust died down, and a report found its way to the Prime Minister's desk he flew into a rage.

"Who put the fucking military on the streets? I'm not having that. Find out who authorised it, and sack the bastard."

The culprit was never found; the military has a wonderful way of obfuscating and muddying the pool when necessary.

The night wore on, and the forces of law and order gradually gained ground, cracking heads that had already been cracked. Local A & E's were so stretched you would have thought it was January not July. Many with minor injuries were ferried out of county. The Chief Constable made an appeal on radio and television for G.P.'s to open their surgeries; some responded, some didn't.

By eleven o' clock the crowds had dispersed. The town looked like a war zone, with shopfronts smashed. The goods, that hadn't been looted, were strewn across the pavements. It appeared that the anger was dissipated – for the moment. A few hundred sustained injuries, but only a handful could be described as serious, and none was life-threatening. Sadly, one person died, an innocent Indian boy passing by on his way to evening class. There had been smaller scale disturbances across the country; not far away in Luton and as far north as Bradford. They were nothing like the bushfire war that had erupted in leafy Bucks for six hours.

The Khan clan gathered in Raza's fine house in Beaconsfield. Mo's mother, Amira, was giving her brother GBH on the ear'ole.

"What are you going to do about it Raza? My boy is in hospital shamed and dishonoured; his *chutar* is black and blue."

Raza shook his head, and grumbled.

"Trouble, trouble, trouble, that boy of yours, sister, has never been anything but trouble to the family…"

Amira tried to interject, but Raza shut her up.

"I know, I know, he's still family. What I want to know is what the fuck is going on. First, the Gurkha and now Mohammed. Is somebody trying to ruin my business?"

"Maybe it's got nothing to do with our business, maybe…"

"What would you know dhal breath? Of course it's about the fucking business."

Usman shut up. Raza sat at the dining table rubbing his chin.

"My money is on the bald headed bastard in Wycombe. He's trying to muscle in on our territory. What do you think Qadir?"

Qadir appeared to give consideration to his uncle's question.

"It is a strong possibility."

Other cogs had been whirring in his brain. Another thought came to him.

Had he been present at the crime scene, he would have concurred with the police that this may well have been a revenge attack. So, who would want to take it out on Mo' for his past misdemeanours. Certainly, the boy made enemies, but they were all kids at heart in a small pond. Violent they may be, but retaliation would only amount to a bashing, or at worst a slashed face. No, the vile word incised into Mo's backside, and its inscription on the Market wall spoke of something more complex. Qadir loved playing the game *'Only Connect'* as a child, and he was the acknowledged champion of the family. His mind recognised a pattern. Before long he was convinced that this mayhem could be traced back to the night Denis Trueman came in for attention from Mo' and his mates.

"Something else on your mind, Qadir?"

Raza interrupted his train of thought, and he came out of his reverie.

"Er no, no uncle, just wondering how Mo' is getting on."

"I'm having him transferred to the private hospital in the morning, Amira. He will have the very best of treatment. In the meantime, I want to know what that shiny-headed *gandoo* in Wycombe is up to. Qadir, you are best-placed to do this. Make enquiries at Mosque, people talk to you, see what they have to say. If that brothel-bred son of a bum fucking Arab is behind these attacks, I'll see that dogs piss outside his house every day."

"Brother, your language gets worse every time I see you."

Raza apologised to his big sister, and diverted her attention.

"Now let's eat."

Usman tried to excuse himself, but Raza was having none of it. He knew only too well about his brother's extra-mural activities with young girls, and exculpated himself from responsibility on the grounds that he himself played no part in the abuse. However, this evening family must stick together, and anyway he had a job for his brother.

With his mouth full of chicken, he started to speak.

"This business with Mo' has left me with a problem, dear brother of mine. Our member of parliament has been on the blower again, or rather his wife has. He needs driving down to that place in Wiltshire again this Friday. What the fuck is the place called?"

"Raza!" Amira exclaimed sharply. He held up a hand in surrender.

Involuntarily, Qadir said, "Tisbury."

Everyone looked at him, because of the almost excited way he had blurted it out. Raza eyed him with a surprised look on his face.

"How did you know that, Qadir?"

He covered his tracks quickly and expertly.

"Oh, Mo' was telling me about his expedition down there, and about the place where he dropped the client off; said it was some sort of castle. You know what Mo's like, easily impressed."

He laughed, looking round the table for confirmation.

The extended family broke into chatter about Mo's excessive imagination and talent for exaggeration.

Amidst the noise, Raza ploughed through his food. He hadn't become a success in business without the ability to read people, and he knew that something wasn't quite right. Qadir's response was convincing, but his demeanour as he gave out the name of Tisbury set off alarms. That boy never laughed out loud, he was one of the most solemn creatures Raza had ever known. Most certainly, he didn't make appeals for approval to anybody. Imam Shirani's report flitted through his mind.

"What the fuck is that boy up to?"

141

He saw his sister looking at him curiously. For a moment he felt guilty, wondering if she had divined the expletive in his head.

"Best treatment we can buy for that boy, eh Amira."

It was said with jollity in his voice, if not in his heart.

"How about this? When Mo' is fit to travel, you and your brood to take a holiday in the Old Country, all expenses paid."

He wanted that boy far away, and this was the solution.

Those members of her 'brood' present gave a whoop of delight. Amira came around to Raza's side and embraced him.

"Oh Raza, you are the best brother anyone could have – even when you talk like a Lahore toilet attendant – blessings be upon you."

"You're welcome. Eat, eat, everyone eats. Usman don't forget, Friday morning at six-thirty pick the Marlborough guy up and take him to his *castle* for the weekend."

Everyone laughed, except for Qadir. He had made his connection. Time was short, but he had a plan that would not just revenge Mo', that was of secondary importance, but all of his people who had been defamed by the writing on the wall.

12

"There is a law in each well-ordered nation to curb those raging appetites that are most disobedient and refractory.
Troilus and Cressida Act 2: Sc.2

Blacow struggled to quieten the House, but his voice resounded enough to control all but the unruliest elements.

"Sir Hugh Marlborough," he cried.

The recalcitrant children who called themselves Members of Parliament reduced their din to that of low-level disruption found in the classroom of a weak teacher.

Hugh didn't want the temperature to rise too quickly, so he began his peroration in a low tone of gravitas.

"Mr. Speaker, we have all been shocked by events of the last two days in, and around, my constituency of Wenbury and Cranchurch; not to say in the sporadic outbreaks of violence across the country. May I extend my sympathy, and the sympathies of this side of the House, to the victims of this disorder. Our sincere condolences do, of course, go to the family of Darshan Kapoor, an innocent bystander, so tragically killed. What is tragic is that early reports suggest he was the victim of those whose origins he shared from the Indian sub-continent."

The House started to murmur. One or two on the Government benches began to see which way the wind was blowing in Marlborough's address.

"Mr. Speaker, may we congratulate, and give thanks, to our police forces for their prompt response to this outrageous civil disorder. Disorder generated by the malcontents and subversives who wish to undermine the fabric of society."

He paused for effect.

"I refer, of course, to those who foment inter-racial strife, and seek the revolutionary overthrow of democracy. Those in communities outside this House, not those residing on the Government benches…"

The House went into uproar at Hugh's sly dig at Tommy O'Donnell. He stoked the fire.

"We haven't yet had to call upon the forces of law and order to enter this Chamber to restore our democracy and its freedoms, which have been, and continue to be eroded, by the gentleman opposite…"

Cries of outrage and delight, in competition with each other, got even louder.

Blacow permitted the din a few seconds grace, in the hope that it would blow itself out, and then he asserted himself.

"Order! Order! Order!"

Gradually the bedlam subsided.

"I really do think that the member for Wenbury and Cranchurch might consider using less inflammatory language. It hardly seems concomitant with his condemnation of those who have so recently perpetrated such terrible acts upon our streets."

A chorus of subdued "Hear, hears," came from both sides of the House.

Blacow tried again.

"Sir Hugh Marlborough."

On the Opposition front bench, Andrew Freddie Forbes had mixed feelings. Hugh had sailed a little too close to the wind for his liking. He hoped that what came next, would be more measured and considered in its expression.

"Mr. Speaker, I apologise unreservedly to honourable members, if my previous statement gave unnecessary offence. However, Mr. Speaker, we have, in the last few days, seen the necessity to draft the military onto our streets in order to assist the police in controlling civil disturbances. Does the Prime Minister not recognise the gravity of the situation? Would he tell the House on whose authority military policemen from the Royal Air Force were deployed?"

"The Prime Minister."

Tommy O'Donnell came to his feet more pissed off than he cared to admit. He had been dreading this question, which was why he had taken the draconian step of having a *'D'* notice slapped on the media.

"Mr. Speaker, I need no lessons from a Tory about usin' the Army to oppress the werkin' people of this country. Their great hero Churchill did tha' in South Wales a century ago..."

Shouts emanated from the Conservative benches.

"Ancient history, ancient history!"

One wag, who knew his musicals, started to sing.

"Let's do the Time Warp again" from the Rocky Horror Show.

"Order, order, the member for South Bentley must really not take to song. I am aware that one of my illustrious predecessors was a member of the Tiller Girls

Dance troupe, but she did not do impromptu Can Cans on the floor of the House."

This reference to the long gone, and much admired, Betty Boothroyd drew appreciative laughter.

"The Prime Minister must be heard."

O'Donnell had not yet managed to remove the television cameras from the Chamber, but it was his intention.

"It is not in the public interest, at this time, to reveal the command structure that resulted in the deployments in question."

To the astonishment of the entire House he sat down.

Even Blacow was nonplussed. He called upon the member for East Backmore.

The excessively lanky Charles Fenwick, dressed in a chalk stripe double-breasted suit, had been briefed in advance by Freddie Forbes.

"Mr. Speaker, we are all aware that, following the decision of the people that we should leave the European Union, there has been a dramatic reduction in immigration from the European mainland. Nonetheless, under the leadership of the present government we have seen an exponential rise in immigration from South East Asia, Africa and the Middle East. One might be tempted to call it an open door policy. Not only has mass immigration occurred at their behest, but we have seen a huge increase in illegal entry to this country."

Fenwick waved a folder in the air.

"Mr. Speaker, this document will be of interest to both sides of the House. It is the transcript of a criminal trial, in which the accused was found guilty, and imprisoned, for people trafficking. The name on the file is Joseph Gerald O'Donnell – the Prime Minister's brother."

A spontaneous "ohh" went round the House like an ill wind.

"Would the Prime Minister not agree, that the violent and sad events we have seen on the streets are a direct indictment of his policy on immigration?"

Charles Fenwick made sit, but halfway he rose and added,

"...and in part the activities of his family business?"

O'Donnell looked desperately to his Home Secretary, a blood brother in their years of activism. He thought the information about his obscure brother had been shredded years ago. How the hell had that no account Tory got his hands on the papers? Unsteadily, and furious, he rose to his feet.

"Mr. Speaker, I protest that the member opposite is using the privilege of the House to slander me and my family with impunity. I demand that..."

He was shouted down with surging anger. Behind him, all he could see was stony faces, and backbenchers with their heads in their hands. The fury and disorder of the House was nigh on uncontrollable, and O'Donnell reverted to type.

Red-faced and roaring, as if he were in a union meeting in the upstairs room of a Liverpool pub, he screamed,

"I'm not 'avin' it, I'm not 'avin' it, not from some lyin' toffee nosed Tory frigger!"

Silence fell like a stone on the Chamber. Such language may have been commonplace in the House during the eighteenth century, but it was unacceptable now. Every eye glared at O'Donnell.

Blacow cleared his throat.

"I must remind the Prime Minister, such behaviour outside this place would earn him an anti-social behaviour order."

There was a handful of people present who knew that it wouldn't have been the first ASBO in O'Donnell's life.

"I would ask the Prime Minister to reconsider his intemperate language to the member for East Backmore."

Blacow didn't actually want to tell the Prime Minister to apologise; that really wouldn't be *de rigeur*.

"I...I...I..." Tommy O'Donnell struggled with himself. Years of getting his own way, and his genetic aggression, prevented him from making the apology.

"I will offer him an apology if I get one from him for the slur on my family."

Before the Speaker could intervene, Fenwick waved the folder and shouted, "...but it's true."

Matters went from bad to worse when the member seated next to him bellowed.

"MY dad's bigger than your dad."

Even Labour members fell about laughing.

The Prime Minister's humiliation was complete. When order was restored, he was asked by the Speaker to retract his unparliamentary language, and refused to do so. The House held its collective breath, but Blacow had bottle. He ordered the Prime Minister to leave the House. When he refused to do so the Speaker invoked the parliamentary procedure called *'Naming'* to vote upon O'Donnell's suspension.

"The question is that the honourable member be suspended from the services of the House. As many of that opinion say 'Aye'...to the contrary 'No.... the 'Ayes' have it, the 'Ayes' have it."

Thomas Patrick O'Donnell became the first Prime Minister in British history to be suspended from entering the House for one day. When he stomped out of the Chamber, Freddie Forbes affected the look of a man engrossed in his papers. Inside his head he said, "A good day's work; a very fine day's work."

13

"A fool thinks himself to be wise, but a wise man knows himself to be a fool."
As You Like It Act 5: Sc.1

It is a sobering thought that as the sun and moon do their rounds each day the hands of love and hate are extended somewhere to bless people, or to inflict pain upon them. The ancient, and unceasing, contest continues in the world between good and evil. Evil will not yield in the struggle. Those who adhere to it believe that their family, tribe, or nation is unique, and those who exist outside their encampment of kinship have no share in the *'noble'* values that only they possess.

We become aware of difference first, and commonality second; colour of skin, religion, ethnicity, nationality, sexuality and gender are ready-made labels to pin on the *'other'* in condemnation. They provide an excuse for making scapegoats of those who are *'not one of us'*. We need someone to blame for our failings, when we haven't the guts to own up to our culpability. So whilst we laud Shakespeare as the wisest icon in our history, we ignore his most pertinent insight. Shylock the Jew in *'The Merchant of Venice'* says: *"If you prick us, do we not bleed?"*

Love is greater, because it faces constant adversity. True courage is needed in the face of fear. Fear of rejection and humiliation; the terror of physical and mental pain; despair that though you may win some battles you will not live to see the war won.

Peter Standish was one of the few. An unknown priest in charge of a handful of village churches with dying congregations. Ministering to good folk who could be encouraged to take the Message out into their communities. Love your neighbour as yourself, and love your enemies. Not an injunction to accept sinful and destructive behaviour, but a creed demanding that, though you will receive blows and curses from the wrongdoer, you must never lose sight of his humanity. There is a cost, always a price to pay.

Whilst laying out chairs in the village hall Peter thought of the famed Lutheran pastor Dietrich Bonhoeffer. He was a German who stood up against the Nazis. They hung him in Flossenburg concentration camp a few weeks before the end of the war. Peter had no such ideas of martyrdom, and he would have demurred if you'd suggested that such an end might be his reward. Nevertheless, he was aware of his minority position in British society. Intensely conscious of the endless barbs from smart-mouthed comedians, polymaths, and intolerant scientists. They sought to demean him and his brothers and sisters in Christ. He would not be deterred; he would run the race. A handful of odds and sods – drawn from fishermen and tax collectors – had persevered in the face of real adversity two thousand years ago. From their seed a great Word that embodied love embraced the world. Peter could do no more than play his part.

Fiona Claymore-Browne's wiry frame was deceptive, and she hefted stacks of chairs around with a frantic will.

"Steady on their Fi', the floor will collapse if you chuck them round like that."

A strained smile stretched her face. She continued to work at a slightly less demented pace. Peter eyed her, whilst he placed a sheet of paper on each seat. He thought she was rather quiet and distracted, a bit out of sorts. Not that Fiona was garrulous, but she was usually good company and ready to chat.

Visitors began to arrive, greeted by Marjorie Whitlock and directed to refreshment tables. When Imam Shirani came through the door, with Faisal Hussain at his shoulder, he had some difficulty detaching himself from Marjorie. With great enthusiasm she accosted him.

"I've always been fascinated by the music you use in your religion. If it's not too much of a nuisance, perhaps you could find a little time to disperse the clouds of my ignorance on the subject?"

The Imam was startled and delighted by this generous introduction to the proceedings.

"It would be a pleasure and an honour to discuss such matters with you...?"

"Marjorie Whitlock."

"Marjorie. A little later then. Excuse me, I must convey my respects to Peter."

Marjorie beamed and carried on with her duties, only to find Derek Fisher at her elbow.

"Getting to know the opposition then, Marjorie?"

She knew he was joking, but she took exception to his terminology.

"Dear me, Derek, hardly in the spirit of the occasion to refer to the Imam in that manner."

"Sorry Marj', only my little jest. What did you make of him?"

"A charming man. We're going to chew the fat about music, if we can find the time."

"Good for you, Marj', good for you. That's the spirit."

He made a bee-line for Jane Standish who was picking up a tea urn in her pregnant state.

"Jane, a lady in your delicate condition shouldn't be heaving that about."

Before he could help an attentive young Indian man leapt to his feet, and relieved her of the receptacle. Together, they plonked it on the table.

Derek was mildly peeved, but managed a smile and a thank you, before accosting Jane further.

"Need help with anything else?"

"A few trays of food to distribute, Derek, if you wouldn't mind?"

"Not at all, not at all. My, my, it is true what they say."

Jane knew what the old goat was like, and over his shoulder she saw Peter smirking in amusement at Derek's panting pursuit of his delicious wife.

"What do they say, Derek?"

"That a woman is never so beautiful as when she's carrying a child."

Jane decided upon a little fun.

"Is that what they say, Derek? I suppose that means when this little mite comes along I'll revert to being plain Jane."

Derek's flushed features revealed both his lust and his taste for scotch.

"You'll never be that, my dear."

His slightly inebriated state got the better of him, and he drew close to Jane.

"If you ever think of getting rid of that husband of yours I'm ready to volunteer for duty!"

"Why thank you Derek, I'll always need a hand with the garden and the ironing. I'll bear you in mind as a candidate for odd-job man."

Before Derek could set his befuddled mind in order she said,

"Come on then Derek, best foot forward."

They exited the small kitchen bearing sandwiches and nibbles.

Lady Marlborough arrived late, interrupting the opening of Peter's address and dispensing *noblesse oblige* as she made her royal progress to the front row. Parking herself in the only available seat, beside a serene young man dressed in Buddhist robes, she beamed her consent for Peter to continue.

"It is so very good of you all to find the time, and the courage, to come here today. We at St. George's thank you; we are truly blessed by your presence. Brothers and sisters, we are one in our common humanity. I will not speak of religion today. Gatherings of ministers are too prone to endless and esoteric talk about the nuances of their faith. No, I do not wish us to imitate the fabled *'Oomigooly'* bird who flew around in circles, and disappeared eventually into a dark and personal orifice."

A dry chuckling filled the air. Debs thought it rather near the knuckle.

"We are keenly aware of the discord that fragments our country. Recent sad events nearby have only served to confirm what we already know about the cavernous divisions in our society."

Peter paused to allow the gravity of the recent disturbances to weigh upon the gathering.

"If not an afternoon of theology, then what? Practical matters. What can we do together to put peoples of different faiths, views and cultures alongside each other?"

"No man is an island, entire of itself,
Every man is a piece of the continent,
A part of the main.
If a clod be washed away by the sea,
Europe is the less.
As well as if a promontory were…"

He glanced at Deborah Marlborough,

"As well as if a manor of thy friend's
Or of thine own were:
Any man's death diminishes me,
Because I am involved in mankind,
And therefore never send to know for whom the bell tolls;
It tolls for thee.

Heads nodded in agreement with the wisdom of poet John Donne.

"Brothers and sisters, let's discuss together the opportunities available to us for joint activities which promote fellowship, goodwill and understanding between peoples of all faiths, and even those of little or no faith. I'd like to start the ball rolling. On the last day of August, we will have what is known traditionally as, *'The Rector's Garden Party'*. Normally, this is held in the grounds of my home, but I'm delighted to say that this year Sir Hugh and Lady Marlborough have kindly agreed to open the grounds of Marlborough House to the event. It is my pleasure to invite you all to participate, and to contribute your own specialities to the day. Let's have a short break to refill our cups. Afterwards we can discuss the practicalities, and widen the discussion to include everyone's ideas for future cooperation."

Tremendous applause followed hard on Peter's heels, and a buzz of excitement made the air tremble. Some of the locals congratulated Deborah Marlborough on her generosity and foresight in hosting this year's unique event. Debs accepted the plaudits with grace, but inside she seethed. She'd had no idea that this damned Rector was going to make her home available to all and sundry. God knows how she was going to break it to Hugh; he would be apoplectic.

When discussions resumed they were quite short. The Hindus would formulate a get-together to celebrate Diwali, the Festival of Lights. Imam Shirani would make sure that others could be included, at some stage, in the celebration of Eid. The Islamic Festival of the Sacrifice honours Ibrahim (Abraham), for his willingness to sacrifice his son, as an act of submission to God's command. All agreed that each occasion would be an opportunity to come to know the *'other'* better; to have fun and to help the poor and needy. Naturally, a committee was formed. So it was that a joyous and profitable afternoon came to an end.

Lady Marlborough did not help clear away, and Derek Fisher was lured home by the siren call of the bottle. Whilst Jane and Fiona attended to the kitchen, Peter, Jack Preston and Marjorie stacked tables and chairs.

"So good of the Marlboroughs to agree to your proposal, Peter."

"Well, actually, Marjorie, they only agreed to be our hosts. I'm afraid it may have come as a shock to Deborah to learn that I was opening the event to wider participation."

Jack laughed until he cried. Marjorie choked on her chuckles.

"I say Peter," she said, "you are a naughty boy."

Jack spluttered through his weeping, "Priceless…priceless. Sir Hugh will need mouth-to-mouth resuscitation."

Marjorie raised her hand to her mouth, "They won't go back on their word will they?"

Jack posited the view that they wouldn't want to be seen to renege, now that it had gone public. Their ruminations were interrupted by the sound of crying from the kitchen.

"That's not Jane is it, Peter?"

"No, I don't think so. Look, thank you both for your help. You potter along now. I'll sweep the floor."

Organist and lay preacher took to their heels, chattering thirteen to the dozen and giggling in complicity.

Peter entered the kitchen with a mixture of curiosity and trepidation. Fiona stood by the sink breaking her heart with Jane's arm around her. He knew better than to launch straight in with a what and a why, and waited for her sobs to subside.

"So sorry, so sorry. I'm being pathetic."

"No you're not."

Jane passed her a clean handkerchief from a pocket in her maternity dress.

"I'd better go, need to prepare dinner. Desmond works so hard, he's such a good husband…"

She burst into floods of tears again.

"Is this just between us Fi, or do you want to tell Peter?"

She blew her nose, and stuttered.

"I'd like Peter to know, but he won't *like* me after I've finished."

Peter straddled a chair, resting his arms on its back.

"Whatever it is, Fiona, it's not for me to judge you."

"Thing is...thing is; I've committed adultery...just the once."

"Not an affair then?"

"No, just a chance encounter, a spur of the moment thing. I feel so ashamed, so guilty. It's awful, I'll never forgive myself."

Crystal tears wended their way down her cheeks.

"Fiona, you know who you can take those feelings to. We do it, every week, during Sunday service. It doesn't need an ordained minister to see that you're truly sorry. Would you like to pray?"

A beautiful quiet fell upon them in the shiny kitchen. After a while Fiona voiced her pain.

"Abba Father, I have done a terrible wrong before you, and to my husband. Grant me your forgiveness in Jesus' name."

Jane took one hand, and Peter the other, and he said,

"You are forgiven Fi, be assured you are forgiven, but there is someone else who *you* need to forgive."

Fiona looked confused.

"Human memory is a fact, and it's a great foolishness to tell another person to forget something that has hurt them. We have it in us to forgive though, to forgive others...and to forgive ourselves. Forgive yourself Fiona. Your Father in Heaven has forgiven you, forgive yourself."

"I'll try; God knows I'll try. Oh my, look at the time. I really must go. Thank you, thank you both."

She embraced Jane and squeezed Peter's hand, then strode out of the building.

Jane took Peter's hand and pulled him to her. They melded into one.

"Come on, Pete, it's a gorgeous evening out there. Let's open a bottle of wine and sit in the garden."

Fifteen minutes later they were reclining on loungers with a glass to hand.

"You were lovely with Fiona, Pete."

"Poor woman. She gave the impression that she thought I'd stone her. We don't do that anymore, thank God."

A light aircraft passed overhead, and its engine droned like one of the multiple garden insects surrounding them.

"Fiona eh, who would have thought."

"Pete! She's a really attractive woman."

"No, no, you misunderstand me. I mean…she's so solid and dependable in all she does. I can't visualise her going off the straight and narrow."

"You spent too much time in the Army with men; you need to get out more."

"You are so right."

He lay back, and inhaled the scents of the garden.

"I like it here. Didn't think I would, but now I'm convinced that God has led us here. There's plenty of His work to be done."

Suddenly, he changed tack.

"Fiona though, Fiona. I wonder who it was?"

Jane went very quiet, considering carefully what she was going to say, or rather if she was going to say anything.

"Thing is Pete...thing is..."

"Go on, spit it out."

"Well, Fi didn't actually say I wasn't to tell."

"Jane, see this thing around my neck? Discretion, confidentiality!"

Jane sat sideways on her lounger facing him.

"It was Julian Marlborough."

Pete stared at her.

"One more thing, darling. He sodomised her!"

14

"I do not set my life at a pin's fee; And for my soul, what can it do to that, Being a thing immortal as itself?"
Hamlet Act 1: Sc. 4

The solar phase of a summer's day sank into darkness, and the baleful lunar cycle was in the ascendant. Qadir and his companions observed the rules of the road scrupulously. The weapons they carried were collected from a lock-up in the back streets of High Wycombe. Qadir was equipped with a Heckler and Koch MP7 submachine gun, whilst his lieutenant, Jamal, carried an Uzi, Bakir and Dawood had the privilege of bearing sawn-off shotguns. The H & K and the Uzi were serious pieces of equipment. It had taken Qadir more than one trip into London to source them and then negotiate their purchase. The shotguns were much easier to acquire. Jamal had a spare time job, burglary. He came across them by chance when he turned over a country property in Hertfordshire; shortening the barrels later.

The Land Rover Discovery was two years old, and Qadir's pride and joy. He was a young man who led an ascetic lifestyle. The money he earned was not dribbled away on fripperies. His one weakness was his shiny motor, discreet and unnoticeable amongst the multitude of four-wheel drives clogging the roads and lanes of Buckinghamshire.

Little was said as they drove, and before long Jamal and Bakir were asleep. Dawood drove, whilst Qadir remained keenly alert beside him. They took the A404 link between Wycombe and the M4. Travelling westward, they soon left the motorway at junction 11, and glided onto the A33, heading for Basingstoke to join the M3. Before long they passed Wellington Country Park. By the light of the crescent moon they glimpsed the towering commemorative column of the Iron Duke, standing at the entrance to Stratfield Saye.

It was four-thirty in the morning. If by chance the police pulled them over they would point to the camping equipment stowed in the back, for their holiday on the Isle of Wight. Dawood could even show them tickets for the ferry crossing from Lymington. To reach that pretty coastal town you follow the M3 until it joins the M27, but after only a few miles on the M3 they exited onto the A303 and headed for their true destination, Salisbury. Once past Andover the countryside got deeper and deeper, revealed in the swoops and rises of the winding dual carriageway.

Dawood was, to all intents and purposes, a gentle young man, but he was on fire for his religion. He knew his history, and when he saw the signs for Stonehenge he spat contemptuously.

"That's where those Pagan fools cavort and bawl their devilish incantations. We'll put a stop to that."

Silence resumed. The great spread of Salisbury Plain was barely visible in the darkness that settled, as the moon passed behind light clouds. Near Amesbury Dawood turned onto the Salisbury Road, the A345. Both driver and front seat passenger were well-educated young men who took an interest in the world, but they remained unconscious of the significance of signs for Old Sarum. The site is the remains of the earliest settlement of Salisbury, a little to the north of the modern city. When the Normans invaded England they had gone in for some heavy duty construction there, including a motte and bailey castle and a great cathedral. A royal palace had been built within the castle for King Henry I. All this passed the travellers by, and they had no knowledge of its history. Like all the grandiose plans of ambitious men, the buildings had come to ruin and dust.

Percy Bysshe Shelley had summed it up:

"My name is Ozymandias, king of kings: Look on my works, ye Mighty and despair!"

The broken remains of the *'king of kings'* giant statue was swallowed by the sands of the desert.

Some of the stone from Old Sarum had been transported to the *'new'* city. It contributed to the construction of the magnificent thirteenth century cathedral. A mighty monument that startled you with its sudden appearance from whichever route you entered the city.

Hugh Marlborough had looked down Pall Mall, and in his evil intent Julian had gazed upon the street of Old Wenbury. They imbibed the air of times long gone. When the great spire of Salisbury Cathedral thrust itself upon you, like the apparition of an alien craft piercing the sky, you felt something much more powerful. It revealed the elemental spirit of an England that stretched back long before its construction. You felt the force of a land forged anew, relentlessly, across centuries. The bedrock of certainty about its destiny never shaken. Its existence -

past, present and future – was gripped by hands burnished in a furnace of immoveable self-will; the reins held by that small cohort who were sometimes seen as effete. Beneath their vestments of cultured and cultivated manners lay sinews of steel.

They parked the Land Rover on Milford Hill, a steep incline leading to the Godolphin Girls' School, a Christian foundation dating back to the eighteenth century. Each member of the party retrieved a rucksack containing their weapon from inside the loosely rolled sleeping bags. They walked down the hill, crossing under the raised A36, christened Churchill Way. Casually, they strolled down St. Ann Street, as streaks of dawn lit the buildings around them.

Bakir spotted it when he glanced to the left.

"Look!"

None of them actually smoked, but Jamal extracted a packet of ciggies from inside his leather jacket and they lit up. It gave them cover to examine what Bakir had pointed out. A white van, with ladders strapped to its roof, parked clumsily within a smallish area called Green's Court.

"That will do," Qadir whispered, "Jamal."

To an old hand like Jamal it took no more than two minutes before he had crossed the road, opened the driver's door and started the engine. He reversed onto St. Ann's, and they piled in. For all the world they looked like a team of builders making an early start.

Qadir had his mobile phone out, and activated an entry for the remote property. As they left the city, and headed for Wilton, he cautioned Jamal.

"Nice and easy, brother, just keep following the A30. We come off at a place called Ansty, and then it's country lanes."

The ever-brightening sky promised a beautiful day. It was little more than half an hour before they took the turn for Ansty, passing the pretty church of St. James and slowly negotiating the twisting lanes. An opportunity afforded itself to pull onto a deserted track. There they dressed in white jumpsuits from their rucksacks. Once back in the vehicle they lay weapons and balaclavas beside them. A sign for Tisbury hove into view, but not long after it they diverted into a lane and climbed the hillside.

The stone columns were devoid of gates, and they sailed through the opening and up the long drive. Chapel House was breath-taking, set back before extensively manicured lawns. It wasn't a castle, but Qadir understood why Mo' had thought it so. The van entered a wide and expansive area of tarmac, and Jamal swept it round with a flourish to face back down the drive, the tyres giving off a distinct squeal.

The noise had been brief, but the old man kneeling before the altar looked up, and heard the vehicle grind to a halt. The Earl of Seaforth was an early riser. Following custom, he began each day with meditative prayer in the stunning chapel that adhered to the East wing of the main house. It had been there for nearly three hundred years, and was a symbol of the Old Religion; the surrounding valley remained Roman Catholic to the present day.

With measured tread, which was all his eighty-seven-year-old legs would permit, he made his way to the fine external doors. Framed in them, he raised a hand to shield his eyes from the shimmering early sun. He made out four figures loafing around a white van. One of them looked in his direction and pointed an outstretched finger. The others turned, and walked towards him. Seaforth's eyes weren't good at the best of times, but as they drew closer he saw the white overalls, and what looked like tools in their hands. His estate manager, Tom Greenough, had said something about work starting on the roof, but hadn't that been scheduled for Monday? They were a bit keen for this time on a Saturday morning.

A fluffy cloud, one of the few in the sky, obscured the sun, by which time they were two metres from him and he realised his mistake. He was about to roar, "What the hell do you want?" when Bakir and Dawood were upon him. The words were stifled at birth. Seaforth was propelled backwards into the chapel, and Qadir closed the doors behind them.

They held the old man with his back against the altar. Qadir strolled down the aisle admiring the marble and ornamentation; he was not without a sensibility for fine art and craftsmanship.

"Good morning, sir."

He greeted the Earl with the courtesy that an elder might rightfully expect from a younger man.

"May I enquire as to your name, sir?"

Edmund Seaforth had no fear. He saw their weapons, and looked Qadir straight in the eyes that glistened through the slit of his balaclava. The colour of their skin on exposed hands, gave him a shrewd suspicion about what was going on.

"I am Edmund Seaforth, and this is private property. You profane the House of God by entering it bearing those arms."

He risked a gambit.

"I would not offend the house of your god by intruding into it in such a way."

Jamal was working up his anger, and he thrust himself forward to answer the old man, but Qadir raised a hand.

"Sir, I apologise for this intrusion, but rest assured we shall soon be gone. We wish you no personal harm. You will please tell us how many others are in the big house, and direct us to their bedrooms."

Eddie Seaforth was nonplussed.

"Hardly a soul in there, we can't afford many staff these days. Anyway, what would you want with them?"

Qadir was sweetness and light.

"Ah, I see that you misapprehend me, it is not the servants we require. How many of the military men are present?"

Eddie frowned, and then it dawned on him causing him to shake gently. It got louder and louder until he was rocking back and forth in his captives' arms in noisy laughter.

Qadir was not amused.

"What's so funny, old man? We know they're assembled for a meeting."

His deference to age was dissipating.

Seaforth steadied himself. In a typically no-nonsense patrician fashion he exclaimed,

"What a cock-up! Me boy rang Thursday to cancel."

He could have bitten his tongue off; he shouldn't have mentioned Freddie. Laughing uproariously again, he tried to cover up.

"What a splendid cock-up!"

The startled leader of the terrorists walked a few steps down the aisle.

Jamal broke the stalemate.

"What are we going to do Qadir?"

The others looked at each other in consternation at Jamal's stupidity in using their leader's name.

Seaforth spoke softly,

"Let me go lads, please, I'm not running anywhere at my age."

Qadir assented.

The game old boy rubbed his chin.

"Qadir eh, fine name."

"What would you know, old man?" Jamal spat.

"Capable, powerful, that's what it means, don't it? One of the ninety-nine names of Allah."

Qadir eyed him curiously.

"You know a lot, sir."

"Be surprised what you pick up in military intelligence. Long time ago, mind you. Nice bit of kit son. Heckler and Koch MP7 isn't it? Make a hell of noise in here. Knock the old place about a bit as well. Be a shame to do that after three centuries."

Aged the Earl of Seaforth may have been, but he retained the wit to try and defuse the unfolding events. He could see a glimmer of doubt in Qadir's eyes, and he was attempting to enlarge his uncertainty now that the day had not panned out as expected.

Qadir came to a decision, "I am sorry sir..."

"No need to apologise, one of those things..."

"No sir, I am sorry for you. We had not intended to harm you, but we cannot leave you behind as a witness to our presence."

A chill went through the Earl, but he held himself together.

"I see. What's it to be, summary execution?"

Qadir hesitated, and his thoughts were interrupted by Bakir.

"Look!"

Pointing towards a small chapel they saw a pair of military colours hanging from horizontal flag staffs. They were not the object of Bakir's attention. He had spotted the gleaming sabre displayed against the wall.

Seaforth's eyes followed theirs, and he breathed a barely audible, "Ahh." Drawing himself upright, he assumed the military bearing of his youth.

"No time like the present. Come on man, you call yourself a soldier. Do your duty."

Dawood strode over to the wall and grasped the sabre.

"Careful young man, we keep it sharp. Don't cut yourself."

The Earl of Seaforth had enjoyed a life of privilege and a life of service, and he was ready to meet his Maker. He was goading them to get on with the job.

Qadir spoke, "Are you sure Dawood? Do you want me to do it?"

Seaforth interjected quietly, "Dawood – form of David. A great king in our Bible, and a prophet's name."

They looked at the kneeling figure, his arms held wide by Jamal and Bakir. Incredulity made them freeze at his calm demeanour, and the sheer look of joy illuminating his face.

Qadir took out his mobile phone, and switched it to video. He intoned into it the usual self-exculpatory tripe that murderers of all races and religions indulge in to justify their tyranny.

Eddie Seaforth picked up where Qadir left off, with the words his Saviour taught him. He never reached *"…as we forgive them that trespass against us…"*

The blade was indeed razor sharp.

The other three left before Qadir. He reversed down the aisle with his mobile filming the scene. The final shot was a close-up of the late Earl of Seaforth's head resting on the centre of the altar.

*

Andrew Freddie Forbes wept for his father, but only his wife saw his tears. They were a lament for his old pa', that his life should end in this way. Seaforth had been a good father; a man who had given his best in all that he undertook. Contained within those tears was a terrible rage.

"Darling, would you leave me now, please. There are matters I need to attend to..."

"Couldn't I help, darling?"

"No, no thank you, one or two official things, you know."

"Of course. I'll fetch you some coffee, shall I?"

"That would be lovely, darling. Do give a rap on the door before entering, would you? Sorry to ask."

Daisy smiled lovingly, and closed the door behind her.

The new Earl of Seaforth brought the tips of his fingers together as he sat behind his desk. He thanked the Lord that they had cancelled their weekend meeting. God knows what would have happened if most of the United Kingdom's top brass had been beheaded in a remote country location. More to the point, it wouldn't have needed a genius to ask why they were all gathered there. They had extensive support undercover in '5', but not enough to prevent snooping that would assuredly have discovered the unpalatable truth. Done and dusted, he thought.

He returned to the present, assembling the known facts. The Chief Constable of Wiltshire informed him that the police were crawling all over Chapel House. He hoped Jenkins, his father's butler, had recovered from the shock of finding his late master decapitated.

"My butler now," he said aloud.

The P.M.'s office had been in touch to express O'Donnell's condolences. Didn't change Freddie's overall opinion of him, but he appreciated the courtesy. The Cabinet Secretary assured him that the Counter Terrorism Unit was on the case, as it had the fingerprints of Isis all over it. Freddie shook his head. The Cab. Sec. should be transferred to the *'Ministry of the Bleeding Obvious'*.

Qadir Khan was not the only one fond of making connections, and the Shadow Defence Secretary's mind positively twitched and whirred. His fingers drummed on the desk. Something wider was going on out there; something nobody had a handle on yet. Sporadic outbursts of inter-racial violence were nothing new, he knew that from his access to the escalating figures on race hate crime. Recently they had stepped across the threshold into a world that made cage fighting resemble a day at the races.

Facts began to marshal themselves like coloured counters falling into place. The riots in Buckinghamshire, Luton, Bradford and elsewhere, all as a result of that Pakistani boy being mutilated in...and he sat bolt upright, in Wenbury, Hugh Marlborough's constituency. Wasn't there something else about that place, something that preceded the carving up of the Asian boy? His Son,

Jasper, had displayed Julian's provocative graffiti to him on his Ipad.

Freddie Forbes had a brilliant mind, honed at Westminster School and Balliol Oxford, aided by a near photographic memory. He closed his eyes, sat motionless, and slowed his breathing. This was his technique when he wanted to recapture something that was close, but not quite within his grasp. A beatific smile spread across his face. Yes, that was it, Jasper hadn't needed to bring this one to his attention, he'd read it in the Telegraph. An old soldier in Wenbury, he too had been mutilated. Where had they found him? Of course, and his eyes blinked open in astonishment, that little village just outside Wenbury. He knew it well, because he'd spent more than one weekend there over the years, a guest of the Marlboroughs. Albert Einstein's words surfaced in his brain:

"Coincidence is God's way of remaining anonymous."

Freddie wasn't certain he subscribed to that, but it made him reflect that there were just too many damned coincidences. Rather more than he cared for seemed to be connected with Hugh Marlborough. Decisively, he picked up the telephone and jabbed out a number.

"Lester, it's Freddie here. Need you to act on something. Yes, yes, thank you, a terrible shock, much appreciated. Lester, I want you to place *'Castle'* on standby. Think we might have to move him out of Town... What? Oh, he could pull the same trick as that arse who got himself turfed out of the hotel...No, no, we won't be short-handed, there's still someone else inside...yes, yes, newly-recruited. We haven't managed to get you up to speed on it yet. Got to attend to family matters this week, but we could catch up in the House next Monday morning; make it early...Right, yes, put *'Castle'* on standby, and I'll confirm with you when we meet. Indeed, dreadful business. Thanks again, Lester."

A light rapping on the door alerted him, and he replaced the receiver.

"Come in."

Daisy Forbes swam gracefully across the room bearing a silver tray, and placed it on his desk.

"Shall I pour?"

He smiled, and thought how fortunate he was to have such a beautiful and considerate wife. She handed him his coffee, and as he sipped she looked at him with pity in her heart.

"Darling, Jasper is outside, he'd like to see you."

"Bit busy now 'D', ask him to pop back in an hour, would you?"

She hesitated, with a look of deep trouble on her face. He put his cup down, rose and went round the table to embrace her.

"There, there, darling, I know. It's been the most awful shock."

"It's not that, I really think that you should see Jasper...he has something to show you."

Freddie released her.

"Okay my love, wheel him in."

"Jasper, Daddy will see you now."

A sturdy young man of seventeen entered the study.

"Pa', so sorry about Grampy. I..."

Freddie smiled and cut him short.

"That's okay son, we'll get it sorted. Now, what do you have to show me?"

Mother and son exchanged glances, mingled with fear and sorrow.

"Jasper has found something on the internet."

"On social media Pa'," and he gulped.

"Come along then, let's see it."

The boy looked beseechingly to his mother for help.

"Darling, they've posted it online."

Freddie knew instantly what she meant. He snapped at his son.

"Show me!"

The boy passed his Ipad to his father, who viewed the death of his father, whilst Qadir Khan's voice echoed tinnily around the large study.

When the obscene video was concluded he walked to the window, and gazed empty-eyed onto the street below. Clever, the bastards had been clever. By all accounts, they should never have been permitted to broadcast it, but Qadir had been astute. At the commencement, he had avoided filming anyone present in the Chapel. Focusing on the internal architecture and ornamentation, he extolled the beauties of the place, as if he were a tourist recording the sights. The swiftness and brevity with which he had turned his diatribe to an exposition of their cause, and shown the beheading of the old man, had caught out anyone monitoring the site. Naturally, they had removed it now, but the horse had bolted, and like Tony the Builder's post of the racial acrostic it had gone viral.

The Ipad skimmed through the air. It hit the far wall, and the screen shattered. Freddie Forbes lifted his head off his chin.

"Sorry, sorry my boy, get yourself a new one, put it on my account."

"That's alright Pa'."

He regained his composure.

"Would you leave me now, please, rather a lot to deal with. Thank you Jasper, you did right to show me that…" and he was lost for words.

Daisy took Jasper by the arm, and fed him out of the room.

"Drink your coffee, darling, before it gets cold."

She closed the door behind her.

He took a substantial glug from his cup, and slowly refilled it from the silver jug.

Carrying cup and saucer to the window, he asked himself,

"Dear God, where are we going with all this?"

Then his strength of will exerted itself, no turning back. He smiled as he recollected words that would have gladdened old Johnny Parkinson's heart in Banksmore, *"You turn, the Lady's not for turning."* He found the number on his mobile. It rang briefly before going to answerphone,

"Hugh, it's Freddie. Need to see you. My office, next Monday, 07:30 sharp!"

Picking up his cup and saucer, he meandered over to his extensive bookshelves, and let his eyes wander over the spines. One in particular caught his attention, and he took it in hand. E. M. Forster's *'A Passage to India'*, an old favourite. Not a book that reflected the antics of the British Empire especially well, but that didn't deter Freddie. He thought it apposite that it should come to mind now with its exploration of the racial tensions and prejudices that beset India under the Raj.

Strange as it may seem, he did not hanker after the days of Empire. He was appreciative of the benefits

Britain had derived from their once Superpower status. He was also aware of the combustible material that is created when conflicting cultures mix, especially when one will not yield to the inalienable rights of the host. That was why they were set on this unstoppable course.

He looked at the author's name, emblazoned in gold lettering, and remembered his sixth form English tutor. *"Only connect,"* he had declared, that's what Forster had said, *"Only connect."* Qadir Khan, as yet unknown to Andrew Freddie Forbes but inextricably connected, had learnt this lesson through a childhood game. Freddie had acquired the wisdom behind his desk at public school. The links were emerging and shifting ever closer to one another. He anticipated his meeting with Lester and Hugh eagerly.

Seated at his desk he set about the task of arranging his father's funeral, and the attendant legal affairs. An hour later he paused for lunch. Striding purposefully to the study door he pulled up short. He was the Earl of Seaforth – that meant he'd either have to renounce the title, or stand down as Member of Parliament. Since the House of Lords Act 1999, passed under the premiership of the *'Smiling Viper'*, he had no chance of sitting in the Upper House. He relaxed his grip on the door handle. Given the pace at which things were moving it might transpire that he could stick with the status quo.

15

*"O, what men dare do! What men may do! What men
daily do, not knowing what they do!"*
Much Ado About Nothing Act 4: Sc. 1

Qadir Khan was not stupid. When he and his party
left Chapel House they journeyed sedately to the
outskirts of Wilton, parking the stolen vehicle in a side
lane on the edge of town. From thence they took public
transport into Salisbury, recovered the Land Rover from
Milford Hill, and headed down the A36 to join the M27 at
junction 2. After a short hop, they exited and ground
their way, with the eternally heavy holiday traffic,
through Lyndhurst and Brockenhurst. Finally, they
arrived at Lymington Ferry Terminal.

The Isle of Wight lies between the Solent and the
English Channel, close to Southampton and Portsmouth.
Throughout England's history it's been near the front-line
of many a conflict, from the Spanish Armada to the Battle
of Britain in 1940. Queen Victoria spent childhood
holidays on the Island, and when she became monarch
she made Osborne House her winter home. She died
there on January 22nd 1901. The old girl's love of the
place kick-started the tourist industry. Tourism boomed,
even Charles Dickens paid a visit. The newly-formed
terrorist cell would spend a few days there, mingling with
the thousands enjoying their fortnight's respite from
work. Qadir was laying a trail that screamed innocence.

Once off the ferry, they drove to a camp site near the popular seaside resort of Sandown. For the rest of the weekend they did what tourists do; visited the nearby Zoo, and the geological museum called Dinosaur Isle, and lay on the beach.

By Sunday evening Dawood was worried. He broached his concern to Qadir as they strolled along the seafront. Jamal and Bakir were holed up in a bar, and as far as the two walkers were concerned they showed too much interest in alcohol and girls.

"Jamal doesn't change, does he?"

Qadir walked on without comment, compelling Dawood to speak further.

"I do not approve of his drinking and womanising, Qadir."

They halted and leant on railings, looking outwards. The serene August waters hold all sorts of mischief for the unwary weekend sailor.

"I do not approve of his mouth, Dawood. He can't keep it shut."

Qadir thought wryly of his cousin Mo' who suffered from the same affliction.

The cries of seagulls and the delighted screeches of small children filled the air.

"Tomorrow morning, Jamal and I will go for a run. When I return his verbal diarrhoea will be cured, one way or the other."

He strolled calmly onwards with Dawood in tow.

Jamal was less than pleased at having to rise at four on Monday morning. Qadir disarmed him with jokes about hard-drinking soldiers who needed to keep in trim. He whispered that they were going to dispose of their weapons in the sea, and he didn't want Bakir and

Dawood to know, just yet. Then he whetted Jamal's appetite with the prospect of shopping in London for some serious new hardware. Jamal positively leapt into his trainers.

They drove across the island, through Freshwater and Totland, to the end of the B3322. There was little traffic, so early in the day. Once parked, they jogged along the strip of land that narrows to an arrow head as it reaches the sea.

Not a living soul could be seen. When they reached the clifftop edge they removed the rucksacks from their backs.

"Here Jamal, do the honours with mine, while I fix this shoelace."

Qadir went down on one knee.

Jamal moved to the edge, a bag in each hand. He looked down, imbibing the beauty of the scene, the glorious scents were intoxicating. Swinging his left arm, he released his grip and watched the heavy rucksack prescribe a gentle and loving arc through the air. It plummeted into the depths of the sea. He looked over his shoulder with a laugh.

"Let's see how far I can launch this one."

Qadir gave an easy smile, stood up and ambled over, standing just behind his left shoulder.

"On the count of three," he said, and together they counted.

Jamal swung once, then twice. Three barely escaped his lips, as he and the bag sailed through the air together. Qadir did not break stride after sending Jamal into oblivion.

When he returned to the campsite, Bakir looked chastened and fearful. It was clear that Dawood had spoken with him. They struck camp efficiently, and drove to Ryde. Qadir was fond of his motor, but he was neither sentimental nor foolish. Whilst the other two ate breakfast, he found a dealer and sold it for cash.

The return journey to Wenbury was uneventful; ferry from Ryde to Portsmouth Harbour, South-West trains into London Waterloo, then Jubilee and Met Lines home.

He popped in to see his Uncle Raza, and asked if he might borrow a car from the yard for a couple of hours.

"What the hell is wrong with yours?"

"Sold it, uncle."

"Boy, I thought you and that motor were going to get married."

"Fancied a change. That's why I need to borrow one of yours. Going to go and browse around in Watford."

Raza was outraged.

"Why you not buy one from me?"

"Could I get the RAC to check out the mileage?"

Raza oscillated with amusement, and tossed a set of keys through the air.

"Cheeky young bugger, here, take the Toyota, and make sure it comes back with a full tank. Away, away, some of us have work to do."

Qadir headed for the door, but was stopped by Raza's shout.

"Hey, how was the holiday? You and the boys have a good time?"

"Fantastic, we did everything we set out to do."

"When is that idle bastard Jamal coming back to work?"

Affecting the look of one who has just been reminded of something, Qadir spoke airily.

"Oh, Jamal is no more. We left him on the Island. Said he'd never seen anything like it, and he was staying. Last I saw of him he was trawling up and down the seafront trying to find a holiday job. You know what he's like, a bit crazy. I think he fell head over heels for the place."

Subduing the temptation to laugh at his own gallows humour Qadir departed, headed for High Wycombe. Lovingly, he stashed his H & K MP47 in the lockup; that was one piece of kit that didn't take a bath.

He had no intention of buying a new car in Watford, and drove up the M40 to Leamington Spa, where he met with a member of his extended family who was in the motor trade. A discussion was in progress on Radio Four about community relationships. Inevitably, the recent death of the Earl of Seaforth was included in the conversation.

"Odd?" Qadir thought, as he passed the junction for Bicester. Given the nationwide coverage of his crime in the depths of Wiltshire why hadn't Raza mentioned it, even in passing? He must be the only Moslem in Britain not talking about the implications of the murder for their communities. He shrugged, and concluded that Raza was too busy thinking about where the next buck was coming from.

In his office, Raza was sipping coffee and working his way through a plate of those sweet confections named *Halwa*. He opened Google Earth on his Ipad, and entered *'Isle of Wight'* into the search engine. Whilst he waited for the screen to zoom in to the location, from the great ball of the Earth, he too was thinking. A worried frown creased his brow. Raza devoured the papers since the death of the Earl of Seaforth, and watched the television news avidly to see if the perpetrators had been identified or apprehended. Usman had shown him the beheading online, and they had looked at each other in fear and dread. The Earl's severed head did not make them queasy, but the familiar voice of Qadir did.

He magnified the image, and was able to hold the names of the two places in shot – Isle of Wight, and, to the West, Tisbury. His gorge rose within him at their close proximity to one another, and he dropped the sweet pastry from his fleshy hand. Qadir's face appeared in front of him. He recollected the glint of excitement in the boy's eye when he had exclaimed *"Tisbury"* over dinner. Raza's stomach churned wildly, and he cursed himself for having given that idiot Mo' the job of driving Sir Hugh.

Westerners rarely understand the concept of honour. To a man like Raza it is sacred. Qadir's mother and father had suffered an horrific car accident when he was a baby. His mother had been killed instantly. Raza sat by his dying brother's bedside for forty-eight hours, powerless to change the will of Allah. It was in the days following Zaheer's demise that he lost his faith. Zaheer drifted in and out of consciousness, and only once was he coherent. It was then that he extracted from Raza the promise to care for his first-born all the days of his life.

Raza sat behind his desk, transfixed by confusion. He was caught between the Scylla of his business ambitions and the Charybdis of his oath to his dead brother.

*

Men and women need respite from the feverish activity of their daily lives. Whilst the Earl of Seaforth's butchers enjoyed the approaching scenic beauty of the

Isle of Wight from a ferry railing, Julian Marlborough prepared himself for a holiday treat.

He was gratified that not a sniff of his encounter with Mo' had found its way to Banksmore. Sitting on the train into London, he anticipated with pleasure an hour's hot and sticky with Charlotte in West Hampstead. The afternoon and evening would be spent on the Town with Billy Conway. Old comrades in arms would keep in touch, whenever Julian was having an away day. Chalk and cheese they were but Julian enjoyed his company.

Charlotte greeted him well enough, but he thought her a trifle subdued. When she removed her clothes he saw why. She was covered with heavy duty bruises.

"What the hell happened to you?"

She did not cry, but trembled and went very pale. He sat beside her, on the bed, and clasped her to him. Odd sensations passed through him. He couldn't quite fathom what it was about this woman that stirred him to feelings of protection.

"Go on."

Charlotte didn't look at him as she spoke.

"I've always worked independently, no go-betweens...no pimp."

"And?"

"Wednesday evening last. I looked through the spyhole when he arrived. One, I could only see one, so I let him in."

She paused, and breathed deeply.

"There were four of them. No messing about, they just raped me..."

"Jesus!"

"...and then the old man appeared in the doorway."

"What old man?"

"He runs the grocer's shop below. He said that from now on I worked for him, and when I tried to argue they did this."

She indicated the discoloured marks on her body.

"There's nothing I can do! The Romanians have got it sewn up around here. If I don't go along with them God knows what will happen."

Julian rose and walked to the window. Peeping through the curtain he could see Billy Conway tucking into his breakfast with a will.

"Get dressed, we're going out."

Charlotte hesitated.

"I'm not sure if...they'll want more money off me if they think you've hired me for the day."

"You can give him something on account on the way out. Here, take this."

She grasped another bundle of notes.

"Wow, do you always carry so much cash?"

"Sometimes it's best not to leave a trail."

"He'll want to know where I'm going."

"There's an old friend of mine waiting for me across the road. Tell this creep that you're going with us to his flat nearby for a threesome. That should do it. Is there anything here that's important to you?"

"Just a bit of jewellery, why?"

"Because you won't be coming back."

Charlotte was wide-eyed in astonishment.

"I don't know why I'm doing this, and I aint asking you to marry me or anything dumb like that."

He adopted an embarrassed *'Mockney'* accent.

"I'm not prepared to leave you here...I can fix it."

She believed him utterly; she believed that this rich boy could fix anything. Emptying a draw of its trinkets, and slipping them into a bag she said breezily,

"Let's go!"

They put on a damn good act together, as they stepped into the street. Julian perused the fruit and veg outside the shop. Looking through the window, he saw Charlotte slipping his father's hard-earned cash into the old man's hand. They caught each other's eye, and he gave the old gangster a gormless grin and a thumbs up.

Charlotte came out of the shop.

"He wants to know the address."

"Can't you make it up? You know the area."

She went back inside, and chose the nearest street that came into her head. She gave him a random number in Fawley Road.

"He bought it."

Julian gave one more look into the interior of the shop, and once again he and the old man were face to face. Both of them were wreathed in jolly smiles, but behind Julian's façade was a promise,

"I'll be back!"

Hardened criminal he might have been, but if Cezar Marinescu had known the real Julian Marlborough he would have opted for a visit from Arnold Schwarzenneger.

"Come on Billy, pay up, we're moving."

Billy Conway heard the authority, and soon the three of them walked around the corner into Fawley Road. Halfway along, Julian called a halt.

"Billy – Charlotte, Charlotte – Billy."

"Seen you around, Billy."

"You too."

"I guess you know what I do for a living then."

Billy grinned, and Julian interrupted this little *tete a tete* to fetch him up to speed.

"Where did you tell him we were going for our *rendezvous,* Charlotte?"

"Here."

"What Fawley Road?"

Billy was alarmed.

"Which number?"

He breathed a sigh of relief, it was on the other side, and farther down from his pad.

"Think we should get our skates on Cap', put some distance between us and them."

Julian took the lead.

"Would you join us for lunch, Charlotte? We have a table booked. I'm sure they can squeeze a third in."

She was in thrall to him, and linked his arm as they strode up the hill to Finchley Road. A taxi was hailed to take them to the Café Royal on Regent Street.

If anyone should have been out of place it was Billy, but he rose to the occasion.

"Been to a few posh places Cap' since taking on the new job."

"Why Cap'?" she enquired over an aperitif.

Julian gestured, and Billy told the tale.

Over pudding Charlotte's problem became the topic of conversation. Before long Julian made a proposal. He had been thinking about it throughout their sumptuous lunch. There was much weighing of pros and cons before he reached his decision. He asked himself why he was doing this. The only conclusion he came to, and it was unsatisfactory, was that though Charlotte was a hooker her background made her 'one of us'.

"You've got money, Charlotte?"

His mother's laugh resounded through the restaurant.

"You asking me to pay for lunch? Only kidding. Lots."

"No chance of those hoodlums accessing it, is there?"

"None whatsoever."

Billy interrupted.

"You got a place to stay? Home to go to anywhere?"

"There is a place, but it's not a question of can't, more a case of don't want to. You can't go back."

They sipped their *digestifs.*

"Got a plan of action Cap'?"

Julian hesitated, he'd rather hoped that Billy could put her up for a while. That was clearly out of the question, given his address. Billy wasn't soft, and he guessed what might be going through Julian's mind. He would have been delighted to give Charlotte a bed for a few nights while she got sorted. Briefly, he considered the safe house in Brixton, but Lester would have strung him up by his balls.

"Charlotte, I can't keep calling you that, what's your real name?"

"I'll tell you mine, if you'll tell me yours, Roddy."

"Roddy!"

Conway exploded with laughter, and Julian threw him a hapless look.

"Julian. Pleased to meet you...?"

"Angela. Pleased to meet you, Julian."

"Thing is, Angela..."

"Angie will do."

"Angie, I can't take you home, and I'm not leaving you in London. Big as it is, it's too risky."

He downed his glass of Armagnac, and set it with precision in front of himself.

"I'm thirty-five minutes out of Town to the north-west. If we get a move on we should still find the estate agents open. There are one or two charming B & B's in the Old Town."

"Which Old Town?"

There was a moment's hesitation, and then he sailed on.

"Old Wenbury. Know it?"

She shook her head.

"You'll like it Angie."

He said it almost in hope.

"If you've got the money, you could put up in a B & B until you find a flat to rent. Doesn't have to be in Wenbury, there are lots of smart places nearby. The men in those parts have plenty of money."

He could have bitten his tongue off at the crass remark, and he found himself apologising to her again.

Billy reclined in his chair, sipping his Cointreau, surprised and amused at the same time.

"What do you say, Angie?"

"Now is always best time."

"What?"

"It's a line from the 'King and I'; the King says it to Mrs. Anna, *'Now is always best time.'* Do you like musicals? I love them."

Julian was all at sea.

"Yes, yes I do, but we never did that one at school. I was in *'West Side Story'.*"

"You were an actor?"

"Amateur."

He looked shy.

"Which part did you play? I'll bet you were the lead, Tony."

A memory surfaced, reminding him of the trouble that ensued when he had been passed over for the lead. Julian shook himself free of the past.

"Riff, I played Riff, leader of the Jets."

She sensed his disappointment, and held his hand.

"I'm sure you stole the show, but your director must have been a dick. You'd have been the perfect Tony."

Billy was entranced by love unfolding before his eyes, but time was getting on.

"Don't wanna interrupt you luvvies, but if you're gonna get some digs for the night shouldn't you be on your way?"

Julian signalled to a waiter, and the bill arrived.

Before he could extract his wallet, Angie flourished notes.

"Ah, ah, ah, this is my treat."

There were protestations, but she was having none of it.

"I didn't give all of my money to that creep. Anyway, I'm flush enough to stand you a meal, and I don't even have to give anything in return."

They knew what she meant. Billy merely smiled, inside Julian felt an odd churning.

Outside the Café Royal they parted. Angie was window shopping a couple of doors down.

"Thanks Billy."

"What for?"

"Being there, as usual."

"No worries Cap', that's what mates are for. You can always rely on Billy Conway."

Julian inched closer.

"I was wondering, Billy. Do you fancy a little extra-curricular activity?"

"What have you got in mind?"

"Soon, quite soon, I'd like to pay a nocturnal visit to West Hampstead. I've got a bill to settle with a Romanian greengrocer."

Billy froze inside, he couldn't afford to get involved in shit like that, so he was non-committal.

"Give me a bell Cap' when you're ready to go into action. We can discuss the details."

"Come on you two. I don't want to be walking the streets tonight."

She clasped her hand to her mouth as she realised what she'd said.

Billy laughed out loud this time, whilst that funny old feeling swept over Julian once more. She skittered over to them, and held Julian's arm as if she'd never let it go. Billy received a kiss on the cheek, and he and Julian shook hands. The happy couple sailed off in the direction of Piccadilly Circus, exuding the joy of those released from the cares of work.

Billy remained rooted to the spot, and waved back to Angie.

"Bye Angie/Charlotte," he breathed. "See you Roddy."

A hand touched his sleeve.

"Excuse me, sir, spare some change for an old soldier down on his luck?"

Billy didn't flicker. He removed the hand from his sleeve and palmed the piece of paper that was in it.

"Here you go chief, get yourself a good meal."

The down-and-out took the twenty-pound note.

"God bless you, sir, for your generosity."

Billy patted him on the shoulder.

"Mind how you go son, it's a bad world out there."

16

"Thou know'st we work by wit, and not by witchcraft;
And wit depends on dilatory time."
Othello Act 2: Sc. 3

"Tyre tracks!" Inspector McInnes exclaimed. "Forensics say they're definitely off the stolen van we found outside Wilton."

Deputy Chief Constables don't normally lurk around the precincts of Salisbury Police Station, but Kathy Bullivant was receiving this report first hand. Headless earls were not something you dealt with every day, especially one whose son and heir was a senior politician.

"What do they have to say about the van?"

McInnes brought her up to speed. Nylon fibres had been found in the rear of the vehicle.

"The owner says he has no idea how they got there. Reckons he's never put anything in the van that they could have come off. The good news is we've got a set of prints off one of the inside walls."

"Identification?"

"We're in the process of elimination. Mr. Burgess, the owner, and his labourer are downstairs being fingerprinted."

"Have they been run through the national database?"

"Thought we'd wait and see if there's a match with Burgess and his lad."

Kathy Bullivant shook her head.

"Time wasted. Get the check done right now."

"Yes ma'am. Sue, get on to it."

D.C. Sue Jeffreys departed to initiate the fingerprint enquiry.

"Now Kenny, it is Kenny isn't it?"

"Yes ma'am."

"What's our reasoning so far?"

Kenny McInnes had been grossly underestimated throughout his life, and left a trail of people behind with regrets. He was an anonymous looking man, and that was his edge. You never paid attention to the wee man, so when he nicked you it came as a complete surprise. Kenny had formidable powers of observation and reasoning. Mentally, he collated what they knew so far and ran it by Deputy Chief Constable Bullivant.

"We have the van, ma'am, stolen from Green Court sometime between 23:45 hrs Friday night and 06:30 hours Saturday morning. From the tyre match we know that this is the vehicle almost certainly used by the killers."

"How can we be sure? It might have visited Chapel House previously."

Kenny shook his head.

"Mr. Burgess assures us he's never been near the place."

"You believe him?"

"I do ma'am. He's a well-known builder in these parts; clean record and of good character."

"So, the van's been nicked; used to convey the terrorists out to Tisbury, or thereabouts. They drive back this way and dump it on the outskirts of Wilton. Why would they retrace their steps, and risk bringing the van close to its port of origin?"

Kenny sighed inwardly, it seemed so obvious, but he restrained himself from saying so out loud.

"Must have had another vehicle parked up nearby."

"Or stolen another one. Any reported missing?"

"No ma'am."

"Do you think they left their getaway in Wilton?"

Kenny bit his tongue.

"Dear God, how do they get to senior rank these days." Once more he shook his head.

"The logistics wouldn't add up ma'am. Park up in Wilton, and then nick the van in Salisbury at that time in the morning. They'd have needed transport to get back into town; unlikely."

"Buses, taxis?"

"No buses at that time, and we're checking the cab firms; negative so far."

"So they've done what they set out to do, and then they get rid of the van. Where to next?"

"For what it's worth, ma'am, my belief is that they returned to Salisbury, and picked their own vehicle up from somewhere in the City. Now, buses and taxis are possibilities for getting in from Wilton at *that* time of day. We'll have word from the last of the taxi firms shortly, the buses will take a little longer. The driver on that route has a hospital appointment, sod's law."

"Assuming they returned to the town, the questions are, where did they collect their vehicle from, and which direction did they take off in?"

"Nothing from CCTV in the car parks, ma'am…"

The door burst open, and an excited detective constable rushed in.

"We've got' em boss. Fingerprints match one Jamal Ahmed, known housebreaker and burglar. Currently resident in High Wycombe Buckinghamshire."

Wheels flew. Within thirty minutes Kenny McInnes and Sue Jeffreys were heading for the A303, and the balmy environs of High Wycombe.

The cordon of armed police surrounding Raza Khan's taxi firm was formidable. A similar team had crashed into Jamal's flat in Wycombe, and communicated that the suspect was nowhere to be seen. When their colleagues assaulted Raza's premises they found two people; Raza, who recovered his composure with admirable speed, and a quivering Usman who thought they had come for him. The commander of the armed unit gave the all-clear.

Chief Inspector Simon Reynolds, accompanied by his Wiltshire colleagues, entered Raza's office.

"Good afternoon, Mr. Khan, and who is this gentleman?"

Raza did not rise from behind his desk, he wasn't sure that his legs would bear him.

"My brother, Usman."

He gave his sibling a baleful look, wondering whether he had been rumbled for his paedophile activities.

"Thank you, Mr. Khan. May I introduce my colleagues; Inspector McInnes and DC Jeffreys from the Wiltshire Constabulary, based in Salisbury."

Raza's mind went into overdrive. When Reynolds continued his bowels turned to water.

"We are assisting them with their investigation into a serious crime committed last Saturday morning close to a village called Tisbury."

Reynolds waved a piece of paper under Raza's nose.

"We have a warrant to search your premises, Mr. Khan. Sue, would you tell my sergeant to proceed, please?"

She left the room, making a beeline for Jeff Durham.

In prior dealings with Simon Reynolds it had been Raza's inclination to bluster and make noises about police harassment and racism. He decided to play this one with a straight bat.

"May I sit down, Mr. Khan?"

Simon Reynolds was inordinately polite. Over the years he had learnt that shouting and screaming at people only raises their hackles, and makes them defensive. A sustained gentle and polite approach often unnerves a suspect. When their nerves are humming like telephone wires they usually start to tell you what you want to hear.

Raza focused upon Reynolds, but was startled by Kenny McInnes.

"Tisbury, Mr. Khan, ever heard of it?"

"Hasn't everybody, Inspector? Been all over the bloody news. Where the old gentleman was murdered."

His tone was sepulchral.

"Jamal Ahmed!"

The name dropped like a barrel bomb into the silence of the office, and Raza's attention returned to Reynolds.

"Jamal is one of your drivers, isn't he?"

Playing the hale fellow well met routine, Raza was derisive.

"If you could call him that. You know these young men, Mr. Reynolds, here one day gone the next, always crying off sick; lazy buggers."

McInnes enquired, "Not reliable then?"

"About as much use as a chocolate tea pot that boy."

"Is he working now?"

195

Raza shook his head; he was making it up as he went along.

"Should be, but the bugger hasn't turned in."

"Any idea where he might be?"

Usman would have been wise to keep quiet, but wanted to contribute.

"Went away on holiday last Friday with…"

An alarmed Raza shut him up.

"That's right, long weekend, went away with friends on the razzle. You know what young men are like, Mr. Reynolds."

  Simon clasped his hands together in prayer, the points of his fingers touching his chin.

"Any idea where he and his friends went, Mr. Khan?"

Raza never flinched, his mind was in full flow, to anticipate where the conversation would go next.

"Not too sure, probably headed for the beach in this hot weather."

He wafted the hot August air with his chubby hand.

"Jamal is a London boy, probably buggered off to Southend or Brighton."

An old taxi hand knows his geography, and he pointed them eastward.

Unfortunately, the garrulous Usman was feeling neglected. Now that he was off the hook he decided to be helpful.

"No brother, don't you remember, he said they were going to an island…"

"Oy, oy, oy, poppadum brain, can't you ever get anything right?"

He smiled knowingly at the two policemen.

"Jamal was boring the balls off everybody last week about sun, sea and girls. I'm sure it was Southend he said they were going to."

He cast Usman a thunderous look.

"Island! He's got relatives on the Isle of Dogs, or Sheppey, or something. Jamal was wittering on about visiting them. That's all we know, sir."

The office door opened with an arthritic creak, and Sue Jeffreys stepped inside. Both senior officers gave her a glance, and she shook her head gently. Reynolds remained in his seat, a light and pleasant smile aimed at Raza.

"Friends Mr. Khan?"

Usman laughed, "Are they still repeating that shite on television?"

Stony stares quelled his nonsense.

"You say Jamal went on holiday with friends. Do you know who they are?"

"Can't help you there, Mr. Reynolds. Jamal doesn't live in Wenbury, so I don't know who he mixes with."

For once Raza was telling the truth, but neglected to mention his nephew Qadir. The other two executioners, Dawood and Bakir, did not work for him. He may have seen them at Cranchurch Mosque occasionally, but they were just faces in a congregation.

"I'm sorry that we cannot help you more."

Kenny McInnes had his face to a wall, leafing idly through an empty calendar that hung there.

"You haven't asked us, Mr. Khan!"

Raza jumped, ever so slightly.

"I beg your pardon, officer, asked you what?"

McInnes studied the fat man.

"Armed police break into your premises, and you submit to a search and interrogation without so much as a squeak. You haven't asked us why we're here."

The old disgruntled and grumpy Raza started to emerge.

"Bloody obvious, isn't it, as obvious as the paint on a whore's face."

McInnes stood next to the seated Reynolds and leant on the desk,

"Humour us Mr. Khan, we're just a pair of plods, what's so obvious?"

"Well, I didn't know what the hell was going on when your marines burst through the door, but as soon as you mentioned that place Tisbury, well…"

McInnes tried a little provocative sarcasm.

"An avid follower of the news, are you?"

"You can't miss it; we've been bombarded with this dreadful business for days."

Sue Jeffreys spoke softly.

"You consider it dreadful, Mr. Khan?"

"Of course I do. Christ almighty, what sort of bloody question is that?"

Simon Reynolds didn't react to the blasphemy, and DC Jeffreys threw Raza a sympathetic smile.

"I can see that you're a compassionate man."

A weighty and lengthy silence embraced them in solemn reflection upon the demise of the Earl of Seaforth.

Raza brought them to attention.

"Is that it Mr. Reynolds? I've got a business to run. This is costing me time and money, not to mention what it's doing to my reputation having gun-toting coppers all over the place. I shall speak to my M.P. about this, he's one of my best customers you know."

Simon Reynolds alarmed Raza.

"Yes we do know. Been having trouble with your business in the last month or two, haven't you?"

Raza remained taciturn, and Usman shrivelled into himself.

"Padam Gurung – you'll be pleased to know he's making a good recovery; slow, but good. What about that other driver of yours; young Mohammed wasn't it?"

Raza finally came to his feet.

"Haven't you found those racists yet? I pay my taxes…"

"I'm sure you do. Enquiries are continuing, and may I assure you, Mr. Khan, that we find such racist conduct and language as reprehensible as you do."

"That boy is family; we are all very upset."

"Naturally Raza. It must be very aggravating to think that someone has it in for you and your business."

Raza pounced on this with alacrity.

"Indeed, indeed, that's what I've been saying all along. Some bastard is out to ruin me; my money is on that *gandoo* who runs the *'Jacaranda'* in Wycombe."

Simon Reynolds kept his counsel, they had long since ruled the business rival out of the frame.

"Thank you for your assistance, Mr. Khan, we'll let you get back to business. You will inform us if Jamal Ahmed shows his face, won't you?"

"You think that boy had something to do with the murder?"

None of the officers responded.

"Of course, of course, only too ready to help the forces of law and order."

The Khan brothers stood at the window, watching the whole kit and caboodle withdraw. When the last one was out of sight, Raza looked Usman up and down before retiring to his chair.

"Shouldn't we find Q...?"

"Don't say that name," Raza blazed, "and learn to keep your mouth shut."

He sat, gazing into space, emotions surging through him like Noah's Flood.

"What is wrong with these people? Bloody religion. If they must worship, why can't they worship in peace, and leave others to do the same?"

In his heart Raza knew that it was nothing to do with religion. If he had spoken with Julian Marlborough they would have agreed. Religious observance was something you just did to hold the fabric of society together. They would have subscribed to the poet Coleridge's philosophy that the visible church's primary role is to be the bearer of the nation's civilisation. Believing that there was actually a God was nonsense.

Unfortunately, Qadir and Peter Standish would have refuted the proposition. As much as their personal beliefs differed, they would have agreed with the theologian Richard Hooker; the first duty of the visible church is to be the embodiment of divine truth and divine action in the world.

The problem was that whilst one person sought it through persuasion, the other was wedded to force. No, these violent incidents weren't really about religion; they were the outcome of men seeking dominance.

"Get the Lexus, Usman. You can drive me to the Mosque."

17

*"Whereof what's past is prologue; what to come, in yours
and my discharge."*
The Tempest Act: Sc.1

Ten Downing Street has seen its share of crises in its
time. The present furore hadn't yet reached epic
proportions, but it was serious enough for Tommy
O'Donnell to foregather with his Home Secretary and
Defence Minister. Henry Longfellow delivered a grim
report. As Home Sec. he knew exactly what the
temperature of the country was. It was his duty to report
it honestly, and make recommendations to the Prime
Minister.

"I'm not telling you anything new, Tom, when I say that
this has been coming for a long time. We've kept the
extent of race crime hidden as best we can, but with the
business in Buckinghamshire, and the death of the Earl
we're on the verge of losing control."

He paused, and lifted a sheet of paper.

"There's not a region in the country that hasn't seen
violence. Every day sizable bodies of people are taking to
the streets in protest. Pakistani businesses are being
attacked, along with mosques, and people being verbally
abused in the streets is commonplace. Some in the
Moslem community are organising and fighting back. The
police don't have the manpower to cope, Tom. If we

don't do something sharpish, we're going to have a bloodbath on our hands."

O'Donnell played with the cuffs of his shirt.

"Why the hell is anyone bothered about some old aristocrat getting his head lopped off?"

Longfellow and Defence Sec. Jacob Greenwood both thought the same thing:

"He doesn't get it does he?"

Tommy O'Donnell's brain was atrophied in dogma, he had no understanding of people.

Englishmen and women – no, Britons – are some of the most cussed people on the planet; opinionated and certain that they are right. There are those who lean to the left, and those who sway to the right, and a body bobbing in the jelly of the centre ground profoundly committed to remaining disinterested. One thing they have in common is a conservative instinct for the preservation of what they see as their way of life. Privileged earl he may have been, but Eddie Seaforth represented an invisible and intangible icon of stability, and the British abhor iconoclasts.

Rightly or wrongly this led to the Kingdom's exit from the E.U. Now a populist rising was taking place at, what the people believed to be, another attempt to undermine their way of life. The flashpoint was unfettered immigration. Add the well-organised extreme right wing groups to the pot, and you had a mixture that was boiling over, and cascading like lava onto the streets of the country.

O'Donnell kept fiddling with his cufflinks.

"I thought that business in Buckinghamshire had died down? Eh, I've 'ad an idea. They're both Tory constituencies aren't thee; the one in Bucks an' the other in Wiltshire. We could blame the Tories for this."

Jake Greenwood was one of the P.M.'s oldest allies, but even he was appalled.

"Jeez Tommy, this is no time for playing politics. Folk are getting hurt out there, our folk."

"I'm surprised at you Jake; it's always time to play politics. Anyroad, you can't make an omelette without breaking eggs."

This folksy wisdom defined O'Donnell's ambition.

Why some men and women turn on their country can be a mystery. Most of the time it is explicable. Some hurt, or slight – real or imagined – has propelled their personality in that direction, and their attitude and actions are motivated by a desire for vengeance. It is not the self-righteous Atheist alone who believes he has the divine right to follow this path; men and women of faith who have decided that only they can speak for God are just as prone to familial hatred. The sin of pride acknowledges but one creed: *'me first'.*

Henry Longfellow drew them back to the task in hand.

"Tommy, we are at a critical point. The ability of the police alone to contain the widespread and ongoing disturbances is not a given."

"So what are you saying, Hank?"

Longfellow sucked in air.

"I know you're not keen on this, Tom, but hear me out. The one thing we can't afford is to be caught on the hop. Now all I'm proposing is just in case –remember that, just in case – we need them. I'm suggesting a strategic regional disposition of troops who can be called upon if push comes to shove."

Longfellow and Greenwood held their breath.

"Not on your nelly! I'm still trying to find out who the bastard was who authorised those M.P.s from the RAF to get involved in Bucks."

Jake Greenwood pleaded with him.

"Tom, we've got to be ready for every eventuality. It's getting nastier by the day out there. The lads will only be on standby…"

O'Donnell retorted fiercely.

"Once troops go on the streets it's a bugger to get them off again. No, no, no. If the day ever comes when we need to do that, it will be because it serves the party's interest first."

He paused for a sip of water.

"Get hold of that tosser at the BBC. I want a ten-minute slot at 6.30 tonight. I'll make an appeal for calm. The country will listen, lads, believe me, they'll listen."

With that he picked up a folder, and examined its contents.

"I've been looking at this police report on Seaforth's death. Seems they think there's some connection with what's been going on in Bucks. Whose constituency is that, Hank?"

There was little point in pressing him further on the distribution of troops.

"Wenbury and Cranchurch, Hugh Marlborough."

"Dat fuckin' fascist. Have a werd with him. See if the old bastard knows anything we don't. Right, I want me dinner."

Off he went, leaving the two of them alone in the Cabinet Room.

Jacob and Henry shuffled their papers in silence. They had never been the closest of party comrades, but in these trying times they had found common ground.

"No need to be too concerned, Henry. His agreement would have been retrospective anyway."

Smiling ruefully, they wandered out of Downing Street together, to breathe freely in the air conditioning of their respective cars.

The Scottish and Northern regiments were already engaged in exercises from their bases north of Newcastle, and in Preston; the Marines were hard at it in the south-west, and Salisbury Plain was alive with forces practicing urban warfare and civil control. Ready to go to all points of the compass at a moment's notice.

*

The 'Brass' had gathered in Hugh Marlborough's Hampstead residence, for their fortuitously postponed meeting. Freddie Forbes held the chair. The gentlemen around the dining table were gleeful.

"There it is chaps; the source is impeccable, our latest *'friend'* within *'Lennon's'* orbit. It seems that *'Grunewald's'* orders to your fellows have brightened our prospects considerably. The present distribution of forces is ideal for what we've planned. It now becomes merely a matter of deciding when we go into action."

The cautious Scotsman, *'Rob'*, spoke with gravitas.

"Not yet. If we're to cross the Rubicon we must be certain that civil order has broken down so badly that the government is seen as no longer competent to hold the country together."

A chorus of support was expressed forcibly. Freddie, wise bird that he was, saw no need to press them further; patience truly was a virtue. He turned his attention to the Brigadier of Paratroopers, *'Connolly'*.

"I can confirm that we have the necessary support for your boys to drop in where and when they're needed. Here's a list of airfields from which you can take off. It would be useful if that were memorised and destroyed. It's a short list, by necessity, of strategic and easily reachable places. '5' inform me that their people within GCHQ have already prepared programmes to reconfigure communications when it all kicks off. We have a sizable group within Hereford who are ready to take over security at GCHQ, and remove any dissenting voices from the premises. *'Frobisher'*, what news on your front?"

The Admiral of the Fleet was concise.

"We're engaged in a programme of goodwill visits at present. Sailing into ports around the U.K. to show the flag, and do a spot of recruiting. All good-natured and innocent, but it allows us to move around freely and be where we want to be."

Freddie Forbes, Earl of Seaforth, thanked everybody for their attendance, and Hugh Marlborough distributed drinks.

'Bernard', Major General of the Household Division, placed his empty glass on the table.

"Damnable business about your father, Freddie."

Murmurs of condolence came from all quarters.

"Thank you, thank you. Yes, one hell of shock for the family. Actually, thank you for reminding me, there is one other matter I should share."

Everyone was keenly attentive.

"There has been a number of, how can I put this, unusual happenings in recent times, and it appears that they may have a common link. You may recall a couple of racial and/or religiously motivated attacks in Buckinghamshire within the last month or so. It transpires that they both occurred within *'Winston's'* constituency; indeed, one was on his doorstep. Now the police believe that one of my father's murderers was a young Asian man who lives not far the scene of the earlier crimes."

"Good Lord, *'Winston'*," *'Frobisher'* exclaimed, "are you stirring the pot?"

Freddie smiled, "Don't think it's our erstwhile friend here up to no good, but someone certainly is, and it's not just one-sided. In many ways they're doing us a favour, by keeping the pot boiling."

The dour tones of *'Rob'* uttered,

"My God, I've known some *sang froid* in my time Freddie, but you take the biscuit. Pot boiling? Would your father's death be an ingredient in that receptacle?"

Freddie had loved his father, but he wasn't paralysed by sentimentality. He would grieve, but he would also act with the resolve his dad would have expected from him.

"A cold eye is required, gentlemen, if we are to put an end to such mayhem. You will recall that we have an agent named *'Castle'*? We have put him on standby to leave *'Lennon's'* service. We want him to pitch up in Hugh's constituency to ferret around."

"Not a bad idea," *'Paddy'* of the Marines chirped.

Freddie looked at Hugh.

"Would you care to tell them?"

"It's a very good idea, but there's a minor complication. By an odd coincidence it transpires that *'Castle'* served under my son in the Middle East, and more remarkably they met by chance in London some weeks back. They've struck up a friendship. Even had lunch together last week."

'Paddy' leapt in.

"How the hell do you know that? Did your son tell you? Who told him *'Castle's'* identity?"

"Hold your horses, *'Paddy'*, you've got it arse over tit."

Freddie explained.

"There hasn't been a breach of security. We had a meeting with *'Castle'* a few days ago. First time he's met *'Winston'*, and when he realised who he is he quite rightly told us about his association with his boy."

The *'Brass'* mulled this over. *'Bernard'* spoke first.

"So where does that leave your proposal to insert him into the community?"

Freddie prompted Hugh to speak.

"I'm going to sound out my lad, and..."

Consternation broke out, and everyone was asking at once if he intended to let Julian in on their plans. Freddie raised his hands to placate them.

"Gentlemen, gentlemen, hear us out.

He inadvertently used *'Winston's'* real name.

"Hugh, pray continue."

He cleared his throat, and said with pride,

"My boy is ex-Sneaky Beaky, rank Captain, and twice decorated in action..." His voice shook with emotion, so Freddie helped him out.

"From the detailed discussions I've had with Hugh, I'm satisfied that this young man would share our views and our resolve. Julian would be an asset to the campaign. So gentleman, with your permission we will proceed in the following manner."

Freddie outlined the simple plan for putting ex-Sergeant Billy Conway alongside ex-Captain Julian Marlborough within the environs of Wenbury and Cranchurch. Little did any of them realise the astonishing rapidity with which events would now unfold, or the remarkable long term consequences of this new liaison.

*

Angela Repton was feeling bright and breezy. The bruises on her body had healed, and she was enjoying a well-earned break from being pounded by all and sundry in the West Hampstead flat.

Sitting in this cute little café in Old Wenbury, it amused her to people watch as she sipped her Earl Grey and limited herself to just one yummy pastel de nata. The firm custard rolled around the inside of her mouth before she swallowed. This was definitely a place where ladies lunched, and chattered at the top of their voices in an effort to impress. Where they were going on holiday; where they *had* holidayed, new kitchens and landscaped gardens, and how well Timmy and Rosie were doing at school. All grist to the mill of one-upmanship.

She observed the way they played up to the strapping young eighteen-year-old who worked the coffee machine and the tables. Their middle-aged lust was palpable, as they salivated over the contents of his tight jeans and t-shirt. She could see the cloud of wistful longing as they remembered the days when their husbands had been so slim and muscular.

She wanted to shout,

"Go on girls, make him an offer over your latte. Taste the early afternoon of youth one more time, before night falls."

Angela rather liked her new name, and was relieved that Julian hadn't questioned its veracity. She was also pleased with herself, because she had fallen on her feet.

Julian had wanted to accompany her in the search for a flat, but she was having none of that. Much as she was grateful to him, she could see the control freak in him as clear as day. Luck followed her around, and she only had to stay in a B & B for a fortnight. Now she resided in a pretty one-bedroom cottage on the edge of the Old Town. The rent was extortionate, but she could afford it for a while. She wouldn't need to go back to work for the foreseeable future. Julian knew very little about her, and she intended it to stay that way.

The most important fact was that she was a lady of property in her own right. When she had gone on the *'game'* it had been to get the millstone of university debt from around her neck. However, she had wised up quickly. The top-end service she gave Julian every punter received. She built-up quite a clientele to keep her busy four times a day, five days a week. At two hundred and twenty pounds a pop that was a sound return. So far, she had been able to acquire two properties around the country, fully paid for and rented out. She was halfway to owning a third. When she had four in her portfolio it would be time to quit.

She finished her pastry. A giggled escaped her. What would the good ladies of South Bucks say if they knew that at this time of the morning she was usually munching on something quite different.

The doorbell tinkled, and admiring glances flew in Julian's direction as he walked over to her table. He bent over and kissed her on the cheek. She allowed him this liberty each time they met. Under the circumstances, she permitted him even greater liberties in the bedroom of her cottage. It was free of charge. How could she ask him for money when he'd done his Sir Galahad act, and rescued her from the clutches of that vile old man? She still shuddered when she thought of the multiple rape she had undergone. Not that it was the first time it had happened. It's more of an occupational hazard for prostitutes than people realise. No, it had happened twice before during the years she'd been in the business. It was never quite so brutal as on this occasion, and never with the consequences the gang intended for her. So she owed Julian a debt. Somewhere along the line she'd have to make it clear to him that it wasn't open-ended.

"Can't stay long, my old man wants a word. Says it's rather important, so I need to be on parade."

Angela was relieved that he wouldn't be in her hair all day. She wanted to go looking for a second hand car. In London she had done without, but here in the sticks it was a necessity. If she needed to move in a hurry she didn't want to rely on public transport.

Her smile dazzled him.

"Ah, that's a shame," she lied. "Time for coffee?"

He caught the eye of the young Adonis at his machine, and mouthed, *'Cappuccino'*.

"So, summoned by the boss. Sounds like you better not be late."

Julian was irked by her mocking tone.

"Oh, five minutes here or there won't matter."

Apologetically, he added,

"He's rather a busy man, is Pa', not fair to keep him waiting too long."

Julian realised he was attempting to justify his subservience to his father. An image of his youth danced before his eyes. When Hugh spoke to him as a boy he would come to rigid attention.

The arrival of his coffee returned him to the present. He took a sip, and fixed his eyes upon Angela. She really was lovely. It disturbed him deeply that it wasn't just the fantastic sex they had that made him feel that way.

"Am I allowed to ask what your father does that makes him such a busy man?"

Julian hoped to make a good impression.

"He's our local M.P."

Angela's life before prostitution had been top-end middle class. Her parents were prosperous people who mixed with the influential of the county. Julian's revelation didn't overly impress her. However, she thought it politic to appear a little awed.

"Gosh, so you're the son of one of our leaders."

Was there just an edge of mockery there, again? It rattled him.

"Look, next weekend we're hosting the Rector's Garden Party in our grounds. Why don't you come as my guest for the day? I'll introduce you to Ma' and Pa'. It's a church…"

"Annual 'do' for the Benefice. We used to attend them in my dim and distant youth."

Angela gazed at him steadily. What was he up to with his invitation? He sounded like a young man who wanted to parade his new girlfriend before his parents. What next, a proposal of marriage? Her more than playful side took a grip upon her.

"Wonderful, sounds like great fun. Should I wear a summer frock and hat?"

"The frock would be lovely; think you can ditch the hat. What about dinner tonight, pick you up at eight?"

"Terrific!"

She noted the flush of lust on his face.

"Hadn't you better be off? Don't want to keep Pa' waiting."

Glancing at his watch, he jumped to his feet.

"Eight then. Where would you like to go?"

"Something simple. Got any good Indians round here?"

"I know just the place. Bye then."

He pecked her on the cheek and carried her musk away with him.

Angela put her tea cup down, its contents were cold. She went to the till to pay. Young Jason zipped the length of the counter to attend to her before his young female colleague could speak.

"Everything alright?"

"Lovely Jason."

It amused her to see his hand shake slightly as she proffered a ten-pound note. In her short residence in Old Wenbury she had frequented the place regularly, and had many a good chat with him. On her fourth visit he had asked her for a date, and she had let him down gently.

"Don't look now, Jason. Table third right; think you've got an admirer."

A rather attractive and well-coutured lady, in good trim, was eying his buttocks over her mint tea.

"Get in there! She looks the sort who'll buy you all sorts of treats. See you soon."

Jason was pained, as he watched her posterior swing through the open doorway. He was still young enough to possess the illusion of love for love's sake, and he abhorred the mercenary tone in her voice.

Angela stood on the cobbled pavement. Time to sort out a vehicle; something small and sporty. She was about to step forwards when a thought occurred to her. When she had made the purchase, she would park it a discreet distance from her cottage. It would be best if Julian remained unaware of her new-found ability to move quickly when needed.

*

The ritual knock on the door was answered, and Julian entered his father's study.

"Ah Julian, come in my boy and park yourself."

In truth, he had no idea why his father had summoned him. He thought he might be in for another ear bashing about not paying his way.

"Thank you, sir."

"Too early for a drink, son?"

"Boy - son!" that put him on alert.

"Er, I'll join you if you're having one."

Hugh had a bottle of Chablis open, and poured a glass for his boy, topping up his own. They sat facing each other in the comfortable leather armchairs.

"Cheers. Mmmm, rather good. Well Julian, don't seem to see much of you these days; always on the go, me that is."

This was a palpable lie. It was only a few weeks since they'd had their lunch in Town. The old boy was leading up to something, and he commenced his fishing expedition.

"How are you finding things these days? Managing to keep busy?"

Julian smiled inwardly.

"Oh yes, Pa', always something to do. No rest for the wicked, eh."

He had no intention of giving anything away.

Hugh savoured his wine.

"How are you finding the old country? Been back in civvie street quite a while now."

Julian was more than a little puzzled. The old man appeared to be asking for some sort of political overview; not something he had ever done before. He made his father wait, as he enjoyed the wine.

"Not quite the place I left when I went overseas."

Hugh couldn't afford the time to fanny around, so he came to the point.

"Bit more than not quite. Country is in a dreadful state."

"Going to the dogs, eh father?"

"Not a laughing matter, Julian. Unless something is done soon we're going to see civil disorder on a scale unimaginable, and then everyone's a loser. The police are already hard pushed to keep control of the streets."

"What, in Wenbury?"

"Nationwide son, nationwide. You don't know the half that's going on; mosques burning, violent public disorder, and the Moslem community organising to fight back. Before long old Enoch's prophecy will become a fact – *'rivers of blood'*, my boy, *'rivers of blood'*."

Julian hadn't wasted his expensive education. He knew exactly what his father was referring to when he used that phrase. It was attributed to Tory M.P. Enoch Powell, in his infamous address to the General Meeting of the West Midlands Area Conservative Political Centre on April 20th 1968; co-incidentally, Adolf Hitler's birthday. Powell had been criticising Commonwealth immigration and anti-discrimination legislation that had been proposed in the United Kingdom. Of particular moment was the fact that the second reading of the Labour

Government's Race Relation Bill 1968 was to take place the following Tuesday.

"Actually, Powell never used those words. He was alluding to a line in Virgil's '*Aeneid*'. What he said was,

'*As I look ahead, I am filled with foreboding; like the Roman, I seem to see 'the River Tiber foaming with much blood'.*

He was a Classicist after all."

Hugh raised his eyebrows.

"My God Julian, your mother is right, you can be surprising. So, some of it did stick at school. I thought you spent all of your time at High Heath poncing about on the stage."

"That would have been profoundly ungrateful of me, to spurn the opportunities your hard work enabled me to have."

Hugh Marlborough was filled with warmth for his son.

"Thank you my boy, thank you, good of you to say so. Here, let me top you up."

Drinks were replenished, and Hugh thought it time to move the conversation into more dangerous waters.

"Shouldn't really have disclosed that stuff about the upheaval going on around the country. Feel sure I can trust you to be discreet."

Julian remained cagy.

"What do you intend to do about it, Father? Not you personally, you understand, I mean Parliament as a whole."

Hugh rose from his seat. He wandered to the window to look over his bit of the green and pleasant land.

"Fact is, Julian, we're hamstrung. O'Donnell and the Labour lot still have the whip hand; we're not in power..."

He turned to look Julian in the eye, and lowered his voice to a whisper.

"Not yet."

Julian thought back to his Drama teacher, and how he always emphasised that an audience would comprehend the meaning of your words if they were delivered in the correct tone; even incomprehensible bits of Shakespeare.

An immense charge went through him, because he detected correctly what his father was inferring when he said, *"Not yet."* He was certain that he was alluding to some sort of action outside the normal intercourse of parliamentary democracy.

"Think I catch your drift, sir. Have to say that in unusual times, unusual measures are called for. Are you in a position to say more?"

Hugh gazed out on his estate.

"Got to be sure about your loyalty my boy. Highest level of security and all that."

Julian stood beside his father in the bow window. It came as a surprise to them both when he linked his father's arm; he and Hugh had never been tactile.

"Look at it Pa', isn't it terrific."

They inhaled the wonderful sight of an almost unchanged English village resting in the valley below. Trees dappled it, as sunlight filtered through the leaves.

Julian made a declaration.

"I will do anything - anything - to protect my country from those who would destroy it, be they foreigners or home-grown wreckers."

Hugh's took his son by the arm and led him to the armchairs. He proceeded to recount everything about the operation he and the top brass were planning.

"What do you think son? Can you see your way to participating? You have some expertise we could use, given your background."

This was what Julian had been waiting for; the chance to bring order out of chaos.

"I'm entirely at your disposal father. There is something I should tell you."

He was about to disclose what he'd been up to with his own little campaign of mayhem. Hugh cut him short.

"Tell me in a minute."

He strode from the room, and Julian was left hanging. Half a minute later, Hugh reappeared.

"Got an old friend of yours here, Julian, he'd like to say hello."

Hugh stepped aside, and Billy Conway walked into the room.

"Billy!"

"Actually boss, it's William these days; Will for short."

Hugh became brisk.

"Sit down, sit down, and let's come to business. Would prefer you to call our friend here Will from now on, William Castle. Will has been on the inside for us gathering information, but we need him here. How did you manage to get your release papers Will?"

"Like I was told. Got pissed up on duty, an' they showed me the door."

"Good, good. Right now, Julian, as you know we've been the centre of some attention here in Wenbury recently. Poor Sergeant Gurung knocked about and then that Asian lad carved up. The Chief Constable tells me there appears to be a connection between someone in this area and the dreadful murder of Seaforth down in Wiltshire. You recall what I told you a few minutes ago, how we were supposed to be meeting down there? Too close for comfort. We decided to pull Will out of Town and put him together with you to see if you can uncover what's going on in these parts."

Julian laughed until he cried, and the other two sat there utterly bemused.

"That's what I wanted to tell you, Pa'. That was me!"

To say that Hugh and Billy were shocked would be an understatement.

"What, you beheaded the old geezer, Cap'?"

"No, no. It was me who branded the Pakistani boy down in Old Wenbury. Revenge, as simple as that, for attacking our Gurkha friend."

Julian related the tale, and Hugh became thoughtful.

"Taxi firm eh? From the information I've been receiving these Khan brothers keep cropping up in all the police enquiries. It would be a good idea if you and Will took an interest in them."

They exchanged a glance of mutual approval. Hugh repaired to the window seat, where he sat in profile.

"What is it you want to come out of this Father?"

"Seems to me that you boys together could cause quite a ruckus in the area. Fires have a habit of spreading if left unchecked. Chances are they will, because O'Donnell won't allow the *'big boys'* to be brought in to help the civilian forces. The sooner we spread discord; the sooner we can reach accord."

He rather liked that, and memorised it for appropriate use in the House.

"Reckon we can do that, sir," Will grinned.

"Yes, well, before you undertake any *'social'* activities I need my grounds in order."

Julian looked at him enquiringly. It was Hugh's turn to laugh.

"Will is our new gardener. Old Horace is on temporary paid leave. Got the Rector's bloody Garden Party at the weekend, with the great unwashed treading all over my flower beds. Get it shipshape for me Will, would you, like to have the old place looking its best."

"It will be my pleasure, sir."

The three of them downed another drink, with Julian proposing a toast to a profitable and successful association.

18

*"He that commends me to mine own content
Commends me to the thing I cannot get…"
The Comedy of Errors Act 1: Sc.2*

"A Muslim should maintain a strong and positive relationship with his family, but he should not favour them unjustly over others."

Imam Shirani let his words sink in, as he stood before his congregation.

"The Prophet Muhammad – peace and blessings be upon him – learnt of a woman whose neighbours were happy with her, he said that she would be in Paradise. See how important it is to be good to our neighbours, in actions and in words."

Shirani was treading a delicate path. Ever since Raza Khan had revealed to him what Qadir had done in Wiltshire he had faced a conundrum. In his heart he knew that he should inform the authorities Yet he believed that no-one was irredeemable; nothing was unstoppable.

"Prophet Muhammad – peace and blessings upon him – said of the rights of our neighbours:

'It is to help him if he asks your help, to lend him if he asks to borrow from you, to satisfy his needs if he becomes poor, to console him if he is visited by an

221

affliction, to congratulate him if he is met with good fortune, to visit him if he becomes ill, to attend his funeral if he dies, not to make your house higher than his without his consent lest you deny him the breeze, to offer him fruit when you buy some or to take it to your home secretly if you do not do that, nor to send out your children with it so as not to upset his children, nor to bother him by the tempting smell of your food unless you send him some.'

Truly this is perfect wisdom."

Peter Standish would have applauded the Imam's address. Jesus' words to His disciples, in Matthew's Gospel, bore similarities. Provide the hungry and thirsty with food and drink; invite the stranger in and clothe the needy, and look after the sick and visit the prisoner. Each of these good men would have been heartened by what they had in common.

"Imam Ali has said:

"A person is either your brother in faith, or your equal in humanity."

Shirani discerned a stirring, and he drew a deep breath before carrying on.

"Islam encourages us to treat our neighbours gently to reflect the true spirit of Islam, and this tolerance is especially true with people of other faiths."

He knew Qadir was present, and felt as if eyes were burning into his heart. This brave messenger continued.

"It makes no difference whether our neighbours are Muslim or non-Muslim. The Prophetic Hadith encourages us not only to kindness with our neighbours, but to exchange gifts with them. The Hadith does not indicate whether the people we exchange gifts with are Muslim or not."

He was relieved to have reached this point, and became almost light-hearted.

"*Within* the scope of Shariah Islamic Law, socialise with your neighbour anywhere; at work, on the street, in your garden. Introduce yourself to those you don't know; you will be amazed how this will reduce fear. Care for people in need, whoever they are. Eat with people and share ideas; bring your families together. Be confident to talk about your religion when the opportunity arises, and if your neighbour shows an interest invite him to visit the Mosque. Even if he goes away still a non-believer, at least a barrier has been broken down."

He had travelled something of a circuitous route, but now he reached the intended destination.

"There is no reason why you should not visit the church where your neighbours attend if they invite you, as long as you are careful not to perform any act which our religion prohibits."

Shirani could feel the damp in his armpits. There it was, he had said it. The last bit would be easier.

"Many of you already know, my brothers, that we have been invited to participate in a social and charitable event at St. George's Church, Banksmore. It takes place this Sunday, commencing at two o' clock. We will contribute stalls with Islamic arts and crafts and foodstuffs. What a fine opportunity, to mix with our neighbours in companionship and harmony."

Shirani looked across a sea of faces. He saw signs of approval and plenty of acceptance, but he also saw young faces that were set in stone. Their bearers sat cross-legged to the right, a dozen or so of them. He picked out Qadir, immobile and intransigent in the centre. Before he could leave, Qadir rose and stared at him, then turned on his heel and strode out with his followers.

The Imam spent ten minutes alone in his office, praying, before departing for his home. He heard the disturbance before he reached the door. When he came into the street he saw people arguing with one another.

Qadir saw him and raised a finger, pointing in accusation.

"See, the apostate is among us; the traitor stands before us. Do we sit and listen to one who has left Islam? Bar the doors to him; he is no longer welcome in our Mosque."

Older men of great faith shook their heads in sorrow.

Faisal Hussain stepped forwards, his hand raised for silence.

"Brothers, brothers, hear me. We must not divide ourselves, because of hot-headed anger and intolerance…"

He got no further, as a stone flew through the air and struck him on the head. Blood poured across his face, and he slumped to the pavement.

All hell broke loose; faction fighting against faction. In the melee, Dawood eased forwards. Gripping Imam Shirani amidst the crush he thrust a knife into his belly, then slipped swiftly away. For a few seconds the Imam was held upright by the density of the crowd, but then he slid to the floor clutching his wound. A cry of horror arose, and a space emerged around him.

Fortunately, there was a local doctor in attendance, who had been at prayer with them. He staunched the flow of blood sufficiently to buy time for the paramedics. They arrived simultaneously with three *'Paddy wagons'* of police in full riot gear. Whilst the ambulance crew were busy, the police found themselves with nothing to do. Many in the crowd had made a quick exit when they saw their injured Imam. Qadir and his team were among the first to slip away.

Simon Reynolds appeared shortly after the riot squads, but was met with a blank wall from those still present.

"Excuse me," a cultured voice said, "I believe I may be able to help you."

"And you are, sir?"

"Dr. Mansour, officer."

"Ah, you were the one assisting the victim. What can you tell me, sir?"

The medic looked nervous, and said quietly, "A great deal...?"

"Reynolds, doctor, Chief Inspector Reynolds."

"A great deal, Chief Inspector – but not here."

"Perhaps you'd care to join me at the station?"

"I would, but with your permission I'd like to walk away from you now, and make my own way to your office. What time?"

"Shall we say four this afternoon?"

Reynolds raised his volume for all to hear.

"Thank you doctor. The paramedics think the Imam will be alright. He'll need surgery, but they reckon he'll pull through, thanks to your swift intervention. I don't believe we need trouble you anymore. Good day sir."

Reynolds watched the doctor stroll away, and saw the pats on his arm from well-wishers.

"Hmm," he thought, "not a bad result to get someone like the doc to talk."

He gave his attention to the man who was being helped to his feet. A plaster covered the cut he'd received from the flying stone.

"You alright, young man?"

"Thank you, yes."

"May I ask your name, sir?"

"Faisal Hussain, Mr. Reynolds."

Simon was taken aback, and not a little suspicious; was our newly-found *'friend'* known to the police?

Faisal managed a pale smile at the Chief Inspector's puzzled frown.

"I teach your son GCSE history Mr. Reynolds. We've met at parents' evenings."

Despite the gravity of events, Simon managed a laugh.

"Did you think that you'd picked me up before, Mr. Reynolds?"

"The thought did cross my mind."

"We all look alike, eh?"

"No Mr. Hussain, that's not what I thought at all. When people know my name it's an occupational hazard to assume that you've met them during the course of the job."

They eyed each other warily, and then laughed.

"Can you tell me what kicked all this off, Mr. Hussain?"

Faisal inhaled a deep breath, and drew closer to Reynolds.

"I can tell you exactly what provoked the disturbance – and a whole lot more. Chief Inspector, would you mind if I left now. Perhaps you could suggest a time when I could call into your office?"

Simon Reynolds would have been amused, if there were anything to be amused about. Two witnesses prepared to speak, but seeking anonymity. In view of the shit that had been going down over recent months, he wasn't in the least surprised that people were cautious and afraid.

"Shall we say ten tomorrow morning in High Wycombe?"

Faisal nodded assent.

Simon Reynolds went into playacting mode again. In the ringing tones of a man who reads the lesson in church he announced,

"Take it easy, sir. Get yourself home and rest. Don't think we'll need to speak anymore."

Faisal walked away, and a concerned friend took his arm, insisting that he would drive him home.

Reynolds shook his head imperceptibly.

"Worried guvnor?"

Sgt Jeff Durham appeared at his elbow.

"The plot thickens, you might say. Come on Jeff, nothing for us here. We'll learn more later."

19

*"All things that we ordained festival,
Turn from their office to black funeral…"
Romeo and Juliet Act 4: Sc. 5*

*S*toking hatred and division between people knows no boundaries. It is the prerogative of any person with a Messiah complex, irrespective of their nationality or the colour of their skin.

Britain in the twenty-first century had become much more divided since the Millennium. Those who wielded the scissors usually came from the educated and atheist soft liberal/left. Naturally, they didn't see it that way, nor was it their intention, but we know which road is paved with good intentions. Proclaiming that they simply wanted justice for all, their modus operandi stirred bitterness and envy by targeting and scapegoating others for the ills of society.

To be fair, the obscenely super-rich are fair game, but they are few and far between and they live in a remote stratosphere. Why not then castigate the extremely rich? This is where the attack dogs of social conscience become disingenuous. It's okay to rail against the CEOs of the FTSE 100 for earning five million pounds a year, but not the Premiership footballer for trousering thirteen millions per annum. You don't question the morality of the peoples' folk heroes, or they might stop agreeing with you.

Problem is, a whole lot of others get tarred with the same brush. No other group has become so despised as the comfortable middle class. Derision is heaped upon them by cheerleaders bred and fed within their midst, to promote class hatred.

On a blazing hot August Bank holiday, the anonymous middle class was out early doing what it always does, in a modest, efficient and companionable manner. Up and about since dawn to prepare for the Rector's Garden Party in the grounds of Banksmore House. They were not all residents of the village, but parishioners drawn widely from teachers and insurance men, painters and decorators. Others had their own small businesses. There were salesmen and women, and the retired. A collection of ordinary folk.

Produce appeared on trestle tables, grown in their own gardens; enough cake to satisfy a glutton, baked in their own kitchens; craft articles, created by their own hands. The everyday achievements of people who paid attention at school, who worked hard at all they did and paid their taxes; building families and caring for their homes. Not mansions, but three and four-bedroom houses in unremarkable urban locations. Possessing an interest in something other than the latest soap opera, and getting *'bladdered'* at the weekend. Teaching their children good manners and courtesy. Passing on the skills to them that they had acquired from their parents and grandparents.

Peter Standish hauled tables with the best of them, and erected gazebos for shelter against the fierce sun. Now and again he would be interrupted with an enquiry as to what he wanted where. Just now, they were on a ten-minute break, and the staff were spread across the lawns enjoying a cuppa.

He looked upon them with immense affection, seeing only their commonality. Not only his parishioners, but the Hindus who had arrived and pitched in with relish, and those Muslims from Cranchurch who had turned up despite the dreadful attack on Imam Shirani. Everyone mixing together in fellowship. Peter admired these people tremendously.

His mind went back to childhood when there would have been a greater social mix and bond. In those days the middle and working class had shared skills and values. He sighed for the times when working men and women pursued education for themselves and passed it on as a great ambition for their children. The ambition that the next generation, through hard work, would stride inexorably forward to a better life than their parents, and their parents would rejoice with pride. Of course, some still did, but the majority of them were from immigrant backgrounds.

Mass media had reduced people to a soporific condition, making them easy meat for the extremists. Christianity received a battering from the wise guys. They played on the inherent selfishness of human beings, and convinced the malleable that they didn't need it any more. No use for hope, joy and love. Feelings that only surfaced when there was a medical crisis or family occasion. No longer accepted, and lived, as the universal creed for humanity entwined in fellowship. That was why this day was so important to Peter, and hopefully the ecumenical projects ahead. It would be living proof that people of different faiths and contrasting colours of skin could unite.

Debs Marlborough appeared with her sunny smile.

"How's it coming along, Peter?"

"Two o'clock we said, and two o' clock it will be, unless the sun gets us first," he joked.

She linked his arm and started to walk him.

"Do show me round, and introduce me to our unknown factors."

Peter knew she meant those from outside the Benefice. He wasn't terribly impressed by the way she expressed herself.

When they approached the stalls erected by the Hindu and Muslim communities she came alive, and Peter was astonished. After he'd introduced her, as the *'lady of the house'*, she was right in there chatting to them about their wares, and displaying insight and knowledge about the materials they used in the creation of their arts and crafts. Debs listened attentively to what they had to say. All-in-all, it seemed to Peter, each made a good impression upon the other.

They strolled on, she attached limpet-like to his arm, until they came to a stall were a young woman was seated in the shade.

"Lady Marlborough, may I introduce you to Jane Standish, my wife. I'm not sure you've met before?"

His eyes twinkled with delight, and all three smiled. Debs played up to him.

"Married Rector! Oh dear, the maidens of the Parish will be disappointed."

Jane couldn't resist it,

"And one or two of the matrons no doubt."

Debs laugh was a fake crackle, but she recovered herself.

"It all looks jolly good, Peter. I'm sure it will be a roaring success."

Her attractive bottom slewed off in the direction of the house.

Peter sat next to the pregnant Jane.

"I should send you to bed with no supper. That was very naughty of you."

"Just marking my territory, darling."

Sitting in silence, he with an arm about her shoulders, they relished a peace they thought would last for ever.

"Penny for them."

"It's a lovely day, Jane, and one which I think we'll remember for a long time."

She put her knitting down and held his hand.

"You are a marvel, bringing these people together. I'm very proud of you. You've had your tea break, go and crack the whip."

They exchanged a tender kiss.

A voice rang out.

"I say, none of that in public vicar."

"Hello Julian, and...? Sorry, terrible to forget a name."

The stocky, muscular man beside Julian carried a sledgehammer.

"No need for apologies, Rector, we've only met once, and that in passing. Will, Will Castle."

"Ah yes, you're the new gardener. How is Horace?"

"Pa' thought he needed a rest. He's been with us thirty years, and he's not getting any younger. Paid leave for three months, and then we'll welcome him back. Now what's next on the agenda?"

"Bouncy castle time." He smiled at Will, "A Castle to build a castle, or inflate one at least."

They groaned at his corny gag, the prerogative of ministers, and set about their tasks. Peter announced the end of the tea break along the way.

Sir Hugh basked in the torrent of applause he received after giving his welcoming address, and declared the Garden Party well and truly open. Peter had already expressed his thanks for Sir Hugh and Lady Marlborough's generosity in opening their home for the day. He had one more thing to say.

"Thank you, thank you Sir Hugh."

The applause petered out.

"What an afternoon ahead of us. We are truly blessed; beautiful surroundings, wonderful weather, and you good people gathered as one in common purpose. It would be remiss of me, however, not to say that one important person is missing. I refer to our good friend, Imam Shirani."

Everyone was so still that a passer-by might have thought he had stumbled upon an art installation of a jigsaw, designed to represent the idyll of an English country garden.

"It is with the greatest pleasure that I can tell you he is out of danger, and recovering remarkably well from his injury. He has asked me to greet you all in brotherhood, and, in his own words, *'spend, spend, spend'*. We have agreed that the proceeds from the afternoon will be donated to our local branch of Samaritans. Enough talk – *'spend, spend, spend'*."

Derek Fisher and Marjorie Whitlock commandeered Peter, as he stepped down from the small dais.

"I say Pete, bloody good turnout!"

"Really Derek, language!"

"Apologies Marj, pardon my French. One heck of a good crowd though, best ever in my opinion."

"Well done, Peter. I knew you were made of the right stuff. Come along Derek, you can help me with the music stands."

They beetled off, with Derek looking wistfully in the direction of the beer tent. The Rector wandered at large, greeting all and sundry with encouragement to buy plants or second-hand books, emptying his own pockets along the way. Jack Preston beckoned from where he was orchestrating the shattering of old china with cricket balls.

"My God, Pete – if I might use the expression in a non-blaspheming sense – you really have done it. Ten minutes into your interview, and I knew you were the guy for me. Boy, have you rattled a few cages, and set the furry felines among the pigeons, if I may mix my metaphors. Not least of which is the gilded cage of high and mighty Hugh and his Lady Bountiful."

Peter stopped Jack abruptly.

"They have been very generous, Jack, in allowing us to stage this event in their home. I really think we should reciprocate that good will."

Jack tried to intervene, but Peter pressed his point.

"Jesus came to save us all, Jack, even the rich. Remember, it's not the righteous who are most in need, but the sinners. *'And now these three remain: faith, hope and love. But the greatest of these is love'.*"

As he moved on, he threw a light-hearted quip over his shoulder.

"King James version, Jack, for love read *'charity'*; same thing, keep up the good work."

The Party had been going for an hour and a half, and they were still pouring in; walkers and cyclists supplementing the locals. With Banksmore being a few miles out of town the occasional taxi rolled up the drive. Heads turned when one deposited a rather delectable young woman outside the big house. She stepped out of the vehicle, and even the sun blinked at the pristine white dress flowing gracefully around her bronzed body. She didn't head for the festivities, but up the steps to the house, into which she disappeared.

A little later, Peter was helping Marjorie Whitlock with a recalcitrant music stand when she exclaimed, "I say!"

He followed her gaze, and saw that she was looking at a beaming Julian meandering through the crowds with the beauty on one arm, and his mother on the other.

"Rather a stunner, Rector."

"Good gracious Marjorie, isn't that rather a modern term for you to use?"

Her giggle preceded a short lesson.

"To stun – old French *estoner 'astonish'*. A permitted extension, I think. Wouldn't the current phrase be, *'a bit of a cracker'*?"

Peter didn't have time to reply, because the Marlboroughs and guest were upon them.

"Peter," Debs drawled, "may I introduce Julian's friend, and our guest, Angela?"

Julian had experienced a frisson when he introduced Angela to his parents. Now he was rather gleeful, knowing that the Rector would shake hands with a prostitute. Unexpectedly, clarity of understanding burst upon him, and he realised that even if he declared Angela's profession far and wide Peter Standish would welcome her and not be judgemental. It rather took the edge off it for him.

"Angela, welcome. May I introduce Marjorie Whitlock, our Director of Music?"

Marjorie extended her hand and her smile.

"My dear, you look like an angel in that frock. I hope Julian realises how lucky he is to have such a beautiful friend."

For the first time in many years Angela was flummoxed, not by what Marjorie said, but by the piercing eyes that seemed to look into the depths of her soul.

"I'm no angel."

"No my dear," the pause made Angela blush to her roots, "none of us are. Or perhaps that's not quite true Rector?"

Peter looked at her quizzically.

"Hebrews 13:2, *'Do not forget to entertain strangers, for by so doing some people have entertained angels without knowing it.'*"

"Marjorie knows the Bible far better than any of us; puts me to shame."

"Ah, now there is a subject worthy of discussion – shame…"

Debs cut her short.

"Not perhaps at the Rector's Garden Party, Marjorie. Where would it all lead?"

Angela took up the theme, and partially recovered her composure.

"It would be a shame not to spend some of the money in my purse. All for a good cause I'm told."

Peter invoked the name of Samaritans, and Marjorie chunnered, "Fine people, fine people."

Angela proffered her hand once more.

"So very nice to meet you both."

Julian led her away. She felt eyes boring into the back of her head. When she dared a quick backward look she saw the old woman studying her, and clung to Julian's arm a little tighter. To her dismay she realised that the overwhelming feeling inside her was not annoyance at Marjorie Whitlock, but a profound and sorrowful disappointment with herself.

The eight-seater taxi, bearing the logo of the Khans, eased gracefully up the drive and made a serene turn in the crescent before the house. Seven young Asian men disembarked, looking for all the world like a group come to join the fun. The driver remained behind the wheel, immobile and watchful, whilst the latest arrivals sauntered towards the stalls chatting and smiling amongst themselves.

Julian and Angela passed them with disinterest, they were absorbed in each other. When they came level with the stationary vehicle Julian felt a chill, despite the blazing summer sun, and every sense came alive. It was the old instinct that warned him of danger when he had gone into battle.

"Don't move!"

He judged the distance between him and the driver to be no more than five metres. They stared at each other; two pairs of stone-cold eyes locked in hatred. Each aware that he was in the presence of his mortal enemy. Angela sheltered behind Julian, wondered what the hell was going on. She tugged at his arm, but he shook her off roughly. The impasse was broken when screams and yells rent the air.

Julian saw what was happening and set off at a run. The young men had made for the stalls run by their fellow Muslims. Briefly, they harangued them and cursed them before they began to wreck and overturn the stalls. Most looked on in fear and horror.

Will Castle reacted swiftly. Picking up his sledgehammer from beside the bouncy castle, he strode towards them.

"Pack it in lads."

His Scouse accent was thick and ripe.

Dawood whipped out his knife and faced the oncoming soldier. Before he could strike, Faisal Hussain leapt over fallen wreckage, smashed the knife from his hand, and delivered a strike to Dawood's neck which brought him to his knees. Another assailant was about to attack Faisal from behind when Will smashed his kneecap with the sledgehammer. The other five came forward in a body just as Julian arrived. He went straight for the largest of them and struck at his eyes, leaving him doubled over and screaming in pain. Time was suspended for what seemed an eternity, but was merely seconds, then a car horn shattered the silence. Warily, the party poopers made for the taxi, carrying the boy with the broken kneecap, supporting Dawood, and leading their temporarily blinded companion.

Debs Marlborough rushed to Julian.

"I'm calling the police…"

"No mother!"

The tone of command in his voice made her shrink within. He looked for Peter Standish.

"Come on Pete, pull it together."

He strode to the edge of the drive with Will and Faisal in tow.

The Rector took a grip.

"Come on folks, let's help our friends to put their stalls back together. Very sorry that happened, but it's all over now."

Testosterone filled young men they may have been, but they barely glanced at Angela standing transfixed near the front door. They had arrived full of vim and piss, thinking that no one would challenge them; just a crowd of soft and effeminate Westerners their leader had told them. The driver negotiated his taxi down the drive, going at the slowest pace he could with his window down. When the cab drew level it was a toss-up who he hated more, Faisal Hussain the traitor to his brothers, or Julian Marlborough; surely that was he, the son of the M.P. who Mo' had described.

The vehicle departed, and Julian said,

"Who the hell is that?"

"Qadir Khan," said Padam Gurung.

It sounded like an echo fracturing the valley, as Faisal said repeated,

"Qadir Khan."

20

"There are many events in the womb of time, which will be delivered."
Othello Act 1: Sc. 3

"Still no sign of Jamal Ahmed?"

Kenny McInnes dulcet tones posed the question for the video conference.

Simon Reynolds was surrounded by his elite team.

"No luck yet, but good news on other fronts; if you can call it good news."

McInnes head was bracketed on the screen with that of DC Sue Jeffreys.

"Bring us up to speed, sir," she said.

"We had an incident at the local Mosque, last Friday after prayers. The Imam has been promoting inter-faith co-operation. Some of his congregation took exception. He was stabbed in a near-riot."

McInnes asked, "Any arrests?"

"None so far, but we've received valuable information from two witnesses. They both identified the person I believe to be the ringleader."

Passers-by sir?" Sue Jeffreys enquired.

"Not at all, two members of the Mosque."

"Wow, that's a result. They usually close ranks when we're on the scene. So who's the guy stirring the shit?"

"One Qadir Khan, by name Kenny."

"Anything known?"

"Not until now, but in the last few days his name has cropped up more than once. A member of the public called us about an incident at a church garden party on Bank Holiday Monday. Seems some lads took exception to a few of the Muslim faithful participating in the event, and smashed up their stalls."

Sue interjected, "Didn't the vicar call for assistance?"

"Not within his remit. This is the interesting bit. It was taking place in the grounds of our local M.P.'s country estate, Sir Hugh Marlborough. Apparently, it was all over very quickly. According to our public spirited parishioner, three of the locals took on seven Asian lads and gave them a going over. They retreated to their waiting taxi and buggered off. Guess who the driver of the cab was?"

Sue got there first, "Qadir Khan!"

"Sue Jeffreys, you have won tonight's star prize! Our belated informant told me that she recognised him. She uses Khan's taxis frequently, and he's driven her more than once."

Simon paused and looked across the room at a crisp and alert fellow who couldn't be seen on screen. They had conferred earlier about what he might reveal to his Wiltshire colleagues, but he wanted confirmation for what he would say next. He raised an enquiring eyebrow, and the Commander from the Counter-Terrorism Unit nodded assent.

"Keep this close to your chest Kenny. One of the witnesses to the stabbing of the Imam tells me that our friend Qadir is planning revolution. He's in no doubt that he's serious."

"Reliable witness?"

"Impeccable Kenny. Moderate and modest young man within the community; his and the wider world. As it happens, I knew him before all this kicked off."

"How so, sir?"

"Forgive me Sue, best I keep that to myself. Strangely, he turned up at the garden party ruckus as well, so our lady friend reported. She knows him for the same reason as I do, and she was very impressed. He was one of the three who sorted out the troublemakers. Disarmed one of them of the knife he was wielding; said he looked like a professional fighter. Quite a surprise to find a schoolteacher so adept."

The Commander coughed, and threw him a fierce look.

"Scrub that, you never heard me mention anyone's profession."

Kenny helped his colleague out.

"Who are these Khans, Simon? You mentioned a taxi firm."

"Owned by Qadir's uncle, Raza Khan. He's a big noise in these parts; fingers in a number of pies."

"Do you think he's in on it?"

"I don't see it, Kenny. Raza and I are old friends. Nothing proven – he's a cunning sod – but we've suspected for a long time that he's at the heart of a number of rackets. Terrorism? Not his style. Raza is notorious for his greed, it's money first and money last with him."

There was an extended silence before Sue spoke.

"So where do we go from here, sir?"

Reynolds eyes caught those of the Commander again.

"Friends, somewhat above our pay grade Kenny, have done a deep clean on Qadir Khan. We know everything down to the colour of his underwear. Until recently he owned a two-year old Land Rover Discovery. According to our friends at DVLA he transferred ownership a couple of days after the beheading of the Earl; sold it to a dealer on the Isle of Wight."

He didn't need to state the obvious.

"Reckon you need to trawl through CCTV footage, Kenny – Wilton, Salisbury and the routes to ferry ports."

"Aye, Portsmouth, Southampton and Lymington. It'll take a while."

"I know Ken. We've made a start on cameras between here and Salisbury."

Sue popped up again.

"So, guv, while we're waiting on that, are you going to pick Qadir Khan up?"

"Nothing substantial yet to confront him with. The witnesses at the Mosque say he was standing well away from the Imam when he was stabbed. As for the business at the church fete, he'll say he was the taxi driver and didn't have any idea what his passengers were going to do."

"What about the intel' on his plans to rule the world?"

Simon smiled at her hyperbole.

"We haven't a leg to stand on. It's hearsay, and he'll claim that it's someone with a grudge against him. No, we need something from the cameras to make a connection. Back to work folks."

The video conference ended, and rooms in two counties emptied. In Buckinghamshire the Commander was last to depart. Simon apologised for his slip of the tongue about Faisal Hussain's profession. The Commander was generous, and told him not to be overly concerned. After all it was confined to a few coppers.

In Salisbury police station Kenny McInnes left his DC in the office whilst he went to the coffee machine, and to update his Chief Super'. The person who leant against his desk was not Sue Jeffreys, but her male counterpart.

"A schoolteacher, eh?"

Not really his business to interfere, they weren't family. He gave the matter further consideration, and said to himself,

"Blood is blood."

The door opened, and Kenny McInnes spilt half of his coffee over the floor.

"Let me sort that for you, sir."

"That's good of you, Monty."

"No worries sir."

DC Monty Abbas went to the toilets for a bundle of tissues.

*

Angela was feeling relieved. During the last few days she'd been finding Julian's attention oppressive. She was neither ungrateful nor dismissive of him, but had lived in her own space for years and was used to dictating her own time. This evening he had excused himself, and she looked forward to being left to her own devices.

Around eight p.m. she had a terrible craving for curry. It was Friday, usually the end of her working week. An evening on which she always treated herself after five busy days on the job. She felt the need to doll up, and at least look as if she were going for a night on the town. On the spur of the moment she decided not to drive, and called for a cab to pick her up at nine.

"Hi, can you recommend a good Indian restaurant?"

The driver was one of Raza's crew, and under strict instructions to always recommend the *'Tamarind'*.

"Great!"

It was a short trip from the Old Town to the New, but far enough to make it worthwhile. She stood beside the driver's window and paid him.

"Hey, could you arrange for someone to pick me up between ten forty-five and eleven?"

"No problem, madam."

"Thanks."

'Madam', she thought, as he drove off. She was slightly concerned with that, was she starting to look old?

"Good evening, madam."

She smiled at the repetition, and decided it was nothing more than beautiful old world manners. The look of the restaurant was modern and shiny with lots of mirrors, no appalling flock wallpaper and dim lighting.

"Table for one, please."

"Certainly madam, this way please."

The handsome young waiter gave her a window table. In the sinking twilight of the evening he thought this decorative young lady might attract some passing trade.

Her time passed pleasantly, despite not having her London-based girlfriends to chat with. The food was excellent. Angela loved her prawns, and decided it was a night to pig out. She ate her prawn Pathia starter with slow relish, and lingered lovingly over her Gurkha Jinga, savouring each mouthful; the king prawns were die for. She put away a bottle of white wine, but remained competent enough to handle the young man who, egged on by his mates at a far table, came over and tried to chat her up. She paid her bill by ten-fifty, and sat with the remains of her wine waiting for the taxi to show up.

"Excuse me madam, your taxi is here. No rush."

Graciously, she said goodbye to the attentive staff, and stepped outside.

A hand waved to her from the taxi window.

"Where to, madam?"

Qadir Khan looked over his shoulder. He saw the extent of her beautiful legs in a short skirt, and felt a sense of arousal. Something else, he recognised her from Banksmore House. His injured friends may not have paid much attention to her, but while he sat waiting for them to smash up the garden party he had examined her closely.

Angela wasn't remotely tired.

"Do you know the *'Pineapple'* night club?"

She had no intention of going on the hunt. Men were forbidden, outside work. No doubt she'd get chatting to some local girls, and they could dance around their handbags.

Qadir was familiar with the club. It was halfway to Watford in a country area, so she gave him the go-ahead. It didn't take long to realise how interested he was in her.

He had made the connection with Julian, and that set his brain racing. There was something else. Qadir had a problem with women. He was a lithe, well-built and handsome young man who could lead others to damnation with unwavering self-confidence, but all his life he became tongue-tied and awkward with girls. He never mastered the art of approaching them. She could see him checking her out in his rear view mirror every hundred metres.

"You need to keep your eyes on the road."

Qadir blushed.

"You are so beautiful!"

"Thank you very much, kind sir; you're not bad looking yourself."

He tried to say something, but could only stammer, so she helped him out.

"Bet you've got a string of girls in tow. What's your girlfriend's name, or are you married?"

"Neither."

He tried to concentrate on the road and ignore his erection.

Angela was astonished, because he really was a good looking guy.

"You're kidding me, a great looking guy like you."

They were on a long road which cut through the countryside. What the hell. She wasn't short of money, but a bit of ready cash would be handy. She leant forward onto the front passenger seat and breathed into Qadir's ear.

"Do you want to fuck me?"

Qadir could hardly believe his ears. He assumed she was Julian's girlfriend, or fiancé or something. That clinched it; what a triumph to screw his enemy's girlfriend.

"There's a lay by down this lane, we could pull in there?"

"Let's do it. Just one thing, this is my business, and I'm not cheap."

A wave of disappointment overcame Qadir. Not because she revealed her profession, but because it must mean she wasn't attached to Julian. Still, he wanted her. For a moment he considered forcing her in this deserted spot. He gave up on the idea quickly. She wasn't one of Usman's wayward and vulnerable teenage girls, and she'd certainly know the name of the firm. Qadir couldn't risk attracting attention from the police, given his recent activities.

"How much?"

"Normally, two hundred and twenty for an hour; one twenty for half an hour. How long do you want?"

"Half...yes half an hour...please."

"Tell you what, I'll do discount for the lack of a comfy bed. Make it one hundred pounds."

They pulled deep into the lay by. Qadir nearly tripped over in his haste to get into the back. Angela had her box of tricks in her handbag out of sheer habit. Poor lad, he was as nervous as a cat. She took command of him and kissed him tenderly. Within a few minutes she was on her knees in the well. She sensed he was teetering on the edge, so she got beside him and unrolled a condom onto his tumescent penis.

Angela looked into his eyes and was nonplussed. She realised that they were a mirror image of Julian's; cold and without mercy. It quite unnerved her, and she wished that she hadn't made the suggestion to Qadir. She would get this over quickly. To her surprise, he didn't demur when she eased him onto his back and sat astride him. She didn't like the idea of being beneath this powerful man in a lonely spot. Angela gave it her best moves, and within five minutes he had ejaculated. She gave him a full and gentle kiss, and eased herself off him.

"That was lovely, thank you so much. How far is the night club?"

Qadir was adjusting himself.

"A quarter of mile down this lane. Do you still want to go there?"

"If you wouldn't mind."

"No, of course, whatever you wish."

She stepped out of the cab.

"How much do I owe you?"

"No, no, nothing."

"Come on, this is *your* business. How much?"

A little cockiness entered his demeanour.

"Tell you what, I give *you* discount. Call it ten pounds."

Angela gave him one of his own tenners back.

She was about to head for the night club door when he said,

"Any chance I could see you again? I mean, do you have a business number?"

Her old skills were in place, and she trotted out a mobile number that didn't remotely resemble her own. She was firm in her mind that she didn't want to encounter this punter again.

"Until the next time then," she lied.

"Will you be needing a cab home?"

"That's sweet of you. No thanks, I'm meeting a friend inside, she's giving me a lift home. Bye now."

He watched her as she exchanged pleasantries with the bouncer. Qadir's radio came alive, and he was in gear and off to another job.

A car had followed them. It too had entered the club car park. Even in the dark, the occupant had been able to photograph the couple, and he was well aware of what they had been up to in the lane.

So, young Mr. Khan had a penchant for screwing his passengers; he'd put that in his report to the guvnor. As for the totty, when he saw her highlighted in the club doorway he was envious, and rather puzzled. She was as smart as they come, real classy. What was a woman like that doing fucking taxi drivers?

"Takes all sorts," he said out loud. "Maybe she likes black cock."

He called in.

"Don't think he's causing any mischief tonight guv, just driving his taxi. Oh, well there is something he did which might qualify as mischief."

He gave a brief run-down of Qadir and Angela's back seat gymnastics, and he and his receiver laughed in concert.

"Yeh, yeh, I'll write it all up. Going off-duty now. They have, have they? Yeh, they'd have picked him up when he got back on the main road; only way out of here. Goodnight."

21

"The childing autumn, angry winter, change their wonted liveries, and the mazed world, by their increase, now knows not which is which."
A Midsummer Night's Dream Act 2: Sc.1

Will 'Conway' Castle drove the white Honda Goldwing sedately down the M25, with Julian *'riding bitch'*. The scion of Banksmore House wouldn't have liked that appellation.

They left Banksmore at one thirty in the morning, and aimed to park the motorcycle a discreet but manageable distance from the target. The Sat Nav was set for a circuitous route. They motored to the Potters Bar exit and then rose up Stagg Hill, heading for New Barnet. From there they cut across to the A406, in the direction of the A5. Closing in on their destination, they relied on the navigation system to guide them through an intricate maze of suburban streets to arrive in Mill Lane, West Hampstead.

Will had his doubts about the expedition, and expressed them openly to Julian. How did an act of personal revenge fit in with the larger strategy?

"We can kill two birds with one stone."

He described the little something extra he had in mind. That satisfied Will enough to follow orders. Whilst they cut through the warm night air he mulled over the personal motive. The Cap' had always been a law unto himself, focus on the job.

The law abiding pace of their journey meant that it was around two-thirty when the bike came to rest in Mill Lane. New York is famously the city that never sleeps, but that applies to any major city. The North London street was quiet when they dismounted and took off their helmets. Black balaclavas beneath were so snug, as to barely reveal their faces. Julian removed a backpack from one of the panniers. Will remained empty-handed, but inside his jacket was a handgun with silencer, and they both carried blades.

Walking briskly down Holmdale Road they approached West End Lane from behind. They met a junction enabling them to stride up Inglewood Road, which should have taken them out onto the Lane. Before they reached it, they swiftly took a left into a gap between the houses of Inglewood Road and the rear of the properties on West End Lane. With extreme caution, and all the skill gained in their experience of urban warfare, Julian and Will negotiated the obstacles between them and the greengrocer's shop. No words were spoken they relied upon hand signals, as familiar to them as their faces.

Without alar'ums or excursions, the companions found themselves pressed against the rear of the building. The alarm system was a joke. Julian extracted a cutter from his bag and snapped the ridiculously exposed cable. Even less secure was the back door, and Will had it open in a trice. Julian entered first, knife at the ready, and Will slid in behind him his handgun nosing ahead. It was so easy that it was laughable. They maintained their caution, passing out of the storeroom into the shop. Eyes became accustomed to the darkness; metal shutters covered the window obliterating the street lights.

Julian removed the explosive device from his bag. Handy having a quarry near home where you could *'liberate'* materials for your own amusement. Time to use his night vision googles, another gift from his former employers. He signalled to Will and they moved a stack of crates, reassembling them under the shop's main light switch.

The exploding-bridgewire detonator is more commonly associated with nuclear weapons, but it is also useful for commercial blasting in mines and quarries. Wikipedia tells us that:

"An EBW has two main parts: a piece of fine wire which contacts the explosive, and a high voltage high-current low-impedance electricity source; it must reliably and consistently supply a rapid starting pulse. When the wire is connected across this voltage, the resulting high current melts and then vaporises the wire in a few microseconds. The resulting shock and heat initiate the high explosive."

To trigger the device Julian had a low energy density capacitor equivalent to a compression generator, and roughly the size of coke can. Using low-impedance coaxial cable he made the necessary connections, the last one to the light switch. Neither were experts in this field, but hoped that when the shop opened the first thing done would be to switch the lights on. Fingers crossed, it would create the necessary current rise rate for the wire in the EBW to connect, and blow the place to Kingdom come. Even if it didn't it would scare the Romanian gangster shitless, as would the other present Julian would leave behind.

At the rear of the building, Julian undertook his final task. He admired his handy work, and thought it improved the place. They moved off into the darkness leaving a phosphorescent glow behind them which read, *'ALLAHU AKBAR'*.

Retracing their steps, they went part way along Holmdale Road, and took a left into Pandora Road. It seemed appropriate when you thought of the hell they were about to unleash from their *'box'*. Will smiled wryly when they turned into Narcissus Road, giving Julian a sideways glance. In a couple of minutes, Billy was firing up the Honda, and the Sat Nav led them away towards the A5. They went beyond Brondesbury, negotiating the ironically named *'Shoot-Up Hill'*, before taking a couple of 'B' roads to join the A404 to Wenbury.

Cezar Marinescu was rich, but old habits die hard. That's why he'd been up since three-thirty, and was heading for the shop. He usually got there for four-thirty and took deliveries of fresh fruit and vegetables. Cezar sighed, he was getting old, but he remembered the poverty and hardship of life under that Commie bastard Ceausescu. Oy, these democratic English with their Socialist prime minister wrecking business for everyone. Were they crazy? Cezar had more in common with Raza Khan than with the English. Take your opportunities to work hard and make money, and look after your family. He didn't have quite the sense of irony to appreciate that most of his hard work consisted of criminal activities. Always moaning and whining the English, and here his view was *Sympatico* with that of Imam Shirani.

What a wonderful country. It had given him a marvellous life, after the miseries of childhood existence in Romania under a totalitarian dictatorship. How the hell had these people managed to create the British Empire? From his sketchy knowledge of history, he concluded that the English owed a big debt to the Scottish and the Welsh for the part they had played in turning the Globe pink. Some of the crazy antics he saw from those living down the road in Kilburn left him unsure about the Irish.

Anyway, best make sure his produce was fresh, these West Hampstead women always badgering him.

"Is it fresh today? How old are these bananas?"

He wanted to reply,

"Stick it up your *pizda,* it's fresher than your husbands cock, and firmer!"

Bloody women round here, they were no better than that *curva* who'd run out on him from the flat above. If he ever found her she'd learn what fear really meant. As for the men, husbands or not, in Cezar's eyes they were all *gaozar* with arses like money boxes.

He parked his Bentley in Fawley Road, making use of the parking permit he'd paid a young couple for in one of the flats.

"Bloody keys," he muttered, but he managed to raise the grill over the door.

The shop door opened more easily, and he entered into the stygian gloom.

"Ouch! Who the hell left those there? That bloody useless English boy. Lazy bastard!"

Cezar had stumbled into the crates moved by Julian and Will. Employing his knowledge of German, he commented as he reached for the light switch,

"Black as the inside of a schwarzers arsehole."

A second later he got all the light he'd ever need.

It took forensics a while to distinguish and separate the remains of Cezar from the pulp of his fruit and veg. By the time they had finished, the gathering heat of the day meant that neither was distinctly fresh.

The Commander of the Counter-Terrorism Unit cast an eye over the Islamic inscription, so dextrously sprayed on the rear wall.

"Pointless to cover it up."

The Assistant Commissioner agreed.

"Yes, I'm told it's already on social media."

The Commander raised an eyebrow.

"Not exactly conducive to community relations."

"Excuse me sir, may I have a word?"

"Yes sergeant, what is it?"

"Well sir, we've knocked on every door within striking distance, and got nothing. Everybody seems to have been fast asleep, but one of my lads has turned this fellow up."

He pointed to a man standing with a constable twenty metres away.

"He's homeless sir, been dossing in doorways. Think he may have something."

The AC looked at the Commander, who said,

"Let's have a word with our sartorially challenged friend."

When the man was brought over he gestured to the inscription on the wall,

"Pakis eh, bastards!"

"Leave that! His name is Des Wilson, sir. Repeat to these gentlemen what you told me earlier."

Like a considerable number who found themselves on the streets, Des was ex-military. He looked the uniform up and down, and noted the insignia; some sort of crown above what looked like a wreath. Des wasn't *au fait* with the particulars of police rank, but he recognised a senior when he saw one. When he looked at the suited Commander his guts turned to ice. This wasn't someone you messed with. When the AC spoke he answered, but he kept his eyes on the man in civvies.

"Yes sarge. The explosion woke me; hell of bang."

"Go back a bit. Where were you pitched for the night?"

"Normally, I settle in this grocer's doorway, but he turns up early every morning and tells me to piss off. He's not a man you ignore, if you get my drift, sir. I've had a kicking off his lads more than once. Reckon they did me a favour."

Grimly, the Commander quipped,

"He won't be disturbing you anymore Mr. Wilson; he's asleep for eternity now. Go on."

Des warmed to the guy.

"Well, there's an empty property at the end of Narcissus Road, just where it meets Mill Lane. I've been kipping in the porch. Can't get in there, locked and bolted to buggery."

The Commander gave him a sharp look, and he decided he'd better come to the point.

"Thing is, sir, the bastards woke me up twice; once when they arrived and once when they left."

"Which bastards?"

"Bloody big motorbike it was, roaring up at half-two in the morning."

"How do you know the time?"

Des flashed his wrist to expose a rather nice watch.

"All I've got left. I kindly donated the house to my ex-wife!"

It raised a chuckle of recognition.

Des became precise, as if giving a report to his old platoon commander.

"Two men, black leathers and balaclavas; one tall and athletic, carrying a rucksack, and the other stocky and well-built. They had the bearing, sir."

The Commander eyed him keenly.

"What bearing would that be, Des?"

Yep, he was really starting to like this bloke; treated you with some respect.

"Military sir, it was written all over them; the straight backs and the step. You'd have thought they was doing drill the way they marched side by side up the street."

The AC spoke, "You said they woke you twice?"

"That's right sir. Punctual buggers, virtually on the half hour again. Back past the house a mite after three-thirty, and then the bike starts up again within a minute."

The Commander smiled sympathetically at Des for having his night's kip interrupted twice.

"Were you aware of anyone else passing by during the night?"

Des shook his head doggedly.

"Not a sausage, sir. Usually, you can't get a full night in around here, the bloody shenanigans that go on. Everyone's knackered though. Is this heatwave ever going to end?"

"Did you get a look at them, Des?"

"Not close sir. Definitely male. Caucasian sir, male Caucasians."

The AC was startled, "White you say. Are you sure?"

"No doubt sir. You couldn't see much of their features with those close-fitting balaclavas, but when they passed the street light you could see clear as day that they were white men."

The Commander placed an arm around his shoulder.

"My dear Mr. Wilson, you have given us treasure. We are going to look after you."

He addressed the AC.

"Would you arrange for your chaps to escort Mr. Wilson to my offices? He'll be received by a Ms Hudson."

Facing Des, he said,

"I'll let Ms Hudson know you're coming Mr. Wilson."

He saw the look of fear and doubt on his face.

"Let me set your mind at rest. When I say we'll look after you it's not a euphemism. We leave that sort of crap dialogue to Hollywood, eh Des. Are you hungry?"

"Yes sir."

He extracted a twenty pound note from his expensive leather wallet.

"Here you go Des. We'll tell the driver to find a café, and pull over on the way. You take your time, no rush. Off you go now."

"Much appreciated sir."

"Oh Des, one last thing. You didn't by any chance get a butchers at the motorcycle?"

"Certainly did, boss. Honda Goldwing, as white as they were. Always loved bikes sir, used to own a gorgeous Ducati. Had to be sold, went into the divorce pot. When I heard that engine I just had to have a gander. After they disappeared up the road I went round the corner, and there it was."

Eyes glittered as brightly as the noonday sun that was beating down upon them.

The Commander's voice had an excited edge, "Registration?"

"Sorry fellers, it was half two in the morning."

"That's alright Des, off you go with the sergeant."

They were not quite out of earshot when Des heard the AC say,

"It'll take a hell of a lot of time and manpower."

The Commander's normally soft voice rose.

"I don't give a fiddler's fart what it takes Gerry! Cameras, cameras, cameras, within a fifty-mile radius. Good day."

*

Julian slumbered deeply after his night's escapade. He awoke and put a hand under the duvet. Stiff as a bat's wing! Showering and dressing at record speed, he was ringing Angela's doorbell forty minutes later.

The bed frame shook alarmingly as he pulverised her. With a great cry he reached his climax, and subsided onto her in a state of blissful exhaustion. Angela felt frightened by the intensity of his passion, and she didn't dare move.

After a couple of minutes, he rolled off her, and stared at the ceiling with a horrible grin of self-satisfaction. If she had known, Angela would have been partially relieved that his smugness was not derived solely from the brutal intercourse he had subjected her to, but principally from the success of his mission.

Whilst taking a leak he listened to the radio. The explosion, and the demise of Cezar Marinescu, was all over the news.

"Put Sky on Ange, would you?"

"Charming," she thought, "almost fucks me to extinction and now all he wants to do is lie back and watch television. Complacent bastard."

She lifted the remote control from the bedside cabinet.

"Which channel?"

"News."

Sure enough, they were leading with the West Hampstead story. The reporter was in close-up, so she couldn't see much of the street. Suddenly, the cameraman pulled back, and the destroyed shop front hove into view as the reporter named Marinescu.

"Oh my God Julian, that's…"

He crossed his arms behind his head.

"Sure is."

"What the hell happened?"

"An explosion, terrorist bomb they say. Heard on the radio before I came out."

Angela sat bolt upright, her pendulous breasts bare and goose pimpled.

"My God! I could have been in the flat. Look, you can see the front of it collapsed over the shop."

She remained upright. Julian stretched out and fondled one of her nipples. When it remained soft he gave it up as a bad job.

"Thought you'd be pleased that the old bastard is dead."

She thought hard, was she glad? Angela was a businesswoman, in a dodgy and potentially dangerous business. Just a way of making very good money at the high end. She could handle herself, as she had done with Qadir. Marinescu's men had hurt her, but did she want people dead in return? No, that wasn't in her nature.

Angela knew that she put herself in the way of trouble all her life; principally trouble for her parents. A holy terror at boarding school, and wild at university. Only infrequently had she asked herself why she behaved in this way. Usually, she gave up the quest for self-revelation after about a minute and a half. This though, this shook her to her foundations.

Back in the studio they were discussing reports from social media that Islamic terrorists were behind the attack. The police would neither confirm nor deny the rumour.

Angela was puzzled.

"What would they want with a Romanian gangster?"

"In my experience, you never know what motivates them to latch onto some poor sod and make him wish he'd never been born. There again, the police won't confirm it, so it may not have been them. Could have been someone else."

He began to shake. In quick stages he reached a crescendo of awful laughter.

Angela looked down on him. He stopped as quickly as he had started. Their eyes locked, and she saw again the merciless pit that she had witnessed in Qadir's. She knew the truth in an instant. The mayhem being discussed on the television was Julian's work.

He pulled her to him, and turned her over onto her knees. This time he took her in more regulation fashion. Kneeling there, she tried to breathe slowly to prevent herself from vomiting.

22

"Shipwracking storms and direful thunder break.
So from that spring whence comfort seemed to come
Discomfort swells."
Macbeth Act 1: Sc. 2

Mid-September, and the unbearable heatwave broke at last. Flash floods tore through the country for four days. Journalists revelled in their usual outraged hyperbole about poor flood defences. Tommy O'Donnell carpeted the Minister for the Environment, who defended his actions with some spirit.

"Shit Tommy, this problem's been around for years. Bucket loads of cash have been sunk into projects by successive governments, even the Tories did their best. It's Britain Tom, it rains a lot. What do they want us to do, build a fucking roof over the Island?"

The P.M. waved a hand in surrender. He urged his minister to use the P.R. team, and assure the nation of their good intentions and best efforts.

One bright spot was that the ferocity of the storms brought a temporary cessation to the civil disorder that spread through the London.

The Marinescu clan took exception to their patriarch being boiled and roasted, like the fine potatoes he once purveyed. For a week, North London was a battleground with Asian shops firebombed and wrecked. Street battles raged outside mosques, as Muslims defended their sacred houses. The East End was plagued by a multitude of fires. Night was lit by the Asian businesses that were smashed and looted. Victims came, principally, from the Pakistani and Middle Eastern communities. The woeful ignorance of religion, of the troublemakers, meant that the innocent Indian community got lumped in with the *'enemy'*.

Seven days of violence left nineteen dead, and innumerable injured. The emergency services were stretched to breaking point. O'Donnell was cornered into permitting the military to render support.

"Support mind you. The Commissioner remains in overall charge, and he reports directly to me."

Surreptitious looks passed between Home Secretary Henry Longfellow and Jacob Greenwood, Defence Minister.

During their journey to the Commons, Jacob expressed his concerns.

"I do sympathise with him Henry. Can't say I'm that delighted to have the military on the streets."

"Absolutely Jake, only as long as is necessary. However, as my dear departed mother used to say, *'needs must when the Devil drives'*. Here we are."

In Banksmore Beelzebub had become an avid fan of the news. He watched the flames of destruction with delight. Soon he would undertake another mission with his trusty lieutenant – sergeant to be precise. Julian was permitting an interesting idea to pass through a period of fermentation before he acted upon it to foment further strife.

*

The second storm of the week was ferocious. Peter Standish considered cancelling the Parochial Church Council meeting. The hardy members responded with British grit, and expressed their determination to be there at eight.

Regular flashes of lightning made them worry that Bela Lugosi might materialise in their midst in the guise of Count Dracula. Marjorie Whitlock entertained the company with her erudition.

"Positively *'Sturm und Drang'*."

The wonderful Marj assumed that everyone else had the benefit of her excellent education. A thirst for knowledge sustained her on her pilgrimage towards wisdom.

Jack Preston enquired,

"Doesn't that mean something like *'Storm and Stress'*, Marjorie? Not sure of its origin."

Derek Fisher stealthily slipped a spot of something into his teacup from a hip flask.

"Sounds Kraut to me Marj."

Lips pursed in disapproval, Marjorie sailed onward.

"The title of a play by Friedrich Maximilian Klinger, 1776. Set during the American Revolution."

She digressed with a twinkle in her eye and her tongue firmly in her cheek.

"That poor benighted nation, lost in a sea of troubles. They wouldn't be in a mess if they hadn't rebelled against their lawful Sovereign."

Even a slightly sozzled Derek got that one.

Marjorie picked up her thread.

"*Sturm und Drang*. Klinger gives rather violent expression to our most turbulent emotions, and worships individuality and subjectivity over the prevailing order of rationalism. An apt metaphor for the prevailing zeitgeist, wouldn't you say Derek?"

"Yes…yes…absolutely Marj."

He hadn't a clue what she was on about.

Marjorie's face was alight with pleasure.

"And that is why we're blessed in having a Rector who draws people together in the fellowship that our Saviour taught us is the metre of our lives."

"What's that you say, Marjorie?"

"Marj was singing your praises, Rector. Telling us that you're our saviour."

Marjorie was mortified, and her cheeks became crimson.

"I say, steady on Marjorie, I'm hardly that."

She was most displeased with Derek.

Fiona Claymore-Browne saved the day.

"I think Derek may have misapprehended what Marjorie said. She was praising your determination to bring people together, and I say *'here, here'* to that."

Hands rapped the table. Debs Marlborough did not join in the chorus of approval.

"How kind you all are. You'll be putting me up for bishop next."

Marjorie's demeanour showed that she more than approved of such a jolly good idea.

"No beard!"

At last, Debs had found something she could agree on with the old girl.

Peter sat at the head of the table, with her ladyship opposite. He saw a shadow flit across her features, to be quickly replaced with her usual rictus-like smile. Perhaps she thought *she* was head of the table? Well that was okay, he didn't mind the lowly position one bit.

"To business. I want to get you off home as soon as possible. If we stay here much longer we'll be marooned, and I'll have to start saying, *"We're doomed, we're doomed!"*

Those old enough to remember laughed at his passable impression of the undertaker from the legendary comedy series *'Dad's Army'*. A tale of ordinary folk facing danger with stoic perseverance.

The mind-numbing agenda of a PCC meeting was waded through with just such determination. Item seven: *'Review of the Rector's Garden Party'*.

Peter thanked the Marlborough's for making their home available. Before anyone had a chance, Deborah Marlborough was into her stride.

"Thank you Peter. When Hugh and I agreed to open the grounds for the event, we were most pleased to do so. However, and I think that I speak for everyone present, as it transpired your arrangements went dramatically awry. If it weren't for Julian, and Will our gardener, things might have gone very badly indeed."

A stony silence sat over the committee. She felt encouraged to prate further.

"I do think that your invitation to communities outside our own was rather ill-judged. I'm sure we all feel that should be an end to these ecumenical activities."

Jack Preston was livid. He scarcely controlled his anger as his hand shot into the air.

"Firstly, Lady Marlborough, how dare you assume that you speak for everyone here. You certainly don't speak for me..."

"Oh well, that's hardly surprising Jack. It's difficult to discover something which you do agree upon – with anybody!"

Marjorie was about to leap to Jack's defence, but the Rector took command.

"Shall we try to keep this civil Jack? Deborah is perfectly within her rights to express her views."

He gave time for simmering blood to settle.

"May I ask if anyone else feels the same as Deborah?"

A terse 'no' came from Marjorie. For good measure she added,

"It wasn't just Julian and your gardener. That young Asian man was very brave."

Peter looked to Jack, who shook his head.

"Derek?"

"Very unfortunate; quite a rumpus, but not your fault Peter. As I said on the day, bloody good turnout of lovely and delightful people; all of them."

He summoned a look, for Debs benefit, that had once terrified board rooms.

Debs looked around, desperate for support.

"What about you Fi, surely you agree with my conclusions?"

Fiona had her head down, and was rubbing her palms mechanically. She wasn't afraid of Deborah. She wasn't really afraid of anything, other than Desmond finding out what had passed between her and Julian in the Snooker Room of Banksmore House.

"No Deborah, I'm afraid that I can't agree with you. What Peter did was wonderful, and I had a terrific day, despite that horrible interlude. Don't you see? Those men weren't attacking us, they were turning on their own brethren. That's why we need to continue to reach out to others, and embrace them in their difference. Dear Lord, haven't you been watching the news Deborah? Poor people dying and being injured in these dreadful disturbances. None of this is going to be solved by driving people further apart."

Fiona was stunned by her own eloquence.

One by one committee members showed their approval by rapping on the table.

When they had finished, Peter said quietly, "Jeremiah 7:

'But they did not listen or pay attention; instead, they followed the stubborn inclinations of their evil hearts. They went backward and not forward...'."

Jack intervened.

"I'd like to propose a vote; that we should continue with our inter-faith contacts and activities."

Fiona seconded the proposal.

Peter didn't want anyone to think they hadn't been given an opportunity to speak.

"We should discuss it before putting it to the vote."

Derek was reinvigorated.

"No need, from what I see, Pete. Got the greatest confidence in you."

"Anyone?"

They remained silent.

"Deborah, is there anything you wish to say?"

"No thank you Rector."

"Right, all those in favour; those against. Deborah, you haven't cast your vote."

Mustering all her dignity, she sat bolt upright and smiled engagingly.

"I shall abstain – on this occasion!"

Odds and sods were addressed quickly, and they went to their homes through the wild storm.

Hugh was livid when she told him how she'd been treated. Julian was in severe agreement, until he left the lounge; then he smiled with delight and said to himself,

"All grist to the mill, all grist to the mill."

Debs reserved especial venom for Fiona Claymore-Browne. She considered her treacherous and disloyal beyond belief.

"I tell you, Hugh, the social opportunities I've created for that woman, and she stabs me in the back. After all, what is she? The wife of a local farmer, a nobody. I'm not having her organising my social diary any longer – are you listening Hugh?"

"What? Oh, yes, damn bad form, get rid of her."

"First thing in the morning Hugh. God, I need a bath. Goodnight darling."

She exited the room with the relentless force of a Panzer division.

To her chagrin, Fiona got in first. Her early morning email thanked Deborah, but expressed regret that she no longer had the time to *'help you out'*, what with the farm and her increasing church involvement.

"Help me out! Help *me* out! How dare she, Hugh!"

For once in his life, Julian was sympathetic to his father, who sat like a mournful bloodhound wanting only peace and quiet in which to eat his breakfast. They stayed out of her way for the rest of the day, until her incandescent rage subsided.

Julian spent the morning in the gardens with Will He couldn't resist telling him what he had done to Fiona on the snooker table. Will thought it politic to laugh, but he was becoming less and less impressed by the Cap'.

"Pity really, I thought that Fiona and I might have enjoyed at least one more frame. See you later Will."

The temporary gardener watched his master's boy eat up the ground to the back of the House.

He plunged the garden fork into the baked earth, most of the storm water had just run off. An uneasy feeling crept over him. Being alongside Julian again revived memories. One in particular was markedly uncomfortable. It filled him with the deepest sense of shame. He closed his eyes, and found himself back in the desert. He heard her screams and moans; the girl, the girl from Bradford who they had violated in that burnt out building. Billy Conway had been a bad boy in his youth, but he'd never done anything like that. When he joined the Army it changed his life for the better. Why had he done that, participated in a multiple rape?

The mental image changed to a close-up of Julian's face. What was it about the guy? He could see the eyes drawing him in; mesmeric and devoid of any meaningful human emotion. Despite the temperature having dropped it was still an Indian Summer, but he shivered. He resolved to contact 'Lester', and see if they could make use of him elsewhere.

Striking the earth, the fork plunged into a soft spot. He recollected a line from a play they'd been taken to see by their trendy Drama teacher:

"I'll dig, but will anything grow?"

*

The mills of the police force resemble God's; they take an interminable time to rotate. Even with the availability of twenty-first century technology, trawling through footage from traffic cameras is incredibly time-consuming and tedious. However, bulldog persistence pays off. The work of the Wiltshire police, and their cousins in the Met, reaped rewards.

Kenny McInnes team had the harder job, having to explore numerous highways and byways; the lads in London got lucky. The Honda Goldwing was picked up twice; once on the A5, and then on the A404 at Harrow.

"Crafty buggers," said the AC, "off one way, then change direction."

Chief Superintendent Stevens risked a remark that might have been interpreted as impertinent.

"That's assuming, sir, that they are the people we're looking for."

"Quite right, Phil, might be perfectly innocent. Looks promising though. Get that registration checked."

It took no time at all to confirm that the motorcycle belonged to one Daniel George of Wendover, Buckinghamshire.

"Thank you Philip," said the AC, "leave it with me now."

He picked up the telephone.

"Commander please."

Daniel George was manager of the quarry. Occasionally, he put on a hard hat, but most days were spent at the computer. He made himself a mug of coffee and stared out of the window daydreaming.

It had been a great summer, out on the bike. The winding lanes of Bucks were a joy to twist through, and the trip down to Southern France with his boyfriend riding bitch had been fantastic.

The coffee went down his shirt front when the door went west. Daniel was confronted with counter-terrorism officers, dressed for the Moon, crashing into the office and screaming at him to get down on the floor. Ferocious looking weapons pointed in his direction.

He was frisked roughly, which in other circumstances he might have enjoyed, but his attention was focused on the state of his bowels. One of the assailants spoke sharply.

"Right, get him on his feet. Clear sir."

Daniel was pinioned between two officers. He was overcome with dread when he saw a shadow cast through the broken opening. It was replaced by a small and nondescript man in a well-tailored suit.

"Mind if I sit in your seat, sir?"

Calm fell upon them. Daniel imagined he had been transported to a cloister, which he was sharing with less than companionable monks.

"Yours, Mr. George."

It was a statement, rather than a question. It accompanied a grainy but distinct photograph lifted from the camera in Harrow; the registration mark was quite clear. His jailers let go of his arms whilst he perused the image.

"Yes...yes sir, it's my bike, but..."

He got no further.

"That's all we need to know...at this stage."

Daniel was detained for questioning under the Prevention of Terrorism Act 2005. Handcuffed and terrified, he emerged into blinding sunlight. His fellow workers watched on in utter astonishment. Two minutes later they drifted back to work, as the convoy of vehicles headed for London.

*

The word 'bugger' is popular with the forces of law and order, and Kenny McInnes expressed himself in a manner similar to the AC. In reference to Qadir Khan's former vehicle he said over the video link,

"First shot is from Cadnam, and the second is the bugger's Land Rover rolling onto the Lymington ferry. It's all a bit grainy, Simon, we can identify friend Khan as the driver, but there's no joy with the others."

"Brilliant result Kenny. So which direction was he coming from?"

He watched Kenny do his familiar chin-rubbing. Then he got all Shakespearean.

"Aye, there's the rub, Simon. He might have come down the A36 from Salisbury, but he could have been travelling east from the Bournemouth area, or coming west from your direction. The position of the camera is no helpful. Still nothing at your end? What about your motorway cameras?"

Simon shook his head.

"Nothing on the M25 or M3, so we checked the M4. I know it beggars belief, but the buggers were switched off for maintenance; sod's law eh. If they went that way they'd have probably cut across to the M3 at Basingstoke. Nothing to help at all; too many cameras switched off at night for cost-cutting."

A gloom spread amongst the officers. Simon Reynolds was having none of it.

274

"I'd say we've enough to pull friend Qadir in for a little light questioning. At the very least, we know he worked alongside Jamal Ahmed. We'll ask him if he enjoyed his hols and who he went with; not to mention what prompted him to sell his motor on the Isle of Wight."

Sue Jeffreys took up the thread.

"Wonder how they got home, Simon?"

"Almost certainly trains and boats and planes – well, not the latter I hope. DVLA has a record of another vehicle he owns. It was bought the week after the Earl's demise, in the Midlands; Audi Q7, black, 2017 mark."

An array of whistles and admiring comments filled the air before Kenny quietened his team down.

"Likes his motors, does this boy. A bit bloody expensive for my pocket."

"Probably for him too, if he's had to buy an older version. They were minimum fifty grand new for that model. Seems he purchased it from a cousin who's in the trade in Leamington Spa. Right Kenny, we've got work to do. I don't think he's going anywhere tonight, so we'll give Mr. Khan a wake-up call tomorrow morning, nice and early."

The video link was closed, and they set about planning Qadir's day.

*

Commander Giles Wentmore led the interview.

"Mr. George, you say you discovered your motorcycle had been stolen when you woke this morning. Why didn't you report it to the local police immediately?"

The room was windowless and oppressive, and Daniel set about some rapid thinking. Damn Julian Marlborough, he had caused nothing but trouble for Daniel ever since they'd met on their first day at High Heath School, Hampstead. It began with relentless bullying, not the physical kind, but persistent humiliation as a daily ritual.

Daniel had known since the age of nine he was gay, and when he saw Julian he fell in love with him. The worst moment came in the second week of the school year. He had trailed after Julian from day one, and couldn't tear his eyes from him in adoration. Julian soon got sick of it, and one break time another boy said in front of the gang,

"Daniel never takes his eyes off you Julian. He looks at you as if he wants to interfere with you."

Everyone screamed with laughter, and another lad cried,

"He wants to toss you off!"

Julian was livid. He gave Daniel a push in the chest, and shouted,

"Fuck off, and don't hang around with us again."

For the next two years they were passing strangers. When they became older, they were accommodated to one another through school productions. Daniel couldn't act for toffee, so he involved himself in stage management. He watched Julian triumph in an array of productions.

"Until that other lad arrived in sixth form…"

For a second he thought he'd spoken the words out loud. Best get his mind in gear. How the hell could he get out of this, without letting them know that he had succumbed to Julian's offer to buy the Goldwing from him for an unjustifiably high price? He paid cash, and the transfer document never reached DVLA.

He adopted an air of self-confidence that he didn't feel.

"Did you see the work on my desk?"

He knew the Commander hadn't. The question was rhetorical.

"Whichever thieving toe rag nicked it would have been well away, so I decided I'd report the theft during my lunch hour. Doubt there's much chance of me seeing it again. The money I spent on that bike; top-end spec' you know."

"My sympathies for your loss."

'Bugger' was growing in popularity by the hour, and Daniel said internally,

"Need to be careful with this bugger."

Then he almost defecated.

"You have access to explosives at the quarry."

The bald statement caused him to become rigid, which did not pass unnoticed by those watching him on camera next door.

"Sod this for a game of soldiers! What's the bugger been doing?"

"Which bugger would that be, Mr. George?"

"Marlborough, Julian bloody Marlborough. I sold him the sodding the bike, and...and the EBW."

"EBW, Mr. Smith?"

Giles Wentmore knew what it meant, but wanted to hear it said for the benefit of the tape.

Daniel gave a run-down on the detonation device and its potency.

"Thank you Daniel, I appreciate you dispelling my ignorance."

Daniel wasn't that stupid, and he cursed this frightening man.

"Now Daniel, who is Julian Marlborough?"

The brown-trousered quarry manager looked at him with incredulity. He couldn't conceive that not everyone was Buckinghamshire county set. Giles Wentmore resided in a rather nice and discreet apartment block not far from Whitehall.

"Hugh Marlborough's boy, of course. I know he's ex-military but, dear God, what the hell has he done?"

Giles was unresponsive, as he marshalled the facts.

"The bearing," that was what Des Wilson had said, "they had the bearing."

The surname rang bells.

Daniel assisted him unintentionally.

"Sir Hugh Marlborough, M.P. for Wenbury and Cranchurch. They live in a village called Banksmore, just outside those towns. Lovely house."

Wentmore had already come to a number of decisions. He would have to run them by 'Lester', and then they could act upon them.

"Thank you, Mr. George, for your co-operation. You've been most helpful; I don't think we need trouble you anymore. We will want a written statement, and you will need to sign the Official Secrets Act."

He drew closer across the table, his hard eyes boring into Daniel.

"I must impress upon you that any breach of the Act, however minor, will result in your detention."

Giles stood and offered his hand, which Daniel took.

"My profound apologies for the considerable discomfort we've caused you. We are required to pass the information you gave us about vehicle irregularities, and the illegal sale of explosives to your local police. It will be up to them how they respond. We will, however, make it abundantly clear to your employers that your arrest and detention by us was merely to assist us in our enquiries. We exonerate you completely of any wrongdoing. Don't worry Daniel, word will soon get round your workplace. Wouldn't be surprised if you don't become some sort of folk hero amongst your mates. If you'd go with Fiona here she'll make all the arrangements, and then she'll drive you home. You must be hungry sir?"

"Bit peckish."

"Fiona, get the canteen to send something up for Mr. George. Glass of wine Daniel, red or white?"

"Red would be perfect, thanks."

Fiona Hudson put him at his ease whilst she drove him to his home in the Chiltern Hills. Soon they were sharing their experiences of the South of France.

She was one of the unit's top drivers. Everyone, who wasn't in the know, asked her how it could have happened.

Cruising along the M25 at a steady seventy she inexplicably clipped the tail end of lorry. It was strange, because they were on a stretch which was almost devoid of traffic. She was able to tell that to the enquiry, because she had checked her rear view mirror very carefully. Her Volvo went into a spin towards the solid concrete barrier of the central reservation. She managed to manoeuvre it so that the passenger side struck first. The impact caused the whole side to cave in, and Daniel was crushed. Fiona emerged with only minor injuries. Somehow the air bag had failed to inflate, so Daniel was entirely unprotected, and dead.

She grunted in satisfaction, and crossed the carriageway to the safety of the embankment.

Thankfully, Fiona had no need to resort to the contents of her handbag to finish the job.

*

Residents of Old Beaconsfield are a cut above – in their opinion. If you live in their midst you are on the *'team'*. Race, nationality, colour of skin and religion are irrelevant. Your very presence shows that you are made of the right stuff; money. That's not to say that prejudice doesn't lurk beneath the surface.

The Khans had lived there for ten years, and to the casual eye they were fully integrated into the community. Raza maintained a high standard of decorum in his household. Whilst he made sure that everyone kept his business affairs within the family, he also insisted upon genuine civility and good neighbourliness.

Simon Reynolds hammered on his front door at six in the morning, having stationed officers round the back. Curtains twitched across the street. If pressed, more than a few of the neighbours would have admitted to a delightful feeling of *schadenfreude* at seeing the police on Raza's doorstep.

Raza was an early bird, like Qadir. He waddled down the hallway, wondering who the hell was knocking seven bells out of his expensive door. When he peered through the spyhole his blood froze. He gathered himself quickly and unlocked the door.

"Good morning Mr. Khan."

Simon was inordinately formal so he responded in kind.

"Good morning Mr. Reynolds, how may I help you?"

Simon held out a paper.

"A warrant to search your premises."

"How many times Mr. Reynolds, I'm just a business man."

"Nothing to do with your business Raza, we're pursuing enquiries into murder and possible acts of terrorism."

The blood drained from his chubby cheeks.

"Is your nephew Qadir in the house? We'd like to interview him."

The Chief Inspector knew very well that Qadir was inside. Special Branch watchers confirmed that he hadn't been out all night. Raza stepped aside without being asked. That boy was going to destroy everything he'd built.

"In the bathroom Mr. Reynolds. Third door on the right."

Raza was torn by his oath to his dead brother, and the folly of his nephew. Sod it, the stupid boy was on his own.

"May I wait in your sitting room, Raza?"

"Seems you can do what you bloody well like if you have that warrant. This way."

Raza wanted to get out of his hallway. He couldn't bear to watch two policemen from the armed response unit padding up the stairs, weapons drawn.

Qadir heard the exchange below, and had no intention of resisting. He reflected upon the situation with admirable swiftness as he dressed, and concluded that though they were on to him it could have been for a number of reasons. Perhaps someone had reported the trouble at Banksmore. Well, he was just a taxi driver, and they were passengers he'd never met.

His mind turned to recent events outside the Mosque, and he connected it with the name Faisal Hussain. The schoolteacher, yes, the cops were here because of his treacherous mouth. Through a trail of distant, and then closer and closer, relatives DC Monty Abbas' information made its way across county boundaries. What was needed was a cool head, and a polite response to their questions.

He entered his uncle's sitting room flanked by the two officers. For all the world it looked like he was inviting them to join him for coffee. Raza stared at him in something akin to admiration. The boy had big balls, he'd say that for him.

"Qadir Khan?"

The proud young man acknowledged his identity.

"We're pursuing enquiries into a recent murder."

"So," he thought, "Shirani has died after all. May his apostate soul burn in a thousand fires for eternity."

"May I ask, who is the victim?"

When he heard the response it was all he could do to retain his equilibrium.

"Edmund, seventeenth Earl of Seaforth."

Reynolds watched him like a hawk, but could discern no reaction.

"We'd like to ask you some questions about Jamal Ahmed."

Though too close to home, he felt like laughing. How they had connected Jamal with Seaforth's execution was as yet beyond him. Jamal was sleeping with the fishes. He doubted they could make too much of a connection between him and the aquatic loudmouth.

"We can question you here, Mr. Khan, or at the police station."

"I would be more than happy to co-operate with you Mr?"

282

"Reynolds, Chief Inspector Reynolds."

Qadir knew who he was; that name too had come through the grapevine of Monty Abbas.

"Thank you Mr. Reynolds. I think that my Uncle Raza has been inconvenienced enough. You wish me to go with you now to your station?"

"If you wouldn't mind Qadir. May I call you Qadir?"

"Of course Mr. Reynolds."

He waited for an invite to call Simon by his Christian name. No such invitation was forthcoming.

"Sorry Uncle, you'll have to find cover for my first shift. See you later."

He led the policemen out of the house and stepped into their car with a friendly smile upon his face.

Simon Reynolds had concentrated on Qadir's eyes throughout their encounter. Amity was absent.

*

Des Wilson was fished out of the Thames by a river patrol near Greenwich. Eventually, the authorities ascertained who he was; another ex-soldier lost and alone in civilian life. Many received excellent care from the numerous charities that did fantastic work on their behalf, but this one had slipped through the net. The pathologist reported that Des was as pissed as a rat when he drowned.

In response to police appeals, a lovely young woman called Fiona said that she and her boyfriend had seen Des around eleven, two nights previous. He was reeling, and swaying far too close to some railings on the riverside. Case closed; drunk as a skunk and fell into the water.

"Poor sod," a fresh-faced constable remarked, "wrong place at the wrong time."

Many a true word is spoken in jest.

In West Hampstead a sergeant and one of his constables had separate interviews with a uniformed Commander. A suited and booted gentleman sat in the background observing.

"This Marinescu business on your manor has become an issue of national security."

He allowed the words to weigh heavily.

"We thought we were on to something with your homeless feller. Good work there, finding him so quickly. All that motorbike stuff turned out to be a red herring. It's out of our hands now. I don't need to tell you this affair has caused all hell to break loose."

He steered the sergeant towards early retirement and a handsome pension.

"After all Bill, you've nearly twenty-five years in, and it doesn't get any easier, does it?"

Bill wasn't permitted time to discuss it with his wife. He could see which way the wind was blowing, and he jumped at the chance.

Neither did Constable Miller demur from the offer made to him.

"Impressive record already, Andy. There's a sergeant's vacancy coming up in the West Midlands, we'd like you to take it."

Andy was a well-educated and perceptive young man. Bill had noted the wind direction, Andy nearly choked on the bad smell it was carrying. It made him afraid.

"When do I start?"

*

The Metropolitan Commissioner of Police and Commander Giles Wentmore sat comfortably, sipping a rather nice thirty-odd year old Amontillado from Bodegas Emilio Lustau, which their host had so kindly provided. The taxpayer contributed handsomely to the lifestyle of some politicians; they would have had a collective fit if they'd known how much the bottle cost.

"We needn't go into detail Giles, I'm sure you've tied up all the loose ends. Ronnie, your boys happy?"

The Commissioner savoured his sherry.

"Mm, one promoted and one retired. Getting like a bloody revolving door these days."

Lester rose from behind his desk.

"Is there anything else I need to know?"

Giles Wentmore wasn't one for mincing his words, and he certainly wasn't afraid of politicians.

"The whole shebang could have gone tits up with your boy blowing the Roma to Kingdom Come; needs putting on a leash. What in God's name made him come swanning into Town to cause bedlam?"

Lester was in absolute agreement, but kept his counsel. He hadn't been party to the decision to team *'Castle'* up with the Marlborough boy. Whilst he agreed, retrospectively, he was starting to have doubts.

"Got it in hand, Giles. You have to admit, it caused a stir. The powers-that-be think it no bad thing for our agenda to be fast forwarded. Everyone's getting a trifle edgy. If we're going through with this, better sooner than later."

Giles wasn't prepared to let it go.

"Covering up indiscretions like that is a hell of job. We've enough on our plate without having to pull our own side out of the self-made *merde*. Confine the bugger to out-of-town activities, or I personally will cut his balls off."

Lester arched an eyebrow.

"Consider it done Giles. Thank you both for popping over at such short notice. Need to get along now, another late-night sitting in these difficult times."

Handshakes were exchanged, and Lester called for his papers from his private secretary.

Ten minutes later he plonked himself on the front benches, and the Deputy Speaker called him to start the debate.

"The Home Secretary, Henry Longfellow."

*

"Nice collection of motors your Uncle Raza has in the driveway. The Jag is a beauty, isn't she? Tell you what though, I'd go for that Audi Q7 every time; a fair bit older, but a gorgeous drive."

Qadir saw no reason to lie.

"That's mine, Mr. Reynolds, you've got good taste."

Simon kept his cool with the cocky young sod.

"Use it in the business do you?"

"Oh no, purely for personal pleasure. As you said, it's lovely to drive – and a beast."

They had danced an opening number. Simon went deeper.

"Owned it long, Qadir?"

The black eyes didn't flicker.

"Bought it quite recently, from a cousin in Leamington Spa. He's in the trade you know, gave me a very nice discount."

Qadir was sure Reynolds knew where it came from. So many people lie when they have no need to, Qadir told him the truth.

"How come you sold your Land Rover Discovery on the Isle of Wight?"

The sudden bluntness of the attack failed to shake Qadir's self-possession.

"Spur of the moment thing. I'm a spontaneous sort of guy."

"Must have been a real drag."

Qadir looked at him quizzically.

"A drag?"

"You and your three mates having to get back home without a car."

Qadir laughed out loud.

"They weren't pleased with me Mr. Reynolds, bitched at me about ruining their holiday."

CCTV must have clocked the vehicle somewhere, that was the only explanation. He'd have to be more careful, next time he went on a mission.

"A good holiday was it - otherwise?"

"Excellent Mr. Reynolds. You know the Isle of Wight? So beautiful and peaceful."

In response to Simon's next question, Qadir gave him a run-down of the highlights of their holiday. Just as Qadir was starting to wonder Simon said,

"The names of your three companions, please."

He had been ready for this, even before they left Wycombe on their murderous expedition. He willingly gave the names and addresses of three cousins in the Midlands who could be relied upon to say the right thing. There was a pause whilst a Detective Sergeant left the

287

room with the piece of paper containing the three jolly holidaymakers' details.

The DS reappeared and resumed his seat.

The name reverberated throughout the room.

"Jamal Ahmed!"

Qadir lay back in his seat, an impertinent grin on his handsome face.

"Jamal, Jamal, Jamal, what have you been up to?"

"Who said he'd been up to anything?"

"Come off it, Chief Inspector, a busy man like yourself doesn't bother with air heads like Jamal unless he's been a seriously bad boy. What's he done?"

"Funny you should mention heads, Qadir. Read the papers do you? Watch the news on telly?"

"Occasionally, Mr. Reynolds, but I try to avoid it most of the time. It's very depressing, such a bad world."

Simon had handled numerous hard cases in his time on the force. He was usually imperturbable to provocation, but this arrogant and sardonic creep was beginning to rattle him.

"The Seventeenth Earl of Seaforth, beheaded in his private chapel by so-called believers in your God!"

He saw immediately that he'd struck a nerve.

Qadir burned with rage; how dare this Christian refer to the name of Allah. He had to struggle with himself to regain self-control.

"You suspect Jamal of doing this?"

"Did Jamal Ahmed travel to the Isle of Wight with you, Mr. Khan? Have you ever been to a place in Wiltshire called Tisbury? Seen the beheading on social media, Qadir?"

The three questions came at him like machine gun fire.

"No, no, and yes. You wish me to be entirely truthful, Mr. Reynolds, so I will tell you this. I have heard of Tisbury."

Simon and the DS waited.

"Our Member of Parliament, Sir Hugh Marlborough, uses the taxi firm to ferry him around. To the best of my knowledge, we have conveyed him to somewhere called Tisbury. My Uncle Raza will be able to fill in the details."

The DS dripped sarcasm.

"Remember every destination your drivers go to, do you?"

Qadir looked at him as if he were dirt beneath his shoe.

"Mohammed Nawaz!"

They were surprised to hear that name.

"My cousin Mo' drove him there, and was terribly impressed by the premises to which he delivered Sir Hugh Marlborough; said it was a castle. Mo' bored us all to death for days. Which reminds me, what progress are you making on finding the animals who inflicted such an outrage on my poor cousin."

The DS let rip again.

"We'll let you know when we think it's appropriate. As for your cousin, he's got a charge sheet as long as your arm..."

Simon rested a hand on his junior officer, they were getting away from the point. He almost admired Qadir for the expertise he had shown in deflecting the conversation away from himself.

"Tell us about Jamal, please."

Qadir gave the request due consideration, and gladly informed them of his working relationship with the late taxi driver. They had socialised a few times, but always as part of a group. No-one in their community would say otherwise.

"Why am I here Mr. Reynolds?"

Simon trod carefully.

"We have received information, Mr. Khan, that – how can I put this – you're not a happy bunny?"

"I am not any sort of creature, and certainly not a rabbit. I am as human as you are."

"That's not what I meant to infer, and you know it. Do you like living in Britain?"

"What an extraordinary question. I've never lived anywhere else; I was born here. This is racist Chief Inspector."

"My apologies, I express myself badly. Are you comfortable with the prevailing values and ways of the society in which you live?"

The question actually gave Qadir serious food for thought. He propped himself up on the table that divided them.

"A philosophical question. Is anyone entirely happy with the world in which they have to live?"

He weighed his next comment carefully.

"I think that your real question is, how far would I be prepared to go to change that which I dislike in my society."

Simon waved his hand in a circular motion.

"Qur'an 6: 151 says:

'and do not kill a soul that God has made sacrosanct, save lawfully.'

What more can I say Mr. Reynolds? I am a good son of Islam, and my life is guided by its teachings."

Simon knew that he was in delicate territory.

"Problem is Qadir, there are some people out there, in your depressing and bad world, who think it's up to them to decide who and what is sacrosanct, and what is lawful. Don't misunderstand me, Qadir, they're not only followers of Islam, you can find them in all strands of society."

He stared deeply into the amused, if unfriendly eyes.

"Are you one of those people, Qadir Khan?"

Another ridiculous question, he was hardly going to admit it, was he.

"Is there anything else you would like to ask me, Mr. Reynolds? We really are shorthanded at the moment. My Uncle Raza will be furious if I miss another shift."

He knew he had won, and his conceit got the better of him.

"Besides I need the money to put fuel into my beautiful car."

He looked down imperiously upon the DS.

"What sort of motor do you drive?"

Simon got in quickly before his purple-faced DS could leap across the table and fetch Qadir a right-hander. He stood up and faced the suspect.

"Thank you Mr. Khan. You've been very helpful, and we've
taken up far too much of your time. If you'd take a seat in the waiting room, we'll find someone to drive you to Beaconsfield."

Qadir's smirk was unbearable.

"No need, I'll call a taxi!"

"Little bastard! Up to his neck in the business."

"A more than apt anatomical reference, Paul."

Qadir had called Bakir, instead of a taxi. He wanted to utter words of caution to his associate. Sitting in the passenger seat, one name went through his head, over and over, Faisal Hussain, Faisal Hussain.

23

"When sorrows come, they come not single spies but in battalions..."
Hamlet Act 4: Sc. 5

So says Shakespeare's King Claudius. He should have known, when he reaped the consequences of bumping off Hamlet's dad and shagging his widow.

What a funny old lot we humans are. We open our mouths with alarming regularity, spouting all sorts of drivel with nary a thought for the consequences. We go about our daily business enacting processes which we believe will satisfy our wants and our desires. Lip service is paid to the rights of others.

The Law of Unintended Consequences affects those who habitually commit themselves to actions in a state of wilful illusion and self-delusion. Some receive unexpected benefits, and some are hit with drawbacks.

This was not the case with Usman Khan. He knew precisely what he was doing and the potential consequences. Like the usurping Danish king, he deserved everything he got. Fictitious king and flamboyant paedophile both knew they were engaged in criminality, of a particularly vile kidney, and got their just desserts.

Sir Hugh Marlborough told the tale with relish, whilst attacking his lamb cutlet.

"Extraordinary to find grammar school girls involved. Usually, it's the more vulnerable types who are seduced into this sort of trafficking. Seems the police have arrested five men; all of them taxi drivers for the Khans. One of them related to the boss."

Julian and Angela lay down their cutlery. With malice in his heart, Julian hoped it was Qadir who was getting his comeuppance. Angela felt sick at the thought she had been intimate with a man who molested children. It was Debs who asked the question.

"Related in what way, darling?"

Hugh looked at her as if she were stupid.

"His brother of course! Osman or Usman, something like that. Anyway, well and truly banged up, and I hope they throw away the bloody key."

Then he was off on a familiar rant.

"How the hell social services miss this sort of thing is beyond me. Fair enough, they weren't involved with the grammar girls, but I understand that the other poor kids were well-known to them."

Debs stemmed his flow.

"Hugh, it's about time you and your colleagues put a stop to this sort of thing. Not to mention the rest of the dreadful behaviour we have to put up with from these people."

He exchanged a significant glance with Julian, that didn't pass unnoticed by Angela. A tiny chill went through her, and she asked herself again what she was doing there.

Debs reference to *'these people'* was a euphemism for those British citizens whose skin was a darker hue, and their religion not her own. Had Peter Standish been present he might have been tempted to assert that she had no religion.

"And your Rector, mother, encouraging us to play games with them."

Hugh shot him a warning look. He couldn't bear another tirade from his wife about the Rector's iniquities. Surprisingly, she didn't rise to the bait, instead she addressed her guest.

"What do you think about this, Angela?"

Hugh beamed at the young woman. She really was a most attractive sort. He envied his son, who he assumed was bonking her something rotten.

Angela had more experience of men at their most intimate than anyone present. Some girls discriminated in who they would accept as punters, but she didn't. Clients were welcomed from a multitude of nationalities and races. So long as they were clean, polite and paid their money they could buy her by the hour. Choosing her words carefully, she said.

"It's a disgusting business, and I hope these men get what they deserve, but…"

Hugh challenged her sternly.

"…but what? There are no buts."

"Darling, do allow Angela to finish. You have no idea what she was going to say. Do go on, dear."

Unknowingly, she shared the view of Padam Gurung. People are to be judged by their actions, not by the colour of their skin, or any other such facile notion.

"What those men have done to these children is wrong and hateful, BUT it's they as individuals who bear the responsibility for the consequence of their actions, not their families or their neighbours, or their entire race."

It was an unanswerable argument, but it didn't go down well. Debs gave Julian a meaningful look, and he couldn't hold his mother's gaze. He was tremendously conflicted between adhering to his warped values, and the feelings for Angela that exhausted him at times. Julian did not possess the personal insight necessary for comprehending what he felt. His sexual encounters were legendary amongst his closest buddies, but no-one had ever satisfied him like Angela. Julian thought he might be in love. Truth be told, he was in a state common to most men and women who reach a point in their lives where they realise they have been alone for too long. He was in lust. Volcanic lust passing through an extended eruption, but whose explosive vibrancy would one day subside.

Debs broke the uncomfortable silence.

"Just look at the time. Hugh, when are you due at the House?"

"Not 'til six. Angela, might I tear Julian away from your side? Spare me ten minutes in the study, Jules?"

The lunch party broke up, and Angela went for a stroll in the grounds.

"What are they complaining about, it had the desired effect?"

Julian's supercilious tone grated on his father. For the first time in his life he realised his son was no longer subservient to him. A revelation fell upon him. This man did things to others that were best left unsaid, or even thought about too deeply. Hugh Marlborough had been a tough guy in the city and in the House, when he was in his prime, but the terrorist activities of his son were a new world to him, and not a brave one. Thinking back to his parents and grandparents he could not discover a penchant for that sort of violence and hatred in his ancestors. Subconsciously, he laid it at his wife's door.

"The Head of the C. T. Squad is livid. It was a complex task cleaning up after you. I'm told that he said he'd personally cut off a piece of your anatomy if you strayed into Town again."

Fear didn't enter Julian's head, but wisdom did. He knew better than to try and ride roughshod over security services.

"Confine yourself to local activities, my boy. You're doing a grand job, and contributing valuably towards our next and final step. Anything on the boil at the moment?"

"It just so happens there is, and your lunchtime chat has confirmed me in an idea I've been mulling over."

"Oh, do tell."

Will Castle watched her following the edge of the lawns, pausing now and again to look at late flowers. She looked unhappy in these surroundings; not so much out of place but uneasy about something. He was in the lee of the trees, clearing up this and that to keep Hugh's grounds in the good order he obsessively liked.

He was happier than he'd ever been. The simple and straightforward work he undertook brought him a peace he had never known. His early life in Liverpool had been all hustle and bustle, and the army much the same. Will thought he might be quite content to live out his days in this present manner, provided it could be far away from Julian Marlborough and what he was being asked to do. He accepted a soldier's duty to kill when necessary, and he felt that the undercover work he'd agreed to do was worthwhile. Watching people and reporting back, well that was all part of the game. Covert operations within your own country to blow people up and murder them? No, he couldn't square that circle.

"Hello Will."

"Hi, Angel," he blurted out of his daydream.

She threw her head back and roared with laughter.

"You're the second person in these parts to mistake me for one of those."

"Sorry love, my mind was somewhere else, it slipped out."

Angela looked at him forensically, and he knew she was assessing him. She was more than familiar with his type; a nice bloke who was lost. They responded to her tenderness with astonishment and gratitude.

"Tell me something, Will, where's the Scouse accent gone?"

She really liked the shy smile he gave her.

"Ahh, I only use that for effect, depending on where I am and who I'm with. *Know worra mean like?* Been around the world so much, it just disappeared for the most part. What about you, enjoying your new life as lady of the manor-in-waiting?"

Angela stared at her feet, and despite her natural tan she looked pale.

"I don't know what I'm doing here, Will. I don't know why I stay. My debt to Julian is well and truly paid."

Will Castle would have made a good Samaritan; he knew when to listen.

"May I tell you something Will?"

He gave her space.

"That business in West Hampstead, you know, the killing of Marinescu – I believe that was Julian's doing!"

Will propped his lopping shears against a tree, and wondered if Angela was aware of his participation. When he was steady enough to look her in the eye, he could see that she hadn't a clue about his involvement.

"What on earth makes you think that?"

"He as good as told me. Not in so many words, but in his manner and his look."

Will thought a prolonged discussion of the issue would not be a good thing.

"I won't argue with you. You know what you saw."

Her eyes filled with tears.

"I'm frightened Billy, I'm frightened."

He believed her, because of the inadvertent use of his old Christian name.

A crisp voice boomed across the lawns.

"Will, Will, a moment of your time, please."

Julian was watching them from the rear of the house.

He picked up the shears automatically. As he walked past her he whispered,

"Why do you stay?"

Angela forbade her tears to come any further, and she turned around to watch Will's receding back. Looking up, she caught sight of Julian's wave. He tapped his wristwatch in an exaggerated manner, then held up his fingers and thumbs twice to indicate that he would be twenty minutes.

She resumed her perambulation, and asked herself repeatedly,

"Why do I stay? Why do I stay?"

Finally, she admitted to herself what she'd always known. She stayed because it was in her nature to stay, when mischief was afoot. Throughout her life, she always wanted to know what would happen next. Whatever the consequences.

24

"By how much unexpected, by so much
We must awake endeavour for defence"
King John Act 2: Sc. 1

Great minds do not think alike. The proverb applies when two people or more discover, independently, a common idea which may be put to good purpose, or used to justify their evil actions.

Qadir Khan and Julian Marlborough latched onto the same notion for a similar reason. Fomenting ongoing civil unrest was where their paths crossed. For Julian its purpose was to keep the so-called Muslim threat in the forefront of the public's mind. Qadir decided upon his course in the naïve hope that the outrage he was about to commit would rouse his brothers to such a pitch of anger that they would rise as one against the Infidel.

Julian and Will reconnoitred Raza Khan's taxi firm for a week. Destroying it in one night did not seem to be too taxing a job. They planned to execute it on Sunday morning around 03:00 hrs. There were numerous vehicles in the compound, from where Raza operated his motor sales business. Julian's parting gift would be to once again spray the foul acronym on a wall that he had first used when avenging Padam Gurung. Given the news of Usman's arrest, with his fellow paedophiles, the public would believe it more than justified.

Using night binoculars, they scanned the premises from their vantage point. The site lay on the boundary between Wenbury and Cranchurch. One side abutted the main road, another an industrial estate, and woodland cradled the remaining edges. It was 02:30 Saturday morning; the day before the attack.

"Same as usual Cap', all quiet on the Western Front."

Julian was about to concur when the sound of an engine breached the stillness of the mid-November night. An Audi Q7 halted outside the compound. A man leapt from the back, unlocked the gates and followed the vehicle inside on foot.

"What the fuck!"

Qadir Khan was visible by the light of the Supermoon; sometimes known as the Frosty Moon and the Hunter's Moon. It looked larger and brighter than usual. Four other men gathered around Qadir. He took out his keys, and let himself into his uncle's office.

"What the hell are they up to?" Julian enquired of himself.

It soon became apparent when they split up, and began prising open the petrol caps on the surrounding vehicles.

"You've got to be kidding me," Will muttered.

"Sssssh!"

A figure flew back to the Audi, and withdrew a jerry can and strips of material from the boot.

Julian and Will lay on their backs and clasped their hands to their mouths to stifle their laughter. Quickly, they resumed the prone position to watch events unfold.

Sure enough, they were soaking the rags in petrol and draping them into the fuel tanks of the cars.

"Oh my, oh my, haven't seen that done for many a year."

"Bloody risky Cap'."

"No worries, might take a few of the buggers with them, if we're lucky."

He took out the camera which Will had requisitioned from the heavy boys.

"Very artistic," he mocked, as he looked at his efforts. "What now?"

A Jaguar drove into the yard. Raza Khan heaved himself out of his smart motor, yelling at the nearest figure.

"What the hell do you think you're doing?"

"It's alright Mr. Khan, it's Imran."

"What the fuck are you doing here? Where is Qadir? He said on the phone you'd disturbed intruders."

Qadir was silhouetted in the doorway.

"Here I am Uncle. Let me show you what we stopped the bastards from doing."

He escorted his increasingly apoplectic uncle around the yard. Raza's eyes bulged at the crude devices set to destroy his livelihood. Standing in the doorway of his office, he shook with rage.

"Bastards, bastards, if I find out who did this I'll cut his *lula* off and make him suck it! Praise be to Allah that you stopped them in time. How many? What did they look like?"

No-one stirred, and five pairs of dead eyes focused upon the fat man. Even at distance, Julian and Will could see the light dawning on Raza's face, though they didn't yet know why. Raza put his arm around his nephew.

"Why, my son, why?"

Qadir moved away from his uncle.

"A small price to pay for the glory of Allah the Merciful One. Our people must come out of their sleep, Uncle. When they see what's been done here they will rise across the entire land to avenge your loss."

Raza's booming laughter was unbearable to him.

"Rise up, rise up? Fuckwit! For the sake of twenty cars. Go ahead you idle dreamer, I'm insured – and for far more than what they're worth. You'll be doing me a favour."

Then he confirmed them in the blood they were about to spill.

"Allah the Merciful One! You bunch of arseholes, there is no Allah; there is no God! If you want virgins you'd better take up Usman's hobby."

The speed with which they acted impressed Julian. Four knives glinted in the fierce moonlight and plunged simultaneously into Raza. He stood there, legs wide apart, with a look of disbelief, and his eyes shifted sideways as he watched Qadir draw his knife. In one motion he slit his uncle's throat. The ground shuddered when Raza hit it. He lay there, an amorphous mass.

Urgently, they ran to the cars and lit the rags. Qadir leapt into the driver's seat of his Audi and made ready for a swift departure. The vehicle farthest from the gates exploded first, and they were already two hundred metres down the highway when the rest began to incinerate. Will saw Julian's eyes ablaze with delight, and he had to drag him away before they were caught at the scene.

On the drive home Julian sat quite still looking positively beatific. The only movement perceptible to Will was the occasional flap of his right hand patting the camera. Will felt nauseous, thinking of the repercussions of what he had just seen.

He heard Julian mutter, "Chaos is chaos."

*

Initially, Qadir's monstrous act had the desired effect. Muslim communities across the nation protested. Most of those good people did so peacefully. The media, as usual, emphasised the negative. Widespread acts of destruction and violence committed by extremists garnered the headlines.

Freddie Forbes, and his acolytes, noted which areas were most volatile, and earmarked them for further strife. *Agent provocateur*s were inserted in both camps. Yorkshire and parts of Lancashire were particularly bad, along with Essex and cities like Portsmouth, Southampton and Bristol. In East Anglia, some took the opportunity to inflict their hatred upon East Europeans who had settled in the region years before, and stayed after Brexit. Troops had to go in with force in places to remove barricades, erected by frightened people in defence of their communities and livelihoods. Needless to say, Accident and Emergency units were overwhelmed, and there were four deaths.

Christian ministers, of all persuasions, put their heads above the parapet and stood beside their Muslim brothers. Even Hindus spoke boldly on behalf of their beleaguered cousins, despite the mutual antipathy that had existed between them for generations.

It was to little avail, because for all the talk of civilised behaviour, founded upon the finest tenets of many religions, they were beating their collective heads against an atheist brick wall. Safe in their sanctuaries, the high priests, who kept the flame of the *'Gospel According to Dawkins'* alive, engaged in sophistry to suggest that what they were witnessing was once more religious conflict. Wilfully, they misrepresented the facts, ignoring the evidence that the atrocities being committed had no foundation in religious belief, but were so clearly the antithesis of the creeds. So they fuelled the indignation of the ignorant who wouldn't know religion or faith if it jumped up and bit them on the arse.

25

"There is a tide in the affairs of men…"
Julius Caesar Act 4: Sc. 3

The first week of December saw the beginning of an additional and secular Advent; relative peace on the streets.

Tommy O'Donnell addressed the Cabinet.

"I don't know who took dem pictures, and I don't much care. Thank God someone gave 'em to the press."

Through the chain of command, Julian reported the events of the night leading to the demise of Raza Khan, and the photographs were transmitted to his masters.

Choosing a moment to suit their ends, they filtered them into the hands of the press and television stations to reveal that the late taxi man had been killed by his own blood. Seeing knives raised in Asian hands, and a very fat man lying on the tarmac threw the public into deep confusion. The apocalyptic scene of exploding cars only added to their astonishment. Within two or three days the civil unrest became sporadic and then petered out.

O'Donnell addressed Henry Longfellow.

"What's the progress on this nephew then?"

He checked his notes.

"Qadir Khan, has he been picked up yet? Jeez, butcherin' your own uncle like that."

With typical Scouse black humour, he quipped,

"Should've paid the lad the full fare and not argued."

Self-appreciative laughter rang hollow around the Cabinet Room in Ten Downing Street, nobody joined with him.

"Come on then, Henry, where are we with this bloke an' his mates?"

Henry knew exactly where most of the assailants were; in the custody of the security services. Raza's nemesis, Qadir, had eluded them, and he related this to the Cabinet.

"They need to get some wheels on Hank, your assets. Can't have this dickhead loose on the streets."

Henry loathed being called 'Hank', though he accepted it was appropriate for a member of this Cowboy government.

"The gentlemen we are entertaining are so far unforthcoming about young Mr. Khan's usual haunts. We hope for an early arrest."

"Worra 'bout that other uncle of his, the one that got banged up for knobbin' gerls?"

More than one member of the Cabinet winced at his coarse expression.

"Usman Khan has been co-operative, Prime Minister, but he has little to contribute to our knowledge of his nephew's whereabouts."

"Okay Hank, keep me up to speed, as soon as you know anything."

He arched back in his chair, and stretched.

"Thank God it's nearly Christmas, that'll calm everyone down. A good bout of shopping, loads to eat and drink, and repeats on the telly. You can't whack it!"

Many sitting round the table shared a similar thought.

"How have we ended up with someone like this as Prime Minister?"

If they had cared to engage with the truth, they could have answered the question easily.

Generations of politicians had ignored the people, believing they knew best. Perhaps they did, but they still should have provided an outlet for the *vox populi*, and not shown open disdain for the wider voice. Resentment had grown from the beginning of the second decade of the century. It reached its shocking expression in elections mid-decade onwards.

Citizens the world over may not have reached the dizzy heights of formal education, but that didn't prevent them from understanding that they were excluded from having their opinion heard. Hence they were easy prey to demagogues. That was why they had a Prime Minister like Tommy O'Donnell; charismatic, and with the gift of the gab that made him sound plausible to the poorly educated. It gave him free rein to encourage their prejudices.

O'Donnell was one of many who had thrived across Europe and America. Each epitomised the words of the Eighteenth Century essayist, Alexander Pope.

"A little learning is a dangerous thing; drink deep, or taste not the Pierian spring: there shallow draughts intoxicate the brain, and drinking largely sobers us again."

Defence Secretary, Jacob Greenwood, would remain an adherent to Socialism until his dying day, but as he sat in that room he couldn't help thinking of words from a play he had just seen. Henrik Ibsen's *'An Enemy of the People'* had been revived in Town. Jacob came away from it thinking over an over about what Dr. Stockmann had said.

"The majority is never right. Never, I tell you! That's one of these lies in society that no free and intelligent man can help rebelling against. Who are the people that make up the biggest proportion of the population – the intelligent ones or the fools?"

He concluded that Ibsen's assertion had merit, but that didn't permit the intelligent minority to ride roughshod over the masses. It was their duty to raise others up. He remembered another line, and it filled his heart with foreboding.

"The strongest man in the world is he who stands alone."

Jacob vehemently disagreed with this, because a man alone is bereft of love. When he is abandoned in that void he loses all compassion. He feared that they were entering a time when so-called strong and lonely men and women would come to the fore, and reap a harvest of hatred.

O'Donnell interrupted his meditation.

"Okay folks, that's it for now. Thanks a bunch."

He waited until he was alone with his private secretary. "Steve Kinsella should be outside, gerrim in 'ere."

The burly Head of Personal Security swaggered into the room.

"Thanks Kev, go and tell my missus I'll be with her in ten minutes, would you? Ta mate."

Kevin disappeared on his errand.

"Sit down Stevie, don't stand on ceremony. Got a job for you, lad, not you personally, but one of your team."

O'Donnell's verbosity would have worn down the patience of saint.

"Say the werd boss."

"All this crap that's been goin' off in the last year has got one common factor."

Kinsella hung on every word, he was intrigued by what was coming.

"You ever come across that Tory M.P. Sir Hugh Marlborough?"

"Heard the name a couple of times. Why?"

"Most of the shit that's been going down started in his constituency; a place called Wenbury and Cranchurch. Just down the road in Buckinghamshire. Our boys in blue are fuckin' useless, they've never turned up nuthin."

He massacred the English language with impunity.

"I want you to set one of your lads up out there for a while, and get him to ferret round. Okay mate?"

"No worries boss. I'll get on to it in the New Year…"

"Fuck that for a game of soldiers! Do it now, today, pronto! Imshi, imshi, jaldi, jaldi!"

He exhausted his knowledge of Arabic and Hindi.

"Who have you got in mind, Stevie?"

Kinsella gave him a name, and proffered the opinion that the lad in question would be mightily pissed off at being away from home at Christmas.

"Tough titty! Give him a big bonus, and I tell you what, bring his wife and kid down and set 'em up in a nice hotel. All the trimmings."

"You're the boss."

"Ta Stevie."

O'Donnell sighed.

"Big meeting with the missus mate. You'll never guess what she wants now?"

"A smacked arse?"

Kinsella was the only one who could get away with such remarks about the P.M.'s better half.

"Says when I retire she wants to be a Lady."

"Bit late in the day for that, isn't it?"

They cackled gleefully.

"Na mate, she wants me to be a lord and make her a lady. I've fuckin' told her, there won't be no House of Lords, so how can I give her a title. Jeez Stevie, the shit I have to deal with."

They strolled out of the Cabinet Room arm in arm indulging in sexist banter.

*

The safe house in Birmingham was in the heart of an anonymous district where Qadir wouldn't stand out.

His heart nearly stopped when he saw his face on the television news. In an instant he was out of the door, and heading up the M40 to Leamington Spa. His cousin Zaheer took command of him, and despatched him to his present quarters after a quick telephone call. The Audi Q7 met a bitter end in a crusher, and the licence plates were obliterated.

An older man welcomed him. In the days of seclusion that followed he took him to task for operating alone and without support. Qadir was now a member of their cell, and they would care for him. At last, this lonely young man had found a home, and people whose views were at one with his.

He was asked why he killed his uncle. After giving a frank description of his Uncle Raza's business and attitude, and the spark he had intended to ignite, they commended him on his action. The only thing bugging him was that he had been unable to deal with the schoolteacher, Faisal Hussain. Promises were made to him that the time for revenge would come, but he must learn patience.

Everyone was on edge, as the two vehicles made innocuous progress down the M40 towards London. The Birmingham cell had been planning this mission for months. Unfortunately, they assigned a novice to make calls to Zaheer in Leamington about the cars he was supplying for the job. In the course of one conversation the idiot had blurted out,

"Yeh man, your cuz will be on the Bicester gig wiv us."

Those listening in to Zaheer's telephone calls danced a jig of delight. Not only would they foil a terrorist plot, but also lay their hands on Qadir.

Commander Giles Wentmore was not happy; his safety first policy was overruled. He wanted to intercept them when they exited at junction 9, with maximum force. The powers-that-be insisted upon a confrontation in full view of the shoppers, irrespective of the risk.

Six snipers were ensconced on shop rooftops, giving them a clear field of fire over the car park. Since early morning traffic marshals directed cars to specific spaces, until most of the area was filled. Giles instructed them to leave one section free. He occupied it with half a dozen cars of his own, plus a breakdown repair vehicle from a well-known organisation. Inside the truck an assault team relaxed, periodically checking their weapons.

Everyone had strict instructions, when the call was made the only person to survive was Qadir Khan.

A relay of cars and vans trailed the terrorists down the motorway. The house they departed from had been known to the services for some time. Telephone tapping, and other listening devices, gave them date and time for the operation.

The A41 from the motorway junction flowed freely. Few of the gang gave more than a cursory glance at the elderly couple standing on the verge, whilst a breakdown man had his head under the bonnet of their car. When they had passed the old woman spoke into her mobile phone, and Giles Wentmore listened.

A bossy-looking young woman in uniform waved the two SUV's towards the empty spaces, and they came to a halt side by side. The drivers were under instruction to remain at their posts with engines running. Eight men began to disembark, bearing arms.

It was over remarkably quickly. Qadir was third out of his vehicle, and the snipers recognised him immediately through their telescopic sights. When the C-T unit burst out of the breakdown van, firing as they went, the assigned marksman put a bullet through Qadir's left kneecap, and he fell to the tarmac, his gun spinning out of reach. Including Qadir, only four got out of the cars, and three of them were dead instantly. Rapid fire extinguished all life in another of the motors, but one driver managed to pull away.

"Get out of the way, get out of the way, stupid woman," he screamed at the car park marshal.

Despite being offended by the horrible uniform she had to wear, Fiona remained at her most efficient. She poured fire into the windscreen of the oncoming car. It slewed to the right and crashed into a barrier where she and three of her companions proceeded to blast it to hell until they were certain the occupants were dead.

On the other side of the car park, uniformed police held back hordes of stunned shoppers, but permitted a young man and woman to pass through the line.

Julian had promised Angela a good day out at Bicester Village, and she was loaded to the gunnels with designer clothes he had bought for her. She was hesitant as they crossed the car park, shocked as the rest of them at what she had witnessed. Her anxiety grew when the police allowed them to pass, and she knew that Julian was caught up in this horror. He unlocked the car, and told her to get in, which she did speedily. Julian remained outside, leaning against the driver's door, lighting a cigarette whilst he waited.

Qadir Khan was handcuffed and held upright by two giant officers. He was in excruciating pain from his shattered kneecap, but they dragged him onward. They passed within five metres of Julian, and in a ringing voice he said,

"Good afternoon, Qadir. Nice day for it."

When Qadir disappeared into a windowless van, Julian threw his cigarette to the ground and climbed into the driver's seat.

"See, I promised you a good day out, and I always keep my promises."

She was silent for most of the journey, thinking to herself that she had wanted to stay around to see how things turned out. Hopefully, that was the end of it. Soon, she could disappear in her little car and be in distant parts before Julian realised she'd gone.

In Hugh Marlborough's Hampstead home there was a small gathering. Hugh and Freddie Forbes were present along with *'Bernard'*, commanding the Household Division, *'Paddy'* of the Royal Marines, and *'Rob'* of the Scottish regiments. At the last minute, Debs had insisted on coming into Town with him. She was entirely innocent of his part in the affair, and he wanted it kept that way. When he tried to talk her out of joining him she was having none of it, but to his relief she went out to lunch with a group of girlfriends.

Freddie held the chair.

"Well gentleman, that young man did us a favour with his antics. Safely under lock and key now, we don't really want him sticking his oar in again."

'Bernard' enquired about Qadir's confederates, and Freddie's suave tones reassured him.

"We have them tucked away. Should they become an embarrassment to us, we'll send them on an extended swimming holiday somewhere off Scapa Flow. "

Freddie's heart was hardened to their fate. Two of them had been involved in the execution of his father.

'Rob's' lilting voice asked, "And the wee man recently taken into custody?"

Hugh interjected, "Going to hang on to him for a while; think we may be able to put him to good use."

'Paddy' had kept his counsel so far, but now he felt compelled to express what was on his mind.

"Don't like to see the country in this shape. The reports from battalion level don't make for pretty reading. Friend *'Lennon'* is keeping the lid on the press, so they're only reporting half of what's going on. The destruction of property around the country is considerable, and injury and loss of life is five times what's being acknowledged publicly."

'Bernard' cried,

"Here, here! We need to enact our plan soon, or it will be one hell of a job to get things back under control. War is war, but what you fail to appreciate Freddie is that civil war is the worst kind. Please don't misapprehend me, I'm not saying we're at that point yet."

'Rob' supported his colleague.

"What Paddy is saying is that though the bulk of the population share characteristics similar to ourselves, other ethnic groups number a few millions. That's not an easy thing to control, if they all decide to get uppity."

Freddie was thinking fast.

"Gentlemen, as you've seen, since we released the photographs affairs have quietened down. The wind went out of the ethnic sails when they saw that some of their ilk were turning on their own."

'Bernard' sounded irritable.

"So what are you saying Freddie? We can all take a break for the Christmas festivities, and kick off again in the New Year? Lovely that you believe in Santa and the Tooth Fairy, Freddie, but this is our arses on the line!"

Freddie needed to spin them a promise quickly, and he latched onto something Hugh had said before the military arrived. He laughed, like a man who can take a joke at his own expense.

"Hold your horses there, *'Bernard'*, I was coming to that next. *'Winston'* and I believe that all we need is one last push, and that it can be accomplished before Christmas, or thereabouts."

317

"What do you have in mind?" a sceptical *'Paddy'* enquired.

Freddie had no idea, but hadn't been a politician all his adult life not be able to manufacture bullshit on the spot.

"Our agents are planning an operation as we speak. I'm told it will be spectacular."

"Can you say more, Freddie?"

"Best kept under wraps, *'Rob'*, operational security and all that, you understand."

"Aye, right, before Christmas you say?"

"Thereabouts."

"You'll be sure to keep us informed, Freddie?"

"Absolutely, every step of the way."

Murmurs of agreement went round the table. A relieved Freddie addressed other business.

"Now, how will your chaps respond at unit level when we give the green light?"

It was asserted that the work done over years to persuade the common soldier of where his duty lay would bear fruit. There had been an unwritten policy for a decade of promoting men and women at N.C.O. level who were sound to the cause. They, cautiously and steadily, indoctrinated their charges with a rabid patriotism, to the exclusion of all else.

'Paddy' bounced Freddie's question back at him.

"What about the police? Where do we stand with them, Freddie?"

"My dear boy, the overwhelming majority has always been of a conservative hue – lower and upper case – and we have been following a similar policy to yours. I feel sure that when push comes to shove they'll be *'on the square'*. Unless there's anything else, gentlemen, we'll leave it there. I understand from *'Winston'* that his dear wife will be returning from her luncheon date shortly. It would be best if he were alone to greet her."

The military men departed swiftly, and Freddie was putting on his gloves when Hugh asked,

"So what's this spectacular operation you've got on the go, Freddie?"

The Shadow Minister had a note of dry humour in his voice.

"I'd rather hoped you'd tell me, old boy."

Hugh Marlborough had rarely looked gormless in his life, but he did now.

Freddie helped him out.

"You said that your boy was mulling something over. Well tell him to stop cogitating – he'll go blind – and to get his arse in gear. Christmas at the latest Hugh, no excuses, and make it memorable."

*

Dressing the Christmas Tree at Banksmore House always took place on the Sunday before Christmas Day. This year Julian insisted on having it done a fortnight in advance. He and Angela were busy as proverbial bees decorating the ten-footer he had purchased.

Angela moved into the House the day before, as their guest for the festive season. When she received the pressing invitation she had been alarmed. Upon reflection she decided that, as abhorrent as Julian's activities were to her, he was unlikely to be active during the season of goodwill. On the quiet, she gave notice on her cottage, determined that when New Year passed she would concoct a reason for a lone trip into Old Wenbury, retrieve her car and make away to pastures new. She was in a great frame of mind as they arranged baubles, and looking forward to a pampered Christmas.

Debs and Hugh relaxed in armchairs ploughing through the Sunday papers, occasionally taking pleasure at the sight of their son, jolly and contented in the company of his girl. Actually, that wasn't strictly true. Debs delight was muted. Arranging the tree was something she and Julian always did together. They invited her to join them in the activity, but she politely declined. Her heart wasn't in it any more when she saw that Julian had eyes for Angela alone.

When Julian was at High Heath School his mother was always by his side. Barely a week went by when she didn't find an excuse to arrive at the premises. It was the only time in her life she got her hands dirty, assisting with the Parents' Guild. When he was in the sixth form some wag, well out of his hearing, christened them 'Oedipus and Jocasta'. If Julian had discovered that his mates thought he was screwing his mother he would have put *their* eyes out, not his own.

Debs examined the girl's legs as she stood on tip toe, halfway up the stepladder. She saw Julian's hand caress them, reaching just under Angela's skirt to stroke the back of her thighs. The envy that filled her was monstrous, and she tried to shake it off by concentrating on the newspaper.

A geezer called Robert A. Heinlein once said,

"Being a mother is an attitude, not a biological relation."

Debs problem was that she couldn't distinguish between the two. She believed utterly that her biological rights gave her the privilege to determine the course of her son's life. Julian's problem was that he paid homage to this. His mother's attitude, from the cradle onwards, had been *'Julian first and last'*. He imbibed the philosophy until it ran through his veins and arteries. She never permitted anyone or anything to stand in the path of her boy. The anguish she felt at seeing him besotted with this young woman was so fierce that she felt like killing her. She cast the thought from her mind.

"Good God!"

So loud was her voice that they all stopped what they were doing.

"Really Hugh, this is too much, look here."

Hugh's lips moved as he read the article rapidly, his features suffusing to a dangerous purple.

"Not again! Look at this Julian."

Julian read a full page article on the Rector of St. George's Banksmore. It lauded his ecumenical efforts to bridge the gulf between communities of different faiths. Beginning with the story of his Garden Party, it continued by describing further communal gatherings. The journalist ended by praising him to the skies for trying to promote harmony in these fractured times. The article concluded by saying that it was significant that a former Army officer, who had served in the Middle East, should be the first to see the need for healing.

"Did you see the final paragraph, Father?"

"Read it to me, Julian."

"Seems our Peter has set off a chain reaction. Churches, Mosques and Temples are at it the length and breadth of the country."

He gave Hugh a significant look.

"If it continues much longer we'll have peace and love breaking out."

321

Hugh understood the implication of his son's words, and chewed a nail in concern. He leapt out of his armchair.

"I say Angela; would you mind awfully if I took Julian away from you for a short while? Debs will give you a hand with the tree, won't you darling?"

Her ladyship smiled, and folded the paper. Alone with Angela, she stabilised the ladder for her whilst she climbed to the top step.

"How dare she have better legs than me?"

It would only take a tiny thrust.

"Don't like the way the wind's blowing, my boy. Time for you to get a push on. What do you have in mind?"

Julian looked at the bare trees from the Study window, their branches arching in the powerful winter wind. He'd been trying to piece something together for the last week. It was Qadir's modus operandi in slaughtering his uncle that gave him initial inspiration. Inciting people to violence by an act of barbarity so beyond the pale, they couldn't help but exact retribution on those they believed to be the perpetrators. Of course, he would make sure that there were no witnesses to *his* act, photographic or otherwise. The exact detail of what to do had eluded him, but the newspaper article opened the locked door. What he was proposing could only be spoken of with men and women whose souls were as dark as his own.

"Like to talk with your Commander, Pa' – today!"

The authority in his voice shook Hugh.

"You can tell me, son..."

"No, sir, the Commander or nothing. Time is getting short."

Hugh twiddled with the pen on his desk, and came to a decision.

"Give me half an hour, my boy. You go and help your girl and your mother. Back here then; thirty minutes."

"Sir."

*

Julian met Giles Wentmore in a quiet pub near the small town of Great Missenden; a stone's throw from Chequers the Prime Minister's country residence. They arrived independently and left so. Two lone men striking up a conversation at the bar. First topic - the weather. Then – England's prospects in the next Six Nations tournament.

"Get you another…?"

"Hugh," Julian said, with a frisson of delight at adopting his father's name.

"I'm Jeremy," the Commander of Counter Terrorism lied.

They shook hands, and affected embarrassment as part of the English male's inability to introduce himself properly to others. In fact, social ineptitude was alien to them, as well-brought up and supremely confident public school boys. Assuming the guise of a couple of provincial middle class chaps was fun.

"Cheers!"

"Shall we find a more comfortable pew?" the older man urged.

Wrapped in the arms of an old wooden settle, they got down to business.

Julian unfolded his scheme in scarifying detail. Giles Wentmore sat there rigid at its audacity and malevolence; he was looking into a pit of darkness which was the equal of any crime imaginable. Giles thought that he had long since abandoned any scruples; they got in the way of keeping his beloved country safe, but even he wavered over what Julian was proposing. Ironically, he spoke to Julian in the fashion of the young man's father.

"My boy, you're certain about this? It will be a hell of thing to live with after you've done it; it could haunt you for the rest of your days."

A mirthless smile stretched Julian's lips.

"Don't believe in ghosts. Can you supply the people and equipment?"

Giles swallowed. He saw that Julian had noticed and was filled with disdain. The kit was no problem, but the people?

"Yes, yes, I can let you have three personnel; the only three who would go along with this...this..."

He wanted to say *'insanity'*.

"Mission?"

Giles ignored the soulless gaze.

"You'll have your answer by seven tomorrow morning."

"Why not now?"

"Even I have to take orders. Need to get confirmation from higher up the food chain."

Tentatively, he suggested that Julian might be rather short on time to organise and accomplish his mission.

"Not at all, it really isn't that complex. So long as I can meet with my personnel within the next forty-eight hours."

Giles drained his pint, stood up and buttoned his covert coat.

"Seven. Good evening."

Outside the pub he strode to his car as if the Prince of Darkness himself was in pursuit.

For once he ignored traffic cameras, and drove over the speed limit. Safely back in his Whitehall flat he phoned Henry Longfellow, on the secure line his technical Praetorian Guard had installed. He became increasingly astonished at the evening's events, as the Home Secretary took it in his stride and sanctioned Julian's proposal.

When he was a child he had been afraid of the dark, but mastered the fear by the time he was eight. That night Giles Wentmore slept with his entire flat lit up like Blackpool Illuminations. His last thought, before sleep enfolded him, was that when this was done Master Julian Marlborough was too bloody dangerous to be left on the loose.

26

"...The wheel is come full circle, I am here."
King Lear Act 5: Sc. 3

Jimmy Allsop was enjoying the luxury of his hotel in Old Wenbury. It was an ancient coaching house on a massive scale, with fine dining facilities. An even greater delight was to share it with his wife Caroline, and their six-year-old daughter Maisie. Jimmy's accent had modified with time and his peripatetic lifestyle, but Caroline and Maisie had that pronounced soft drawl of St. Helens; an accent indicative of good humour and kindness.

The hotel staff were lovely, and did all they could to make them comfortable. Tony, the manager, gave strict instructions that only the very best was to be provided for the Allsops. They were going to be there for three weeks at least, and the money had been paid up front. Payment was by cheque, which arrived through the post. A clerk had slipped up by including government headed notepaper in the envelope. Tony raised an eyebrow when he saw *'Ministry of Defence'*. He assumed he was playing mine host to a VIP; he wasn't far wrong.

The family finished lunch in a café across from the hotel. The first snow of the season fell ever so lightly.

Jimmy looked at his daughter.

"Come on, let's go on a mystery tour. We can take a ride into the country, it's only a couple of miles away.

You never know Maisie there might be enough snow to make a snowman."

The little girl squealed with delight, as she swung between her parents on the way to the car.

Whilst he drove, Jimmy pondered his situation. Steve Kinsella had been crystal clear in his briefing, but he didn't really see what he could find out in Wenbury and Cranchurch. Security man he was; spy he was not. Heck, he'd just enjoy the time with his family. The motor pool provided a family-sized Vauxhall, run of the mill and anonymous.

Jimmy arrived a few days before his family, and took the opportunity to explore the area. He drove along the now familiar arterial road through an urban landscape of pleasant houses, and soon emerged into the countryside. After half a mile he signalled left, and passed through a small village before descending to the valley floor.

It was early afternoon of a Sunday in December. For the first time in years, the trees and fields bore the hallmark of a genuine English winter; cold, frosty and a low sun in a peerless blue sky.

"Oh, let's go that way."

Caroline pointed at the sign indicating right at the crossroads.

"Look at that big house on the hill. I'll bet there's a nice village just round the bend."

A contented Jimmy followed his wife's instructions, and in three minutes they entered Banksmore.

"Daddy, Daddy, look a church!"

Maisie spotted the grand old place, and he and Caroline exchanged a smile to warm any one's heart on a freezing winter's afternoon. They were Christian, and

Maisie had taken to church with a will and great delight. She loved to sing and join in the activities.

Before long the child was scampering through the graveyard examining every tombstone that took her fancy.

"Daddy, Daddy, look at this one. How old is it?"

Jimmy was thrilled to be summoned by his daughter, and she was delighted to have the opportunity to do so, because Daddy spent so much time away from home. Caroline was hopping from one foot to the next, trying to keep warm.

"Hurry up you two, let's see if the church is open. They might have the heating on."

Fortune favours the brave. St. George's decrepit radiators managed to give off just enough heat to make it worthwhile going indoors. Maisie demanded explanations for everything, and her parents were happy to respond to her enquiring mind.

"Time to go Maisie."

She didn't seem to hear him. She stood on the altar steps gazing in wonder at the crucified Christ and his sorrowing mother, depicted in stained glass.

Caroline caressed her precious child.

"Shall we say a prayer together, Maisie?"

"Can I say it, please?"

Jimmy stroked her long dark hair.

"Of course you can darling."

"Well go on then, you two, kneel down."

A family filled with love and simplicity sank to their knees, and the piping treble of a child rang like a bell.

"Dear Lord, we've got a lot of trouble in our town right now. People keep fighting and hurting each other. Make them stop, not just in our town but everywhere. Let's all have a Happy Christmas, and remember Jesus. Amen."

Repeated attempts failed, the engine whirred in chronic pain and then died.

"What's wrong with it Daddy?"

Despite the nuisance, Jimmy retained his good humour.

"Maisie my love, it is no more, it is dead, deceased, it's snuffed it!"

His paraphrase of an old comedy routine provoked giggles that fluttered on the frosty air.

"Not to worry, we've got breakdown cover. Let me give them a call."

Jimmy tapped the number into his mobile three times. In northern self-mockery he declared,

"Ee, ecky thump, no signal."

Caroline was off, pulling Maisie along.

"Follow me, my gang."

Marjorie Whitlock opened the Rectory door, with the welcoming smile she gave all and sundry.

"Good afternoon, are you expected?"

Caroline explained their predicament, and asked if they might use the phone to summon the AA.

"We're really sorry to bother you, I can see you're busy."

People were passing through the hallway, from the sitting room to the kitchen. They returned the same way bearing plates of sandwiches and cakes.

"Nonsense my dear, come in out of the cold. Hello young lady, what's your name?"

"I'm Maisie, what's your name?"

Marjorie didn't normally approve of forward children, but she was in high good humour, and Maisie's forthright approach tickled her.

"I am Marjorie. We already have something in common, our names begin with the same letter. How about that? Now in you come, the Rector won't mind one bit. Put your coats and bits there while I go and inform him."

Jimmy detained the bustling and jolly lady, pointing at the landline on the hall table.

"May I make that call?"

"Please do, no time like the present."

Marj took off like an Exocet missile in search of Peter Standish.

The Rector appeared in two shakes of a lamb's tail with Marjorie in tow, his hand extended to greet his guest.

"You're most welcome. Did you get through to the AA? Forgive me, I'm Peter Standish the Rector."

Jimmy stared wide-eyed, and could scarcely get his words out.

"Yes…yes thank you. An hour to an hour-and-a-half they said."

He was stuck for words. Marjorie gave assistance.

"This is Maisie, Rector."

"Hello Maisie. I think you can help me out. Would you tell me your mummy and daddy's names; I think they're a bit shy?"

"Me Mum's Caroline, and me Dad's Jimmy."

"Allsop, Caroline and Jimmy Allsop – Captain Standish!"

Peter stood bolt upright, and peered intently at Jimmy, and then he recollected.

"By all the saints, Rifleman Jimmy Allsop. What on earth are you doing in these parts?"

Before they went any further, Marjorie put her oar in.

"Over tea and cake Peter."

"Absolutely Marj, first class thinking."

Peter had been uncertain about hosting a tea party, but Jane insisted that she wanted a good feed and a natter with their dear friends before she gave birth; which was imminent. Introductions were effected, and Maisie gave Jane her less than comprehensive knowledge of childbirth, involving gooseberry bushes and lots of hot water.

Jimmy answered Peter's questions about what he'd been up to, but was circumspect about revealing details of his work. Eventually, the Rector had to circulate, but his parishioners took good care of the unexpected guests. Maisie made a great friend, who was entranced by the little girl.

The Marlboroughs had been invited, but declined. Will Castle overheard Julian and Angela talking about it in the kitchen, whilst he took his morning break. Angela was keen to escape the too genteel atmosphere of her hosts' home, if only for a couple of hours.

"I'm going Cap'. It would be my pleasure to accompany your lady."

"You've been invited?"

"Yep, I was surprised too. Got to know Pete Standish at his Garden Party. Had a pint with him once in the local."

Julian was guarded, and spoke quietly out of Angela's hearing.

"Careful he doesn't recognise you - from former times."

"It was a big place Cap', and there were lots of bodies. Anyway, I was never a God-Botherer. He might have seen me around, but I'd be one face among many."

So it was that Angela found herself occupying a bit of floor space, and entertaining Maisie with paper and crayons that Jane had dug out.

"Mind your backs, folks, logs coming through."

A voice with a hint of Scouse cried out over the babble of fellowship.

The stocky man made his way to the log burner and put the basket down. Will danced through the throng towards the kitchen, and bumped into the back of a man chatting with the seated Jane Standish.

"Oops, sorry friend."

Jimmy turned to reassure him that no harm was done, and they looked at each other in utter astonishment. It was Jane who prevented the gardener from being compromised.

"Will, this is Jimmy Allsop. Jimmy, Will Castle. Thanks ever so much for fetching more logs."

"No worries Jane, any time."

Jimmy went fishing.

"Do I detect a bit of a Scouse accent there, Will?"

His eyes twinkled as the game progressed.

"Yep, an' I reckon that accent of yours isn't far from Liverpool?"

"St. Helens."

Will couldn't resist.

"A woolyback, eh Jimmy. What brings you to these parts?"

"Family holiday, Will, Christmas and New Year away. No cooking for the wife, that's her, and that's our little girl."

"She's a cracker, Jimmy – both of them."

"What about you, Will, do you live around here?"

Jane joined the conversation.

"Will lives in very grand circumstances."

"I'm a live-in gardener. That big house on the hill, you must have seen it from the valley road."

"Sounds like you've fallen on your feet. Good employer?"

Jane was in there again, with a lightly mocking tone.

"Sir Hugh and Lady Marlborough, no less – our local M.P. and his lady."

Jimmy was on full alert, this was why he'd been sent to Wenbury and Cranchurch.

"Oh, not forgetting their delightful son, Julian."

Will's steely look held Jimmy's attention.

"That's right Jane, Julian Marlborough."

With as much emphasis as he dared, he said,

"Ex-army officer dossin' around and spongin' of his old man. That's his girlfriend, over there playin' with your daughter."

Jimmy clocked the association. He was unsure of the origin of words that hummed tunefully in his befuddled head,

> *"God moves in a mysterious way*
> *His wonders to perform;"*

If he'd had time to research it he would have discovered that it was the opening of William Cowper's eighteenth century hymn. If the entire nation studied the next two lines they would have taken them as a prophetic cry for what was to come, if they abandoned utterly the two great Commandments.

*"He plants his footsteps in the sea
And rides upon the storm."*

"Eh mate, I need to wash my hands. Come and keep me company. Scuse us Jane."

"Whereabouts in Sint Ellins do you live?"

Will teased, as they walked away.

They secluded themselves, talking quietly. The AA man interrupted them, requesting the car key. He too was provided with a mug of coffee and a slice of cake.

Will and Jimmy danced a tarantella, neither revealing too much. By the time the AA man advised the Allsops that their vehicle had a new battery, they each assumed the same two things: both engaged in missions specific to them, and both on the same side.

Jimmy didn't know whether to address him as Captain, Rector or Peter, so Caroline waded in.

"Say thank you to Peter and Jane, Maisie."

"Thank you."

She rushed down the hallway shouting,

"Where's Angela?"

She flung herself into her new friend's arms with a huge hug and sloppy kiss.

"Happy Christmas, Angela!"

The beautiful young woman could scarce keep the tears from her eyes.

"And a Happy Christmas to you too, darling Maisie. Happy Christmas everyone," and she fled to the conservatory.

"I never asked. Where are you staying?"

Jane clung to Peter's arm.

"Very posh, eh Caroline, *'The Cromwell'* in Old Wenbury."

"We've got Midnight Communion on Christmas Eve. Why don't you join us, it's a wonderful celebratory service?"

Caroline was enthusiastic.

"If we can organise a babysitter, we might just do that. Thanks again, it's been lovely. Good luck with the baby, Jane. Oh, look at that sky."

It was laden with snow, and darkness was falling.

"Talk about *'all the clouds that lour'd upon our house'*, eh Jimmy?"

Quick as a flash he replied,

"Richard III!"

Another time when England festered in murderous turmoil.

"The benefits of an Education Corps, Mr. Allsop. Bye."

"Bye everyone," the Allsop family chorused.

Caroline strapped Maisie into her seat, and sat in the back of the car with her.

"Whenever you are ready chauffeur," she attempted a posh accent.

"Jimmy, Jimmy, 'ang on a mo'!"

Will Castle ran across the graveyard, and went to Maisie's window which she buzzed down.

He produced a ten-pound note.

"Here you go Maisie, Angela says I've to give you an early Christmas present, and I'll tell you what, here's another one from me."

Maisie's delight was palpable, and she plonked a kiss on the snowy cheek of the aging ex-soldier, whose head was in the car. Tittering she said,

"You look like someone's cut your head off. Give Angela a big kiss from me. Mind you, I expect you'd do that anyway."

"Maisie!" Caroline exclaimed. "You are a cheeky young madam."

Everyone laughed, and Will thought wistfully,

"Out of the mouths of babes and sucklings…"

"Maisie, put your window up. Thanks Will…and to Angela."

"You're welcome Caroline."

He moved to the other side of the car to Jimmy's open window. This time it was Jimmy who extended his neck, and his bare head was whitened by snowflakes.

"Safe journey mate, good to meet you."

"You too Will, take care of yourself. Might see you on Christmas Eve?"

"Don't know about that mate, I'm not much of a church goer."

He came to a spontaneous decision. Pressing his mouth to Jimmy's ear, he hissed,

"Get away from here, and don't come back. This is no place for family, or you. Steer clear of O'Donnell; his days are numbered."

Will Castle held his head down, to prevent the whipping snow from blinding him, as he circumvented the tombstones.

27

"If it were done, when 'tis done, then 'twere well it were done quickly..."
Macbeth Act 1: Sc. 7

Julian's meeting with his three new friends was brief.

It took place in a house set well back from the road, protected by high walls and CCTV. It lay discreetly off the A404, between Rickmansworth and Northwood. Having NATO Allied Maritime Command close by was useful for finding a safe house.

The conduct of the meeting was formal, and they listened to Julian with fascination. None was especially concerned by the scale of the mortal sin they were soon to commit. Giles Wentmore had run over the lie of the land with them in London, so they focused upon sequence of events, timing and weaponry. They were remarkably unconcerned about the aftermath. Although the local police would attend they would be sent away in short order. The Counter Terrorism Unit would deal with all matters pertaining.

"Happy? Any questions?"

Fiona flashed him her most seductive smile. He really would have to see what else she might be up for once the dust had settled.

"Sounds a doddle, boss."

He liked the *'boss'*, especially rolling off Fiona's luscious lips.

"Right, I'd like to meet our guest. Fiona, would you be kind enough to lead the way."

She took him to the kitchen, and unlocked a door. Behind it was a further door, armour-plated and soundproofed. They descended the stone steps. She pointed back to the top of the stairs, and Julian saw the men on the screen. Fiona pressed the remote control three times, each image revealed the occupants of the cells below. Bakir was at prayer, whilst Dawood prowled the boundaries of his confinement like a zoo animal gone stir crazy.

Qadir sat on a chair, his injured leg resting on the bunk. He had been treated, cursorily, for the gunshot wound to his knee. It really required reconstructive surgery, but they patched him, and kept dosing him up for it to be sufficiently bearable. He was occupied with the copy of the Quran he always carried. It was on his person when they captured him. Giles Wentmore examined it with a respect that surprised Qadir. The Commander saw the look on his face.

"I don't abuse any man's religion Mr. Khan, or his lack of faith. My only argument is with those who hide behind their beliefs to justify the pain they inflict on others. Here, you are welcome to keep your Holy Book."

"Hello brother."

Qadir immersed himself deeper in Scripture. He certainly didn't dignify Julian's presence with an angry response. He might well have done, because he would have regarded a ravenous lion more of a brother.

How wrong he was, and how right Marlborough's provocation. One man had purified his religion to a point where he had bound himself to laws which suited his skewed view of the world; the other was devoid of faith in anything but his own self-aggrandisement. Both had strayed so far from humanity that they had become jackals, scouring the world to feed off innocent flesh.

"How's the leg, comfortable?"

No response.

"Hope you can manage to hop about a bit. We're going to have you out of here soon."

Qadir turned the page more slowly, his interest aroused.

Julian was getting bored, and had other things to do.

"You're going to get the opportunity to show what a hard man you are."

He turned on his heel to leave.

Qadir's voice bounced around the thick wet walls.

"Ask your girlfriend how hard I can get!"

Julian stopped in his tracks. Qadir assaulted the back of his head with a graphic description of what he had done to Angela in the back of his taxi; the tale grew in the telling.

Julian found enough strength to maintain self-control. He climbed the steps, trailed by Fiona, and mocking laughter from his captives pursued him. The last words he heard, before the door slammed, was Bakir shouting.

"Qadir said her *pudi* was so big he had to tie a plank to his arse in case he fell in. *Eik dolla raande*!"

Julian had served sufficient time in various parts of the world to know that Angela had just been called a *'one-dollar whore'*. He was inclined to agree.

28

"I go, and it is done; the bell invites me.
Hear it not…for it is a knell
That summons thee to heaven or to hell."
Macbeth Act 2: Sc. 1

St. George's Church Banksmore was bathed by the light of an opaline moon at ten forty-five on Christmas Eve. It shone like translucent glass, and shifting patterns of colour swirled across its face.

The service of Midnight Communion brings people out of the woodwork. Naturally, regular parishioners attend, and the aged were able to find their footing along the path with the help of festoon lights strung either side. Everyone picked their way carefully, crunching the crisp snow beneath their feet. The sidesmen and women greeted worshippers with great cheer, and distributed carol sheets. Many attended to fulfil their ritual second visit of the year; Easter morn was the other favourite.

Jack Preston stood beside the organ. Marjorie Whitlock was providing the burgeoning congregation with pre-match music.

"You see, Marjorie, they come twice a year to sustain an illusion."

Marjorie beamed, but focussed on her stops. Jack was encouraged to explore his theory further.

"What is the English disease, Marj?"

Out of the corner of her mouth, she said, "Alcohol?"

"Plenty of that been imbibed tonight, by the look of some of them."

"My dear, I've had a sherry myself. All in moderation."

She played the *'Birth and Annunciation to the Shepherds'* from Bach's *'Christmas Oratorio'*.

"Nostalgia Marj, unadulterated nostalgia. A race memory wrestles them from their caves at Easter and Christmas to sup on the illusion that they're not such bad people after all. A visit to church is to absolve them of the sins that disturb their sleep. For an hour they make the past their present."

Marj rooted out her next piece of music.

"Hmm? I think you're a tad off beam with one part of your thesis. Nostalgia is never unadulterated; it's soiled with all manner of dirty linen. I believe they come not so much to wash their sins away, rather to have the Rector whitewash them with words of joy and love. It doesn't change their lives, because they have made themselves immune to the power of reason and strength of will. They embrace the Word in the cloying grip of sentimentality for temporary respite; by January 2nd their sleep is disturbed once more. Poor, poor people. Excuse me, Jack, I must press on."

"...I press on to take hold of that for which Christ Jesus took hold of me..."

She came back quick as flash, "Philippians 3."

"I'll stump you one of these days."

He wended his way to the vestry at the rear of the church. *'White Christmas'* resounded from the organ, and a number of jolly voices crooned the lyrics.

"Perhaps Marj has a thing for Bing?"

Jack was amused at his use of alliteration.

Last five minutes before the service began, and they were flooding through the doors; bonhomie and goodwill in abundance. A rather noisy young couple bounded in, so obviously in love with each other. Wendy Fisher followed, a look of annoyance darkened her features.

"Hello Wendy, no Derek tonight?"

Wendy pursed her lips.

"Derek is indisposed."

Sandra Henshall knew what that meant. Wendy had tried to rouse him, but he was as pissed as a fart by ten o' clock. She left him comatose before the log burner.

Sandra scanned the congregation, trying to keep count of the number for the vestry register. She saw Padam Gurung and his wife, and there was that nice young Asian man, sitting alone on the end of a row. Faisal had decided to attend. Earlier in the day he recollected Imam Shirani's words about visiting a church. He tried to convince Abir to join him. She wouldn't have anything to do with her own Mosque, so she was hardly prepared to join him in a church. Sandra glanced at the rear pews. Oh good, those nice people whose car broke down had managed to get along. Caroline Allsop caught her eye, and nudged Jimmy; they gave Sandra a wave.

The Marlboroughs entered *en famille*, including Angela. Debs swept forward grandly with Hugh in tow. Julian steered Angela along, a look of blissful serenity on his face. He noted familiar faces amongst the congregation.

"Good, we can tie up loose ends tonight."

Rarely does anyone race for the front pew in the Church of England. Deb's supreme self-confidence in arriving late was borne out. They settled themselves immediately in front of the pulpit.

Sandra closed the door to prevent heat loss, but opened it for a chap in his early fifties who entered alone. She sized him up; there were always a few like him, unknowns who turned up out of the blue and were never seen again. She wondered what pain and loss there was in his life; it was written across his sad face. At least he was wrapped up warm in a heavy overcoat.

Jack Preston emerged from the vestry alongside the Reverend Peter Standish, who was resplendent in cassock and surplice with a purple stole draped around his neck. Marjorie acknowledged his signal, and began to play *'Once in Royal David's City'*. Jack sang the first verse beside the ancient font, and the congregation rose in readiness to essay the ensuing verses.

Will Castle closed the door, careful not to make a noise. He picked up a carol sheet. Spotting Jimmy Allsop tucked away at the back, he padded across the stone floor to sit with him and his wife. The penultimate verse of the carol covered his entrance,

"And our eyes at last shall see Him,
Through His own redeeming love;
For that child, so dear and gentle,
Is our Lord in heaven above;
And He leads His children on
To the place where He is gone."

Will was deep inside himself. How would Jesus recognise him? He hardly recognised himself. Was he Will Castle, or was he Billy Conway? Was he even...? He came back to the reality of his surroundings.

Jack Preston was reading the lesson:

"Matthew 22: 34 to 40:

Hearing that Jesus had silenced the Sadducees, the Pharisees got together. One of them, an expert in the law, tested him with this question: 'Teacher, which is the greatest commandment in the Law'

Jesus replied: 'Love the Lord your God with all your heart and with all your soul and with all your mind. This is the first and greatest commandment. And the second is like it: Love your neighbour as yourself. All the Law and the Prophets hang on these two commandments'."

Jack retired to the font whilst Marjorie struck up Christina Rossetti's reflective and haunting '*In the Bleak Midwinter*'. Angela had taken one more glass of wine than she should have.

"Julian, is there a loo in here?"

He looked bewildered, and repeated the question in his mother's ear.

"In the vestry at the back."

As inconspicuously as possible, Angela walked down a side aisle, and Jack showed her to the facility. By the time she was done the carol was finished, and Peter Standish was mounting the steps to the pulpit. She decided to stand beside Jack.

A face looked up from a pew in front, and Will mouthed, "Hello."

Julian also caught her eye. Across a sea of heads, she mouthed,

"I'll wait here."

It mattered not a jot to Julian. She could be dealt with there as much as in any other part of the church.

"May the words of my mouth, and the meditations of all our hearts, be acceptable in your sight; O Lord our rock and our Redeemer. Amen"

Peter Standish surveyed the congregation; expectant faces, bored faces and those resigned to a sermon.

"You may have been surprised when Jack Preston read the words of a fully-grown Jesus, rather than the usual Scripture for the Eve of our Saviour's birth."

He gripped the surround of the pulpit.

"What use have we for those traditional forms when the world on our very doorstep is riven with violence and conflict? How can we in all conscience celebrate the Coming of our Redeemer when we turn our face away from him; when we do not love our neighbours as ourselves."

He let the weight of his words hover over them.

"A clever man wrote a book called *'The Selfish Gene'*; a bleak treatise that leaves us spinning in a universe without love. He asserts that we behave altruistically only when it suits our ends to do so. Unwittingly, he confirmed the second greatest commandment, *'Love your neighbour as yourself'*. Friends, do you not want what is good for you? Do you not want that which feeds you with joy, fulfilment and love? I tell you that you can never attain it through the exercise of wilfulness. In the selfish pursuit of your own freedom you will trample on everyone else's freedom."

The power of Peter's oratory held them spellbound.

"It is *always* in your interest to love your neighbour as yourself, but you will not do so if you separate yourself from God. Without God's presence in your life you will *try* to live by precepts which have the limiting status of mere ethical values. You will regard them as a user's

345

manual, and we all know what we do with a user manual – stick it in the draw to gather dust, taking it out to scrutinise only when our need is desperate.

So it is that you condemn yourself to live alone without higher guidance. Engaged in battle with your base desires which generate conflict and strife. We all fight the same internal war.

Why does Jesus say these are the two greatest commandments on which hang all the Law and all the Prophets? Because loving God and loving your neighbour are inseparable. When we break the bond between them we create a fearful world."

He took a glass of water from the shelf beneath the lip of the pulpit, and sipped.

"And who is your neighbour? Acts 10: Peter says,

'I now realise how true it is that God does not show favouritism but accepts men from every nation who fear him and do what is right...'

The Salvation that came into the world on a Christmas morn is Salvation for all nations; it has no eye for gender, ethnicity, colour of skin or sexuality. So it is that we – men, women and children of all nations – are all brothers and sisters in Christ. We remember that He came amongst us to be the Light of the World. Only you as an individual can decide whether or not to accept that light, to live your life as a creator yourself in the midst of Creation. Which decision will you take this night? Will you accept His light, or will you extinguish the spark, and plunge yourself into fearful and destructive darkness?"

Peter gathered his papers, making ready to descend from the pulpit. A mocking handclap echoed throughout the building. Raising his head, he saw Julian Marlborough standing below.

"Very good Peter, very good," sarcasm dripped from every word.

"Thus conscience does make cowards of us all."

Marjorie Whitlock took him to task.

"Out of context; besides a deranged Hamlet is hardly a good role model. Sit down, young man, your behaviour is inappropriate."

Julian had known Marj since he was a boy, and funnily enough she was the only person to whom he showed any genuine respect. Even he recognised integrity.

Hugh rose to his feet.

"I say, not now my boy. Time and place for everything."

He got no further. His son withdrew a silenced pistol from the depths of his coat and shot him through the forehead.

The torrent of screams was silenced by a threatening cry from the young woman who had entered the building all lovey dovey with her young man.

"Sit down, NOW!"

Fiona stood in one aisle, and her partner, Dougie, in the opposite. Wendy Fisher tried to run for the door, and was felled by a blow to the neck. Her assailant was the older man who Sandra Henshall had thought so sorrowful. Jeremy always regretted what he had to do, but did it unwaveringly.

The first Uzi submachine gun was designed in Israel in the late-1940's, with the prototype finished in 1950. It has been lethal in any number of wars since, and also in the hands of hoodlums worldwide. Compact, and with a rate of fire of six hundred rounds per minute, they appeared in the hands of Julian and his three murderous colleagues before anyone realised. The congregation was rigid with fear, and the only sound was of children crying.

Debs Marlborough looked upon her husband, dead at her feet. With her usual grace she stood and walked to Julian. For five seconds they held each other's gaze. She turned sideways, linked his arm, and looked defiantly at the mass of people.

Julian barked,

"Bring him in!"

Jeremy walked briskly out of the church, and everyone waited, watching the guns to see if they were trained on them personally.

The metal ring of the church door latch made them jump, and Jeremy re-entered. He was prodding a man in front of him, who was handcuffed and shackled with leg irons. They moved along the central aisle towards the crossing. To a few the face of Qadir Khan was more than familiar, and even to those who had never met him personally he resembled someone they thought they'd seen on the television news.

Qadir stood between Julian and Jeremy. Whilst the former covered him with his Uzi, Jeremy knelt and unlocked the leg irons.

"Peter, down here please."

The Rector descended from his pulpit, his footsteps resounding on the wooden stairs.

Julian's politeness would have been a credit to him, in other circumstances.

"Peter – Qadir; Qadir – Peter. To the altar, please."

Julian detached himself from his mother's arm. He and Jeremy drove the two captives towards the altar like shepherds guarding prize sheep.

"Free his hands, please."

Jeremy removed Qadir's handcuffs, and then held the muzzle of his gun in the small of his back.

Julian faced eastwards, obscuring what he was doing. When he faced westward a gasp warmed the air of the cold church. He was brandishing a gleaming machete, withdrawn from a sheath attached to his body. Julian lay the savage weapon on the floor between himself and Qadir, and took a pace backwards. Two guns covered the stony-faced man, and their bullets would cut him in half if he made the wrong move.

"Pick it up!"

With utmost delicacy, Qadir lifted the blade from the flagstones, and admired the cut-throat edge glinting in the light.

"Don't keep your back to the Rector, Qadir, be respectful to a man of the cloth."

Julian preened himself, it was the main flaw in his otherwise good acting skills. His old Drama teacher told him repeatedly that he over-egged the pudding.

His view never changed.

"Sod him! I'm the centre of attention, and I intend to make the most of it."

He waited, and he waited, and then his words exploded,

"Behead him, hard man!"

Many came to their feet in spontaneous protest. Two men with experience, partially hidden by the shadow of the organ loft that hung above the font, remained still and watchful. Will Castle stayed as cool as a cucumber.

"Well, well, Jimmy, he is full of surprises."

The protesters sank into their seats in fear of Julian's associates.

"Go on then."

Qadir weighed the weapon in his hands, and found its balance.

"Kneel down, Peter," Julian ordered.

Qadir shuffled sideways, and raised the machete high.

"No brother, no, for the love of Allah don't do it!"

Faisal Khan leapt into the aisle.

"It is a sin my brother, it is not lawful."

Dougie was restraining Faisal, but Julian ordered him to let the schoolteacher come forwards.

"Good evening friend. Does the schoolmaster have a lesson to give?"

Faisal spoke softly to Qadir.

"This is not the way, my brother, it is never the way."

In those seconds he became the first person ever to see the real man in Qadir Khan. The softening was momentary, but unmistakeable, and a clear message passed between them. Qadir held the blade high above Peter Standish's head.

Jeremy was the oldest hand present, but he was taken by surprise. He did manage to drop Qadir dead at his feet, but not before he had struck Julian a blow to the head with the machete. It was far from fatal, and as Faisal attacked him Julian was able to defend himself. A grade two Krav Maga instructor is very adept, but he's no match for a man who has been trained in Commando Krav Maga. Julian shattered Faisal's windpipe with one blow, and his life ebbed away as he choked on his own blood.

Julian placed a hand on his scalp and shrugged; a fair bit of blood, but he'd live. Debs Marlborough removed her scarf and wrapped it tenderly around her little boy's poorly head.

"Thank you mummy," and he kissed her.

"Well Pete, if you want a job done, do it yourself."

He picked up the fallen machete.

Peter Standish smiled at his would-be assassin, and Julian amused himself by asking,

"Any last words."

"Actually, yes," and Peter gestured to his congregation, "may I?"

"Keep it short."

Reverend Standish came to his feet, and spread wide his arms,

"Be self-controlled and alert. Your enemy the devil prowls around like a roaring lion looking for someone to devour. Resist him, standing firm in the faith, because you know that your brothers throughout the world are undergoing the same kind of sufferings."

Peter raised his arm in blessing,

"And the God of all grace, who called you to his eternal glory in Christ, after you have suffered a little while, will himself restore you and make you strong, firm and steadfast. To him be the power for ever and ever. Amen,"

A rejoinder of *'Amen'* sounded mightily from the nave.

Matching whispers of Marjorie Whitlock and Jack Preston weren't heard,

"1 Peter: 5."

The living Peter fell to his knees and awaited his fate. Julian's arm rose, and a military voice bellowed,

"Captain Marlborough, sir. Rifleman Allsop reporting for duty."

Julian lowered his arm in utter amazement, and peered the length of the church.

"Should I know you?"

Jimmy named the small Middle Eastern town, and the girl from Bradford who they'd captured.

Julian cut him short when he mentioned the name of Fatima.

"We don't need the details rifleman, might frighten the horses. Let him through."

Jimmy kissed Caroline; his back masking her seated person.

"One for you, and one for Maisie."

The Light Infantry march at one-hundred-and-forty paces to the minute compared to the Army standard of one-hundred-and-twenty, so he covered the ground rapidly. The handgun was issued to protect O'Donnell, Jimmy put it to better use and fired two shots at Julian before Fiona cut him down with a sharp burst from her Uzi.

One shot took Julian in the shoulder and he reeled backwards. Everyone was on their feet, screaming and crying. The counter terrorism operatives tried to restore order. Nobody noticed Jack Preston grab hold of Will Castle. In the melee, they rushed into the vestry, dragging Caroline and Angela behind them. It took seconds to open the outer door and run for their lives.

Julian rose to his feet, and an awestruck silence fell.

Marjorie Whitlock had not moved from her organ stool throughout the proceedings.

"The Devil looks after his own," she said to herself.

"Enough, enough! Everyone, in your pews, and kneeling; arms by your side. Anyone moves, shoot them."

Striding to the altar, he grasped the machete and severed Peter Standish's head from his body.

When he raised it for display a low moaning sounded, like animals in distress. Julian looked at the eyes, and was dumfounded. He couldn't possibly know that the look of love on those lifeless features was for a wife asleep at home and an unborn child.

To Julian's astonishment, Marjorie Whitlock stepped into the crossing.

"We will sing the carol printed on your extra sheet of paper, verses one, four and five."

She sat at her organ and played. Sixty-two people kneeling in the carnage of that small church raised their voices in praise:

> *"I heard the bells on Christmas day*
> *Their old familiar carols play,*
> *And wild and sweet*
> *The words repeat*
> *Of 'Peace on earth, good will to men!'"*

Julian saw only an opportunity in the noise of the singing. At his nod submachine guns raked the congregation, but on they sang:

> *"And in despair I bowed my head;*
> *'There is no peace on earth,' I said,*
> *'For hate is strong*
> *And mocks the song*
> *Of peace on earth, good will to men!'"*

An ambulance roared by, its engine loud and its bell clamouring even louder. A pregnant woman had gone into labour. Whilst her husband was only next door he was busy. She called for help herself.

The shooting and organ stopped simultaneously. Four State terrorists surveyed their handiwork of corpses. A faint scuffing drew their attention. Marjorie Whitlock took her sheet music and placed it neatly into her case. She stood upright, and sang the last verse of the carol to Julian unaccompanied:

> *"Then pealed the bells more loud and deep:*
> *'God is not dead; nor doth he sleep!*
> *The wrong shall fail,*
> *The right prevail,*
> *With peace on earth, good will to men!"*

She stepped forward, and the tiny woman placed her hands lightly either side of his face. The kiss on his forehead mesmerised him, but he still put a single shot through her heart at close range. He wasn't remotely conscious of the irony that the carol was the work of the American poet; Henry (Wadsworth) Longfellow.

Derek Fisher woke from his alcoholic stupor. A combination of emergency vehicle bells, and an array of lights, set up around the cordoned crime scene, disturbed his slumber. Fiona, Dougie and Jeremy had slipped away into the night. The twice-wounded Julian instructed his mother to help him into the graveyard, and there he sat on the Whitlock grave.

"You have your mobile phone, mother?"

"Yes."

"Stand in the middle of the green, it's the only place you'll get a signal; police and ambulances. Off you go."

While Debs followed orders, Julian extracted a mobile from his pocket. It was more refined than his mother's; a present from Commander Wentmore's department. He sent a one-word text:

"Accomplished."

Chief Inspector Simon Reynolds arrived first, accompanied by a superfluous armed response unit. All Debs could do was point, as she knelt beside her son.

The armed response guys were first into St. George's, and an ashen-faced officer reappeared outside.

"Better have a look, sir."

Reynolds stood by the font.

"Dear God! Jeff, more ambulances, as many as they can spare."

Jeff Durham was glad to get out of the charnel house.

Simon gave instructions, "Check for signs of life."

"All of them, sir?" a young constable enquired.

"Yes, all of them!" Simon screamed.

They need not have bothered. The professionalism of the executioners had seen to it that no-one was left alive. Methodically, they had gone round, and anyone who was still breathing was finished off with a neck shot from silenced pistols. Josef Stalin's Commissariat for Internal Affairs, the vicious and feared NKVD, couldn't have done a better job.

Simon was so aghast that he didn't notice the man at his shoulder.

"And you are?"

"Reynolds, Chief Inspector Reynolds."

Giles Wentmore pre-empted the question in reverse by flashing his identity.

"Thank you, Chief Inspector, this is now a matter of national security. You and your men will withdraw, and establish a cordon which you will maintain. No-one is to enter the area without my say so, that includes you and your men. If you want confirmation of my authority, you'll find your Chief Constable in the graveyard."

Simon withdrew, and took the armed response team with him.

What followed had been subject to rigorous planning. Giles knew that procedure had to be seen to be followed, and the first people allowed into the church were his forensic boys. He asked them to wait until ambulances started to arrive. A team was instructed to demolish a section of the church wall, to permit an ambulance to reverse up to the church doors. Giles' appointed traffic marshal stood on the church path helping a driver to reverse his vehicle. It bore the correct right livery, but the two men who dismounted didn't normally dress as paramedics.

Derek Fisher sought out Wendy, but couldn't find her anywhere. Grabbing his overcoat, he wandered outside, and circumvented the cordon to acquire a position in the Rectory garden. From his vantage point, in the lee of the trees, he watched events unfold.

"Bloody odd!"

He assumed that his alcohol befuddled brain was playing tricks with his eyes. The paramedics looked as if they were taking bodies *into* the church.

There was nothing wrong with Derek's optics. Dawood and Bakir were arranged decorously around the church, and weapons placed with delicacy adjacent to their lifeless bodies.

That would be the story released on Christmas Day evening, and photographs would provide back-up. The men who slaughtered Raza Khan and Eddie Seaforth would take the blame for this horrific outrage; Faisal Hussain's inert presence was an unexpected bonus.

By the end of the day, the name of ex-Captain Julian Marlborough would be a household name throughout the nation. His attempt to prevent the massacre, and his SAS background would be more than hinted at, lending plausibility to his heroics. Photographs of him in his hospital bed made the Boxing Day papers. At his private debriefing he put Jimmy Allsop's hat in the ring, as a protector of the righteous. When Jimmy's connection with the P.M. was ascertained he became a posthumous hero.

Thomas Patrick O'Donnell was taking his festive pleasures at Chequers, no more than thirty minutes away. He turned up in Banksmore at mid-day for the television cameras. He had been briefed, and they showed him some of the photographs so recently taken. In the words of the song, he turned a whiter shade of pale. O'Donnell mouthed his platitudes and concerns for the benefit of T.V and radio, and expressed his sorrow for the families of the victims. He reserved especial praise for the Late-Sir Hugh Marlborough, telling the British people what a fine public servant they had lost, and how tragic it was that the son had been unable to save the father. On the journey back to Chequers he telephoned Henry Longfellow.

"This is in your hands now Hank, keep me up to speed."

It took until nine that night before all of the bodies were removed. The once rural idyll returned to a surreal reality, for those residents who were still alive. The cordon remained around the church, its doors under twenty-four hour armed guard; more show than necessity.

The forensic team worked through the night, but not following their usual procedure. They ensured that everything was in place to make the story watertight. Giles Wentmore left around midnight. As he headed for the M25 he felt that the job had been done well. Any inconsistencies about time, participants and ballistics could be explained away, if necessary. There again, it wouldn't be necessary; his people were handpicked and each one of them subscribed to the inexorable direction in which events were moving.

When Jack, Will and the women had fled, Jack had wanted to call the authorities.

"Jack, they are the authorities!"

The three of them stared at him dumbfounded. Will pressed them with urgency.

"A car, we need to put distance between ourselves and this place."

Caroline was in a state of shock at seeing her husband gunned down, and didn't make sense of Will's appeal.

"Over there!"

They tumbled into Jack's VW Golf.

"Where to, Will?"

"Anywhere. Just drive."

Caroline became hysterical.

"Maisie, take me to my Maisie!"

Angela held her.

The car halted across the road from *'The Cromwell'* in Old Wenbury.

Silence bound them, until Jack said,

"But that's too fantastic to believe."

He was trying to get his head around everything Will had told them.

"I believe you Will; I'd believe anything about Julian Marlborough."

Angela whispered through her tears,

"We don't need to imagine; we saw for ourselves. They'll come after us, won't they Will? What shall we do?"

He pondered their situation in the darkness of the car, until a plan of campaign evolved.

"Caroline, they won't be after you. In all that mayhem I don't think they'd have clocked that you were with Jimmy. Anyway, there'll be enough witnesses to make you redundant."

Will said this to reassure, but watching Julian terrorising the congregation, and seeing his backup, he knew immediately the enormity of the crime that was to be committed. There wouldn't be a single survivor to tell the tale. Still, he more than hoped that Caroline had escaped their notice.

"Caroline, time for you to join Maisie. You spent the night babysitting…"

"What about the young woman who's been with Maisie?"

"Here, give her an extra twenty quid, and tell her to keep her mouth shut. Say you were off on the razzle while your husband went to church."

Caroline half-opened the door when Will held her back.

"Give us your address in St. Helens."

"Why?"

"My place is only a few miles from yours. Nobody knows about it, and that's where me and Ange are headed."

She scribbled her address on a slip of paper from her handbag.

Jack cried plaintively, "What about me?"

Will looked away, "You're in trouble pal, you need to disappear."

"I've nowhere to go."

Caroline found a solution, and for a woman in the grip of terrible grief she showed remarkable clarity of thinking.

"Here's my house keys. You can all travel north together. Let yourself in, and use the spare bedroom. Any neighbours get nosy, and they will, you're my cousin from London. I'm always talking about him, and moaning that he never visits. His name's Eddie Jackson, he works in computers – make the rest up. Me and Maisie'll see you soon."

She opened the door fully and got out.

Will leaned over Jack.

"Stick to your story, Caroline, when they come to tell you…"

His voice dribbled away in sorrow, and she took up his theme,

"…when they tell me that Jimmy's dead."

A strong and powerful woman stood tall in the moonlight.

"Never fear lad, I will. There'll be no need to play act, the grief is real enough."

She sped across the road to hold her Maisie.

Jack drove them north. They would have come too close to Banksmore to join the nearest motorway, so he fiddled his way along A and B roads and joined the M40 at Oxford.

The journey was uneventful, and they stopped the once at Hilton Park Services on the M6.

Well before dawn Jack was safe inside 13 Alexander Road, St. Helens. Will convinced him that the car should get lost, and he could arrange for it to happen. By eight, on Boxing Day, it was in the hands of Liverpudlian *'businessmen'*, and was no more.

First, the car took Angela and Will to Whiston. He parked it in an inconspicuous side street near the hospital. It wouldn't be noticed amongst the numerous vehicles littering the road and he could retrieve it later.

They had a twenty-minute walk to his place. The snow was deeper in the north, and the pavements were treacherous. As they picked their way along they held hands. For all the world resembling a couple returning from a good night out on Christmas Eve. One or two early risers passed them, and cries of *"Merry Christmas"* rent the air.

Will held the front door open to allow Angela to enter.

"Welcome to Paradise Lane."

29

"...civil blood makes civil hands unclean."
Romeo and Juliet: Prologue

Boxing Day is usually reserved for the Gadarene Swine to rush headlong to the shops, in search of bargains that commit them to penury throughout January. This year they flew recklessly into the streets, and committed themselves to disastrous action that had far longer term consequences. Demons of anger and hatred possessed their souls.

West Yorkshire and the old mill towns near Manchester were the flashpoints. The heavy concentration of Muslim communities provided the source for outraged citizenry to enter those districts, and commit violence and destruction upon the residents on an unprecedented scale. By mid-afternoon, the extent of the pogroms against thousands of innocent people was nationwide. Leicester and Birmingham, Portsmouth and Southampton, Newcastle and Sunderland, Bristol and its environs. London, and many towns were in uncontrolled riot with the police ill-equipped and too small in number to be effective.

The news from that tiny Buckinghamshire village had seared the entire nation. Right wing extremists and the terminally mindless roamed in gangs, dealing out revenge. By the law of averages there must have been some among them who claimed to be religious, the overwhelming majority was not.

The reason they reacted in this way had been unwittingly defined by Jack Preston before the fatal Christmas Eve service began. They weren't even religious fellow travellers, they were the English in the grip of nostalgia and sentimentality. The church they'd never dream of going to, except for a funeral or a wedding - when they would stumble about with no idea of when to sit or stand, and mumble their way through hymns and responses - was *their* church in their minds. Ask them why and they would struggle to articulate an answer. Jesus? Yep, heard of him. Judas? Wasn't that what you called your favourite footballer when he transferred to another club? By any measurement they were atheists, it would be charitable to call them faithless.

The cabal, headed by Freddie Forbes and Henry Longfellow, had its finger tightly on the pulse of events. They held the military back until the evening of December 27th It wasn't until late the following day that some semblance of order returned to the streets of the nation. The Army had to turn out in huge numbers to re-establish control. Finally, their objective was achieved, and the presence of soldiers was fully justified.

O'Donnell asked Henry Longfellow to make the television broadcast on the morning of the 29th. The Home Secretary explained that the continued presence of soldiers was to protect life and property, and their proximity to Muslim communities was in a protective capacity. He also announced that Parliament had been recalled, and the House would sit on New Year's Eve.

When dawn broke on the 31st the citizens of major ports were surprised to see warships in their waters; the

Mersey, the Tyne, the Solent and Avonmouth were occupied with Guided Missile Destroyers and Frigates. In the early hours an SAS detachment secured GCHQ Cheltenham, and all UK military bases were in the hands of the *'Saviours of the Nation'*. Anyone who resisted was placed under close arrest.

At 10:00 hours, as Members of Parliament jostled for seats in a packed House, paratroopers fell from the skies and took control of the major airports, whilst the Royal Marines provided the same service for the ports.

"Order, order!"

Members responded to the cry, and Speaker Blacow called the Prime Minister.

Thomas Patrick O'Donnell rose slowly to his feet, but no-one looked at him. They were trying to determine where the sound of marching feet was coming from. The crowd of M.P.'s standing near the door was crushed into an even smaller space as Major General Mike *'Bernard'* Montgomery, accompanied by Major General Roy *'Rob'* McKinnon, Brigadier General William *'Connolly'* Rodgers, and a detachment of thirty officers and n.c.o.'s in full battle dress and bearing arms, entered the Chamber.

Montgomery shattered the silence.

"Mr. Speaker, this sitting is suspended indefinitely, and its members will leave immediately. The United Kingdom is now under Martial Law."

Protests began, but were silenced when the soldiers spread themselves before the benches, and raised their weapons in the direction of the M.P.'s. It began as a trickle, and turned into a deluge. The nation's elected representatives fled.

Fifty-nine members remained resolutely seated. Those of them on the Opposition benches stood, and moved to the Government side. Freddie Forbes sat beside Henry Longfellow, and they looked around at their fifty-seven supporters. In number they matched the fifty-nine who had been signatories to the death warrant of King Charles I.

*

Abir Hussain was alone on New Year's Day, in her house in Old Wenbury. The grief she felt for her dead husband, Faisal, would pass eventually, she knew that. How she would cope with having him branded a terrorist, who had participated in wholesale slaughter, was quite different. Already she had protested, but nobody wanted to listen. The radio said the new Prime Minister would speak to the nation at 11.00 a.m. She carried her mug of coffee from the kitchen to the sitting room. A brick shattered the front window, and she screamed and dropped her drink. When she recovered sufficiently to peer through the broken pane there was nothing to see.
In the next street a young man strolled with his tiny dog. Denis *'Poodle'* Trueman had exacted his one and only piece of cowardly revenge.

Abi stood distractedly as the cold air blew into the room. She reached her decision quickly. The house would go on sale by the end of the week. By the following weekend she would be with her parents in Edinburgh; professional people of good standing in their multi-cultural community. Scotland had seen its share of the disturbances, but nothing like the tempest that raged across England. Abi picked up a broken photograph frame from the floor, and held the torn photo' of her beloved Faisal to her bosom.

*

"The Prime Minister, the Right Honourable Henry Longfellow."

The anonymous voice of the television announcer intoned the name with gravity.

"I am speaking to you from the Cabinet Room in Ten Downing Street."

Henry looked foursquare into the camera, with absolute self-confidence; no longer necessary to hide behind the code name *'Lester'*.

"The grave events of recent weeks are, as you know, little more than the eruption of a suppurating boil that has festered for many years. As a nation, we have suffered economic and political turmoil on an unprecedented scale."

He paused, as if trying to stare the nation out.

"Simultaneously, we have stood by as an assault on our values has bereft us of our identity. Cultural values have been swallowed into a mess of potage, religious values mocked and derided, and above all our easy-going tolerance taken advantage of and abused."

What he said next surprised a populace used to obfuscation and evasion from their politicians.

"I, as a government minister, must share in the blame for this sorry state of affairs. Along with other elected representatives I decided some time ago that it must stop. Today I am pleased to announce that we have taken the first step towards the reunification of the peoples of this Island. The coming year will see us flourish in hope, and in the prosperity that follows a people united in common purpose."

Henry's voice deepened.

"Recent events have scarred us all, and our hearts go out to the victims of terrorists everywhere, but particularly to those murdered in the quiet Buckinghamshire village of Banksmore. The provocation of this dreadful act brought a degree of civil disorder to our cities and towns unseen since the days of the English Civil War, four centuries ago. Our courageous police could not hold back the tide alone. That is why I, and my colleagues, called upon our brave military forces to assist us, not only in restoring immediate order on the streets, but with the longer term project of leading our country back to political, economic and cultural sanity."

He assumed a look of regret.

"It is a grave decision in the conduct of any nation to ask its military forces to intervene in its political life, but we have been left without any other option."

Suddenly, he appeared more cheerful.

"However, these are your sons and daughters, who have gladly accepted the responsibility to guard the lifeblood of the United Kingdom. Like me, I feel sure that you will have the greatest confidence in their sense of duty, loyalty and love for this land."

His chameleon face altered.

"It is my duty to tell you that I have been asked to lead an interim government of national unity, and it is my privilege to accept the awesome responsibility. Members of Parliament, from both sides of the House, have united to maintain stability in these troubled times. Nonetheless, we are no substitute for a properly elected government by you the people. We have set a timetable, which we hope to keep to. In May of this year we aim to hold a General Election, at which you can give your mandate for a new and full Parliament.

If we are to return to settled times we are all going to have to accept the temporary inconveniences of the intervening months. For the foreseeable future, this means that the United Kingdom must function under the diktats of Martial Law. Permit me to explain what this means."

Strictly speaking he was not accurate. Under Martial Law the highest ranking military officer is imposed as head of government. Henry explained that his national government would operate in close relationship with the military. He named the Admiral of the Fleet as military governor. A run-down was given on the new laws of curfew, and the suspension of civil law and civil rights, along with habeas corpus. It was made as plain as a pikestaff that civilians defying martial law would be subject to military tribunals.

"Whilst it is regrettable that we must resort to such an extreme measure, I feel certain that you will agree that it is necessary. With the common-sense, for which we Britons are rightly famed, I see no reason why the normalities of our Parliamentary democracy cannot be restored in a short space of time."

The Prime Minister drew breath, and sipped from a glass of water.

"British soldiers will be a common sight on our streets for some little while yet, and you are asked not to hinder them in their duty. Their first task is to maintain order. To that end, predominantly Muslim communities will be under protective custody; non-residents of those areas will be prohibited from entering them without the written permission of the local military commanders.

Outside of those districts, anyone engaging in acts of racial or religious abuse will be subject to the most stringent punishments under military law."

He came to the most volatile section of his speech.

"Residents of Muslim communities must report to registration centres, which will be announced after this programme. There you will be issued with identity cards, which you must carry at all times. Further to the setting up of these processing centres, we are preparing internment camps on a number of islands off the British mainland. Illegal immigrants will be detained there, along with those subject to deportation orders. From there they will be returned to their countries of origin. There is no right of appeal."

The silent majority sat awestruck before their screens. Those given to the long-held right of protest on behalf of civil liberty took to the streets within hours. They received short shrift from the soldiers who faced them. It was their privilege to be the first to be dealt with by military tribunal.

"Finally, I turn to the question of terrorism. Any persons assisting terrorist acts will be sentenced to life imprisonment; those who commit acts of terror will be subject to Capital Punishment. There is no right of appeal."

Henry leant across his desk, and spoke with sincerity.

"The government we have replaced was proto-Marxist; a failed creed that leads only to poverty of body, mind, heart and soul. I remain a Socialist, convinced that it is the duty of all forms of government to create a land of opportunity for their people. Yet government alone cannot make a nation prosperous; politicians cannot dispense successful and fulfilled lives for each individual, like a doctor's prescription. You have your duty also; to seize the opportunities provided and make good lives for yourselves and your families. This is the inheritance your forefathers passed down to you."

In his passion he made a slip of the tongue, excluding three other countries in the Union,

"This is England!"

30

"There are more things in heaven and earth...
Than are dreamt of in your philosophy."
Hamlet Act 1: Sc. 5

August Bank Holiday was all you could ask for, and folk were out and about rejoicing.

Protests against the imposition of Martial Law and an unelected government came to nought. The British people accommodated the situation, and made the best of a bad job. The majority embraced the sense of order and safety as a blessing. Henry Longfellow's promise of a May General Election was optimistic, but the temporary government and military combined managed to create conditions conducive to the democratic process by the end of July. In a break with tradition the people had gone to the polls on a Friday, and the Bank Holiday weekend was used for a leisurely count. The result was to be announced on the Monday.

In Edinburgh Abi Hussain was settled into her new home and job. She doggedly persevered in trying to clear her husband's name, but it was slow-going. She occupied her Monday preparing evidence for the letter she would address to the new Prime Minister. He had declared on the campaign trail that slates needed to be wiped clean, and a fresh start dispensed to everybody, so Abi lived in hope.

At opposite ends of England two widows played with their children, keen to be away from the hot air and furore of the election. After all, they thought, the result isn't in doubt.

Caroline and Maisie Allsop were in Taylor Park enjoying a picnic. Maisie squealed as Uncle Eddie swung her in an aeroplane spin. Watching on, Caroline felt wistful as she thought on her dead husband. The manager of 'The Cromwell' had woken her, and the police had broken the news which she already knew.

Jimmy's body was transported back to St. Helens, and his ashes scattered behind the posts at one end of the Totally Wicked stadium, home of his beloved St. Helens Rugby League Football Club. They gave him a minute's applause before the game against Wigan. Jimmy was with the Saints in glory. She was pleased that Jack had decided to make his home with them, and he felt safe in the guise of Eddie Jackson. No-one came looking.

Down in Hampshire the New Forest hummed with visitors. Among them was Jane Standish, accompanied by her parents. She placed her sleeping baby, Sophie, into the pram, and stood over her with a deep gaze of concentration. She seemed to be searching the child's features, in the hope that her late husband would materialise. The rage she felt would not subside, and she whispered to the child,

"Someone will pay, someone will pay."

A voice interrupted her thoughts.

"Glass of prosecco darling?"

"Thank you, daddy."

Samantha Calvin and Paul Baxter also broke with tradition, and walked hand in hand to church for their marriage ceremony. Paul doted on her, she looked beautiful in her ivory dress.

Through that dark winter, they had stuck closely to each other in the little house in Paradise Lane. Nobody pursued them. Julian Marlborough simply assumed that Will Castle had disappeared into the ether at the behest of his paymasters. As for that whore, he had no intention of identifying her corpse, which he assumed was carted away with the rest from St. George's Church.

Paul Baxter aka Will Castle aka Billy Conway was a happy man, though prone to nightmares. Samantha soothed them whilst she lay beside him. In Whiston he had always been Paul Baxter. He bought the house when he left the army, and wanting a fresh start had changed his name by deed poll. Charlotte aka Angela had simply reverted to her real name. The neighbours liked her, and she took to the straightalking northerners, with their dry humour. She was sorry to leave the area, but it was too close to Liverpool where her husband-to-be might be recognised by those who remembered him as Billy Conway.

Cartmel is a village in Cumbria, and the home of sticky toffee pudding. They pooled their resources and purchased a lovely old house on the outskirts. There was a substantial garden for Paul to grow his vegetables in, and wider grounds in which Samantha could paint. It was blissful, and the property was not overlooked.

The small troop of newly-made friends came to a sudden halt, when Paul stopped abruptly.

"What is it?"

He was a trembling mass of emotions, and took her face in both hands, kissing her lightly.

"I love you."

"Come on," she said with visible delight, "we can't both be late on our big day."

They had considered marrying in the magnificent Cartmel Priory. Founded in 1190 by England's greatest knight, William Marshal 1st Earl of Pembroke, a man who had known turbulent times. It towered over the village and attracted a good income for all in and around Cartmel. Upon reflection, they thought it too public a place. A snap happy tourist might conceivably post a photograph on Facebook. They had worshipped for the last three months in a modest and discreet nearby village, and now they headed for the Church of St. Nicholas. Friendly villagers were gathered for a gawp, and applauded the happy couple and their new-found friends through the lych gate.

Walking down the aisle to the strains of *'Jesu joy of man's desiring…'* Samantha and Paul felt the sudden memory of that dark night of the soul in Banksmore. It slid insidiously into their minds. Thankfully, the service began, and the Vicar led them through the mutual promises of eternal love.

Once they were officially man and wife the Vicar gave a short talk. He linked the joy of their day with that of the entire country, about to return to normality with the impending election result.

The organ thundered as it introduced the final hymn. Samantha and Paul had come to love Charles Wesley's glorious words:

"And can it be that I should gain
an interest in the Saviour's blood?
Died He for me, who caused His pain?
For me, who Him to death pursued?

Amazing love! How can it be
that Thou, my God,
shouldst die for me!"

Sammy and Paul smiled at each other, as they sang the second verse. It was the third that did for them. A waterfall of tears baptised his face first, then hers:

"Long my imprisoned spirit lay
fast bound in sin and nature's night;
Thine eye diffused a quickening ray –
I woke, the dungeon flamed with light..."

With their inner hands clasped, their outer arms lifted to Heaven and palms open, they surrendered the terrible burdens of their lives, and accepted the yoke of He whose burden is light

"...my chains fell off; my heart was free.
I rose, went forth, and followed thee."

The congregation sang the final verse as a forgiven people, without dread of condemnation. Paul Baxter's eye was held by the Burne-Jones stained glass, ablaze with powerful sunlight. Even so, he could make out the images; Moses receiving the Tablets of Commandments, and the story of Moses leading the Israelites out of bondage.

Maisie was in bed at one end of the country, and little Sophie sound asleep in her cot at the other. Caroline and Eddie were mid-barbecue with a few of the neighbours, and Jane Standish's father served evening drinks to his daughter, wife and guests in the sitting room. The open French windows revealed the full glory of his garden.

"Time for the result," he intoned, as he pressed the remote.

Elsewhere a St. Helens voice shouted from indoors,

"Eh Caroline, alright if we stick the telly on? The election result'll be comin' on abart now."

The anonymous guest didn't wait for a reply and tuned in to the BBC.

Abi Hussain sat on her small terrace in Edinburgh, still working at the papers strewn about her. Radio 3 was playing Mahler's Fifth when it was interrupted.

In an ancient pub-cum-hotel in a Cumbrian village, a wedding reception halted when the landlord turned on the big screen. Television and radio presenters were in full flow.

"The result of the General Election has come as a surprise to nobody. We have a Conservative Landslide, with an overall majority of one hundred and nineteen seats. Here, in Downing Street, we await the arrival of the new Prime Minister. I can report that in the last hour a seismic shift has taken place in the leadership of the Conservative Party. In a statement delivered through his press secretary, Andrew Forbes, who has led the party throughout the election campaign, has announced that he is stepping down with immediate effect. To honour his late-father, cruelly murdered by Islamic terrorists, he has decided to retain his title as Earl of Seaforth. We understand that he has been guaranteed a seat in the House of Lords. We are yet to learn who will replace him, and lead the government of the United Kingdom."

The buzz and chatter of the gathered journalists grew, and cheering was heard from beyond the Downing Street gates. The voice of the Beeb's man shouted over the noise.

"The new Prime Minister's car is approaching, and a sense of excitement is palpable."

The car glided majestically to a halt before the door of Number Ten. An unheard of hush fell upon the TV and radio crews and the multiplicity of cameramen.

A bevy of stern looking men emerged from accompanying vehicles and scanned the crowd. One nodded, and the rear door of the limousine was held open on the far side. An elegantly dressed older woman emerged, and beamed at the puzzled crowd; a tall and stylish man rose as he stepped out of the vehicle and stood beside her, his back to the feverish journalists. In the still pulsating heat of an English summer's evening he turned and smiled easily before the flashing cameras. Sky's lady was heard across the nation, and for a moment she echoed around Downing Street.

"It's the hero of Banksmore; the new Member for Wenbury and Cranchurch! Julian Marlborough is our new Prime Minister. Ladies and gentlemen, Julian Marlborough."

Her words were lost in a cacophony of competing voices, which failed to elicit a response from the Premier. He proffered his arm to his mummy, Debs Marlborough, and they wallowed together in their triumph on the steps of Ten Downing Street.

Abi Hussain felt the chill of an Edinburgh night creep upon her. Mahler's Fifth resumed and the heart-breaking adagietto, famous for its accompaniment to stricken emotions in the film *'Death in Venice'*, tore her soul.

Eddie Jackson clasped an ashen-faced Caroline to his breast.

In Hampshire Jane Standish stood, drink in hand, as her parents and their neighbours chattered their excited approval. Her emotions moved between mild astonishment and uncertainty.

"The next round is on the house!" cried mine host to the wedding party, and bodies scrambled to the bar.

Paul Baxter stood alone before the sixty-inch screen, disbelief painted on his face.

"Excuse me, ladies."

Samantha crossed to Paul and took his hand.

Two pairs of eyes were glued to the screen.

The monstrous figure of Julian Marlborough raised a hand on the steps of his new home, and the press fell silent. With the DNA of public school and Oxbridge fortifying his very marrow, he asserted his inalienable right to proclaim but not to believe:

"Where there is discord, may we bring harmony. Where there is error, may we bring truth. Where there is doubt, may we bring faith. And where there is despair, may we bring hope…"

He did not credit the words to either St. Francis of Assisi, or the Iron Lady who had trotted out the very same mantra years before. After all, he thought, who gives a toss about a social climbing grammar school girl.

Paul was transfixed by Julian's cavernous eyes, but Samantha experienced something else. The face of her old punter metamorphosed into a kaleidoscope of glorious technicolour.

During the wedding ceremony Paul had revelled in the stained-glass image of Moses, but when they walked out of church Samantha had glanced upward at the West window.

Now The God of the Old Testament loomed over her once more from the television screen, a flash of lightning in His hand. The summer sunlight revealed the legend beneath Him in arterial red:

"Vengeance is Mine, I Will Repay," says the Lord.

*

In THE PROVIDENT EYE (book 3 in the COUNTING the SPOONS trilogy), Julian Marlborough reigns supreme.

His ambition is to create a 'Golden Age' in the U.K.

The severity of his policies against his own people foments rebellion, and violence of cataclysmic proportions.

Julian's fiercest opponents are the women he has wronged.

Printed in Great Britain
by Amazon